Hot Wings and Homicide

Also available by Carmela Dutra:

The Food Truck Mysteries

A Murder Most Fowl

Hot Wings and Homicide

A FOOD TRUCK MYSTERY

Carmela Dutra

NEW YORK

Books should be disposed of and recycled according to local requirements. All paper materials used are FSC compliant.

This is a work of fiction. All of the names, characters, organizations, places and events portrayed in this novel are either products of the author's imagination or are used fictitiously. Any resemblance to real or actual events, locales, or persons, living or dead, is entirely coincidental.

Published in the United States by Crooked Lane Books, an imprint of The Quick Brown Fox & Company LLC.

Crooked Lane Books and its logo are trademarks of The Quick Brown Fox & Company LLC.

Library of Congress Catalog-in-Publication data available upon request.

ISBN (hardcover): 979-8-89242-441-7
ISBN (paperback): 979-8-89242-442-4
ISBN (ebook): 979-8-89242-443-1

Cover design by Heedayah Lockman

Printed in the United States.

www.crookedlanebooks.com

Crooked Lane Books
34 West 27th St., 10th Floor
New York, NY 10001

First Edition: May 2026

The authorized representative in the EU for product safety and compliance is eucomply OÜPärnu mnt 139b-14, 11317 Tallinn, Estonia, hello@eucompliancepartner.com, +33757690241

10 9 8 7 6 5 4 3 2 1

To my boys, Levi and Lucas, who remind me that laughter makes everything better. Even deadlines.

Chapter One

A few years ago, if someone had told me I'd be driving a bright yellow food truck with a giant chicken riding shotgun, passionately butchering Lady Gaga's "Bad Romance" in two languages, I would've laughed. But that was before Seth and I inherited our Aunt Dolly's truck and built a chicken empire.

Okay, maybe "empire" is a stretch, but Kluckin' Good is a household name in our small town of Clementine, California, just outside of San Francisco.

I hum along to the upbeat pop song blasting from the radio as I pull up to a stoplight, but Rylie—my copilot and best friend, who is currently wearing our truck's chicken costume—isn't content to hum. She rolls down her window and, in full mascot regalia, serenades the bewildered driver in the next lane with a wildly off-key Portuguese rendition.

I join in with dramatic backup vocals as Rylie points a chicken wing at the elderly gentleman.

"*Eu quero seu amor*!" she belts, shimmying in the passenger seat like this is her personal stage. The man blinks, mouth agape. The second the light turns green, he peels out like he's fleeing a poultry-themed curse.

I stifle a laugh. Whether it was the warbling vocals or the shock of being serenaded by a dancing chicken, he wanted no part of it. Rylie Cortes is one of the perks of taking over my aunt's business. Sure, I wish she could cook, but I knew what I was getting when I hired her.

"I don't understand why *she* gets to sit in the front seat when I called dibs first," Seth complains from the back. He's my twin brother, business partner, and a part-time lawyer who is *always* full of opinions.

"Because I won best two out of three at rock-paper-scissors," Rylie shoots back, spinning in her seat to glare at him through her chicken head.

"Why are you still wearing that ridiculous outfit? Our shift ended thirty minutes ago," Seth grumbles.

The chicken suit came with the truck and is now essential to Rylie's brand. She's become *one with the chicken* and wears the outfit to attract more customers. Not that we need help drawing customers. Competing on *The Food Truck Showdown* put Kluckin' Good on the proverbial food map. Sure, it involved two murders, one attempted murder, and my kidnapping—but business tripled after the finale aired.

"It's called branding, *meu amor*," Rylie says, using Seth's nickname that makes me gag every time.

Neither Seth nor I were ready to take over after Aunt Dolly's sudden death, but we've made it work—thanks to Rylie. She helps me with day-to-day operations while Seth splits his time between lawyering and food trucking.

And now she's dating Seth.

Gag.

I'm still adjusting to my best friend and my brother becoming a couple. Half the time, I laugh at their banter; the other half, I dry heave at their mushy nonsense. We really need to have a team meeting about workplace behavior.

"*Vire à esquerda*!" Rylie shouts at me to turn left.

"Relax," I say, turning onto my parents' street. "Sugar and Spice Bakery doesn't close until four. We can drop off the truck first."

Sugar and Spice Bakery is a Clementine staple. It's part cozy bakery, part cat café, and the owners, Chris and Helena Wynn, are fully committed to helping the local shelter find *furever* homes for its feline residents.

It's more of a comfort stop now, reminding me of Saturday mornings with Aunt Dolly. Seth's allergic to cats, so as a teen, she'd pick me up and we'd go to Sugar and Spice. I'd get a cupcake and pick a cat to cuddle while she sipped her hazelnut latte and caught up on small-town gossip.

I pull into my parents' driveway carefully, avoiding my mom's long-dead hydrangea bush.

One condition of parking our truck here is delivering leftovers to our dad twice a week. Another is steering clear of the hydrangeas. Those poor plants are victims of her "natural fertilizing" gone wrong. She insists they'll revive with enough time and positive energy. I'm surprised the HOA hasn't fined her yet.

I stash the wings and sliders in the fridge, stub my toe, and hobble toward the door—just as I hear the stairs creak. No way am I getting trapped in another "now that your brother's found someone, it's your turn" talk with my mom.

I limp-run down the driveway and gag at the sight of Seth and Rylie making out by her Jeep. "Seriously?" I choke. "Children play in these streets!"

"You need to grow up," Seth says, stepping back.

"That was disgusting. Parents wouldn't approve of you leaning your girlfriend over the hood like that."

"You're so dramatic," Rylie grins, hopping into the driver's seat.

I sulk into the back while Seth takes shotgun. "This is my life now—my best friend dates my brother, and I'm relegated to the back seat like unwanted baggage."

"You wouldn't *be* in the back seat if you'd ditch that clunker you call a car," Seth says.

"Don't insult Audrey!" I punch his arm. "She's a *lady*."

"That lady wheezes worse than a chain smoker," Rylie quips, taking a sharp left onto Maple Avenue.

"Pedro said she just needs a little TLC," I counter.

I wouldn't care if it were just the usual check engine light that's been on since I bought Audrey, my beloved red Volkswagen Rabbit. But two weeks ago, she started making a loud rattle that was worse than normal. So I took her to Rylie's cousin's dad's shop. "There's good news!" I say too brightly. "It's a simple fuel line repair, *and* it won't cost me a dime because it's a recall notice . . ."

"I'm sensing a but." Rylie speeds through a yellow light.

"But . . . Pedro found a bad oxygen sensor. He thinks that's why she idles rough and the light's always on."

"Did my cousin say when he'll be done?" she asks.

"Soon . . . ish." I avoid her gaze in the rearview mirror. "The parts are back ordered. It's going to be at least another week and there's still no rentals."

Seth twists in his seat to glare at me.

"Looks like both of you are my chauffeurs a little longer." I smile sweetly.

"*Seriamente*, Beth," Rylie complains, pulling into the Sugar and Spice parking lot. "Put that car out of her misery."

"Never."

Rylie parks, and Seth jumps out to help her down from the Jeep. Not that she needs help—it's her car—but my teddy bear of a twin is grossly in love.

The bell over the door jingles as we step inside. The smell of cupcakes and coffee wraps around me like a sugary hug.

"Well, well, well," Helena Wynn calls from behind the counter. "If it isn't my competition and favorite chicken girl."

"Hardly competition," I grin. "You've got the trifecta: coffee, cupcakes, and cats."

Seth sneezes. "And allergies," he whines, popping a pink pill from a blister pack.

Seth's immune system rejects anything with fur. We learned that when we adopted Mr. Muffins when we were eight. A gorgeous, fluffy, gray and white tabby, and the feline overlord of air biscuits. I was smitten. Seth lasted three days before turning into a sneezy, wheezy mess. Dad rehomed Mr. Muffins to a coworker, and I was devastated. I still haven't totally forgiven Seth for being allergic to joy.

Dad tried other animals. Dogs, rabbits, even hamsters. Same problem. Fish were the only pets that didn't trigger a sneezing fit—but try cuddling a goldfish bowl. Not the same.

Helena beams from behind the counter like she's got a secret. It's probably just caffeine and cat hair. She's become a solid friend since I took over Aunt Dolly's food truck. Helena understands the hustle of the business. She and her husband, Chris, started in a food truck before opening this charming little café, now home to espresso, flaky croissants, and twelve rescue cats who judge you for ordering decaf.

Basically, it's everything I aspire to—minus the litter boxes and the arrogant orange tabby who once slapped a scone out of my hand.

"Can I get a flat white with soy? Are those Chris's homemade chocolate s'mores cupcakes?" I ask, eyeing the display case.

Helena nods.

"I'll take two."

"Two?" Seth sneezes again.

"Cupcakes are the lunch of champions."

"Sure, *spinster* champions."

I elbow him in the stomach, eliciting a satisfying "Oof." "Seth will take anything covered in fur."

"Rylie already ordered his food through the app," Helena says. "It'll be out soon."

Of course she did. They're one of those gross in-love couples who order for each other. I'm happy for them—in a barfy kind of way.

"Thanks, Helena," Seth says, recovering from my "abuse." "Tell Chris I looked at the papers. It all checks out. Stop by the office for the official sign-off."

Seth practices law part-time at Buford and Myers, one of two law firms in Clementine. People constantly ask him legal advice. And I'm happy to volunteer him if it gets me free food.

On my way to where Rylie is sitting, I scratch a silky black cat snoozing in a sunbeam. She opens one eye, purrs, then goes back to sleep like I'm invisible.

"You would've loved Mr. Muffins," I whisper, giving her one last stroke.

Seth sits beside Rylie and kisses her temple. *Yuck.*

"I get enough spinster comments from Mom." I glare at Seth, taking the seat across from them. "You didn't need to call me one too. And Rylie, why didn't you order my food? You know what I like."

"Last week was iced coffee. Before that, macchiatos," she says, ticking off my obsessions. "Two days ago, you switched to matcha for 'health reasons.' How was I supposed to know today's craving?"

"You could've asked." I sulk.

"Or I could get your favorite table."

She's right. This is my favorite table, under the hanging pothos. The open window is a perfect spot to be with cats like Mrs. Whiskerton, who is currently napping in a cat house.

"Thanks," I drone. "Now, what about Mom?"

"Mom? I thought this was about work?" Seth sniffles.

"We'll get to that." I wave him off. "First, you need to get Mom off my back about dating. She started again last week when I dropped off leftovers for Dad."

"Why me?" He rubs his nose.

"You started dating Rylie, now Mom thinks I need a partner too."

"To be fair, she's always thought that," Seth says as our orders arrive.

"It's worse," I hiss, spooking the teen holding our food. Mumbling an apology, I grab the plates. "She's setting me up on blind dates."

"Here's a thought: don't go," Seth says, biting into his sandwich.

"Can't be worse than that maniac you dated," Rylie says, digging into her spinach soufflé.

"*Klepto*maniac," I correct her. When our bowling date ended, my lipstick, hand lotion, and glasses case were missing from my purse. When I went to swap my rented shoes for my flats, I caught him red-handed, trying to tuck my left shoe into his messenger bag.

"Or that guy who kissed like a . . . what did you call him?" She snaps her fingers. "A wet fish?"

"Sloppy. James kissed like a sloppy fish," I say, reliving my trauma. "It was wet too. His teeth gnawed on my bottom lip while his tongue waged an unwanted war against mine." Propping my elbow on the table, I point at Rylie. "I was the unlucky victim of too much tongue and not enough common sense."

"I don't want to hear this." Seth throws his hands up as a fluffy Maine Coon brushes up against his leg. He freezes. "Oh, no."

The cat winds around his ankle, purring loudly. Seth twists away, sniffling and waving a hand in a weak attempt to push the cat off.

"Shoo!" he says—only it comes out all nasally, like "Shnuh!"

"*Pare com isso*," Rylie swats him. "Be nice to your sister. She's going through a rough patch."

"Sure, if you call 'life' a rough patch." Seth dabs at his nose with tissue, sounding like a congested cartoon character.

"If you'd take allergy shots you wouldn't be miserable," I sip my drink and Seth grumbles. Blowing his nose into a napkin.

"Ignore him," Rylie says. "Are you considering one of your mom's matches?"

"Already did." I recount my most recent disaster. "His name was Larry"—I look around, then lower my voice—"K-U-N-T-Z."

Seth nearly chokes on his coffee, and Rylie groans.

"How is that pronounced?" she asks.

"It's gotta be a long U, right?" Seth says.

"I don't know!"

"Wasn't the name a red flag?" Seth laughs.

"We don't judge people by their names!" I defend. "I just wanted Mom off my back. How was I supposed to know Larry's mom would join us with their prom photos?"

"You mean *his* prom photos?" Rylie asks, hopefully.

I shake my head. "Theirs. Larry was homeschooled."

Seth's laugh becomes a sneeze attack. Serves him right.

"I had Rylie fake a call so I could leave."

"What did you tell them?" Seth's tone is suspicious.

"That you were in the ER with explosive diarrhea," I say.

"You what?" Seth yells, startling a few customers. And cats. "That's why Mom keeps sending me gut health articles!"

"Yeah, wehh," I say around a mouth full of cupcake. "She won' shtop ashing when I'm gonna shee Larry again." I swallow. "What do I do?"

"Don't see him," Seth says flatly.

"I wish it were that simple." Between Mom's meddling and the repair costs for my car, life feels overwhelming. At least I have a silver lining. "Let's talk about Flavors of the Bay."

Flavors of the Bay is the unofficial start of summer—three and a half days of food, music, and family fun under the trees at Green Family Farm.

There's a main stage with live music and a (mildly chaotic) amateur talent show on Saturday evening with a grand prize of $1,000. There's a shaded picnic zone and more food vendors than you could possibly sample in one weekend. Our truck has a coveted vendor spot, and I'm determined to make the most of it.

Seth's face scrunches. "Ah . . . ahh . . . achoo! Achoo! A-achoo!" He groans. "Why is it always three?"

"Your Benadryl's wearing off," I say as the doorbell jingles.

Right on cue, a plump calico with a clipped ear hops up onto our table like she got a personal invitation.

"Hi, sweet girl," I coo.

"*Gata bonita*," Rylie says, stroking her back. "Isn't she the cutest?"

Seth stiffens as the calico vaults into his lap.

"No, no, no! Get off," he tries to lift her. "This is not mutual!"

He's touching her like a ticking bomb, but she chirps, stretches, and settles in.

"Achoo! ACHOO!"

The third sneeze launches the calico like she's been shot from a cannon. She flies off his lap, bolting across the room, her tail puffed up like a bottle brush.

"I'll be back," Seth groans, rubbing his eyes and stumbles to the bathroom.

"Do you know which vendors will be there?" Rylie asks, watching me devour a cupcake.

I gesture toward the bathroom with my half-eaten s'mores cupcake. "Not even a flicker of concern for your sneezing soulmate?"

Rylie shrugs, totally unbothered. "I suggested he get allergy shots. He said, and I quote, 'I will not be injected in the butt for a cat.'"

"Honestly," I pause, licking frosting off my thumb, "that sounds exactly like something he'd say."

Before Rylie responds, a familiar voice cuts through the café, freezing us in place.

"We'll head to the farm and get the lay of the land," the voice says. "I want you to film me exploring."

My lungs seize. *That voice.*

"Maybe it's not him?" I whisper.

"Oh, *meu Deus*." Rylie pales, her eyes fixed behind me. "Beth, don't turn around."

"Don't be dramatic," I say, more for my benefit than hers. "It's not him, it's a doppelgänger with the same voice."

"And matching height and hair?"

"It's not him," I insist.

"Beth," she says urgently.

I look and instantly regret it. "I *told* you not to turn around," Rylie says.

Heat floods my skin as I whip back around in my seat, every nerve buzzing. Those eyes—warm brown, deceptively kind—are burned into my memory like I saw them yesterday, not three years ago. Three years since he dumped me during karaoke . . . for his step-cousin. They sang "Secret Love Song" as a duet while my heart shattered into tiny, off-key pieces. Peeking over my shoulder again, I curse and my heart pounds.

My ex-boyfriend, Brad Dawson, is standing ten feet away with another woman.

I duck low and hiss to Rylie, "I can't believe he has the audacity to be within a one-hundred-mile radius of here! Sugar and Spice is mine!"

Okay, technically, Sugar and Spice belongs to the Wynns. But it's always been my comfort spot. The place when I need quiet solace or a cupcake the size of my face. Plus, the memories of Aunt Dolly bringing me here. I'd sit by the bay window, sketching cats as they napped in sunbeams or tried to steal sips of unattended coffee. I still have a drawing of a chonky Manx trying to squeeze into a teacup. His name was Cinnamon. He had no shame.

Aunt Dolly even threw our high school graduation brunch here when Seth and I graduated. There were cat-shaped pancakes, personalized mugs, and a glitter banner that read "Paws-itively Proud of You!"

Seth broke out in hives before the pancakes arrived. His face puffed up like a marshmallow Peep, and a cat mistook his duffel bag for a litter box. In Aunt Dolly's defense, she didn't know the severity of Seth's allergies.

After that, Seth admitted defeat and started carrying allergy pills everywhere, like a Victorian woman with smelling salts.

This place isn't just coffee and cupcakes. It's memories, fur and warmth. Brad knows what this bakery means to me, we came here weekly when dating. He doesn't belong here. He's the guilty one. The heartbreaking, dream-crushing, soul-stabbing devil.

"Give me your keys." I slink lower in my chair. "I can't face him. Not when I look like this." I gesture at my grease-stained shirt.

"You mean like a confident queen who doesn't care how she dresses?" Rylie digs in her purse.

"Where's Seth?" I scan the room, panicking. "I can't get up and walk out. Brad will see me." My eyes drop to the floor. "I could army crawl out of here."

"Yeah, that's subtle."

"But I'm not leaving this." I stuff the rest of my cupcake in my mouth and stand—right onto Mrs. Whiskerton's tail. Her yowl makes everyone look at me.

Everyone including Brad.

Chapter Two

Brad Dawson slipped into my life before I inherited Kluckin' Good. We met at a backyard party with string lights and questionable sangria. He was an intern at the *Clementine Gazette*, already talking like a household name—destined to tackle hard-hitting stories that would change the world. Brad had an easy charm about him, weaving tales that made you feel like the only person in the room, even if he did all the talking. I fell for him in under a minute. We stayed up until one AM, swapping stories on a creaky porch swing, passing stale popcorn back and forth like it was a five-star meal. I thought it meant something. I thought we meant something. Apparently not enough to stop him from dumping me onstage in front of a full house at the Tipsy Cow. The humiliation's dulled, but it still simmers.

Whatever warmth I had left evaporates as I stare at him. Last I heard, he was living in Southern California with his step-cousin-slash-girlfriend. And yet here he is—in Sugar and Spice Bakery—jaw slack, frozen mid-step like someone hit pause.

Then I notice the way his arms are curled in protectively, the way he's wheezing.

Oh. Someone did hit pause.

Or more accurately, Seth hit him in the stomach.

"Seth!" Rylie yells. Lattes are forgotten, as everyone in the café is staring. Brad doubles over, coughing, but he recovers unnervingly fast.

He rubs his stomach, straightens, grimaces, then laughs dryly. "Okay. Fair," he says, clearly more annoyed than hurt. He stoops down to collect his things in one smooth motion. "I probably deserve that."

"Probably?" Seth flexes his fingers.

"Hey, Beth." Brad's voice is smooth and steady, like he wasn't just punched. "It's good to see you again."

I hate and admire him in the same breath for acting unshakable.

"You're still carrying that thing?" I point to the worn poker chip keychain that fell when Seth punched him.

Brad flashes the same grin he used to practice in the mirror. "What can I say? Lucky charm. Won it the night I met you." He spins it once on his finger, casual as ever.

"You didn't win that the night we met," I call him out on his lie. "I was with you when you bought it off a street magician outside some taco bar in Fremont on our second date."

"It was serendipitous."

"You were drunk on five-dollar jalapeño margaritas."

Classic Brad: charming, confident, and total bull. "Well, its luck still works. Here you are." His tone is playful, but there's that annoying undercurrent of faux charm, like he thinks he can still sweet-talk me.

I fold my arms. "I don't believe in luck. But if you're banking on it now, you're already broke."

"Let me be the judge of that."

"What are you doing here?" My voice comes out sharper than I mean, all the hurt I thought I'd buried rushing back.

"Work," he replies. He gestures toward a woman in an sweater. She's holding a to-go cup and looking anywhere but at us.

"I thought you were at some magazine down south."

"Moved on," Brad replies, rocking on his heels like we're catching up over brunch instead of me glowering at him. "Better position. Better reach. More creative freedom."

"Creative freedom?" I ask. "Weren't you planning to do some 'serious journalism'?"

"You'd be surprised what people will pay for," he gives an arrogant smile. "Content is content."

I don't know what that means, but it feels like an insult.

"Good for you," Seth says, grabbing a black bag from a server and shoving it at Brad. "Take your food and leave."

"Uh," the server says, "that's garbage."

"Garbage likes garbage," Seth says, disgusted.

Brad ignores Seth and shoves the bag back at the server, then looks at me. "Beth, could we talk?"

"No," Seth answers for me, arms crossed like he's about to referee a wrestling match.

"I didn't ask you," Brad says. "Last I checked, Beth can answer for herself. Or does your twin bond let you dictate her life?"

"Last *I* checked," Seth matches Brad's tone, "you humiliated my sister. You don't get to walk in and expect to talk to her."

Brad's always hated how close Seth and I are. And Seth's always hated Brad, period.

"Seth, stop," I say.

"No, he needs to stop," Seth says. "He's a conceited jerk. Don't talk to him. And you"—he shoves Brad in the shoulder—"leave my sister alone."

"Or what?" Puffing out his chest, Brad stands toe-to-toe with Seth.

"*Vamos*," Rylie says, tugging Seth away. "Beth can handle herself. Here," she hands me a napkin.

"What's this for?"

"Frosting." She points to my cheek.

Great.

As if I needed extra embarrassment.

Brad steps closer as I scrub at the frosting on my face. "How are you?" The softness in his voice sends a fresh spark of anger through me.

He wants to talk? *Now?* Three years after I begged for an explanation?

Fine.

"How's *Tiffany*?" I ask, loading her name with enough venom to drop a horse.

"Don't," Brad says. "That's beneath you."

"No," I snap. "You know what's beneath me? This conversation." I chuck the napkin at his chest. "You don't get to dump me in front of a karaoke crowd because you fell in love with your cousin—"

"Step-cousin," he corrects.

"IT DOESN'T MATTER!" I gesture wildly. "You don't get to leave me for a family member, stick me with a two-hundred-dollar bar tab, then show up years later acting like everything's fine. Especially not with her"—I wave in the general direction of Sweater Woman—"here. Who is she, anyway?"

"No one," Brad says, annoyed. "Beth, look—"

"Here's your order," Helena interrupts, holding a to-go cup and a paper bag.

Brad steps closer. "Beth, I—"

"No!" I cut him off, holding up a hand. "You don't get to do this. But you *do* get to give me your drink." I snatch the to-go cup from Helena. "Let me guess—double espresso with cream?"

Without waiting for a response, I march out the door, with Rylie and Seth following.

The late-afternoon sun hits my face, its warmth doing nothing to cool the fire in my cheeks. I'm halfway to Rylie's Jeep when Brad calls my name.

But I don't look back.

He can drop dead for all I care.

Chapter Three

"I don't know why I let you talk me into these things," Seth complains from the driver's seat. "If I'd known what you planned, I wouldn't have come."

We're parked in the vendor section at the Flavors of the Bay food festival, squeezed between a cupcake trailer shaped like a whisk and a barbecue rig belching hickory smoke. The sun is hot, and Seth's patience is already thin.

"I didn't talk you into anything. You agreed," I remind him as Rylie and I prep for the afternoon and evening ahead.

It's the first day of the festival. Well, half day. The gates open to the public at three PM, but vendor load-in started at one. We pulled in right on time, and it was already a mad dash for parking and setup.

Which is why I wanted to be here the second we're allowed through the gates. Prime real estate doesn't snag itself. We're close enough to the stage for foot traffic but far enough that the live music won't rattle the fryers. Flavors of the Bay is the unofficial summer kickoff for the Bay Area and is part food lover's dream, part county fair chaos. Live music, carnival games, and specialty food trucks stretched out under the trees. All I want is steady foot traffic and hungry people with cash to burn.

"*Ela está certa*. She's right," Rylie says, jamming a potato through the slicer attached to the edge of the counter. "We all sat down last week to discuss the plan for the festival." She finishes the potatoes, then washes her hands in the prep sink.

Her licorice-black hair is pulled into a tight ponytail that somehow still looks perfect in this heat. She's tall, lean, and effortlessly graceful—even in her chicken costume, which she slips into now, minus the head.

At five-two, I feel like her pocket-sized sidekick. I'm a full foot shorter than Seth, who sucked up all the good genes in the womb. Seth takes after our father, tall and handsome with thick dark hair. Whereas I look like our mom. Short with freckles and curves that no chicken suit could ever fully disguise. My strawberry-blond hair frizzes if someone so much as whispers the word *humidity*.

"Your lack of listening isn't my problem," I add, heating the oil for the deep fryer. "And don't start with me, Seth. I'm already stressing, knowing Brad's gonna be here."

Despite my better judgment, two nights ago, after seeing Brad, I went down a Google rabbit hole. Six months ago, he apparently moved from Southern California back to the Bay Area. He writes for *The City and Beyond*, covering Bay Area life and culture. The magazine has a cult following and major social reach.

Naturally, they're covering the festival. But why did it have to be Brad?

I found an article titled "Rise of the Foodie." Brad's reinvented himself as a food critic. Gone is the guy who ranted about journalistic integrity while double-fisting stale popcorn on a rickety porch swing. Now he writes pieces like "Love It or Lump It," handing out five-star reviews or health department warnings. It's ironic, when we dated, he thought crème brûlée was soap.

I can't help wondering what changed. What made him switch gears? Did he have a quarter-life crisis and discover aioli? Not that careers can't shift—look at Seth: law school to part-time line cook—but Brad's pivot feels calculated.

His reviews run hot or ice-cold. No room for nuance. In a recent promo video—hair perfectly gelled, ego oozing through the screen—he promised to reveal his top five food trucks from the festival. And which ones to avoid.

A glowing review from *The City and Beyond* could be huge for Kluckin' Good. But considering our history, I'm not holding my breath.

"You're a new level of crazy," Seth says, yanking me out of my thoughts. "Even for you. I never agreed to dress like a sexy cow!"

"First off, you're just a cow—"

"My udders are hanging out!" Seth cuts me off, standing dramatically.

"Phwwht phwoooh!" Rylie catcalls, fanning herself. "Careful shaking those around, this is a family event." She gestures to the pink udders.

"Would you stop it?" Seth grabs my sweater to cover himself. "This is what I'm talking about. People are going to ogle me all day."

"Weekend," I correct. "How else are we supposed to promote our sliders?"

He looks like a grumpy bull, tugging at the edges of the fuzzy costume. For the record, I found the cow costume online during a late-night scroll—and Seth lost a very specific jalapeño poppers and hot sauce bet. A deal's a deal.

Rylie whistles again. "I can't help myself, my man's a fine-lookin' bovine." She wraps her wings around Seth's neck, nuzzling his cheek.

"Knock it off!" I shield my eyes. "This is not the time or place for whatever . . . animal fetish this is. And people better ogle you. Ogling customers means more sales."

"Can we please stop saying the word 'ogle'?" Seth groans, dropping my sweater. "It's hitting my ear the way 'moist' does. And I'm *not* going outside like this. Rylie can parade around dressed like a piece of meat, but I refuse."

"Why is it okay for Rylie to parade around dressed like a chicken, but you won't dress like a cow?" I ask.

"Yeah, why is that?" Rylie narrows her eyes.

"Oh no, you don't," Seth raises his hooves. "I'm not falling for that trap. You know I'm team female and support equal rights. Rylie's used to ridiculous costumes."

"And for this weekend, so are you." I slap a few patties onto the sizzling flattop, the sound punctuating my statement.

Rylie bawks and gently nuzzles Seth's neck again.

"Stop it!" I snap a dish towel at them. "You're ruining farm animals for me."

I really *need to schedule that team meeting.*

"Having you dressed as a giant beefcake—literally—is the visual edge we need. There's a lot of competition here"

A sharp pound on the truck's side interrupts me.

"Beth Lloyd of Kluckin' Good!"

"Finish the sliders," I tell Seth. Wiping my hands on a towel, I swing the serving window open to find Kaydee Foley, one of the festival organizers. Her tailored pant suit is as crisp as her tone.

"Thanks for being on time. I wish all my vendors were this reliable." Her eyes land behind me, smile spreading. "And you've brought a mascot! I love it!"

"Two, actually. Buckawk!" Rylie flaps her wings and struts into view.

Kaydee laughs, her bun perfectly intact as she shakes her head. I first met her a couple of weeks ago when she stopped by our truck for lunch. After one bite of our Klucked in the Bayou wings and Juan and Only sliders, she begged me to fill a last-minute vendor spot at the festival.

So here we are, ready to impress.

"Thanks again for including us," I say.

Kaydee starts to respond but stops short, her smile fading as she looks to the right.

Two trucks—one bright orange with Roller Burger scrawled in bold lettering, the other a sleek tan with the logo Coffeeology and a beaker-shaped mug—are squared off like two roosters at a county fair, waiting for the other to peck first.

The Roller Burger driver slams her door and storms up to the tan truck. "Back up!" she yells.

"We were here first!" the other driver shouts through his window.

Seth leans in. "I thought foodies were supposed to be chill."

"Have you forgotten *The Food Truck Showdown*?" I ask.

The Roller Burger driver plants herself by the other truck's door. "Move it or else!"

Kaydee marches over. "Layla, what's going on here?"

"They took my spot!" Layla snaps, pointing at Coffeeology.

"I did not! She wasn't even in the lot when I started backing up!"

"Pack up and get out of my spot or else!" Layla threatens.

"Or else what?"

"Enough!" Kaydee shouts.

Rylie crosses her arms, her chicken feathers ruffling. "I already don't like this Layla person."

"Both of those food trucks should've come earlier," I say. "Who waits until the last minute and expects a prime spot?"

As Kaydee tries to calm things, I google Roller Burger. Layla Gafford runs it, usually parking at Jack London Square in Oakland. Her Yelp reviews are mixed. Some rave about the burgers, others gripe about the quality and spike in prices. Every review agrees on one point: the owner is a loudmouth.

Eventually, Kaydee gets Layla back in her truck and points to another parking spot on the opposite side of the festival. Layla crawls forward slowly, daring anyone to challenge her.

"She's trouble," I murmur, watching her snail-like compliance.

"No kidding," Seth agrees.

Trouble is the last thing I need. Festivals like this can catapult our business into new customer bases. If I can steer clear of Layla and her dramatics, everything should be fine.

With Layla moved and the road rage show over, Rylie slips her chicken head on. "You sure you're going to be okay?" she asks through the beak.

"Why wouldn't I be?" I look at her.

"Because of *o idiota estúpido*," Rylie says, referring to Brad.

"Don't worry about me. I have other things to worry about than the biggest mistake of my life."

I glance at my phone. 3:07 PM. When I look up, small groups of festivalgoers are already trickling through the entrance—some holding maps, others craning their necks to scan the food truck lineup.

"Looks like the gates are officially open." I point at a woman and man walking past our truck wearing matching shirts. I hand Seth a stack of flyers. "Start handing these out before the crowds really hit. Work the main path, get them into as many hands as possible. Then hustle back—we'll be slammed soon and I'll need your help." Rylie grabs a tray of samples and hops down from the truck.

Seth hesitates at the open door, still brooding about his costume, then lumbers after her in his cow suit, his udders swaying with every step.

"Wait!" I shout, leaning halfway out the back step, waving a black leather strap like a flag. "You're gonna need this."

Seth turns, body stiffening when he sees the cowbell dangling from my fingers. "You've got to be kidding me."

"If you're going to commit to the bit, then commit," I say, hopping down the last step with the bell in hand. "Now lean in."

"No way." He stands firm, holding his cow head.

I sigh, channeling our mother. A quick twist of his ear brings him down to my height.

"Ow! What is wrong with you!" He slaps my hand as I loop the cowbell around his neck.

"There. Festival-ready," I give the bell a little pat.

Rylie cackles from across the path. "You look udderly delightful!"

"Go," I wave them off. "Moo and mingle. Hand out samples, and don't embarrass me, Seth!"

My brother grumbles as they disappear.

Once they're gone, I duck back into the truck to finish working. I knock out the last of the sides, stack the extra napkins, and wipe down the counters—again. I grab the chalkboard menu and nudge the door open wider with my hip. With a grunt, I hoist the sign and carry it awkwardly, waddling like a penguin as I balance it against my knee.

Sunlight catches the still-smudgy chalk letters as I position it in front of the truck, anchoring it with a small crate and a rock I borrowed from the nearby flowerbed.

I check the time: 3:25.

We got here at one, but I've been playing catch-up ever since. The fryer jammed after we plugged in the generator, and the point-of-sale system decided to throw a tantrum and wouldn't boot.

So much for a smooth two-hour prep window. Between troubleshooting and last-minute prep, I'm only now adding the final touches. The gates have been open nearly half an hour, and the crowd is growing fast.

I wipe my hands on my apron and take a deep breath. Ready or not, it's go time.

I angle the chalkboard toward the path to catch foot traffic from both directions. It advertises our festival-exclusive specials. Beats and Bites Basket: beef sliders with truffle fries. Golden Gate Heat Wings: our spiciest wings with a sweet zing. Last, our Guac the Line Fries: crispy avocado fries for our vegan crowd. Regular flavors are listed below the specials.

Under our serving window, I hang a small chalkboard sign on a hook Seth installed, labeled Kind Bites, with cheerful script and little chicken footprints.

The board explains how it works: Customers can prepay for a meal I'll later serve to someone in Clementine who needs it. No questions asked. It's my way of keeping things local and personal, even at a big festival.

Instead of collecting names or hanging notes, I track donations and honor each one after the weekend. Whether it's a regular who's hit a rough patch or someone new who needs a little grace, I make sure those meals get into the right hands.

The festival donates a portion of ticket sales to regional food banks, which is amazing. But our Kind Bites board lets people contribute in a more immediate, boots-on-the-ground kind of way. One meal at a time.

The crowds are moving now, slowly at first—families scanning food options, teens posing for selfies, and couples mapping out their snack plan for the night. It's not packed yet, but the foot traffic is steady.

I finish adding a few touches: a mini pennant banner I made last night out of twine and old takeout menus, plus a tiny bouquet of wildflowers in a glass jar on the far end of the serving ledge to make it feel homey.

As I adjust the chalkboard sign one last time, a woman in a sunhat approaches the truck. "Hi," she says. "Sorry, do you know if there's a real bathroom somewhere? Like, not a porta potty?"

"Yup—head toward the red barn past the flower pavilion. Restrooms are over there," I say, pointing the way.

"Thank you," she says, speed-walking away on a mission.

I turn around as I hear. "Beth, stop me, or I'm going to snap the man in two!"

Helena Wynn, owner of Sugar and Spice Bakery, is there. Helena, normally so upbeat, looks troubled. Her black hair is in a messy bun, and her usually warm eyes are shut as she rubs her temples.

"Did Chris forget something?" I ask.

"Chris is holding down the bakery. I'm here with Trina." Trina is one of their best servers and Helena's go-to for events like this. "The problem is *him*." She hands me her phone.

"'Bakers Beware,'" I read aloud.

"Read the whole thing," Helena says, resuming her temple massage. "But first, got anything strong to drink? I'm gonna need it."

"Lemonade or iced tea."

"Give me an Arnold Palmer. I'll pretend there's vodka in it."

I give her back her phone and duck inside the truck. As I pour equal parts lemonade and iced tea into one of our Kluckin' Good tumblers, I glimpse my reflection in the serving window. Flushed cheeks, already frizzing hair peeking out from under my blue baseball cap, and a flour flecked shirt. Yep, festival chic.

Popping the lid on her drink I head back outside.

"Here."

"This is cute," she turns the cup and smiles at our laughing chicken logo. "That's the other thing. We forgot cups. Trina went back to pick some up, but she's late."

"I might have an extra sleeve of compostable cups you can have. Want me to look?" I offer.

"Thanks, but Trina should be back any minute. Read what that jerk Brad Dawson wrote about my café." She hands her phone to me.

My stomach clenches as I skim the review. Brad wrote terrible things about Sugar and Spice, claiming the baked goods use cat hair instead of sprinkles.

"That's awful," I say, handing her phone back. "Why would he write that?"

"It's because of the other day," Helena says, pocketing her phone. "After you left he tried to play the victim, claiming you wouldn't let him explain himself. Not that he deserves a chance after humiliating you like that. I gave him a fresh drink and told him to take his business elsewhere."

"I appreciate that, but you shouldn't let my personal life interfere with your business."

"You're my friend, as was your Aunt Dolly." She reminds me. "No, I did the right thing. But if his online review affects my sales this weekend, he better watch himself."

"Careful what you say," I warn. "Heat of the moment words have a way of coming back to haunt you. Trust me."

She waves a dismissive hand. "Don't worry about me. If anything, you should worry about Seth."

"Seth?" *What did he do?*

"On my way here, I saw him and Rylie talking to a group of people. Some kids tried to milk him. He didn't look happy."

I laugh, picturing Seth fighting off thirsty toddlers.

Then—

Pop!

We both flinch as a balloon bursts. Followed by a small child's wail and a flurry of "Shhh, you're okay, you're okay," from the parents.

"Poor kid," I say, watching the festival buzz around us. Music drifts from the main stage and vendors shouting over one another about kettle corn and mango slushies.

That's when I see him walking toward us.

Tousled hair, ripped jeans, flannel at his waist. Something about him tugs at my memory. Helena points at him. "You're Ivan Parks, right? 'The new face in alternative rock'?"

"Yep." He nods, then looks at me. "But Beth might remember me as Adam Parker."

Recognition hits like a freight train. Brad's best friend. The life of every party and the guy who drank as much as he smoked. The last time I saw him was the night Brad dumped me.

"Adam. Wow," I say, surprised. "You've . . . changed."

And he has. The Adam I remember had bloodshot eyes, beer breath, and a knack for quoting bad stand-up comedy. This Adam—or Ivan—looks like he stepped out of a music video.

"Maybe a little," he says, sheepishly.

"What are you doing here?" I ask.

"Living the dream," he says. "A talent manager discovered me at an open mic night, now I'm the lead singer for the Silver Stones."

"Your name is Adam?" Helena asks.

"Ivan is my stage name," he explains. "We're playing here this weekend."

"Nice to meet you," she says before leaving.

"So, Adam, why are you here talking to me?" I ask once Helena is gone.

He shifts on his feet, looking uncomfortable. "I saw your name on the vendor list and wanted to apologize."

"Apologize for what?" I laugh. "You never did anything to me."

"But I did," he insists. "I should've said something that night when Brad dumped you instead of bailing."

"It's not your fault Brad was an idiot," I say. "He's a dumb mistake from my past who I've moved on from."

"Yeah, but," Adam pauses. "I need to make amends for any part I played that night. What Brad did was wrong and I should've stepped in."

"Adam, you don't—"

"Please," he stops me. "It's part of my recovery program. I've been sober for almost a year now."

I take a closer look. He does seem clearer. Grounded. Like someone who's crawled through something heavy and made it out the other side.

"Back then, I was partying hard," he says, softer now. "Like . . . blackout hard. I used it to justify my stupidity. And to avoid taking responsibility. But I've been doing the work and realize what Brad did to you was wrong. I'm sorry I didn't speak up. I wasn't a good friend to anyone back then."

I swallow the lump in my throat. "I forgive you, Adam. And I'm proud of you for getting sober. That takes real strength."

"Thanks," he gives a grateful smile.

"Yo, Ivan!" A stout man in flannel matching Adam's jogs over.

Adam gestures to him. "This is Van Ambrose, the drummer for the Silver Stones. And Reggie Douglas is our guitarist, but he's," Adam looks around, "somewhere."

"Nice to meet you," Van smiles at me. "We gotta go, man," he tells Adam.

Adam nods. "It was nice seeing you, Beth." He pauses, then hugs me awkwardly. "You look happy."

"I am," I smile.

Adam turns, then says. "You're better off without that scumbag."

"That's a nice thing to call your best friend," I joke.

"We're not friends anymore. Haven't been since . . . well, he knows what he did."

Adam leaves with Van, and I'm left with a tangle of emotions I'd rather not have.

Looks like I wasn't the only bridge Brad burned.

Shaking it off, I step back into the truck to refocus.

I then hear an unwelcome voice. "Was I really a mistake?"

Chapter Four

Outside my truck, Brad is giving me a goofy grin. Once upon a time, that grin made my heart melt. Now all I feel is lava boiling in my veins.

"What do you want?" I demand, crossing my arms tightly to keep from throwing something.

"I'd like to talk."

"I'm busy," I snap.

"Can't you spare a few minutes? You know, for old times?" His nostalgic tone makes my skin crawl.

"Old times?" I slam my hands on the counter, the sharp sound startling even me. That stupid grin is still there, and my resolve shatters. Years of frustration bubble up.

"Is one of those old times when you dumped me for your cousin? Or when you left me to pay for your tab at the pub? Maybe when you ghosted me for a week? Oh, wait—" I clap my hands. "I know which old time. The week I called you over and over, only to hear from your assistant you were on vacation. In Florida. WITH YOUR COUSIN! She also told me you'd instructed security to remove me if I showed up at your office." I'll never forget her warning about being forcibly removed and banned from the building. "I can't believe you!"

The crowd outside the truck thickens, and I hear a faint "Ooh." Good. Let them hear.

"Step-cousin!" Brad shouts, as if that makes it better. "There's no blood between us."

"That doesn't matter," I spit.

He throws his hands up. "You can't be mad we broke up. We didn't know what we wanted. *I* didn't know what I wanted."

"We didn't break up, you *dumped* me! We dated for just over a year, Brad. We talked about our future together!" I scream.

"Beth—"

"That was *our* Florida trip," I cut him off. "I planned the entire thing! Then you dumped me in public without an explanation. You're a piece of—"

"We broke up," Brad interrupts. "And for the record, Tiffany dumped me. Seven months ago."

"Daaang," someone says, and I spot a woman munching on popcorn like she's at a matinee.

Brad's phone rings. He looks at the screen, silences it, and shoves it into his pocket. A second later, it rings again. He stares at the screen before silencing it once more, visibly annoyed.

"What do you expect me to do with this information? Say I'm sorry? That I understand? Maybe grab a drink so you can talk about your feelings?" My voice drips with mockery.

A festival worker has stopped sweeping to lean on his broom, utterly engrossed. "Could we, you know, continue this conversation in private?" Brad asks, lowering his voice.

"Nope." I cross my arms. "Say whatever you need right here." From inside the truck, I have the high ground—literally and figuratively.

"It was a mistake. I never should have left you for her," Brad says, voice thick with regret.

Once, I would've killed to hear those words. Now they land too late. He disgusts me. How could I have ever fallen for him? "Too little, too late—"

"Beth, please."

"Goodbye, Brad."

"You tell him, girl!" someone shouts from the crowd, and applause follows.

"Don't be like this, Beth," Brad pleads, stepping closer to my serving window. "We had some good times. Why can't we—"

"I believe the lady has made her feelings clear."

My stomach flips at the gravelly voice behind him.

Not him too.

Detective Drew Kane steps into view, his blue eyes locking onto mine before turning to Brad.

Brad pivots sharply. "This doesn't concern you. Mind your own business."

"See, that's where you're wrong," Detective Kane says, calm but firm. "Anything involving the residents of Clementine is my business."

Resident? That's all I am to him? After everything we went through together on *The Food Truck Showdown*, me practically solving the case on my own because he was too tight-lipped to share anything. You'd think I'd rank a little higher than *resident*. Especially after all the meals he's had me "put on his tab."

He's one of two detectives in Clementine. His partner, Jerry Hamstead, talks more than he thinks and is always ready to spill the tea. Detective Kane, on the other hand, plays things close to his chest. Frustratingly close. But he's thorough. Smart. And unfortunately, *very* attractive. Which makes this whole situation deeply inconvenient.

"And who do you think you are?" Brad jabs Detective Kane's chest.

Big mistake.

He flips open his wallet in that classic cop move, flashing his badge. "Detective Kane."

Brad's eyes widen. "Th-this isn't what it looks like."

"It looks like you're harassing an upstanding member of my community," Detective Kane replies.

"Upstanding?" Brad snorts. "She once stole a red thong from a department store!"

Oh, for the love of . . .

"I told you that in confidence!" My cheeks burn. One accidental theft in high school and suddenly I'm the town menace? I didn't even mean to take it! I was holding it for Rylie as a joke, got distracted and walked out with it still hooked on my wrist like a deranged bracelet. Seth thought it was hilarious when he had to pick me up from mall jail because I was too embarrassed to call our parents.

I can't believe he brought that up now!

Detective Kane arches an eyebrow, his lips twitching. "Do you still have said thong?"

"That's none of your business!" I snap.

"It is. It's called evidence."

"No, it's called my mom threw it out after Seth tattled like the traitor he is."

Detective Kane lifts both hands. "Sounds like case closed."

I glare at Brad. "It's time for you to leave." I shoo him.

"Let's go," Detective Kane clamps a hand on Brad's shoulder to steer him away.

"Hang on." Brad twists free, grabbing the orange lanyard around his neck. "I have a right to be here. See this?" He shakes the lanyard in the detective's face. "I'm press. Covering the festival. My job is to interview the food trucks, and I'm starting with Kluckin' Good."

His gaze returns to mine, and I want to throw up just looking at him.

"Fine," I say through gritted teeth. "Talk to my brother when he gets back. Seth handles all media inquiries. Now, if you'll excuse me, I have a customer." I wave the woman forward, but Brad blocks her way. His face twisting with anger.

"C'mon," Detective Kane says, nudging him with a look that leaves no room for argument. "Go interview another vendor while you wait."

Brad clenches his jaw. "We're not done talking, Beth."

"Whatever," I mutter as he stalks off.

The woman approaches the serving window as I'm trying to calm down. She's maybe early thirties, with shoulder-length hair streaked teal to match her chunky glasses. Her bubblegum-pink T-shirt features a cartoon dinosaur in a tutu that reads *Fierce but Fancy*. I like her already.

She scans our chalkboard menu. "Two Kluck-a-Doodle Classics, a basket of Plucked and Truffle Fries, and three lemonades, please."

"You got it." I tap her order into the point-of-sale system. "By the way, we've got a special on our Kluckin' Good tumblers." I gesture toward the display by the serving window. "Free refills today, and just ninety-nine cents the rest of the weekend."

"You sure know how to upsell a girl," she says, handing me a credit card. "I'll take three tumblers."

"They're festival exclusives. Once they're gone, they're gone."

"Even better. I love merch with a mysterious expiration date." She glances in the direction Brad disappeared. "So . . . you and the guy. That was either a breakup or an audition for *General Hospital: Food Truck Edition*."

I give a tight smile. "Ex-boyfriend. Long story. He dumped me for his step-cousin in the middle of karaoke night. His timing is almost as bad as his decency." I hand her back the credit card.

"Oof," she says, wincing. "Been there. I once had an ex dump me via Venmo. Left a $7 payment labeled 'for your emotional damage.'"

"Shut up!" My mouth falls open. "Okay, that might actually top mine."

"Nah, public ex drama at a food festival wins on sheer chaos points." She leans closer, stage-whispering, "Especially in front of a hot cop."

"Trust me, I didn't plan it," I say, passing her the receipt. "But I've said my peace. It's over."

"You handled it like a pro." She watches me set the fry basket on the ledge. "Those smell amazing."

"Freshly tossed," I say. "Real truffle oil, none of that fake stuff. Let me get the rest of your order."

The fryer hisses as I remove the tenders and give them a good shake. I transfer the Kluck-a-Doodle Classics to the waiting baskets on the counter. Then I grab three tumblers, scoop the ice, and fill them with fresh lemonade.

"Here you go." I secure the drink lids and pass her order through the serving ledge.

"Thanks." She snaps a photo of her tumblers on the counter. "I'm documenting this weekend," she explains. "My husband's competing in the chili cook-off on Sunday and he's made me taste-test twelve batches. Pretty sure I have cumin trauma."

I laugh. "You're doing the Lord's work. Also, those tumblers are dishwasher-safe."

"Good to know," she starts gathering her order.

"Will you be able to carry all of this?" I ask.

She waves me off. "I was a server in college at a German restaurant. During Oktoberfest, I carried thirteen steins without spilling a drop. I can handle a few baskets of food and some lemonade."

I watch, impressed, as she balances three baskets in her elbow and arranges the lemonades without breaking a sweat.

"Thanks again," she smiles. "And hey—if you decide to publish your breakup memoir, I'll preorder."

"I'll call it *Love, Lies, and Chicken Thighs*."

She laughs. "See you tomorrow. I'm definitely coming back."

I watch her go, narrowly avoiding a man chasing a toddler chasing a bounce ball.

"She's got her hands full." Kaydee says, a tight smile on her face.

"She's my first customer of the weekend," I say, pointing at the woman who left. "What can I do for you?"

"Coffee," Kaydee says, reaching into her pocket.

"Coffee?" I doubletake. "I don't sell coffee. We have a coffee maker in the truck, but that's just for us. Why don't you try Helena's truck? Or Coffeeology?"

"I did, Coffeeology had a line wrapped around their truck. Helena doesn't have cups. She sent me here for one of yours." Kaydee eyes the display. "The yellow one's cute, I'll take that one."

"Oh, right." I grab a Kluckin' Good tumbler from our merch display. "They're usually $14.9—"

"Keep the change," Kaydee hands me a twenty. "Add whatever's left to your Kind Bites board for someone after the festival."

"Thank you," I smile, taking her twenty. "Tell Helena I've got a few sleeves she can have."

Kaydee takes the tumbler but doesn't say thanks. Her fingers drum along the lid.

"Cute cup," she mutters, distracted. She's not really looking at it.

"Double-walled and dishwasher-safe," I say. "Highly recommend Helena's graham cracker latte."

That gets a flicker of a smile, but it vanishes fast.

"What was that shouting match about earlier?" I nod to where those two food trucks had been.

She exhales sharply. "Vendor turf dispute. We'll sort it out once Conner arrives."

Of course. Her boss, Conner Green. His family owns the farm hosting the Flavors of the Bay food festival. You wouldn't know Conner was her boss. Every time I've seen him he's in a different graphic tee and has the energy of someone who thinks showering is a scam. Kaydee's dresses are pristine, and Conner looks like he sleeps in laundry.

"Hopefully it's all settled between those two food trucks and the festival runs smoothly," I say.

"I hope. Last thing I want is a fistfight over fryer space."

She tries to sound breezy, but she fiddles with the tumbler. Something's bothering her.

"Speaking of problems . . ." Her tone shifts. "I heard you had . . . words with a food critic."

Ugh. News travels fast here.

"Sorry about that," I say. "Won't happen again."

"Should I be concerned?" she presses. "This is my first major event working here. I don't want things going sideways."

She stiffens, like she's bracing for bad news. I suddenly feel on trial for my public emotional outburst.

"Brad's my ex," I admit. "He showed up at as the festival started and stirred up . . . stuff. I never got closure after things ended." Kaydee's eyes flicker with something unreadable before she masks it.

"It's fine," she says. "You're not the only one here to dislike him." She tries to sound casual, but the words drop like stones.

"Have you met him?" I ask.

She grips the tumbler tightly.

"You could say that," she says flatly. "Conner thought having someone from *The City and Beyond* would be a smart PR move. I disagreed."

"Why?" I ask. "I mean, I don't like Brad, but isn't any press better than none?"

I flash back to when the *Clementine Gazette* ran a full-color image of me in Rylie's chicken suit, walking out of the police precinct. The headline? "Local Chicken Flees the Coop!" Not exactly Pulitzer-worthy, but it did lead to a bump in sales. Go figure.

"Personally, I didn't think we needed him, especially after—" She stops talking.

"After what?"

"It's nothing," she waves her hand. "Brad and Conner didn't get along. That's all."

"Then why is he here?" I ask.

"Conner wanted an edge. He called Brad 'clickbait with a notepad.'"

"Charming."

"Conner thrives on buzz, and Brad thrives on drama. Conner thought it would make for good coverage."

"But something happened?" I guess.

"They clashed fast. Conner didn't like Brad's condescending questions during the walkthrough. Brad said the festival had 'county fair energy in a Silicon Valley zip code.' I had to step between them."

I blink. "Seriously?"

"Mm-hmm." Her phone rings, but she silences the call. "They shook hands afterward, it was nothing."

"Sounds tense," I grab a rag to clean some spilled flour I missed earlier.

"Don't let Conner know I told you. He hates looking unprofessional."

Funny, since I've only seen him in ripped jeans and wrinkled shirts.

"Honestly," Kaydee continues, "I think Brad just likes getting under people's skin."

"I agree."

"He's always been that way," she mumbles.

"Wait"—that catches my attention—"did you know him before the festival? Because that is spot on."

Kaydee licks her teeth. "This festival has been a lot of work, and he's not been easy to deal with," is all she says.

That's not an answer.

I study her face, but she's closing off. Whatever she knows, she's not sharing.

"I don't want drama," she finally says.

"Neither do I."

"Then do me a favor and stay professional," she says. "If Brad hassles you, call festival security. They're here for situations like that."

"I don't think that will be necessary," I assure her. "My only plan this weekend is selling to hungry customers."

"Good plan." Her phone rings and she groans. "Conner. Again. If I don't answer soon, he'll start sending messages via drone."

She clutches the tumbler so tightly her knuckles blanch as she walks off. I'm left holding a rag and a hundred questions.

What did she mean I'm not the only one who disliked Brad? Did she hear about his review of Sugar and Spice Bakery? Or what Helena said about him?

Or . . . was she talking about herself?

And Conner Green. She said he brought Brad in for PR but didn't get along. So why keep him?

It feels like something more than festival logistics is happening. But I shake it off. "Not my problem."

Then I see him.

Brad.

He walks up to a man standing next to a decorative lemon tree—why do all festivals have those? I don't recognize the man. Tall, broad-shouldered, wearing a "Wrap City" T-shirt and worn apron around his waist. They stand too close, heads almost touching as Brad holds out his left hand. The guy reaches into his apron pocket and hands Brad what looks like a letter.

Brad tucks whatever was handed to him into his jeans pocket. A second later, both men walk away like nothing happened.

What the heck?

I squint after them, fighting the urge to yell, "I saw that!" But what did I even see?

Still. I clock the vendor's face, just in case. Something about it feels off, but I can't explain why.

I turn away from the serving window, but the image lingers.

Whatever Brad pocketed didn't look like lunch.

Chapter Five

Knock, knock.

I spin around, nearly knocking over a stack of food trays. Detective Kane leans against the doorframe at the back of my truck. His smile equal parts amused and exasperated.

"Hi," I say, my voice a little higher than usual. My gaze lingers on him for a second too long, and I almost forgot how handsome he is. The dappled shadows from the tree above seem to conspire against me, emphasizing his sharp jawline and those eyes that always look like they're keeping a secret.

"You're making a habit of this," he says, stepping into the truck. "Arguing with men in public. That's the third time I've seen it now."

I also forgot how annoying he can be.

"It's not my fault jerks have a radar for me and my food truck," I say, stacking food trays.

The truck shifts as he moves, closing the door behind him. He surveys the small space like he's on duty, even though he's wearing casual clothes. "Was he harassing you?"

I shake my head. "Brad's many things, but dangerous isn't one of them. He's also my ex, unresolved issues come with the package."

Detective Kane leans against the counter, close but not too close. "Even calm people snap under pressure. If he comes around again, let me know."

"I didn't know the festival hired detectives for crowd control."

"They didn't," he shrugs. "My sister and nephew are here. Family tradition: deep-fried everything, cotton candy, and then seeing how many times I can take my nephew on the carousel before he pukes on my sister's fiancé."

I laugh loud enough to turn a woman's head. "You don't like the guy?"

"He's fine." His mouth quirks up. "I did a thorough background check and interrogation over Thanksgiving dinner. He's solid, just . . . dragging his feet on the whole wedding thing."

It's the longest non-murder-related conversation we've ever had, and it's oddly nice. I picture him, sleeves rolled up, lifting his nephew onto his muscular shoulders. It surprises me how easy it is to imagine him like that.

"Anyway," he continues, interrupting my daydream. "I knew Lauren would be here the second the gates opened. Good thing I planned to meet my sister today, considering your ex can't read the room."

"Thanks, but you don't need to worry. I don't plan on seeing or talking to Brad for the rest of the weekend."

A bell jingles faintly, and our heads swivel as the back door flies open.

"Moo!"

Detective Kane hooks a thumb at my brother. "Did he just moo at me?"

I sigh as Rylie struts up, her beak bobbing. "*Oi, como vai*? How are you, Detective Pretty Boy?"

Heat floods my face. *Why, oh why, did I ever call him that?*

I hadn't meant to say it out loud when I first met him. In my defense, I was under duress.

Being arrested while dressed as a giant chicken tends to rattle a person. I learned two important things that day: one, it's considered "assault" to ruffle your feathers in someone's face. And two, if you're going to use poultry profanity, don't do it while dressed as a larger-than-life fowl. It's hard to be taken seriously while looking like a character from a fast-food commercial.

Back then, I didn't know who Detective Kane was. I was just thinking, *Wow, that's one ridiculously good-looking officer*, and the words "Officer Pretty Boy" slipped out. Loudly. In front of him. And another cop. The nickname stuck with his colleagues, and once I learned he was a detective, the title was upgraded.

Yay me.

Detective Kane laughs. "I'm fine, Ms. Cortes." He snags a basket of fries as he steps past Seth, still in his full cow regalia, glaring with his hands—I mean hooves—on his hips.

"You forgot to pay!" I call as he heads down the steps.

"Add it to my tab!" he shouts.

I grab my moleskin, flipping past pages labeled "Detective Kane's Tab" in increasingly aggressive block letters. His running total: $301.67. One day, he'll owe me a truck's worth of wings.

"What was Kane doing here?" Seth asks. "Why were you alone? With the door closed?"

"Ignore him," Rylie says. "He's just mad some kids tried to milk him."

"One actually latched on!" Seth stomps a hoof. "I was assaulted!"

"He was two," Rylie says. "Calm down, *amor*."

"Two or not, he had a death grip."

I laugh. "Sucks when people treat you like a walking side of beef, huh?"

"I don't appreciate your lack of sympathy." Seth huffs.

"And I don't appreciate you cow-blocking me," I say.

"So, you admit I blocked something?" Seth points a hoof at me.

"No!" I shake my head, but I feel my cheeks flush. *Do I want anything to happen with Detective Kane?* I brush the thought away. "Even if there was something, you have no right to meddle in my love life."

"What love life?" Seth snickers.

"That's it!" I untie my apron, hanging it on the hook by the door. "You two can handle things for a while."

"Where are you going?" Rylie asks.

"To get some fresh air. Away from the giant jackass." I point at Seth.

"I'm a cow, thank you!"

"My apologies to donkeys everywhere," I say, stepping out of the truck.

My stomach growls. Craving something sugary, I make a beeline for Helena's truck.

Chris's cupcakes are the best, so when Helena says Trina brought back a dozen sugar cookie crumble cupcakes, I order two without hesitation. I inhale one before my coffee soda's ready, then the second. Halfway through my drink, I urgently need a bathroom.

Porta potties dot the grounds, but the barn's public restroom is worth the walk.

Fluorescent lights flicker as I push the door open, casting a dim glow over the yellowing walls. The place smells of damp industrial cleaner. It's as if someone hit mute on the festival. Music and laughter seep through, but the hush inside feels too still, too expectant. Someone could scream in here, and it wouldn't carry far.

I take two steps inside when movement in the dimness makes me freeze.

A shadow shifts near the sinks.

My pulse spikes, and my hand twitches for the door. Then the lights steady, revealing a familiar figure.

"Kaydee?" My voice is sharper than I intend.

Last time I saw her, she was leaving to answer a call from her boss. Now she looks like she's been through a shredder.

She stands motionless, half turned, expression unreadable. A dark jagged smear mars her pristine maroon shirt, spreading near her waist. My stomach clenches looking at the fabric.

I glance from the stain to her face. "What are you doing in here? The lights were off."

She looks as if she's just noticing me. "I—I just needed a minute." Her voice is thin, stretched tight. "Didn't realize it was that dark."

The automatic light sensors should have switched on when she walked in. Unless she's been standing still in the dark.

I nod at her shirt. "What happened?"

She looks down, tugging at the fabric. "Oh. Spilled something."

I've never seen a stain like that before. Could it be sauce, wine, maybe juice? But the shape of it . . . It doesn't look like a splash or drip.

"Are you feeling okay?" I ask.

Her face is pale, and her posture's all wrong—too rigid, like she's holding her breath.

"I'm fine," she says, closing her eyes briefly.

She doesn't look fine, but I don't push it.

"Did you get that situation sorted out?" I ask.

She hesitates. "Which situation?"

"The phone call from Conner. Back at my truck. Your phone rang twice while we were talking and you said it was him. It sounded like it might've been important."

There's a flicker of something across her face I can't place before she tamps it down. "Oh. Yeah. It's . . . handled."

"With Conner?" I prod.

Her jaw twitches. "Yeah. Him."

She doesn't elaborate, and I don't press, but something about the way she says *him* feels thorny—like there's history there. Or resentment. Or maybe fear?

She crumples a paper towel and tosses it in the trash. She looks upset.

I should leave it alone.

But I don't.

"You sure you're okay?"

Her lips press into a tight line. "I'm fine, Beth."

The words are final. A clear dismissal.

I let her have the final word, but something in me itches. The weird stain. Her robotic movements. That look when I brought up Conner.

What's going on between her and her boss?

And why does it feel like I just interrupted something I wasn't supposed to see?

I linger for a second longer before nodding. "All right. See you out there." I step into a stall and a second later I hear the door creak open and bang shut.

She's gone.

Finishing up, I wash my hands and mull over how strange Kaydee was acting. There's something about that stain. It didn't look like a food stain. Then there was the flatness in her voice earlier when she talked about Conner.

Conner thought having someone from The City and Beyond *would be a smart PR move. I disagreed.*

Brad and Conner didn't get along.

The words stick like peanut butter on the roof of my brain. What happened between them? And why did Kaydee grip her tumbler like she wanted to throw it through a window? More importantly, why do I care so badly to know what went down between her and my ex-boyfriend? He's my ex for a reason. I shouldn't care this much what he's been up to since he dumped me.

If Seth were here, he'd tell me this isn't one of my true-crime podcast episodes. But still, Kaydee's reaction, the stain on her shirt, the way she stood there in the dark—it all gnaws at the edges of my mind.

But that's not my problem. My problem is to focus on selling wings to hungry festivalgoers.

Outside the bathroom, I can hear the festival buzzing in full swing. Families wander toward the flower pavilion, and music drifts from the stage. The festival sprawls out before me in a lively horseshoe formation. Game booths, pop-up shops, and merch tables make up the outermost area, while the heart of the festival belongs to the food trucks, over seventy vendors strong. Beyond the stage, where live music and a variety of acts perform, sits the historical Green Family Farm red barn. This year, it's open to visitors who purchased advance tickets, allowing them to feed the rescue alpacas and sheep housed inside.

Even though it's technically just a half day, the festival is already packed or close to it. Festival workers dart across the grounds, vendors fine-tune their setups, and the crowds are trickling through the inner paths, clutching tote bags and snapping selfies.

Pulling out my phone, I check the time. I need to get back to the truck. My pace slows as I start to send a quick text. Only my phone loudly ba-gawks with a new message from our group chat.

Seth: We need you. A line is already forming.

I'm about to reply when a figure ahead catches my eye. It's someone in an oversized brown sweater and a wide-brimmed hat blocking their face standing still in the middle of the path ahead of me. They're staring at something I can't see.

My phone ba-gawks again with another message. The person jerks, their body stiffening, and they rush straight for the flower pavilion. Vanishing behind the colorful displays.

Weird.

My thumbs dance on the screen as I text and walk.

Me: I'm coming back now, just finished in the bathroom.

Rylie sends a gif of a chicken running, and I laugh.

Then I stop, midstep.

"What the . . . ?" I look at the grass to the left just off the dirt and gravel path.

There's a pair of worn Chuck Taylors—red, white, and blue plaid. Shoes I once gifted years ago.

My stomach drops.

"Brad!" I shout, rushing forward.

He lies still, his eyes wide and unseeing. A bloody rock lies by his temple, staining the grass red. I gasp, and the world tilts.

I don't want to confirm what I already know, but I have to. Trembling, I reach for his wrist. No pulse.

"Oh, no, no, no."

His familiar keychain lies next to his hand—a lucky Ace of Spades poker chip.

Guess I was right. Its luck ran out.

I fumble for my phone, but before I can dial 911, a scream rips through the air. I whirl around, heart hammering.

Layla Gafford, owner of Roller Burger, stands a foot away, eyes enormous as she points a shaking finger at Brad.

"What did you do?"

Chapter Six

I barely feel the stump beneath me as Grover County officers cordon off the area, stretching yellow tape between the trees. It flutters in the breeze, jarring against the greens and browns of the farm. Brad is dead.

I blink, but the words don't feel real. Our last conversation replays in my mind—the anger in my voice. Him telling me we're not done talking. I was furious with him and wanted him to know it. I wanted him to feel even an ounce of the humiliation I felt when he dumped me for his step-cousin. And now?

Now he's gone.

I don't regret what I said. I just didn't know it would be the last thing I said. I feel a sudden chill. I should feel something more, shouldn't I? Not grief—because I'm not grieving him—but something. Guilt? No, I didn't kill him. Sadness? Not really. But maybe . . . unease. The kind that settles in when the past catches you off guard. *How did this happen? And why did it have to be me who found him?*

An officer stands nearby, arms folded, listening to Layla Gafford. Layla's voice is too low to catch, but her expression says enough. Anger, suspicion, maybe even triumph.

I clench my hands together, my nails pressing into my palms. She'd screamed at me before the police came. I'm surprised her screams didn't draw the entire festival to us. Layla demanded to know what I'd done, as if I had anything to do with Brad lying there. Now she's calmer—too calm.

The officer nods, typing on her phone, her face unreadable. Layla purses her lips as she glances in my direction. A flicker of satisfaction? No, I must be imagining it.

Finally, the officer steps aside. I think she's a detective. She's in plainclothes, unlike the others in the vicinity. Another officer walks over, escorting Layla away from the scene. She doesn't look back as she strides away.

I stare at the spot where Brad fell. It's unsettling, knowing that the last words I ever spoke to him were said in anger. That I meant them. That I never wanted to see him again.

And now I never will.

My eyes follow who I assume is a detective—she's the same officer previously conversing with Layla—as she approaches Brad's body. Crouching with precise movements, she brushes away leaves and gestures to a tech. She hovers her gloved hand near his head for the tech to look at. The camera clicks in rapid succession.

She stands, moving methodically around the perimeter of the scene, stopping at a bush a few feet away. She bends down and picks something up. A pause—just long enough to study whatever it is—before she lays it on the grass.

A cup?

Dread coils in my stomach. Did Brad drink something, faint and hit his head? Somehow, I doubt that. And why do I have the sinking feeling that cup is about to make everything worse?

My phone ba-gawks with a text from the group chat with Seth and Rylie.

Rylie: Where are you?
Seth: Customers are slamming us. We need you!

My stomach twists. Looks like a dead body hasn't delayed the festival. I quickly reply.

Me: Held up. Be back as soon as I can.

Three dots appear, but I silence my phone and shove it in my pocket. The officer peels off her gloves and approaches. Her stride is brisk, her expression unreadable. She's wearing a pair of fitted black slacks with a navy jacket zipped halfway and a plain white shirt peeking through. A forced smile tugs at her lips but doesn't reach her eyes.

"Detective Wilcox," she says, shaking my hand before sitting on the log across from me.

I knew she was a detective.

"Beth Lloyd." Her firm, no-nonsense tone yanks me back to reality. Brad is dead, and I'm here again, sitting across from a detective.

"Can you tell me what happened? How did you find the body?" Her calm tone feels heavy.

I fidget, my gaze drifting to the yellow tape still fluttering in the breeze. "I was walking back from the bathroom while texting. That's when I found him."

"And you went to check it out?"

I nod, swallowing hard. "I thought . . . I didn't know . . ."

Didn't know what? That he was dead? That it was real?

"Take your time," she says.

She leans forward slightly, elbows on her knees. Beneath her jacket, I glimpse the edge of a shoulder holster. A quiet reminder of her authority and the situation I'm in.

Again.

"Did you touch the body?"

"I did," I admit. "I was checking for a pulse. I needed to be certain."

I hadn't wanted to touch him, but in that moment, I couldn't stop myself. Maybe it was instinct. Maybe it was something else—something I can't quite name. Because no matter how much I resented him, how much I wanted him out of my life, I never pictured him like that. Dead. Still. Empty.

A flicker of something crosses her face before disappearing. Understanding? Doubt?

Why isn't she taking notes with me like she did with Layla?

"I'd have done the same," she says, assessing me. "Did you know the victim?"

"Brad Dawson," I say. "He was my ex-boyfriend." I bite back the rest—about our unresolved breakup and the argument we had at my truck earlier.

Her brow lifts just slightly. "Were you the only person here when you found him?"

"Yes. I mean no," I blurt. "Layla Gafford showed up maybe a minute or two after I found him. You were just speaking with her. She owns the Roller Burger food truck. She was screaming her head off and pointing at him."

"And why are you here?"

"I was using the bathroom." I point behind me.

"Perhaps Ms. Gafford was doing the same thing," she says. "These bathrooms are open to the public, right?"

She's right. Everyone has access to these bathrooms.

Which means anyone could have been here at the time of Brad's death.

"So, why are you here?" she asks again.

"I just told you, using the bathroom."

"No." She shakes her head. "I mean, what are you doing at the festival?"

"Oh. I'm a food vendor like Layla. Kaydee Foley hired me."

"And who is Kaydee Foley?" she asks.

"I think she's the PR person for the farm or something," I say. "She's involved with the festival and organizing the food trucks."

"And which truck is yours?"

"Kluckin' Good. I own it with my twin brother."

"Kluckin' Good?" she repeats.

"It's chicken-themed. We sell sliders too," I add.

She pauses, a glint of something unreadable in her eyes. "Interesting."

"What is?"

"There was a Kluckin' Good tumbler in the bush not too far from where your ex-boyfriend was found."

"That can't be right." I shake my head. "I never gave him one."

But I gave one to Helena . . . No. No way. Helena wouldn't—

Goosebumps prickle my arms.

Helena was furious after Brad's review of her bakery. She was really upset when she said, "If that little online stunt of his affects my sales this weekend, he better watch himself."

I warned her to be careful what she said in the heat of the moment. Helena seemed dramatic at the time. But now there's a tumbler from my truck at the scene of Brad's death?

My stomach twists, unease creeping in around the edges.

"Well, somehow it made its way over there," Detective Wilcox says. "Any guesses?"

"No. I mean, I give those tumblers out sometimes. I gave one to Helena Wynn."

"And who is she?"

"Another food truck vendor here." I think back to when the festival first started. "And I sold one to Kaydee Foley earlier. And three to a mom in a dino tutu whose husband's doing the chili cook-off on Sunday."

She seemed chill, totally normal. But sometimes moms snap. I've seen it. My own mom used to go full banshee when Seth and I ignored the dishes for too long. One minute she's humming along to ABBA, the next she's launching wooden spoons like ninja stars.

I swallow. "It could be anyone, honestly."

"Anyone with a connection to you," she says, not unkindly. But the implication lands hard.

I shake my head. I don't like the direction this is going.

And Kaydee acted weird when we talked about Brad. Said she told her boss, Conner Green, they didn't need him. Said they didn't even get along. And yet . . . here he was.

"Is there anything else?"

"No," I say, too quickly.

And even if no one's pointing fingers—yet—I need to know what one of my tumblers was doing here near his dead body.

"Do you know if anyone else was here when you found the body?" she asks. "Was anyone in the bathroom with you?"

I replay my steps. Then it hits me. "Wait! Kaydee was in the bathroom before me." I remember the vacant look in her eyes, the way she was just standing near the sink. "She seemed . . . out of it. And there was a strange stain on her shirt."

Was it Brad's blood?

There's a beat of silence. "Strange how?"

I try to explain. "She's wearing a maroon blouse, so it was hard to tell the color of the stain. But it was around her waist, jagged and irregular. It didn't look like a food stain."

"You said she was at the sink when you found her?"

I nod.

"So, is it possible the stain was just water that splashed on her while washing her hands?"

Well, when she puts it that way . . .

It hadn't looked like water, though. Not the way she'd reacted. Not the way she tugged her shirt like she'd forgotten it was there.

I shift my weight and glance at the detective's hands. Still no notepad. No recorder either.

"Excuse me," I say, "but don't you need to be writing this down?"

Detective Wilcox doesn't blink. "No, I can remember everything just fine."

"But you were taking notes earlier. With Layla."

Irritation passes across her face, but she smooths it over fast.

"That was a formal statement," she says. "This is just a preliminary conversation."

So Layla gets the official version, and I just get the casual chat. Interesting.

"So, I'm not being taken seriously?"

Her lips twitch, but it's not a smile. "Ms. Lloyd, we're still in the early stages. I'm collecting background. Observations. When and if this becomes pertinent to the investigation, it'll be documented."

"That stain could be pertinent."

"Could be," she agrees. "Or it could be spilled sauce, or coffee, or water. I can't know that based on a glance from someone under stress."

I clench my jaw. "I wasn't under stress when I saw it."

Detective Wilcox studies me for a long moment, like she's trying to decide whether I'm helpful or just a nuisance.

"I'm not dismissing you," she says finally. "But I can't chase shadows. I need all the facts to move forward."

No notepad. No real interest in digging deeper. Just cataloging me, like a box to be ticked.

I want to press her, but before I can, she leans in slightly. "Did you see anyone else in the area? Someone who looked suspicious?"

"There was someone," I say. "Whoever it was, was standing on the path a few feet ahead of me."

The detective's posture sharpens. "Can you describe them?"

"I'm sorry, no." I shake my head. "They never turned around. All I remember is the person was wearing an oversized sweater and a wide-brimmed hat. It looked like they were headed to the flower pavilion."

"Do you think it was a woman?" she asks.

"Maybe. But their back was to me, so I'm not sure."

Detective Wilcox pulls her phone, taps rapidly, then holds the screen up. "Is this what the hat looked like?"

I shake my head.

She swipes and shows me another image. "This one?"

"Neither. Now that I'm thinking about it, those are too dark. The one I saw was light tan."

"Maybe something like this?" She shows me another picture.

I look at a safari hat. "Maybe? I'm sorry. I wish I could be of more help, but they were too far away."

"Did they seem to be acting strange to you? Fidgety, maybe on alert?"

"Not that I recall." I think back. "Whoever it was left pretty quickly when my phone ba-gawked."

"Ba-gawked?"

"My text tone." I shrug.

"What about their hair?" she asks. "Were you able to tell if the person you saw had long hair sticking out from under their hat?"

"Again, I'm sorry, but that's all I have."

"Hmph." She tucks her phone back into her pocket.

"Is that all?" I ask, hoping to leave.

"Not yet. You mentioned you and the deceased dated."

"Yes," I say. "Are you sure you don't need to write any of this down?"

"Would it make you feel more comfortable if I did?"

"I just think it's important to help with your investigation," I say. "Suppose you mistake my statements for someone else's—what then?"

"I won't," she says, a challenge to her tone.

A quiet beat stretches between us. She's studying me again, as if she already has an opinion.

"How long ago did you and Brad Dawson date?" Her question comes out tersely, as if my presence annoys her.

"Three years ago," I reply, feeling the weight of her scrutiny.

She studies me, gaze sharp as a hawk's. "Did you know Brad would be here today?"

"I did."

"And did you see him today?"

I take a deep breath. "Yeah. I saw Brad earlier."

She tilts her head, waiting.

"We . . . talked," I admit, my throat tightening around the word. "At my truck. This afternoon."

"What did you talk about?"

I hesitate. The fight replays in my head—Brad's voice laced with frustration, my own cutting response. I could tell her the truth. But the truth, out of context, makes me look bad.

"We argued." I blurt out without thinking. "But it wasn't anything serious."

"An argument with your ex-boyfriend before he turns up dead?" Detective Wilcox muses. "That's quite the coincidence."

I feel heat creeping up my neck. "You're twisting it. Brad and I had unresolved stuff. But I didn't—" I stop myself, exhaling sharply. "I didn't kill him."

Her expression doesn't shift. If anything, she looks almost . . . patient. Like she's waiting for me to slip up.

"Tell me about the argument," she says.

I think she wants to keep things "preliminary" while she builds her list and gets me talking. This way she can see where I fit and save the formal statement for later.

I shake my head, pressing my lips together.

A sudden wave of déjà vu crashes over me, so intense it leaves me momentarily dizzy. I've been here before. Not here, exactly, but in this same awful position, sitting across from a detective who believes I have something to hide. Detective Kane had looked at me like this when Benji Mayhew was murdered. That was bad. But this? This is worse.

I wasn't the one who found Benji's body. And we weren't exes.

Brad and I were.

And I had argued with Brad—publicly—twice before he died.

My stomach knots so tightly I feel like I might be sick.

How did I end up in this position again?

I'm not just a witness, I'm going to be a headline. Again. The ex with a motive. The girl who fought with the victim before he died. I don't care what Detective Wilcox thinks. I can't sit around and wait to be the next name on her suspect list. I need to figure out who really did this—before she convinces herself it was me.

I straighten, planting my hands on my thighs to keep them from fidgeting. "Not to be rude," I say, "but if this talk is going to continue, I need to call my lawyer."

A flicker of something—amusement or maybe annoyance—crosses her face, but it's gone before I can pin it down. "There's no need to get defensive. It's my job to understand what happened here." She shifts in her seat on the log with slow, deliberate movement and lifts one hand. "You're here." Her other hand rises. "Your ex-boyfriend is here." Her palms hover at uneven heights like scales weighing guilt and innocence, just waiting to tip.

My shoulders tense as I stare at her bun. It's pulling so tightly at her forehead it's stretching the skin. "But now he's dead. Let's be honest. It looks dodgy."

Her cold voice makes my skin prickle. She's acting like she hasn't already boxed me into a theory, but I can see it in her eyes. She's the shark and I'm her prey.

I glance again at her empty hands—still no notepad, still no recorder. "You keep saying this is just a conversation, but it sure feels like more than that. You're not taking notes, not logging what I'm saying. Why is that?"

"Because I'm not treating you like a suspect."

"Right," I say, my tone sharper than intended. "You only do that when you *are* writing things down."

Silence hangs between us, taut as a fishing line. "I can remember everything I need to," she says. "But if you'd prefer to give a formal statement, I'm happy to bring you down to the station."

I grit my teeth. "I didn't say that."

"Then let's keep talking."

I steady myself. "I'll admit I talked with Brad this afternoon—"

"Argued," she interrupts.

"But I wasn't alone," I ignore her. "There was a Clementine detective there too."

She crosses one leg over the other, her knee bouncing slightly. "And what's the name of the detective?"

"Detective Kane," I say.

Her head tips up. "Wait . . . are you talking about Andy?"

"Who?" I ask. The name is foreign, unexpected.

"Detective Andrew Kane," she clarifies. "We went through the academy together. I've always called him Andy. But these days he goes by Drew."

"Funny," I say. "He just introduces himself as Kane."

She shrugs. "He does that. Keeps people guessing."

My mind spins, trying to reconcile Detective Kane's stoic, unreadable presence with someone this woman calls "Andy."

"Is this officially a homicide investigation?" I ask.

"Right now, we're just looking into the unusual circumstances of your ex-boyfriend's death. Anytime a body is found under unclear or suspicious conditions, protocol says we bring in CSI to process or to clear the scene."

That's not a no.

But it's also not a yes.

She reaches into her jacket and pulls out a business card, offering it to me.

"That's all the questions I have for now."

I take the card, brushing my fingers against the crisp embossed lettering.

Grover County Sheriff's Department
Patricia E. Wilcox
Grover County Area Detective Division

The gold emblem of a badge gleams under the light, the numbers and email sharply printed.

"Do you know if the festival will continue?"

She regards me for a moment. "Why are you asking?"

"Well . . . I mean Brad was killed," I say. "Wouldn't *force majeure* cause the event to close?"

"*Force majeure*?" She quirks a brow.

"It's a legal term that means—"

"I know what it means," she interrupts, "and I'm not at liberty to say."

She didn't correct me when I said Brad was killed . . .

I shift my weight. "What about security cameras? Around the barn or the festival grounds?"

The last time I found a body, the warehouse cameras were practically ornamental. Glitchy at best, offline at worst. But when they did record? They caught exactly what we needed.

"There aren't any cameras on that side of the barn. Nothing that shows what happened."

I cross my arms. "So let me get this straight. No footage. No eyewitnesses. Just me discovering the body."

This time, she doesn't argue.

"If anything else comes up, even if it seems small, call me," she says.

I nod and tuck the card into my pocket. "Hopefully, you won't need to talk to me again." The words are half a joke, but the weight of my worry makes it fall flat.

"One last question for you." She stands, brushing the dirt from her trousers. "That Kluckin' Good tumbler. You really have no idea how it got near the body?"

I feel nauseous. "No."

"You didn't give it to him?"

"No."

"Did you ever see him with one?"

"Not that I can remember."

"What about your brother? Would he have given one to Brad?"

That throws me. "Seth? No. He never even liked Brad."

Darn my stupid mouth.

"Hm." Detective Wilcox purses her lips, like she's mentally noting that for later—even though she still hasn't written down a single thing.

"That's not what I meant," I say, quickly trying to backpedal. "Seth didn't like Brad from a protective brother's standpoint, that's all. Seth wouldn't hurt a fly."

Again, all she says is "Hm."

With that, she walks away, her heels crunching against the uneven ground as she stops to speak with another officer.

Exhaling slowly, I stare at the dirt, hoping for an answer. Did Brad fall? Did he hit his head? Or did someone pick up a rock and swing?

A chill snakes around me, squeezing me tight. We don't live in biblical times. Stoning people is a thing of the past.

Right?

My gaze drifts toward the police tape. Beyond it, techs are crouched over markers and evidence bags while snapping photos. One of them steps aside, revealing the familiar yellow glint of a Kluckin' Good tumbler, lying half buried in the grass beside a bush.

It hasn't been bagged.

It's still there.

Still on display. Like a silent accusation.

How *did* that get there?

I gave one to Helena this afternoon.

And Kaydee, and the dino tutu customer.

But Helena wouldn't have left it here. She couldn't have.

Right?

I push to my feet, my muscles stiff, my pulse hammering in my ears. I need to clear my head. *Keep moving.* The best way to shake the tight grip of Brad's death looming over me is to focus on something, *anything* else.

As I step toward the edge of the scene, I spot Kaydee a few feet away. She's already being questioned by Detective Wilcox. Color has drained from her normally bright face. Her shoulders slump, and her mouth presses into a thin, bloodless line. She looks like someone who's just seen a ghost.

Does she know I mentioned her to the detective?

Kaydee told me this is her first big event for the Green Family Farm, and she didn't want any drama. How will Brad's death reflect on her?

Her strained voice carries over. "I heard Brad didn't get along with a few people here," she says. "Particularly one man. I was told he punched Brad at Sugar and Spice Bakery the other day."

My feet freeze midstep.

Her words hit me like a slap.

Seth.

She's talking about *Seth.*

My stomach drops. This isn't just a passing comment—this is a lead. A direction. And Detective Wilcox is taking it.

The detective's gaze meets mine.

Despite my forced casualness, I'm sure she sees my inner panic.

I want to scream at Kaydee to shut up. To leave my brother out of this. Seth is innocent, and I won't let anyone—not Kaydee, not Detective Wilcox—try to pin this on him.

Panic threatens to claw its way out of my chest, but I swallow it down. Seth is my brother. I know him better than anyone. And yet, here they are, quietly whispering his name like it's a secret accusation. I can't just stand idly by while they drag him through the mud.

But now's not the time to lose it. I need to be smart.

I turn away, casting one last glance at the tumbler in the grass. CSI is still photographing it. Still calling it evidence.

Fine. Let them collect their clues and take their time. If Detective Wilcox is so quick to point fingers, maybe I can't trust her to find the real killer.

I can't let them pin this on Seth—or me, or anyone else—without real proof.

And while everyone's busy throwing around theories and pointing fingers, maybe someone should be asking one simple question: What's on Kaydee's shirt? Because she's still wearing it and the stain is still there. Dark, irregular, and definitely not water.

Chapter Seven

"Oh God, my eyes!" I slap my hands over my face like I've just witnessed the apocalypse.

"*Oh meu Deus*," Rylie moans.

"Haven't you heard of knocking?" Seth asks.

"It's my truck. I don't need to knock," I say. The sight of my twin and best friend making out while dressed as farm animals makes me wish I could bleach my retinas. Carefully, I peek through my fingers, praying the horror show is over.

"There's a bell on the back door," Seth says, still holding Rylie. "When the food truck is a-rockin', don't come a-knockin'."

Gag!

"Emergency team meeting. First item on the agenda: banning workplace PDA." I jab a finger into my palm. "You don't see me making out in the kitchen where we prepare food. And where are your heads?"

"In the driver's seat," Rylie says.

"Maybe you'd be less grumpy if you had someone to kiss," Seth says.

Grabbing a hand towel, I snap it at him. "Enough!"

"What took you so long to get back, anyway?" Seth asks, untangling from Rylie. "We were drowning during a rush of customers."

"I offered to help cook," Rylie says.

"No," Seth and I say in unison, glancing at each other—both a little too quick with our response.

"You guys are so unfair," Rylie pouts. "I can do more than just mix sauces and peel potatoes. Last week I made mac-and-cheese poppers, you know."

"You mean the batch you burned?" Seth asks.

I chuckle, then remember why I'm late "I'm sure you were a help," I say. "Seth's just dramatic."

"So? What took you so long?" Seth presses.

"I stopped at Helena's truck for a coffee. Then I went to the bathroom."

"Ah," Seth says. "I see."

"See what?"

"Coffee. Then bathroom. Obvious."

"Seth!" I scream.

"What? We're adults. Everybody poops. There's a whole book about it," Seth says, completely unfazed. "Still, an hour is a bit much. Are you getting enough fiber in your diet?"

"Oh, my God." I bury my face. "I'm not discussing my fiber intake with you. I don't appreciate the toilet humor. We're twenty-nine. Grow up."

"Correction: *I'm* twenty-nine. You're technically what? Seven? Maybe seven and a half."

I hate his trump card. "It's not my fault I was born on Leap Day. You were just fortunate enough to make it out two minutes later!"

"*Pare com isso*!" Rylie shouts. "You two are older than me by six months, you're both ancient." She turns to me. "What happened? You said you were held up."

"With her luck, she probably found another body," Seth jokes.

"Well . . ." I say, opening the truck's fridge to grab a yogurt.

"Bethany," Seth says, using my full name like our mother does. "Tell me you didn't."

I focus on peeling back the yogurt lid very intently.

"Seriously?" Rylie throws her hands in the air.

Seth looks half horrified, half resigned. "Wasn't one body enough for you?"

"It's not like I planned it!" I jab my spoon into the yogurt. "The first murder investigation scarred me for life. I didn't exactly go looking for another."

"Do you know who it was?" Rylie asks.

"More importantly, you didn't talk to anyone, did you?" Seth asks.

Before I can answer, a couple approaches the truck. Rylie shoos me away and walks over, plastering on her best customer-service smile.

I shove a spoonful of yogurt in my mouth as the couple lingers, glancing between me and my two farm-animal-clad coworkers with visible confusion.

"What happened?" Seth demands the second they're gone.

"Everything is a nightmare," I say, rinsing my yogurt cup in the prep sink. "I'm late because I had to talk to the police. About Brad."

"Brad?" Rylie asks sharply. "Did he do something? Did he try to—"

"Brad's dead," I interrupt. "I found him near the barn on the way back from the bathroom."

Rylie shrieks, wings flapping, while Seth curses under his breath.

I rub my temples.

I should feel *something*.

Instead, there's just this strange hollowness. A quiet, unsettling hum beneath my ribs.

One minute he was alive. Now he's not.

Gone.

And no matter how I turn it over in my head, I can't make sense of it.

"I don't know how it happened," I say. "When I left the bathroom, I was walking and texting. There was someone standing in the middle of the path, then they left."

"Did you get a good look at them?" Rylie asks.

I shake my head. "Too far away. All I could make out was a sweater and a tan, wide-brimmed hat."

"That didn't seem suspicious to you? Someone standing in the middle of the path alone?" Seth asks, slipping into full-on lawyer mode, despite still being dressed like a cow.

"I was there alone too. Does that seem odd to you? Why should I think someone standing there is weird?" I defend myself. "Yes, in retrospect, it seems odd, given what I found. But why would I conclude something bad was happening?"

"Big mistake, *irmã*," Rylie wags a wing at me. "Rule number 57 on *Murder and Mayhem*: Anticipate the worst, hope for the best."

I almost laugh. Almost.

The *Murder and Mayhem* podcast got me through the last investigation. Rylie and I quote it like scripture. The host, Inga Nevarez, breaks down every case and provides practical life rules to keep you safe. It was following her rules that helped me catch a killer once.

And now . . . it might have to help me again. "She's right," I admit, recalling the exact episode where Inga Nevarez coined that rule. "But my only focus was getting back here to help you guys. It wasn't until I saw Brad's shoes lying in the grass that I knew something was wrong."

Seth's eyes narrow. "What else happened?"

"I called 911. Layla saw what was going on and started screaming. The police showed up not long after."

"Please tell me you didn't speak to them?" Seth's question isn't really a question.

"Layla?" Rylie asks.

"Roller Burger chick," I say.

Rylie mumbles in Portuguese.

"Answer me," Seth demands. "Did you speak with the police? *Again*?"

"Yes, I did. Happy now?" This conversation feels the same as last time. He'll lecture, I'll argue, and in the end, it's easier to be honest with him.

Seth exhales. "Was it at least Detective Kane?"

"Her name is Patricia Wilcox." I hand him her card. "She's with the Grover County Sheriff's Department. I kept our conversation as short as possible. Bare bones only," I add quickly, watching his expression darken.

Seth pinches his nose with a hoof. "If she's a good detective, bare bones don't matter. She'll consider you a suspect the moment she learns about your history with Brad."

"I'm pretty sure she already does," I say.

"What do you mean?" Rylie tucks her wings across her chest.

"She asked me if I knew the victim—"

"And you answered her?" Seth roars. "What is wrong with you? How many times do I need to tell you not to speak to the police without me?"

"Stop yelling at me!" I shout back. "Yes, I told her who Brad was. And, yes, I told her he was my ex-boyfriend." I quickly hold up a hand to stop Seth from yelling more. "But I was quick to tell her we broke up three years ago." I shrug, trying to indicate it's not a big deal.

But I know I'm wrong. It is a big deal. A tight knot forms in my chest as I replay the conversation in my head. I can't help feeling like I've painted a target on myself.

But it wasn't like I had a choice. I couldn't exactly lie, not when she was already staring me down like I was the one holding the murder weapon. And I know, logically, admitting we had a past doesn't make me a killer. It just feels like it does, with all these darn eyes on me.

"That's where you're wrong," Seth says, confirming what I know deep down. "It is a big deal."

His gaze drills into me, his silence a warning that he doesn't trust this. I don't blame him. It feels like I'm setting myself up for something bigger than I can even see right now.

"It's her job to consider everyone at the scene of the crime a potential suspect," he continues. "Once she looks into you, she'll find out about Benji and Sloane."

Rylie swears in Portuguese. Silence hangs in the air as we all reflect on the two murders that happened during *The Food Truck Showdown* last year.

"Well, that's not the only problem," I say. "I think she's gunning for you too."

"Me? What did I do?" he asks, genuinely confused.

I wince. "I may have accidentally let it slip that you didn't like Brad either."

Rylie swears again, and Seth looks like he wants to break something.

"But!" I hold up both hands. "Great news!"

That actually stops them both for a second.

"I'm not the only one who told her that!" I say brightly. "So it can't all be blamed on me!" I nod to encourage positive reactions.

Seth looks incredulous. "Do you have greater news than that?"

I look between them, their expressions full of anticipation. "No."

Seth scowls, then narrows his eyes. "Who else?"

"After I finished talking to Detective Wilcox, I overheard Kaydee telling her that you punched Brad in the stomach."

"Kaydee?" Rylie asks. "Why were the police speaking with her?"

"I don't know. Maybe because she's helping run the festival. Or she was still in the area after leaving the bathroom. Who knows?"

Why was Kaydee still hanging around the bathrooms if she left before I did? Why talk about Seth at all?

Seth scrubs a hoof over his jaw as Rylie swears again. "How does Kaydee know about that?" he says, more to himself than anyone else.

"Probably the same way all news in Clementine spreads. Gossip." I glance at Rylie, who looks the most upset. "Sure, the festival is being held here, in Grover County, but I met Kaydee in Clementine. She might live there for all I know."

"You punching Brad was the talk of the town," Rylie adds. "My sister and brother-in-law already knew about it when I got home that night."

"I lost my temper," Seth admits. "I shouldn't have let him get to me, but I did. But that doesn't mean I had anything to do with what happened to Brad today."

"You're right, it doesn't," I say. "But you said it yourself. If Detective Wilcox is any good at her job, she'll look at Brad's past and consider you a suspect too."

"I'm not worried," Seth says.

"It's my job to protect you. You're my little brother," I remind him.

"By two minutes." He holds up his hoof and separates it like he's Spock telling us to live long and prosper. "That's all."

"Did you just Vulcan salute me with your cow hoof?"

"Live long and graze," he deadpans.

"Moo-ve over, nerd," I joke, and for a second, everything feels almost normal. "I'll be darned if I let anything happen to you, Seth."

"Nothing will," he tries to reassure me.

"What are the chances they'll cancel the festival?" Rylie asks. "I mean, a death happened at a public event. An event with families in attendance. It can't be ethical to continue with a celebration of food where someone died. Especially under suspicious circumstances."

"Ethics didn't stop a TV network from continuing a reality show after two people died," Seth reminds her. "I doubt a festival that's been planned for a year is going to be shut down because of one death."

"Seth's right." The memory of Brad's lifeless body flashes behind my eyes, and my stomach lurches.

Dead. Just like that.

"But still . . ." I hesitate.

"Are you okay?" Seth asks, the earlier anger gone.

I force a smile. "I'm fine." Falling apart won't change anything.

"No, you're not," Seth says. "You found your ex-boyfriend dead. No matter how much I disliked him, he was still someone you once—" He clears his throat. "Someone you loved. We can pack up and go home."

Loved. Past tense. We were over years ago, but hearing it put like that feels strange.

"I signed a contract with the festival," I remind him.

"The festival won't blame you for needing to leave."

"And if they're going to be jerks about it, then it's not a contract we want," Rylie interjects, tugging at the wings on her gloves before finally peeling them off and flexing her fingers.

"Besides," Seth says, giving my shoulder a little shake, "don't forget I can get you out of any contract."

I snort, feeling a little lighter. "I appreciate it, but I'm staying. Leaving now won't change the fact that Brad is dead—and that I'm the one who found him." My fingers tighten around the edge of the counter. "At least it wasn't as gruesome as the last body I found."

The words slip out before I can stop them, and I wince.

"Promise me you won't say stuff like that to the police." Seth sighs. "I get it. But it doesn't mean you have to push through this alone."

"She's not alone," Rylie says, like she's making a promise. "She has us."

I glance at Rylie, then at Seth, feeling the weight of their gazes on me. I know they really mean it. It's not just words—they're here. I don't have to carry this on my own.

Seth doesn't say anything, just pulls me into a quick side hug. "I know. But you've got us, okay? No need to carry this by yourself."

I lean into the hug for a second, letting it sink in. "Thanks," I whisper.

Rylie pulls her phone out of the pocket of the chicken suit. "What do you remember when you found him? We'll start a new Kluckin' Clues list and build a timeline."

Our good ol' trusty clues list. We made one last year when we were trying to piece together what was happening on the set of *The Food Truck Showdown.* We solved the case by meticulously tracking clues and suspects, as instructed by Inga Nevarez on *Murder and Mayhem.*

"Good idea." I nod, chewing my lip. I hesitate, my stomach turning. I don't want to say the rest. The image of his lifeless eyes staring up at me is burned into my brain, but I can't let it stop me now.

I force myself to keep going, pushing the discomfort aside. "When I found him, his eyes were open, and there was a bloody rock next to him."

"How did his head look?" Rylie asks.

"His temple was smashed in." I swallow, the taste of the words awful in my mouth. But I keep steady, turning my focus to the facts.

Seth frowns. "You think he fell and hit his head?"

"Maybe?" My confidence is at zero. "But Detective Wilcox didn't seem to think it was an accident. She said they're investigating 'the unusual circumstances'—and in her tone, 'unusual' definitely seemed to indicate foul play."

Rylie shudders. "Murder rule number 8: *If there's blood and a rock, assume it's not natural causes.*"

"Exactly," I say. "But . . . I hate to think someone stoned him to death. I mean, who does that?"

"What else could it have been?" Rylie asks. "A heart attack? A stroke? But neither of those would account for a bloody rock."

"As far as I remember, Brad didn't have a family history of medical emergencies," I say. "When we dated, he was in perfect health. He ran 5Ks, ate kale salads, and drank those disgusting green smoothies that smelled like lawn clippings."

"That was over three years ago," Rylie reminds me.

"True." I chew on my bottom lip. "I hate to admit it, but Brad didn't let himself go after he dumped me. Which honestly feels like an extra slap in the face. Like, couldn't he have gained fifty pounds or something?"

"At the very least, lost his hair," she adds.

"It's important to study all angles." Seth says. "We have to consider the possibility that someone, maybe the person standing on the path, may have used the rock to kill him."

"Could the person I saw have found Brad, panicked, and fled for no other reason than fear of what they found?" I ask.

"It's plausible," he says. "Fear and flight are common reactions for many people."

The thought of abandoning someone in need is inconceivable to me. Even if that person was my awful ex-boyfriend.

My stomach churns with the question I can't seem to answer.

Did Brad fall?

Did he hit his head?

Or did someone pick up a rock and swing?

Rylie finishes typing her notes. "There," she says, as our phones ping simultaneously with a message. "Each of us has a copy of the Kluckin' Clues list."

"This isn't your true-crime podcast," Seth says. "This is a job for the police. My job is to handle things *legally*. Your job"—Seth shakes a hoof at us—"is to let the police do theirs."

Rylie and I share an eye roll.

She grabs a tumbler with our laughing chicken logo on it and pours herself lemonade. We rarely serve fresh drinks—bottles are easier—but Rylie convinced me that summer drinks like lemonade and iced tea would sell well. I caved and bought aftermarket drink dispensers for the festival. Who knows? If we land regular catering gigs, they could come in handy.

I hesitate, watching her take a long slurp. Then I say it.

"They found one of our tumblers near Brad's body."

The words land like a bomb.

Rylie chokes mid-sip and nearly drops the cup. "What?"

Seth straightens. "What do you mean, they found one of our tumblers?"

I swallow, the acid rising in my throat. "Detective Wilcox pulled it from a bush near where I found Brad. When I left, CSI was documenting it as evidence. She knows it's ours."

"Perfect," Seth scowls. "Because *that* doesn't look suspicious."

"*Você deve estar brincando comigo*!" Rylie slams the cup down, lemonade sloshing over the rim. "You have got to be kidding me!"

"I don't know how it got there." The words tumble out in a rush. "I didn't drop it, and I didn't hand it to Brad. Someone must've—" I pause, heart twisting. "Could someone have planted it?"

"Did you sell any this morning before the festival started?" Rylie asks, tapping a new note in her phone.

"Five," I say, counting on my fingers. "One to Helena. Three to a woman who showed up right after Brad tried talking to me at the truck. And one to Kaydee."

"So, to sum up," Seth says, throwing up his hooves in disbelief, "a guy you used to date ends up dead. You find him. The cops already know about your history. And now one of our branded tumblers—one of only five you sold today—is found right next to his body."

I nod, stomach twisting tighter than a dishrag. "Yeah. That . . . basically covers it."

"Great," Seth groans. "So we're all on their radar now."

"I didn't plan for this—"

"Beth, if you get yourself tangled in this again, I swear—"

"I'll be careful."

Seth groans. "That's what you said *last time* before you nearly got yourself killed!"

"I survived, didn't I?"

Seth points a hoof at me again. "This is how it starts. A clue here, a lead there, and suddenly you're dodging syringes in dark warehouses while wearing a wire under your chicken suit!"

"I really doubt a syringe is going to get pulled on me again," I say.

"She's right, you know," Rylie says. "The chances of that seem low."

Seth glares. "Not helping."

I press my palms to the counter. "Look, I know you want me to leave this alone, but I believe someone killed Brad. If I don't at least keep my eyes open—"

Seth sighs in defeat. "Fine. But this time, I want to know *everything* you're doing. No secrets. No sneaking off."

I meet his eyes, guilt gnawing at me. I scared him last time. I won't do that again.

"Deal," I say.

Seth looks skeptical but doesn't argue.

Rylie claps. "*Perfeita*. Now, let's figure out: of the three people you sold tumblers to, which one left theirs behind at the crime scene?"

"Not Helena," I say immediately. "We've known her for years. I can't imagine her doing this to Brad." Although she *was* furious about his online review of her café.

I told her to be careful what she said. That heat-of-the-moment things have a way of coming back to haunt you. She didn't even blink. Just waved me off and said, "Don't worry about me. If anything, you should be worried about Seth."

At the time, I thought she was just being her usual blunt self. But now I can't help wondering—was she deflecting? Turning the conversation to my twin before it got too close to something real?

"Agreed," Seth says. "What about the customer who bought three?"

"Was one of those possibly a plant?" Rylie suggests, tapping her chin like she's solving a tricky escape room.

"I don't think it was her either." I shake my head. "She was a mom wearing a dinosaur tutu. Her husband is competing in the chili cook-off on Sunday. That doesn't exactly scream 'killer.'"

Rylie makes a *tsk* sound.

"I'm serious," I defend our customer. "What motive did she have to harm Brad? I'll bet fifty dollars she didn't even know the man."

"Don't you remember the *Serial Mom* episode from season two of *Murder and Mayhem*?" Rylie asks. "She was an unassuming middle-class housewife with a husband and teenage kids. Secretly? A serial killer. She murdered people over trivial offenses."

"Rylie's right," Seth says. "It's the unassuming people you have to watch out for."

I sigh. "Fine. If the tutu mom turns out to be a criminal mastermind, I'll eat my blue baseball cap." I run a finger over the brim.

Seth grins. "I'll hold you to that."

"Maybe it was Kaydee," I say. "When I went to the bathroom, she was zoned out at the sink, standing in the dark. And there was a strange dark stain on her shirt."

"Strange like blood?" Rylie asks without looking up from her note taking.

"I'm not sure," I admit. "It was a maroon shirt. When I shared my theory with Detective Wilcox, she pointed out that it was possibly water had splashed on her while she was washing her hands."

Seth nods like that makes perfect sense.

But the more I think about it, the more it doesn't sit right.

Because Kaydee was still wearing that shirt when I left after speaking with Detective Wilcox. And the stain was still there. It looked like something smeared or wiped.

Why would she stay in a soiled shirt?

Maybe she didn't have time to change, and she tried to clean it as best she could. Hiding what really happened and blaming it on spilled sauce.

But why stand there in the dark?

The detective might have dismissed it, but I can't. Something about Kaydee's expression when I walked in—blank, dazed—has been needling at me ever since.

She said she was fine. But what if she wasn't?

What if she had something to hide?

"Everything will be fine," Rylie says, finishing with her notes, clearly determined to look on the bright side. "The food truck gods are watching over us. Nothing's gonna keep this cock and bull down."

I smile, but it's fleeting. I can almost *feel* the weight of Detective Wilcox's presence before she even shows up.

Sure enough, through the serving window, I spot her heading our way, and my shoulders tense.

"Here we go," I whisper to Seth under my breath. "That's the detective." I point at the woman, making a beeline for our truck.

I walk up to the serving window, plastering a painfully fake smile on my face. "Hello, Detective Wilcox. Care for some wings?"

Seth moos loudly from the back of the truck, giving me a knowing look. Our twin bond takes over as we have a silent conversation.

Remember, don't answer questions, he says with his eyes.

Do you think I'm stupid? I squint.

A little. He squints back.

"I'm not interested in food." Detective Wilcox stands on her tiptoes, peering into the truck. "Is Seth Evan Lloyd here?"

My brother steps forward, his jaw clenched, looking more like an angry bull than a cheerful cow. "And who are you?" he asks, giving her a cool, pointed stare.

"Detective Wilcox with the Grover County Sheriff's Office." She flashes her badge. "I have some questions for you regarding your relationship with Brad Dawson."

"I don't have a relationship with him," Seth informs her, his tone deliberately neutral. "Not sure how I can be of any help to you."

"Maybe we should find a more private place to talk," she suggests.

"Go on," I say. "Rylie and I have the truck under control."

Seth tips his head, and Detective Wilcox follows him to the back of the truck. He purposely keeps the door open, just enough for Rylie and me to hear everything.

"I'm sure your sister has informed you about what happened to Brad Dawson," the detective says.

"She has."

"Witnesses observed you arguing with Mr. Dawson at Sugar and Spice Bakery two days ago," she says. "Mind telling me what that was about?"

"'Arguing' implies a mutual exchange," Seth replies. He's in full lawyer mode now. "I'd describe it more as a brief, one-sided conversation."

I wonder if the detective finds it distracting that he's dressed as a cow during this conversation. Does she think that's a power move, or just him being . . . Seth?

"I'm sorry," the detective amends. "I meant to say you *assaulted* him."

"Assault is a legal conclusion," Seth says smoothly. "You'll have to be more specific."

"Did you or did you not punch Brad Dawson?"

"What I recall is a situation where Mr. Dawson created a disturbance, and I took steps to remove myself from it," he says, and I swear there's a grin in his voice.

"That disturbance being your fist?"

"I'd characterize it as a reflexive gesture of personal space enforcement," Seth says. "Mr. Dawson seemed to have issues respecting boundaries."

"You don't deny physical contact occurred?"

"I'm not in the habit of denying verifiable facts. But I am in the habit of letting my attorney—me—advise caution when asked to characterize events with legal implications."

Rylie lets out a short laugh that she tries to turn into a cough.

Detective Wilcox's silence indicates she isn't amused. But Seth? He's unshaken. It's not bravado, it's strategy. He's giving her nothing, and she knows it.

"I heard you fought with him over your twin sister," Detective Wilcox presses. "Calling him a conceited jerk and threatening him to leave her alone. Is that true?"

"Detective, those are emotionally charged characterizations, not facts." Seth clicks his tongue disapprovingly. "Did I express my personal concerns about Mr. Dawson's past treatment of my sister? Certainly. Did I do so using nonviolent, constitutionally protected language? Also yes."

Rylie and I both grunt at the word *nonviolent*.

I move to the far end of the truck, keeping behind the window hatch, watching from the shadows. Seth's spine is straight, chin high, lawyer shields up. But I clock the flex in his jaw. This isn't casual anymore. It's a chess match. How did she look at me during our chat? Did I look guilty? Seem twitchy? Defensive? Or just like another spiteful ex with terrible taste?

Maybe I should ask Detective Kane how I rank on the Cop-O-Meter of Suspicious People. Would he tell me?

"You really expect me to believe you *calmly* spoke to the man who humiliated your sister in front of a room full of people?" Detective Wilcox asks, her voice skeptical.

"It wasn't a *roomful*," I whisper to Rylie. "And how does she *know* about that?"

"Uh-oh," Rylie whispers as Seth laughs. But there's an edge to his laugh, one that makes me think this isn't funny anymore.

Does the detective view his laugh as guilt?

"Well," Seth says, his voice tightening, "I guess it's my word against a dead man's."

"I guess so," the detective replies.

If Detective Wilcox suspects there's a connection between Seth and Brad's death, then Kaydee must have given the detective a *very* convincing statement after I left. A secondhand statement because Kaydee was not at Sugar and Spice when Brad showed up. So that makes me wonder who told Kaydee what happened there? And why did they tell her? Was it for gossip? Or was there a motive to telling her about Seth?

To my knowledge, Brad and Seth hadn't crossed paths until the other morning at Sugar and Spice.

Unless there's something Seth *hasn't* told me.

Chapter Eight

"I think we should stay and discuss everything," Rylie says, as I hand her the chicken head, the feathers drooping like they're also emotionally drained.

Across the lot, Detective Wilcox walks away, not sparing a glance back at our truck or at Seth, who is huffing like an angry bull.

"We need a plan of action," Rylie says, her voice low but firm.

"What is there to plan?" I ask while arranging a tray of samples and coupons for her and Seth to hand out. "My ex-boyfriend is dead. I found him, and the police are sniffing around me and Seth like bloodhounds on espresso. That about covers the highlights."

But my hands shake as I realign the tray for the third time. There's no clean way to say it: I found Brad's body in a field. His face—those empty eyes—are still stuck in my head, like my brain insists on replaying the moment like some kind of trauma slideshow. I don't even know how I feel, but I know I don't *want* to talk about it. I want to hand out chicken wings and pretend this weekend didn't veer sharply off a cliff.

"Rylie's right, these can wait," Seth says, pushing aside the coupons I painstakingly printed.

I snatch the cow head from the driver's seat and thrust it at him. "I promise not to unearth any more corpses while you're gone."

"Don't make promises you can't keep," he stares at the costume like it has personally wronged him. "That thing is stuffy. I can't breathe in it. And more importantly, I'm worried about you talking to that Grover County detective again without me."

"I don't plan on speaking with her, unless the conversation is about her ordering a basket of wings and fries." I wiggle the costume head at him, urging him to take it. He doesn't. "If you want to stay and talk, we can discuss employee conduct," I add, all syrupy-sweetness as I jab the cow's head at his chest again.

"We're going," he grumbles, shoving the head over his face. "Call me if *anything* happens." His voice is muffled from inside the polyester dome. "And do *not* talk to Detective Wilcox without me. Am I clear?"

"Yeah, yeah, I'm your client." I push him out the back door. "Don't forget your bell!"

He pauses, comes back, and snatches the little cowbell off the prep table with a theatrical sigh, like I asked him to give a closing argument in clown shoes.

"Alone at last," I say to the empty truck, adjusting the serving window with a heavy exhale.

This isn't how I imagined the festival weekend going. When we signed up, I pictured long lines, new customers, maybe someone posting our mac-and-cheese poppers on social media with a trending hashtag. Not finding my ex-boyfriend dead in a field.

Not being watched like I'm next in line for a mugshot.

I take a breath. Deep. Sharp. The smell of fried chicken, funnel cakes, and overly salted popcorn wafts from the surrounding trucks. There's laughter. A twangy country tune playing over the loudspeakers. Kids squealing as they chase bubbles and each other. It's everything a summer festival should be.

But it feels wrong. Off. Like someone shifted reality a degree to the side and forgot to take me with it.

My hands curl into fists at my sides.

Seth being considered a suspect isn't just unfair, it's dangerous. This could ruin his career as a lawyer. I need to keep my head on straight, focus on the business, the customers, the food. We've worked too hard to build Kluckin' Good into something real. I don't want our truck associated with another murder—especially one involving my ex-boyfriend. I have big plans for our business, and gaining a reputation as a "killer ex-girlfriend" isn't part of them.

I take another breath and let it burn in my chest before I release it. I didn't plan on spending my weekend investigating another suspicious death. But if it means protecting my brother I'll do whatever it takes.

Even if it means facing the past I never wanted to revisit again.

Two men approach the serving window, their hair dyed bright orange and yellow and their faces adorned with lip piercings. They each order a basket of Golden Oldie sliders and two Kluckin' Good tumblers filled with lemonade.

That makes seven tumblers sold today, and I still have no clue how one of them ended up near Brad's body.

A flicker of jealousy sparks as I watch them rejoin a group of friends sitting around a picnic table. All of them are laughing and carefree. They're here to enjoy the festival, while my weekend has been completely derailed.

Rylie's voice echoes in my head, urging me to put on my big-girl feathers and suck the kluck up. Leaning on the serving window, I watch the crowd of people mingle. We arrived here at one PM to start setting up. The festival officially opened at three. Now it's almost six, and the place is packed. Strollers are weaving between barbecue lines, teens taking selfies in front of funnel cake stands, and kids losing their minds over balloon swords.

One of these people—one of these cheerful, cotton-candy-eating attendees—may have killed Brad.

But why?

Someone picked up a rock and hit him. That's not an accident. That's rage. Or fear. Or something worse.

Rylie floated the idea of a medical emergency. A stroke, heart attack, a tragic stumble onto a conveniently placed rock. But that doesn't sit right. Brad was thirty-two, relatively healthy, unless hay fever finally came for him with a vengeance.

Whatever happened, it wasn't random. I *feel* that in my gut. This wasn't an accident. It was murder.

I close my eyes, trying to picture the scene exactly as I found it. But all I can see are Brad's eyes, wide and unseeing, frozen in a stare that's going to follow me for a while.

On *Murder and Mayhem*, Inga Nevarez always says to focus on details. That the devil doesn't just wear Prada, she carries a checklist. Lists help reveal patterns. Connections. Motives.

Right now, all I have is a growing suspicion and a dead ex-boyfriend.

I pull out my phone and open the shared Kluckin' Clues list. I scroll past Rylie's observation about Detective Wilcox's "weird cop energy" and a bullet point that says, "THAT ROCK???" then tap the screen to start a new list.

Suspects:

Kaydee Foley: Festival manager. Had access to the grounds before anyone else. Major control-freak energy. She didn't seem normal in the bathroom with that weird suspicious stain. She also purchased a tumbler this morning.

Conner Green: Event manager. Family owns the farm. Conner didn't like Brad's questions during the

walkthrough. Called him condescending. Kaydee had to physically step between them.

Mystery person from the path: Saw someone walking away before I found Brad. No ID yet. Sweater, large tan hat, fast pace, looked like they didn't want to be seen. Classic murdery behavior.

Layla Gafford: Roller Burger food truck. She showed up right after I found Brad. Could she have been there all along and arrived pretending to be innocent?

Dino tutu customer: I sold three Kluckin' Good tumblers to her. Could be eccentric. Could be a killer. Honestly, it's a toss-up at this festival.

Helena Wynn: Owner of Sugar and Spice Bakery and food truck vendor at the festival. Gave her a tumbler this morning. Brad also gave her a bad review, and it made the rounds on social media. I wouldn't blame her for being salty, but would she go full murder over it?

I hesitate. My thumb hovers over the screen. There's one name I haven't added yet.

Seth.

Do I think he did it? Absolutely not.

Do I know for sure he didn't?

My gaze flicks to his apron hanging on the hook by the back door. I think of how he punched Brad the other day, his lawyer-speak when he was questioned by Detective Wilcox, the tight little laugh that didn't reach his eyes when she pushed.

He's my twin. My ride-or-die. But that doesn't mean I get to ignore reality.

I look back at our shared note and type:

Seth Lloyd: Argued with Brad publicly. Punched him two days ago. Was furious over what Brad did to me. Had motive. Had opportunity.

I don't believe he'd do it, but if I'm honest . . . I don't know what I believe anymore.

The thought curdles inside me, bitter and wrong. Like I'm betraying my own blood—even if it's just for the sake of being thorough. I know my brother. He wouldn't hurt anyone. He barely kills spiders unless I scream.

But the facts are facts: he recently punched Brad. In public. Witnesses saw it. And now Brad's dead. It's the kind of thing that would definitely make the list on *Murder and Mayhem*. Inga Nevarez would be disappointed in me if I didn't consider all the angles.

Still . . .

I stare at the screen, my finger hovering over the option to remove Seth from the shared note. His profile picture—grinning in sunglasses from our last beach trip—stares right back at me, and guilt twists in my stomach.

He doesn't even have time to keep up with this list, not with his caseload at Buford and Myers eating up every spare second. He barely pays attention to the notes we share about groceries, let alone suspects in a murder. It's not like Seth ever really keeps track of this list anyway. Back when Benji Mayhew and Sloane Owsinski was murdered, it was just me and Rylie trading names on the Kluckin' Clues List. Seth never said a word about being left out then, so why would he care now?

"Sorry, Seth," I murmur, and tap remove access. "I'm doing this for you," I whisper aloud, needing to hear it.

If something does come up later—some twist I didn't see coming—at least I'll be ready. I'll know I didn't let blind loyalty cloud my judgment. I'll know I did everything I could to clear his name before someone else points the finger.

This isn't betrayal. It's strategy.

It's love . . . in a slightly messed-up, suspicious kind of way.

Removing his access from the list will keep him from going into a tailspin or give him a reason to lawyer up on me. If Rylie asks why he's missing from the shared list, I'll do my best to lie. Say it was an oversight.

But my voice always goes high-pitched and squeaky when I lie—like a cartoon chipmunk having a panic attack.

I pray I don't betray myself by squeaking.

I hate including Helena on my list. She and her husband, Chris, were friends with my Aunt Dolly. They even brought us homemade peach cobbler when Aunt Dolly died. But Helena was furious with Brad over the scathing review he wrote about her bakery. Could she have been angry enough to kill in a moment of passion? God, I hope not. If she did, who would take care of Mrs. Whiskerton?

"Oh no!" I clamp a hand over my mouth.

Could Helena have been the one who told Kaydee about Seth punching Brad?

I hadn't considered it until now, but Kaydee seemed so confident when she brought it up to the police. As if she wasn't offering info—she was armed with it. Kaydee was not at the bakery that day. I'm sure of it.

I never told her about the incident there. Seth sure didn't. That means someone else did. Helena saw the punch. She was nearby. If she's the one who told Kaydee . . . what does that mean for her? What does that mean for Seth? It would explain why Detective Wilcox is zeroing in on him. Why the tone shifted during questioning. What if Helena's trying to deflect suspicion from herself? Or worse, if she genuinely believes Seth had a motive and decided to help the investigation along?

Bile rises in my throat, and I have to force a swallow.

I want to believe Helena means well. But if she's stirring the pot, even unintentionally, she may have set something in motion that can't be undone.

Then there's Kaydee. On paper, she's the festival manager—tight-laced and perfectly lip-glossed. But her whole bathroom freak-out earlier right before I found Brad still doesn't sit right with me. The stain. The zoned-out look. The way she snapped back into PR mode like nothing happened. And the way she threw Seth to the wolves without blinking . . . that wasn't festival protocol. That felt personal.

Conner Green is Kaydee's boss, technically. But I've only ever met him once or twice in passing. Kaydee's been my main point of contact since day one. Still, I remember the way she talked about him and Brad during their walkthrough before the festival. How Conner didn't appreciate Brad's questions, how she had to step in between them. Kaydee's description suggested more than annoyance. Maybe Conner's problem with Brad was deeper.

And Layla Gafford . . . well, she's got claws. Her meltdown over a parking spot with Coffeeology made that clear. The woman practically vibrates with intensity. But is she intense enough to kill someone? That's the question. I don't know her well enough to say. Not yet. But she arrived suspiciously fast after I found Brad. Something tells me if she had a run-in with him, it might have been more than just a bad review. I need to find out what her story is.

As for the mystery person I saw on the path, I still don't know who they are. Sweater, big hat, fast pace. Who are they? Were they in the wrong place at the wrong time? Or were they trying *not* to be noticed.

If so, that's exactly the kind of person who *needs* to be noticed.

Then there's the dino tutu mom from this morning. I sold her three Kluckin' Good tumblers, and one of my tumblers was found at the scene. Yeah, she was quirky, but not in a "shove a body into a flower bed" kind of way. More like "has a Pinterest board for bento box lunches" kind of way.

I mean, sure, Ted Bundy may have been convincing as a normie, but this dino tutu mom with funky glasses and teal highlights doesn't scream "murderer" to me. Still, the only thing worse than a murderer who looks suspicious is one who doesn't.

Smoked brisket drifts in the warm breeze. The air hums with laughter. My truck is parked near the heart of the action, a prime spot for business, but right now, food is the last thing on my mind.

I open my text thread with Rylie, eager to share the updated list with her.

She replies with a gif of a chicken holding a magnifying glass. At least I know Rylie is going to help me uncover what happened.

Opening my other group text with Seth and Rylie I share a theory.

Me: If we're considering all scenarios, any attendee could be involved.

Rylie: Would someone go as far as buying a festival ticket to kill Brad?

Seth: Leave it to the police.

Rylie: *Fique quieto!*

Me: They'd have to *really* hate him to do something like that.

Closing the app, I set my phone down and lean on the prep counter, mulling everything over. I'm struggling to accept Brad's death so soon after seeing him.

A young family passes by my truck, the little girl giggling as her mom adjusts her sunhat. The scene tugs at something in me, and I reflexively grab my phone.

Me: Just wanted to let you know before you see it on the news, I found a dead body at the festival.

My phone immediately rings as my mom's name flashes across the screen.

"Hi, Mo—"

"What do you mean, you found a dead body?" Her shrill voice cuts me off. "Wasn't one enough for you? You're supposed to be working and selling food, not wandering around looking for trouble."

"Mom!" I raise my voice to match hers. "Brad Dawson is dead."

Silence hangs heavy on the line.

"I found him on the way back from the bathroom."

Finally, she says, "Hmph."

"Are you kidding me right now?" I can't believe what I'm hearing. "I found my ex-boyfriend dead, and all you say is *hmph*?"

"What would you like me to say? 'Oh, poor Bradley, the world will miss his shining light? There's going to be one less star in the sky tonight?'" Even though I can't see her, I know she's making dramatic hand gestures.

"Right now, you're being incredibly callous," I snap.

"Well, what do you expect?" Mom snaps back. "He broke my baby girl's heart and sent you spiraling. You acted like a lunatic."

"I did *not* spiral!"

"You started dressing like a glorified street-corner prostitute."

"It's a chicken costume! Big difference between me and a prostitute."

"Oh, do tell."

"They make more money than me!"

Silence. Outside the truck, a mortified mom shields her son's ears. I give her an apologetic wave and turn my back to the window.

"Well," Mom finally says, "that was vulgar."

Instant guilt reflex.

"Sorry, Mom," I sigh.

"Did you at least keep your promise?"

"What promise?"

She groans. "The one where you swore you'd call me first if you ever found another dead body."

"You can't be serious!"

"Oh, I am!"

While she rants, I hear soft clucking behind me. I turn to find a real, fluffy white chicken hopping into the truck like it's on the payroll.

"I don't think the health department allows live poultry in the kitchen," I say.

"Who are you talking to now?" Mom demands.

"No one," I squeak and quickly clear my throat to cover my lie. The chicken settles into a box of towels like it owns the place. "I promise if I find any more bodies, I'll call you first."

"A mother always knows when her kids are lying."

"Uh-huh." I crouch, trying to shoo the chicken out.

"Not that you'd know," she continues. "Seeing as how you're not a mother yet. What was wrong with Larry?"

"Not this again."

"You barely spoke to him and his mother at the store the other day. He's kindhearted. If you gave him a chance—"

"Larry," I say flatly, "is thirty-seven, unemployed, and still lives with his parents. He has a bad comb-over and an unfortunate last name. Also, his mom tagged along on our date."

"Well," she sniffs, "not long ago, you were two of those things yourself."

"Wow, Mom." I pause. "I lived in the garage apartment. That's not the same."

"When your mailing address is the same as ours, you live at home."

I open my mouth to argue, but she barrels on. "Anyway. A mother's superpower is knowing when her kids are lying. Yours is apparently finding dead bodies."

"Not funny." I shiver. "I have to go, Mom."

"Give Larry another chance!"

"Goodbye!" I hang up and turn my full attention to the fluffy intruder curled in the box. "Did you come from the barn?" The chicken leans its head. "You're fluffy. What kind of chicken are you?"

Opening my camera app, I snap a picture and reverse search the image. "Ooh, you're a Silkie chicken," I tell her. "Sounds fancy. I assume you're a girl."

Do chickens have preferred pronouns?

The chicken clucks softly in response, and I reach over, stroking her purplish comb.

I hear customers outside the truck, so I get up and leave my small kitchen crasher to take their orders. A steady stream keeps me busy, and my newest fluffy buddy's innocent eyes make me feel guilty about the number of chicken wings I sell. But like Aunt Dolly used to say, "If God didn't want us to eat them, he shouldn't have made chickens so tasty."

Twenty minutes later, the chicken is still here, her beady black eyes fixed on my every move. "I guess I should name you instead of just calling you chicken."

"Bawk!" She fluffs her wings.

I tap my chin, brainstorming. "Pom-pom? No, too cutesy. Snowball? No, still not right."

Squatting down, I make eye contact with the chicken, though its feathers make it hard. "Your name needs to be something punny to match our brand. I got it!" I snap my fingers, "Teriyaki!"

The chicken stretches her wings and purrs, as if approving her new name.

"Welcome to your new home, Teriyaki," I say. "At least until I figure out what to do with you."

Chapter Nine

"Naming a chicken after a dinner dish seems morbid."

Looking up from my newest feathered friend, I spot Detective Kane standing at the back of my truck. Without hesitation—or permission—he steps through the propped-open door.

"You're violating health codes," I say, seated on the floor with Teriyaki nestled in my lap.

He looks at me before glancing at the chicken.

"Touché." I tuck Teriyaki back into her box and stand. "Stay," I tell her, pointing a finger before I wash my hands at the sink. "What brought you back, Detective?"

"There's a rumor going around that you found a dead body." His usually clear blue eyes darken, taking on a stormy hue as they lock onto mine. "Is it true?"

I dry my hands slowly, searching for a distraction. "Can I get you something to eat? Maybe one of our weekend specials?"

"Yes. But don't think I didn't notice you dodging the question."

Grabbing a tray, I busy myself preparing a basket of Beats and Bites sliders and fries. His gaze burns into the back of my head, and the thought of Teriyaki watching makes it impossible to serve him chicken wings.

"Here you go." I hand him the basket. "On the house this time."

"Thanks." He takes a bite of a slider, finishing it in one go. "Delicious. Now, about those rumors." He licks his fingers.

I cross my arms, watching him with mild disgust—mostly to cover up the fact that I find the way he enjoys his food strangely attractive. "Are you asking as Detective Kane or as a friend?"

"A little of both."

I sigh. "It's true. I found my ex-boyfriend. As soon as I realized he was dead, I called 911." I keep my answers brief, recalling how intense Detective Kane was the last time I ended up smack dab in the middle of a murder investigation.

A customer approaches the serving window, giving me an excuse to escape. A sweet older couple orders two Arnold Palmers in our laughing chicken tumblers and prepays for two meals on the Kind Bites board.

Detective Kane waits until they're gone. "I know there's more you're not saying." He pops a fry into his mouth.

I glare at him. "Why are you here, really? This isn't your case, is it?"

"No, but I heard things."

"What things? Who told you?"

"Trish."

He says the name like it should mean something to me. "Trish?"

"Patricia Wilcox. We were in the academy together. Trish and I are old friends."

The way he says her name stirs something uncomfortable in my chest. "Old friends?"

He shrugs, picking at another fry. "Something like that."

"Something like that," I echo. "What did you say to her about me and Seth? Did you tell your cop friend how Seth punched Brad the other day?"

His eyes flash. "No, but thanks for confirming he did."

Me and my stupid mouth.

"She called me after she spoke with you and your brother," he says, offering no further explanation.

Teriyaki shifts in her box, pecking at the edge. I reach over to settle her, but she suddenly flaps her wings wildly, startling me. I stumble forward, colliding with Detective Kane's solid chest. His hands instinctively catch my arms, steadying me.

"Easy there," he murmurs, his voice close. His breath brushes against my temple, warm and smelling faintly of coffee and something woodsy.

My breath catches. For a split second, our eyes lock. There's a flicker of amusement and curiosity . . . something I don't quite have a name for. Then his hands drop, and the moment's gone. I clear my throat and step back, pretending my face isn't suddenly volcanic.

"Tell me what happened, Beth."

The way he says my name makes me spill every last detail—from running into Brad at Sugar and Spice Bakery two days ago to finding him this morning.

"Detective Wilcox seems competent," I say. "But I'm sure she'll soon see she's barking up the wrong tree with me and Seth."

Detective Kane gives me a look, like I'm being naive. "Once a detective gets wind of something, they latch on. Finding your ex dead doesn't look good. Nor does your brother punching him."

"Neither does one of our truck's tumblers being found nearby," I mumble.

His expression darkens. "Jeez, Beth."

"I didn't drop it, if that's what you're thinking. And neither did Seth."

"I wasn't thinking that." He takes a bite of his second slider.

"So, what do you suggest?"

"Be careful when talking to the police." His tone bristles Teriyaki's feathers, making her let out a small, offended cluck.

"Correct me if I'm wrong, but aren't you the police?"

"You should always be careful of what you say to me." He grins.

I roll my eyes. "I'll keep that in mind."

He backs against the counter. The space in the truck is tight, and with him posted there, tall and broad and entirely too calm, it somehow feels even smaller. His arms are crossed, his stance casual—but the energy between us isn't.

"Be honest," he says. "You're not gonna let this go, are you?"

"Do I look like Elsa to you?"

He gives me a slow once-over, the corner of his mouth twitching. "More like Anna."

"Anna? I like Anna. Is that a compliment?"

"Sure," he smiles. "Impulsive. Talks too much. Trusts the wrong people."

"Wow. Flattery from a man who's clearly Kristoff."

He snorts. "Kristoff?"

"Total buzzkill. Plays it safe. Grunts instead of talks. Probably thinks a romantic gesture is lending someone a shovel."

He tries to look wounded, but he's losing the battle with his smile. "Could've been worse. Could've said Sven."

"Oh, you're Sven on a good day. Strong. Silent. Slightly judgy."

He chuckles. "What if I told you I see myself as Olaf?"

I blink. "You? Olaf? Please. You don't do warm hugs. You don't sing. And your head is very much screwed on."

"I can be warm."

"Mm-hmm. You radiate exactly the energy of someone who'd call a hug 'a security risk.'"

"Is that so?" He arches a brow, and then—oh no—his left dimple makes an appearance.

That dimple should come with a warning label.

Before I can blink, he steps in, close enough that I have to shift back an inch just to breathe—and then, with quiet certainty, he lifts his arms and wraps them around me.

Not a side hug. Not a quick pat-and-release.

A full, solid, intentional hug.

One of his hands settles low on my back, the other curling gently around my shoulder, holding me like I'm something to keep safe. Like he's done this before and knows exactly how to make it count.

I hesitate, my arms frozen between us, palms grazing the front of his shirt. Crisp cotton, warm from his skin.

Then I give in.

Slowly, I slide my hands up over his chest and lightly around his back, fingers brushing the ridge of his shoulder blades. He's solid all the way through—no give, no pretense—and something inside me stutters at the feel of him.

He smells like cedar and black coffee, like early mornings and focus and quiet loyalty. The kind of man who shows up and doesn't need applause for it.

I melt against him before I can stop myself.

My cheek rests against his firm chest. My breath hitches.

Then, too soon, he steps back—calm, unreadable—and says, "See? Not a security risk. This time."

I stare up at him, my brain a complete blank slate.

"Anyway," he adds, like he didn't just turn my spine to warm applesauce, "this isn't my case, so I can't tell you what to do. But if I could? I'd tell you to back off."

"Noted," I say, voice slightly higher than normal. "I'll sleuth carefully."

"That's not a thing."

"It is if you wear gloves."

"Call it what you want, but it's still being a busybody, and you should stay out of it." He points at me. "Besides, we both know you'll forget to wear gloves anyway."

My mouth opens and closes like a guppy.

He's right, I'd forget gloves.

"You hold no legal authority over me." Detective Kane arches a brow in challenge. "In this situation," I amend. "I'll take your suggestion under advisement, but you telling me to stay out of it is not legally binding."

Shaking his head, he plants his fists on his hips. "I knew I should've arrested you when I had the chance."

"You already have," I half joke, half remind him of the time he arrested me outside City Hall after an altercation with my old food truck nemesis, Benji. Did I mention I was wearing the giant chicken suit?

"I meant again."

We stare at each other in a silent standoff, both of us too stubborn to blink first.

He sighs and shifts back against the prep counter. The metal lets out a groan under his weight, all six-plus feet of broody muscle pressing into the steel. He's already a foot taller than me, but in this cramped space, that difference feels exaggerated—like the walls are closing in. I'm still hyperaware of our earlier hug. Of how warm and solid he felt pressing into me. How *right* it felt. Like his arms were made for hugging. The scent of him—cedar and black coffee—lingers faintly in the air, and I catch myself leaning slightly forward, like my nose might snatch it up before it disappears.

I sniff deeply.

Focus, Beth!

"Fine," he says, his voice laced with reluctant patience. "Tell me what you think is going on."

I cross my arms, tilting my head. "Are you going to run and tattle to Detective Wilcox?"

He narrows his eyes, the corners of his mouth twitching like he's suppressing a smirk. "I've already told her plenty of what I think about you." He pauses, letting that sink in before adding, "And your brother. Now spill it."

I hesitate, fingers twisting the hem of my apron. The truck suddenly feels warmer, like someone turned on the heater.

"I think someone killed Brad," I say. "I think it was murder."

Detective Kane's posture straightens, his casual stance sharpening into something more attentive. "Why do you think that?"

"His temple looked pretty smashed," I say. "And there was a lot of blood on the rock next to him. Way too much for it to have been a simple accident."

He folds his arms, considering. "Maybe he tripped. Hit his head on the way down. That spot you found him? It's tucked behind the vendors and a bit of a dead zone. If something happened, there might not have been anyone around to see or help."

I nod, then shake my head. "Sure, it could've been an accident. But Brad wasn't the kind of guy who wandered off by himself. Especially not at a crowded event with a press pass around his neck. He liked an audience."

Detective Kane studies me, like he's weighing how much to believe. "What were you doing over there alone?"

"Using the only actual bathroom here," I say. "I don't like porta potties."

He nods, filing that away. "When was the last time you saw him before this weekend?"

"Over three years ago. When he dumped me."

"It's possible you didn't know everything about his health or personal life," he says. "People change. Maybe he had a condition—heart issue, dizziness, anything that could've caused a fall. Maybe he was seeking solitude and tripped while he was staring at his phone."

I narrow my eyes. "I don't believe it was natural causes."

He doesn't push back, just says, "We don't know yet. Until the ME's report comes in, all we've got is speculation. If something feels off, trust your gut. But don't stir the pot too much. You might end up making yourself—or Seth—look worse."

"Did she say something to you?" I ask. "Detective Wilcox. Are we her prime suspects?"

He doesn't answer right away.

My throat tightens. "Is that why you're really here?"

He sighs, rubbing the back of his neck. "I never said you were a prime suspect."

"Do you think I did it?"

He lets out a soft laugh. "No. You and Seth aren't killers."

"You don't know that!" I snap. "I mean—Seth did punch Brad. He's protective of me."

"Is there a point you're trying to make?"

"I . . ." *What point am I trying to make? Why do I have to be such a contrarian?*

"It's a brother's job to protect his sister," he adds.

"You sound like my mother."

And like he's speaking from personal experience.

"Your mother's a smart woman," he says, swallowing the rest of the slider.

"Don't let her hear you say that," I tease. "If she finds out I'm semi-friends with a handsome cop who thinks she's smart—" I let out a low whistle. "Hope you like Sunday dinners."

Detective Kane chokes on his food. Coughing. Gasping. He grabs a cup and downs lemonade like it's an emergency. "Wow."

"Wrong pipe," he croaks, eyes watering. He sets the cup down and avoids looking at me.

I hold up my hands. "Okay, relax. I wasn't inviting you to dinner. I was making a point."

He whispers something under his breath, barely audible. "It's not dinner I'm worried about."

That makes me pause.

But he doesn't elaborate, and I pretend not to notice the shift between us. Instead, I say, "Thanks. For believing I didn't do it."

"But that doesn't mean someone won't try to make it look like you did." He leans in slightly, voice low. "A tumbler from your truck was found near the scene. Maybe someone already is." He meets my eyes. "Be smart, Beth."

I shiver. If someone planted something from my truck, then this isn't some messy coincidence. It's calculated. Personal.

"I might really be in danger," I say, and this time it's not sarcastic. It's true.

"Which is why I'm telling you to go home. Close up the truck. Let the detective in charge do her job."

"She's the one sniffing around me and Seth like we've got bodies buried in the fryer," I complain.

"She'd be sloppy if she wasn't. It's hard to overlook you two, especially given your connection to two recent murders. That's not nothing."

"Nice. Really comforting."

"You're not her only lead," he says. "But you're not off her list either. Which is why poking around is only going to make it worse."

I glance toward the window and freeze. "Is that a llama?"

Detective Kane follows my gaze. A llama in a top hat struts past, led by a handler in a tuxedo shirt.

"Alpaca," he corrects.

"How do you know?"

He lists the differences. "Llamas are bigger, angular faces, banana-shaped ears. Alpacas are smaller, fuzzier, and look like they have a mop of hair."

I stare at him. "Huh."

He shrugs. "My nephew's eight."

"So that's how you know so much about *Frozen*," I grin. I have a joke for him. "What do you call Olaf when he's singing off key?"

He sighs. "I don't know."

"A meltdown!"

He groans. "Terrible."

"Rude." I shove his shoulder—his very solid, muscular shoulder.

His phone beeps. He checks it, then grabs a basket of fries from the warming station. "These are for my nephew. I've gotta go. But do me a favor—stay out of this."

"No promises," I say, walking him to the back door. "Bet your nephew would love my joke."

"I'm sure he would."

Chapter Ten

The next morning, the fryer's hot, the sauces are prepped, and I've triple-checked the foil wrap on every single tray of backup wings. For a few brief, golden minutes, Kluckin' Good is running smoother than my favorite lemon butter glaze. It's only the second day of the festival, but it already feels worlds apart from yesterday. The biggest difference, of course, is that I haven't found any more dead bodies.

At least not yet.

Outside, the morning sun peeks over the top of the barn, casting long shadows across the gravel path that runs between the food trucks. The gates have only been open about thirty minutes, but already, the early crowd is drifting in. Pass holders with branded tote bags, local news crews with big cameras and bigger coffee cups, and vendors taking advantage of the lull to scope out the competition.

I wipe my hands on my apron and lean on the counter. "Okay," I say to Seth, who's arranging water bottles with the grim focus of a man solving a Rubik's Cube blindfolded, "we're set for the first rush."

"Cool," he replies. "I'm gonna pretend to be doing inventory so I don't have to talk to anyone yet."

I roll my eyes. "You're a shining ambassador for the brand."

He gives me a thumbs-up without looking up from the cooler.

"You got about ten minutes before it's time to get dressed and join Rylie," I remind him, handing over a bottle of his cold brew like a peace offering.

Seth grumbles in response, stacking the bottles with a bit too much force. "I still think this constitutes sibling abuse."

"Hey, no one made you challenge me to Jalapeño Roulette," I flick a crumb off the counter.

He scowls. "I thought you'd tap out by round three."

"You thought wrong." I grin. "I still can't feel the roof of my mouth, but it was totally worth it."

Seth complains about betrayal and ghost peppers under his breath and grabs the last bottle, slamming it into place with the finality of a man accepting his bovine fate.

Outside, Rylie is already working the path in her full chicken regalia. She's handing out Kluckin' Good flyers, posing for photos, and working that chicken strut like she's on a feathered runway. She's in her element.

I step down from the truck and stretch, taking in the scene. The air smells like freshly cut grass and fryer oil. In the distance, someone's testing the speakers in the carnival zone. The distorted notes of an eighties pop song float over the fields before cutting off abruptly with a squeal of feedback.

Time to stretch my legs.

I wander past a couple of food trucks I recognize. Fat Al's Burgers and Bao Chicka Wow Wow, whose bun game is criminally underrated. Danny, the owner of Fat Al's, gives me a casual salute from behind the counter. He's neither fat nor named Al, which he claims is part of the branding mystery. I lift a hand in return, catching a whiff of grilled onions and peppers.

Next to him, Bao Chicka Wow Wow is already puffing steam through its roof vent. Jules, the owner, is outside dancing while setting up serving tables like she's choreographing a cooking show, earbuds in, ponytail bouncing, completely in her own world. I'd kill for one of her spicy kimchi baos. Probably not the best mental phrasing given current events.

As I approach the coffee stand, I slow my steps. A small group of vendors has clustered near a folding table stacked with complimentary Danishes and thermoses labeled "Vendor Fuel." They're deep in conversation, voices pitched low, like they're trading secrets instead of stories over mini croissants.

"I heard someone died yesterday," says a guy in a green Vegan Ventures hoodie, glancing around like he's expecting a health inspector to pop out of the bushes.

"No way," someone else replies, wide-eyed. "Here? At the festival?"

A third voice—female, older, probably from one of the BBQ trucks—chimes in. "I talked to Conner this morning. He said someone tripped. Fell. Total freak accident."

"Wasn't it one of the food critics?" asks a man dusted in powdered sugar, his apron looking like it lost a snowball fight.

That stops me cold.

I linger near the edge of the group, pretending to scroll through my phone while I listen. They're not saying his name, but they don't need to. My pulse kicks up.

"That's what I heard," answers another vendor. He has a tangle of salt-and-pepper curls and a faded Rolling Stones tee. His truck, Wrap City, is next to Layla's, and now that I see him up close, I realize he's the same guy I saw yesterday. The one who passed something to Brad when they thought no one was looking.

"Doesn't make sense," the woman says. "You fall and just . . . die?"

"If he landed wrong," Vegan Ventures guy guesses. "Could've hit his head."

I use my phone for real this time, swiping to the local news app. If someone at the festival died, there's gotta be something online. But all I find is weekend weather, a ribbon-cutting for a new community garden, and an outdated article previewing the food truck lineup. Nothing. Not a whisper about Brad.

"I haven't heard anything about this," someone else says.

"Figures they're keeping it quiet," Vegan Ventures guy replies. "Bad press for the festival."

"Maybe they don't even know who it was yet," another adds. "Or they're still trying to notify next of kin."

Instantly I think of Janice, Brad's mom. Losing her is my biggest regret after the breakup. She tried to stay in contact, but it was too difficult. She would've been a wonderful mother-in-law. As I'm sure she's a great step-aunt to Tiffany.

I can't imagine how she must be taking the news of her son's death.

That's when the crowd parts like a shark just glided through.

Layla Gafford enters, owning the pavement, sunglasses on, lips pursed, her ankle boots clicking like punctuation. She doesn't say a word as she shoulders past the vendors. She just grabs a pastry before leaving, ignoring everyone.

"Good morning to you too," someone says, all huffy.

"She's been like that since she got here," another says, not bothering to lower their voice. "Acting like she's above the rest of us."

"She's acted like that as long as I've known her," the powder sugar apron guy says.

"I heard Layla yelling at a food critic yesterday," Wrap City guy says, lowering his voice a little. "Told him he had no right to comment on her food. Said she wouldn't do an interview with him, not after that hit piece he wrote about her a few months ago."

"Was it *the* critic?" someone asks him. "The Foodie Guy? The one everyone's been talking about?"

What is everyone saying? My brain kicks into high gear.

"Um, I'm not sure who he was," Wrap City guy replies.

"You know," a woman wearing a dancing potato shirt says. "The guy with influencer-level following, and the ego the size of a bounce house."

"The tall guy?" someone replies. "Dark wavy hair, always smug? Wore those ridiculous red, white, and blue Converse like it was his brand."

Yep. That was Brad. Subtle as a parade float.

"It had to be him," the dancing potato shirt woman says. "I think his name was Chad?" She snaps her fingers. "No, no, Brad! He had a reputation for tanking businesses with a single snarky post. But if you played nice—and by nice, I mean paid up or offered extra incentives—he'd sing your praises. Was that who Layla was arguing with?"

"Um, I couldn't tell ya," Wrap City guy says, voice wobbling. "Never met him before."

He's lying!

I saw him pass something to Brad yesterday when they thought no one was looking.

"What I can say is she was fired up," Wrap City guy goes on. Almost like he's trying to deflect attention from himself. "I mean, Layla always runs hot, but this was next level."

Vegan Ventures hoodie guy shakes his head. "This Layla person seems like a hot pot ready to blow. You heard about the fight she tried to start with Coffeeology yesterday, right?"

"Oh yeah." The powder sugar apron guy nods. "Layla's always ready to blow. She nearly got banned from the Savannah Street Eats Rally last year. Took a swing at a churro vendor, I kid you not."

"If someone did push the Foodie Guy, I know who my money's on," someone murmurs.

The group chuckles, but it's a tight, nervous sound. Nobody wants to say it out loud—but they're all thinking it.

Including me.

Because I feel deep down that it wasn't a freak accident.

I drift away before I get caught eavesdropping and head back toward Kluckin' Good, but not before someone else catches my eye. A woman standing alone near the edge of the path, staring at the food truck signs like they're in a foreign language.

She's wearing a brown sundress, matching cardigan, canvas tote slung over her arm. Her coral sandals are the only splash of color, more cheerful than daring. She looks vaguely familiar. She approaches the truck as I do, and I slip in through the back door while she looks at the menu. Seth is already gone, his leather cow bell conveniently left behind.

I go to the order window. "Hi, can I help you?" I smile.

She blinks, startled. "Oh. Sorry, I—uh—I'll have the Golden Gate Heat wings."

"Sure thing," I say. "Anything else?"

Her hand tightens on the tote strap. "I'm trying to decide. Do people like the avocado fries?"

"People love them," I say, warming to the pitch. "Our Guac the Line Fries are dipped in panko and deep-fried till they're golden and crispy. They're a festival special. Plus, they're vegan-friendly, if that matters."

Her brow lifts slightly. "Do you use a separate fryer?"

"Yep, totally separate. Canola oil only."

"Okay, then . . . I'll get those too. And the wings. And a lemonade, I guess?"

"You want that in one of our festival-exclusive double-walled tumblers?" I'm striving to match Rylie's upselling proficiency. "You'll enjoy free refills all day with your receipt and get refills the rest of the weekend for only ninety-nine cents."

"Sure," she laughs. "It looks cute, why not?"

"Coming right up!" I reach for one of our happy yellow tumblers and scoop some ice into it.

I watch as she digs in her bag for her wallet, and something scratches at the edge of my memory.

Her voice, maybe. The shape of her face.

She hands me her card, and I ring up her order. "Sorry, have we met before?" I ask, handing her back her card and receipt. "We have," she says, almost apologetically. "Well, kind of. We were both at Sugar and Spice Bakery the other day."

And just like that, it clicks.

She was with Brad, but he never introduced her. She hovered behind him like an afterthought, smiling faintly but not saying a word.

"He never introduced us," I say, remembering the weirdness of that day.

She gives a lopsided shrug. "He didn't always . . . bother."

I pour her lemonade and hand over our Kluckin' Good tumbler.

"I'm Beth," I say.

"Peyton Nelson," she replies. She adjusts her grip on the cup, then awkwardly sticks her hand through the window. "I work—worked—at *The City and Beyond*. With Brad."

"How are you holding up?" I ask, not sure why I bother.

"It's been . . . strange." A pause. "I keep thinking he'll text. That this was all some scheduling mix-up or something." She gives a humorless laugh. "Or find an email from him with a typo in the subject line."

I try to smile, but it catches.

"Anyway. Sorry. That was weird."

"No, it's okay," I say. "It's been a weird week. Give me a minute while I get your order together."

I move to the prep counter, working quickly. Panko-covered avocado slices hiss in the fryer, their garlic and herb scent mixing with the spicy wings.

I slide the basket through the serving window. "Here you go! The fries need another moment."

"Thanks," she murmurs but doesn't reach for the food right away.

"Being here after his death must be hard for you." The words are out before I can second-guess them.

Peyton nods, adjusting her tote again. "It was a shock. Brad took care of himself, more or less. He drank those awful green smoothies every morning. Swore by them."

I wrinkle my nose. “Did they smell like grass clippings?”

That gets a quiet genuine laugh out of her. “Yes!”

Her fingers shift slightly on her lemonade cup. Something unreadable flickers behind her eyes. I almost miss it. I watch her adjust the wings and snap a photo. “I’m covering his assignment this weekend for the magazine. It’s the least I can do.”

“Oh, are you a food critic too?”

Peyton shakes her head. “No. I actually went to school for multimedia journalism. I am—or was—his editorial assistant.” Her thumb hovers over the shutter. “Mind if I grab a photo?”

I give her my best food truck owner smile. “Go for it.”

“Thanks,” she says, lowering her phone once she’s done.

“You should stop by later when my twin is here,” I say. “Seth and I own the truck together, and he’s dressed as a giant cow this weekend.”

She laughs, and the sound lights up her face. “I bet the magazine would love that.”

“So, an editorial assistant, that sounds exciting. I bet you’re spinning a lot of plates. Is it fast-paced?”

Ding!

The timer for the deep fryer finishes. “Be right back.” I remove the freshly cooked avocado fries, giving them a gentle shake before transferring them to the basket. “Here you go—fresh from the fryer.”

“Ooh, those look amazing.” She snaps a couple photos. “It can be fast-paced. A lot of scheduling, proofreading, fact-checking, keeping projects on track . . . not always glamorous.”

“Try the avocado fries with our Zesty Verde Lime sauce.” I gesture toward the little container on her tray.

She dips one and takes a bite. Her eyes go wide. “Oh, wow.” One hand flies up to cover her mouth as she chews. “These are incredible.”

I grin. “We get that a lot.”

She swallows and leans on the counter, more relaxed now. “Before I joined the magazine, I had a lifestyle blog. Wellness stuff, mostly. Recipes. Interviews with small local businesses. Nothing huge."

"What happened? Did you want something more stable?"

She shrugs. "Kind of. A friend passed my name along to one of the editors, and I started freelancing. Then they brought me on part-time and then full-time. But it's changed a lot."

"That sounds tough. I'm sorry," I say, unsure what else to add. "But at least they kept you on."

"Barely." Her voice lowers. "They fired the last food critic when the magazine changed ownership. I was next. Brad . . . he went to bat for me."

"Really?"

"Yeah." She glances down at her tray, not meeting my eyes. "Said they'd need someone who actually knew the system if they were going to clean house."

"That was . . . kind of him."

"It was," she says quietly. "He didn't have to. Most people wouldn't have." I watch as she fiddles with her sweater, looking down at her shoes.

"So despite the layoffs, you got to keep your job? That's great."

Peyton nods. "It was so stressful. The new leadership wanted a rebrand with edgier tones, tighter writing, more trending Bay Area content. They started cleaning house fast."

"And Brad?"

"Brought in for the overhaul," she says. "Mr. Collins—he's the managing editor—hired Brad specifically to replace our food critic. They liked what he was already doing on his own and thought it would work well for the magazine's new direction."

"Wow! That sucks for the person he replaced."

"Yeah," Peyton drags the word out. "The old food critic was a total Karen. Literally. Only she spelled her name with a C, and always emphasized, it's Caren with a C," she says with air quotes.

"That tracks for a Caren," I half joke.

Peyton laughs hard, then winces like she doesn't want to speak ill of the formerly employed. "She was . . . hard to work with. Brilliant palate but constantly butting heads with everyone. Caren was edgy but not in a good way." Peyton takes another bite of her fries. "I guess she wasn't a good fit for Mr. Collins's vision."

"So they booted her and brought in Brad to make food content go viral?" I ask.

"Pretty much. I don't think Brad was out to take someone's job. But Mr. Collins loved that Brad was all about the snappy one-liners, bold headlines, and had TikTok-worthy writeups. It made the brass happy."

"But you survived the purge," I say.

"Barely," she says. "Mr. Collins told me they were 'going in a different direction.' That direction was out the door."

"And Brad stopped it?"

"Yeah. Walked in while I was ugly-crying into a box of file folders. Told Mr. Collins I was 'top-notch.' When that didn't work, he asked to make me his assistant instead."

I blink. "Wait. Brad hired you?"

"Kind of. I went from writing essays to ghostwriting captions and editing Brad's reviews."

"That sounds . . ." I hesitate.

"Crushing? Demoralizing? A betrayal of my literary soul?" Peyton supplies with a sardonic smile. "All of the above. But hey, still a writing job."

"What's it like working there?" I ask. "At *The City and Beyond*?"

"It's mostly online now. Big push for social media, but they still do a limited print run. Glossy, boutique-style. It's weird seeing your work in print next to a $15 hotdog review."

I laugh. "I didn't know they still printed anything."

"They do," she says, proudly. "Enough to say we're 'multimedia.'"

"Do you like it?"

She hesitates. "I like writing. The job's . . . fine. I still blog on the side—indie spots, events the magazine won't touch. I'm hoping it leads somewhere."

"Like where?"

"Somewhere bigger. National would be a dream. Or even just better pay. But writing jobs are like parking in the Mission—you take what you can get and pray you don't get towed."

"That bad, huh?"

"Brutal," she says. "But a crummy job is better than none. Sometimes you have to suck it up."

"I get that," I say. "For what it's worth, I'm sorry Brad is dead."

"Me too," she says. "He wasn't bad to work with. Good at making people think he cared."

Ouch!

"We weren't close. But he saved my neck. I won't forget that."

Her phone chirps. She checks the screen and sighs. "I have to meet with a detective. Wilcox, I think. Joy."

As Peyton disappears into the crowd, I stare down at the order window, my mind racing.

So. Caren-with-a-C got fired, Brad got her job, and Peyton got demoted to keep hers. It's a mess, and messy situations breed resentment.

And if Karen—sorry, *Caren*—was half as difficult as Peyton described, I wouldn't put it past her to hold a grudge.

Is she still lurking in the wings? Watching Brad take her spot, watching her bylines disappear one by one, watching him enjoy the spotlight that used to be hers?

Gripping my phone, I scan the festival.

I shake off the thought, but it sticks like grease on a fryer basket.

And then there's Peyton.

She said it herself—Brad saved her job. He fought to keep her when she was on the verge of getting fired. It didn't sound like she had any reason to hurt him. If anything, she owed him.

I tuck my phone back into my apron as Seth sidles up to the window, his giant cow head tucked under one arm. He's sweaty, out of breath, and looks like he barely escaped the slaughterhouse.

"Please," he pants. "Tell me we have a cold drink that isn't lemonade."

I glance pointedly at the soft foam udders bouncing against his stomach.

"You're not funny!"

Grinning, I gesture to the drink tray outside the truck, filled with ice and bottled water. "You're right. That costume looks suffocating."

Seth clomps over to the drink tray in his full cow regalia, the fake udders bobbing like they've got somewhere to be.

"See!" He groans and holds up his costume hooves, clumsily trying to grip a bottle of water from the tray. "Hooves. Beth. I have literal hooves. Help me out here."

Laughing, I grab a bottle from inside the truck, twist the cap off, and hand it to him.

He gulps down half of the water, then squints at me. "You've got that face again."

"What face?"

"The one that says you're mentally pinning red string to a corkboard," Seth says, pointing at me with his bottle. "You're about to Nancy Drew your way into trouble."

I ignore him, my gaze drifting toward the refreshment table. "I overheard some vendors talking earlier. They'd heard someone died yesterday, but nobody knew the details. One woman said she talked to Conner Green."

"And?"

"Well, Conner told her it was a freak accident. Someone tripped and fell. No mention of a murder, no name, nothing."

"So they're keeping it quiet."

"Yup. I couldn't find anything online either. And then this other vendor, the one with the Wrap City truck? He said he's parked next to Layla and overheard her screaming at a food critic yesterday. Said she refused to do an interview with him, that he had no right to review her food after what he wrote about her last time."

"I wonder what that's about?" Seth takes another swig of water.

"It gets better," I lean forward, looking around before I continue. "Wrap City guy totally lied."

"About what?" he asks, not really interested.

"About Brad. Some of the other truck owners were asking if the food critic Layla was screaming at was the Foodie Guy, and Wrap City guy played dumb. Said he didn't know him. But I saw him, Seth. I saw him hand Brad an envelope on Thursday, right when the festival started."

That gets Seth's attention.

"You're sure?"

"Totally! It was fast, and low. Like a drug deal with a Yelp rating. You don't pass off mystery envelopes to total strangers. He knew who Brad was. But he didn't want the others to know he knew. Why?"

Seth furrows his brows. "He lied about knowing Brad. That doesn't mean he killed him."

"No," I admit. "But it might mean he was one of the last people to see Brad alive. Doesn't that matter?"

"It matters to the police. Not to you." He gestures toward me with a hoof. "You can tell Detective Wilcox what you saw and then leave it alone."

Ignoring Seth, I continue with my story. "Then Layla showed up—no hello, no smile—she stormed through, grabbed a Danish, then left like she was auditioning for a villain role in a telenovela."

"Charming." He drinks some more water.

"Once she left, people started whispering stuff like 'she's always nasty' and 'if someone pushed the guy, I know who my money's on.'"

Seth lowers the water bottle, his expression sharpening. "They think she did it?"

I shrug. "They don't know. But there's suspicion."

"Are you adding her to your list?"

"Already did yesterday," I say, guilt gnawing at me for adding Seth to the list too. "I'm going to add Wrap City guy too."

"Great, add him to the list, then tell the cops."

Fat chance of that. I'm not handing over a suspect list to Detective Wilcox with Seth's name on it.

I shift gears. "Did you know Brad wasn't the first food critic for *The City and Beyond*?"

He shrugs. "I mean, it's a magazine. I figured there were critics before him."

"No, I mean, they *fired* the last one just to bring Brad in. Her name was Caren with a C."

"And you think she—what—took him out in a revenge-fueled crime of passion?"

I press my lips together. "I don't know, but think about it. If you got fired and someone else waltzed in and took your job, wouldn't that sting?"

"Sure." Seth takes another gulp of water. "But I wouldn't *kill* someone over it."

"Maybe she wouldn't either," I admit. "But what if she's here?"

That gets his attention.

"What if Caren showed up yesterday, cornered Brad somewhere private, and something went wrong?"

"You think she came here to kill him?"

"Not necessarily. Maybe she tried talking with him, but things got out of hand. Maybe it *was* a revenge-fueled crime of passion. Or maybe it was an accident—"

"Or maybe she's innocent and not even here," Seth interjects, "and this is all speculation."

"This is not your courtroom," I remind him. "I'm not a judge you can yell 'objection' at. I'm trying to cover all possibilities.

Because right now, you and I"—I motion between us—"are looking pretty good as far as suspects go."

Seth pulls a face. "Okay, first, I'm a man of the law. Second, if I were a murderer, I'd like to think I'd at least be smart enough not to do it at a festival with a thousand potential witnesses."

"Wow. I'm so comforted right now," I say.

Seth waves a dismissive hoof. "My point is, if this Caren person did kill Brad, it would be risky to do it here, out in the open. And if it *was* her, why now? He's been at that job for a while, right? Why not go after him months ago?"

I frown. "That's . . . actually a good point."

Seth grins. "Say it again. Louder."

I roll my eyes. "I *said*, that's a good point."

"You should pay more attention. I'm full of 'em." He smirks, then crumples his empty water bottle and tosses it into the recycling bin. "How do you even know about this Caren person?"

"A woman named Peyton stopped by the truck before you got here. She was Brad's assistant. Apparently, she was there Wednesday at Sugar and Spice Bakery, but I don't really remember because it's not like Brad introduced her. Besides I only cared about getting out of there and not seeing his stupid face for a second longer."

"What is your point?"

"My point is that Peyton told me about Caren. She also told me a lot of people liked Brad."

Seth snorts like a bull. "You're looking at Caren, but maybe the real motive came from someone closer. Someone who thought Brad liked them back."

"Then she said he was good at making people think he cared about them." That part still sticks with me. "Brad *looked* like he cared," I murmur. "But maybe it wasn't real."

Seth nods. "And if it wasn't real, maybe some of those people thought they meant something to him—until they found out otherwise."

I chew my lip. "Maybe Caren isn't the only person with a grudge."

"Exactly," Seth says. "Maybe there's someone else you're missing. Someone who *thought* they were special to Brad . . . until they weren't."

The words hit me like a gut punch.

I *knew* that feeling.

I lived it.

The moment Brad left me for his step-cousin, I realized I'd never actually mattered to him.

I swallow hard. "If Brad had enemies we don't know about, then we're looking at a way bigger suspect pool."

Seth watches me for a long moment, then exhales. "Look, I get that you want answers, but maybe—and hear me out—you let the *police* handle this?"

I let out a dismissive *pfft*.

Seth groans, rubbing his face with one fuzzy hoof. "Yeah. That's what I thought."

I cross my arms. "If I can figure out what really happened before anyone else—"

"And there it is." He points a hoof at me. "That attitude is what gets you in trouble." His udders sway slightly as he sighs at me. "At least don't get tunnel vision. If you're gonna play detective, keep your options open. And don't Nancy Drew yourself into a situation you can't get out of."

Chapter Eleven

The customer from yesterday with the funky purple glasses and dino tutu approaches my truck. Only today her tutu is neon green. Flashing a grin, she hands over her credit card.

"Back again?"

She laughs. "I told you. I've got two little boys who only eat chicken tenders, and you're the only chicken truck here who serves chicken they'll eat. You're gonna see me a lot this weekend."

We share a laugh as she rattles off her order—two Kluck-a-Doodle Classics with an empty tray for extra ketchup.

As I ring up the order, she glances at the suspended food board. "What's that?"

"That's our Kind Bites board. It's our way of giving back to those in need. Customers can prepay for a meal, a drink, or a side dish," I explain. "Next week, I'll add the prepaid items from the festival to our food board for those in need."

"I like that," she says, her eyes fixed on the board. She pulls a twenty-dollar bill from her pocket. "Here. Please use this to prepay for whatever you think will help most."

"Thank you," I say, taking the money and adding a note to our food log. "That's really generous."

She donated to our kindness board. That doesn't exactly scream "murderer."

Then again, she was here yesterday when the festival first started and she did buy *three* tumblers from me. Was the tumbler found near Brad's body possibly hers?

"Oh! Could I get a refill?" She lifts one of the tumblers she bought, the design still crisp and bright.

I take it from her and the dollar bill she's holding. "Lemonade?" She nods, and I begin the refill.

"I love these. I was worried they wouldn't keep my drinks cold yesterday, but they're fantastic. My lemonade still had ice in it over an hour later. My sons even agreed to try plain water from their tumblers. They call it 'chicken water,' but who cares as long as they're staying hydrated?"

"Do you want to me refill theirs with water for you?" I offer, handing her the refilled tumbler.

"Oh no, they're good." She points behind her to two little boys on a bench, happily drinking from their bright yellow cups.

All three tumblers. Still accounted for.

Well. That theory failed.

Actually, I feel . . . relieved.

I like her. I didn't want her to be a killer. She's kind, she tips well, and she somehow manages to wrangle two kids under ten without looking like she's about to lose it. Her boys look less sticky than most children I've encountered, which honestly feels like a small miracle. That says something, right? About how much she cares. About the kind of person she is.

Not a killer. Just a mom in a neon tutu doing her best. As I start prepping her food, I keep my tone casual. "Hey, out of curiosity, do you follow any food critics? You know, the influencer types?"

She inclines her head, thinking for a moment. "A few. Mostly for recipes, though. I love watching those hands-in-bowls videos where everything gets chopped up in fast motion."

"I get stuck down those rabbit holes too." I drop baskets of fries and chicken strips into the fryers. "Does the name Rise of the Foodie ring a bell?"

Her brows pull together. "Sounds familiar. Wait—isn't that the guy who does brutal restaurant takedowns? I think I saw a video of his floating around a few months back. Something about overpriced mac and cheese?"

"That sounds like him."

"Ugh." She wrinkles her nose. "I remember now. He ripped some poor place apart because their cheese sauce wasn't 'complex enough' or something ridiculous. Food snobs annoy me."

"So, you never met him?"

She shakes her head. "Nope. After I learned one of his viral reviews caused a small restaurant to shut down, I blocked his accounts. Didn't really care for them, to be honest. Why?"

"Oh, no reason." I brush off the question with a shrug as I remove her food from the fryers. "Just curious."

Because that's the guy who ended up dead yesterday, and I'm still trying to figure out who hated him enough to make that happen.

I line the baskets with red-and-white checkered paper before putting in her chicken tenders and fries. "Here you go—fresh and hot."

"You're the best," she grins. "See you in a few hours when my kids start asking for round two."

I watch the woman walk off, my fingers already reaching for my phone.

Me: Scratch our dino tutu customer off the list. She still has all three tumblers.

Me: Also, she only knows Brad as a guy with an obnoxious food account.

Rylie: She may have been a bust, but there are still two more tumblers that need to be accounted for.

I tuck my phone away. One less suspect to worry about.

Now I need to figure out who actually *is* worth worrying about.

A person in a full unicorn outfit, complete with a horn and hooves, trots up to the counter. I can't tell if they're male or female, but they whinny and point a hoof at a tumbler on the ledge, then at the lemonade jug.

Pouring the drink, I do my best not to judge their dedication. When I hand it over, they let out another whinny, drop a twenty-dollar bill on my ledge, and trot away.

"People are really leaning into the crazy this weekend," I say as a new wave of customers approaches, each one dressed wilder than the last.

Somewhere between boxing up orders and dodging the advances of an aggressively sparkly cowboy, I notice two unicorns across the way battling over a single plastic chair.

Seth groans as he stomps up to the truck, dragging the cow mascot head under one arm. His hair is damp with sweat, and his face is set in a deep scowl.

"I'm quitting. I'm done. I refuse to be an object." He throws the cow head onto the driver's seat dramatically. "I got groped by a woman dressed as a sexy Oompa Loompa. And I have been asked to take no less than *twenty* photos with strangers."

"Did you make sure to tell them to tag our social pages?"

Seth's scowl deepens. "Oh my God, can you not?"

I grin. "This is the price you pay for being the younger twin."

"By two minutes. Two. *Minutes.*"

"Still counts."

He groans and grabs the open bottle of water I've extended to him, complaining about twin injustices, as Adam Parks, Brad's former best friend, better known to his legions of fans as Ivan Parker, the lead singer of Silver Stones, approaches the truck. He's traded yesterday's faded green tee for a crisp white one with *Silver Stones* scrawled across the chest in bold gray letters. The shirt might be fresh, but he's still wearing that same plaid overshirt from yesterday. His whole posture seems heavier, like he's been carrying around something more than festival fatigue.

"Hey," Adam says, handing me a credit card. "I'll take an Arnold Palmer, please."

I notice the tiredness in his eyes, the kind that doesn't just come from a long day. Something compels me to offer a small kindness. "How about some fries on the house?"

His lips twitch, and for a fleeting moment, a real smile breaks through. "Thanks, Beth. You're a lifesaver."

"I'm surprised to see you here again," I say, handing him a disposable cup filled with freshly squeezed lemonade and tea.

"There are a few trucks here peddling my drug of choice," he replies, a faint smile tugging at the corners of his mouth. "But I can only drink so much coffee before I start vibrating like a jackhammer."

Seth chimes in, "Not interested in beer pong anymore?"

Adam's expression shifts, his grip tightening slightly around his cup. "Nah, man, I got clean a year ago." He hesitates, then adds, "And I won't do drugs and risk messing up my voice. Besides, if I were high right now, I'd be totally flippin' out, wondering why a headless cow is talking to me."

Seth yanks at the Velcro on his costume. "That's it. I'm taking this thing off."

I smile. "You look like something a sober person would hallucinate after too much dairy."

Adam chuckles, but his amusement fades quickly.

"Gotta be honest," I say. "I'm surprised you aren't living up the party-boy lifestyle. Isn't that what most musicians do?"

"They do, and for a while, I did too." Adam's voice turns serious, his gaze distant. "But I met someone who made me realize if I didn't change my ways, I'd plunge into the abyss." He exhales, a faraway look in his eyes.

I step around Seth, who is still trying to disrobe, and grab an order of regular fries from our warming station.

When I hand Adam the basket, I hesitate. "You holding up okay? Losing Brad had to be hard."

Adam's jaw tightens as he takes his food. "He and I weren't friends anymore. Hadn't been for months. Last time I saw him, I told him our friendship was over."

"Oh."

That's . . . not what I expected.

He gives a tired half laugh. "Don't feel sorry for me. I should've walked away long before that. What he did to you should've been a wake-up call."

"What do you mean?" I ask.

He leans against the edge of the food truck window, rolling the cup between his palms. His whole vibe is off—edgy, almost brittle. Not the guy who came by yesterday with apologies and awkward smiles.

"Brad took a nosedive after he lost his job during the pandemic," Adam says. "The paper let everyone go. Said he wasn't 'essential.' He took that personally."

I glance at Seth, who raises a brow but stays quiet. Adam's voice has that faraway edge people get when they've been holding a story in too long.

"He tried freelancing for a while," Adam says, turning his cup slowly in his hands. "Then he started posting food videos, simple stuff at first. Recipes, reviews. Some of them went viral. Suddenly, he was 'the food guy.'"

"So that's what happened?" I say more to myself. "I'd been wondering why he made the switch from journalism to food critic."

"At first, I was happy for him. He needed a win. But it stopped being about the food real fast. It became about the clicks. The drama. Stir the pot, rack up views, rinse and repeat."

"He did something to you," I guess. "Didn't he?"

"Brad didn't care who he hurt. As long as it kept him trending." Adam takes a slow sip from his cup. "After Tiffany dumped him, it got worse. He spiraled. Hooked up with fans, people he barely knew."

"You make it sound like Brad had groupies," I joke.

Adam doesn't smile. "You'd be surprised."

His lack of humor wipes the smirk off my face fast. He grabs a fry, chewing slowly, like he's chewing through something far tougher than fried potatoes.

"I tried to talk to him," he says after a long silence. "But you can't help someone who doesn't want help."

Seth leans in slightly, resting his elbow on the counter. "So he pushed everyone away?"

"He did." Adam's tone sharpens. "Didn't even flinch when the rest of us backed off. Once he landed the gig at *The City and Beyond*, it was like he hit the jackpot. Big platform, big following. They didn't hire him for his opinions. They wanted his online clout. His whole edgy, tell-it-like-it-is bad boy food critic persona."

"That sounds like Brad," Seth agrees.

Adam scoffs. "Brad loved the sound of his own voice. Especially when he had a platform to project it from. I know addiction when I see it. Brad was addicted too. To all the attention. And he'd do anything to get it. Mr. Collins—his editor—gave him his pick of assignments. He fed his addiction. Brad always went for the splashiest ones. The ones that would get the most eyes."

And the most drama, I think. Drama equals attention.

"This is what influence does to a person?" I'm disgusted thinking about it.

"If they let it," Seth says.

"But he crossed lines," Adam goes on, his voice lowering. "Burned people. Betrayed them."

I know that tone. It's the shift right before a truth you've been holding on to breaks loose.

"What did he do to you?" I ask, softly.

Adam doesn't answer right away. He stares at the basket of fries like they might say it for him.

"He made a joke about my sobriety once. Publicly." His voice tightens. "Said it was cute I thought I could stay clean." I can almost hear Adam grinding his teeth in anger. "But that wasn't even the worst of it."

He picks up a fry but doesn't eat it. "He slept with someone I cared about. Someone I thought . . . might've been it for me."

My chest aches. Not just for Adam—but for the version of Brad I used to know, who keeps disappearing the more I hear about who he became.

"When I confronted him, he laughed," Adam says, picking at his basket of fries. "Said I was being dramatic. That me and her weren't even technically together when it happened. Like that made it okay."

Seth shifts beside me, arms crossed tight over his chest. I don't need twin telepathy to know what he's thinking. *That's low.*

"She and I were always off and on," Adam says quietly. "But she was . . . she was it. And Brad knew that."

He looks down at the broken fry in his hand like he doesn't remember picking it up.

"He wasn't Brad anymore," Adam says. "Not really. He was 'The Foodie.' This persona he built. All snark and swagger. He said what people wouldn't say and didn't care who it hurt. That's what got him the clicks. But the real Brad?" Adam shakes his head. "I don't think he knew who that was anymore. Maybe he never did."

Seth shifts beside me, his casual lean gone rigid.

"Maybe this was who he really was all along," Adam finishes. "And we were all too blind to see it."

The air turns heavy, like someone sucked the sunshine right out of the day.

I think back to my time with Brad. How easily he'd fill a room, pull focus, draw every gaze without even trying. Or maybe he was trying, always. Maybe the charm was just a well-polished performance.

He stole my spotlight more than once. Claimed credit. Made jokes that left me red-faced. I used to tell myself it was part of his charm. But charm shouldn't feel like shrinking.

Maybe I didn't want to see the truth back then. Maybe I wasn't ready.

"Wow," I say quietly. If we'd stayed together, I wouldn't have just lost myself. I'd have been erased. "I thought he broke me when he left. But now I can see it clearly: I dodged a bullet."

"You really did." Seth squeezes my shoulder.

"Do you think he realized what he'd become?" I ask, not sure if I want the answer.

Adam watches the crowd again, his expression unreadable. "Maybe. But by then, he was too far gone. And he didn't know how to come back." His gaze flicks to mine. "I tried, Beth. I really did. But he betrayed me."

The word cuts through the morning like a cold wind.

Betrayed.

"I'm sorry." The words feel hollow. "You didn't deserve that."

Adam shrugs like he's trying to shake it off. "That was it for me. I blocked his number. Told him we were done."

He pops a fry into his mouth and chews slowly, as if it might help him swallow the rest of it down too.

"So no love lost then," I say quietly.

He looks at me, something exhausted and honest in his eyes. "I didn't want him dead, if that's what you're asking." A muscle ticks along his jaw as he looks away, like he's trying to swallow something bitter. "But I'm not mourning him either."

Adam lingers just a second longer, like he wants to say more. But then he grabs his food, turns, and walks off.

I watch him go, a dozen questions catching in my throat. The Adam I remember wasn't the level-headed one in Brad's circle—he was the wild card. The guy who drank too much and was always down to party. He was the one who said things at the worst possible moments. But he was also the one who made you laugh when you were ready to cry. Sloppy, maybe. But never cruel.

Since I saw him last, he cleaned himself up. Got sober. Found someone worth changing for.

And then Brad took that from him.

Adam's bitterness went beyond heartbreak. It was a pain buried deep, leaving only sharp fragments. Something *dark*.

A betrayal like that doesn't just *hurt*—it *shatters* a person. And from the way Adam talked, Brad had *taken* something from him. Someone important. Someone that might've been his future.

Maybe he took more from Adam than I know.

I shake my head, unsettled.

Could that kind of hurt drive someone to murder?

Did Adam hate Brad enough to make him pay the ultimate price for breaking the bro code?

The thought chills me.

And as I add Adam's name to my growing list of suspects, I can't shake the way his voice sounded when he said it.

Betrayed.

Was it enough to push him over the edge?

Chapter Twelve

"What is that?" Seth asks, his eyes widening as he spots a fluffy white chicken waddling confidently through the back door and nudging against my leg like she owns the place.

"Meet Teriyaki," I say with a laugh as the Silkie chicken turns and rubs against my shins, a soft clucking purr vibrating in the air. "We bonded yesterday after she wandered into the truck. I thought she'd gone back to her owner when she left about an hour before the gates closed. But apparently she's decided we're soulmates now."

"You named it?" Seth says, like I've personally betrayed him. "Beth, you named our next lunch special."

"She is *not* a menu item," I say, stroking her ridiculous pom-pom poof of a head.

"She's a chicken," he says flatly. "What else are we supposed to do with her? Teach her tricks and let her work the register?"

"She's smarter than you think," I say, lifting Teriyaki into my arms. "Aren't you, sweet girl?"

"Bawk!" Teriyaki clucks.

"Does she understand you?"

"Of course she does!" I attempt eye contact with Teriyaki, but her feathers are in the way again. "You understand me, right, Teriyaki?" I coo.

"Bawk, bawk!"

"I knew it!" I hug her tight.

"Oh God," Seth groans, eyeing the bird like she's going to start judging him out loud. "She knows I said 'lunch,' doesn't she?"

As if on cue, Teriyaki squawks in sharp protest and flaps her wings, her poofy head bobbing in righteous fury.

"See? She's offended!" I say, holding her protectively. "Apologize."

"I'm not apologizing to a chicken. And unless you're planning to add her to the menu, that chicken is leaving," he demands.

I huff, standing to my full height of five-foot-two, which is still several inches too short to be properly intimidating. "Seth Evan Lloyd! You stop that right now."

"Beth. You brought a live chicken into the truck." He gestures wildly, like he's trying to process what life choices led him to this moment. "Now you're adopting farm animals?"

I nuzzle Teriyaki's feathers as she lets out a soft *brrrkkk* of contentment. "Some people stress-bake. I stress-rescue."

Seth laughs. "You *also* stress-bake. Or do you think I forgot about the dozen brownies you made last week after Pedro said your lemon of a car needed to stay in the shop?"

I scowl. "Audrey is not a lemon."

"Beth, your car has been in the shop more than she's been on the road. If she were a horse, they'd have turned her into glue and sold her reins on Etsy."

Gasp!

I clutch my imaginary pearls—and Teriyaki. "You take that back! Audrey is vintage. She has character. Charm. A deeply misunderstood soul."

Seth raises an eyebrow. "She doesn't have brakes."

"She's delicate!"

"She's a death trap."

"How dare you!"

He pinches the bridge of his nose. "You can't keep every stray thing you find. Unless she lays golden eggs or makes espresso, she's not staying."

"Until I find her owner, she's with us."

Seth groans, already massaging his temples like he's getting a headache just imagining the Yelp reviews.

"Don't worry," I add, walking toward the open front window and scratching Teriyaki behind her little puffball ear—do chickens have ears? I'll google it later. "If she lays an egg in here, I'll cook it just for you."

Seth points a dramatic finger. "If Teriyaki lays an egg, I'm naming it Kung Pao!"

"Ignore him." I squat down, cooing gently to Teriyaki as I place her in her box. "Are you ready for a few fries?"

"I'd love some," a voice says from outside the truck. "Two orders of truffle fries, actually."

I jump, nearly knocking over my stack of baskets. At the window stands a handsome bearded guy, smiling like he knows the effect he has. He's got serious early-seasons *Grey's Anatomy* Patrick Dempsey energy—before all the emotional baggage.

Relief washes over me. Thank goodness it was him and not the chicken that spoke. Now *that* would've been weird.

"Coming right up!" I quickly wash my hands and grab two baskets of fries from the warming station, topping them with truffle oil and sprinkling them with parmesan cheese and chopped parsley.

"That'll be $14." I set the two baskets on the ledge. As I do, I glance around for Teriyaki, but she's nowhere to be seen. Maybe she's gone back to napping—or has an appointment with a petting zoo.

"Keep the change." He hands me a twenty-dollar bill. "I love what you're offering," the man says, pointing to our chalkboard menu. "There's something for everyone. Do you have a regular location?"

I pull out a flyer from under the counter. "This lists all the upcoming food truck nights we'll be at. But if you're ever in downtown Clementine, we're usually parked by City Hall on Wednesdays and Fridays."

"Be sure to follow us on social media too," Seth adds. "Sometimes we host special events where the first ten customers at a specific location win free swag. Like a tumbler or a shirt with our logo."

"That's awesome!" the man exclaims.

"Here." I hand him a coupon. "Come back later, and you'll get a basket of wings on the house."

He tucks the flyer and coupon into his back pocket, nodding appreciatively. "You've just earned a customer for life." He grabs his order, then winks at me.

I squint and try to wink back, determined to look effortless. Instead, it feels like my face is spasming. My eyelid twitches, and I quickly drop my gaze, hoping he didn't notice.

"Are you okay?" he asks, his voice tinged with concern.

"Oh, I'm fine!" I blurt, trying to sound nonchalant as Seth stifles a laugh. "Just something in my eye." I rub at my eyelid, as if that will lend credibility to my excuse.

The man raises an eyebrow, clearly unconvinced. "See you around," he says, walking away with a bemused smile.

As soon as he's gone, Seth leans against the counter, grinning like a cat with cream. "Nice wink, Sis. Real smooth. You've got all the charm of a blinking traffic light."

Heat rushes to my face. "Shut up, Seth. It was just harmless flirtation."

"More like a harmless seizure. I was tempted to call an ambulance. That wink looked painful."

Blushing furiously, I grab a rag and start wiping the counter to avoid his teasing. There's no denying the guy was attractive, but my disastrous wink likely ruined any chance at leaving a good impression. But I also know the wink he gave me probably means nothing. Detective Kane winks at me all the time while flashing those delicious dimples of his, but they're just that—winks.

"What are you doing now?" Seth asks, watching me blink rapidly.

"Practicing," I concentrate on narrowing my eyes at him.

"You look like a malfunctioning robot."

"Rude!"

Clearly, winking is not my forte.

Glancing down, I see that Teriyaki didn't leave. She's just curled up in a cozy little ball by the fryer.

"No, you cannot adopt her," Seth says, half amused, half exasperated.

"You don't adopt pets, they adopt you," I reply, pulling out my phone to snap a picture of her fluffy, napping form.

"She's not exactly the brightest, is she? Look. She's curled up next to a fryer. These could be her relatives."

After a series of mini rushes that leave my arms aching and my mind buzzing, I barely have a moment to catch my breath before Conner Green, the festival's top banana, strides up to my serving window.

It's only day two of the festival, and already he looks like he's aged a decade since I last saw him. His man bun is coming undone, his talking tomato T-shirt is rumpled, and there's a streak of dirt along his elbow like he's been digging a trench somewhere instead of running event logistics.

"Tough day?" I ask as he leans against the counter, his brow furrowed.

"You can't even imagine." He exhales sharply, rubbing his temples. "It's been a nightmare of mega proportions. Staff no-shows, a delivery truck sideswiped a car on the way here this morning, and oh yeah, someone I know dropped dead on my family's farm."

I can't believe his wording. *Dropped dead?* That term doesn't usually refer to murder.

"I'll take whatever's hot," he adds, eyes bleary.

I turn to Seth. "Can you prepare Conner a basket of Golden Gate Heat Wings?" Facing Conner again, I ask, "How well did you know Brad?"

"A few weeks, tops." He grimaces. "*The City and Beyond* reached out for a press pass. Interviews, some promo on the festival. You know how it goes."

I fold my arms. "Funny. Kaydee said it was your idea to bring him in."

Conner's brow lifts, a wary flicker in his eyes.

"She said you were excited until he made some offhand comment about the farm. Something like 'county fair energy in a Silicon Valley zip code.' She said she had to step in before it got worse."

Conner lets out a dry laugh. "Brad was a real tactful guy."

"But Kaydee also made it sound like she didn't want him here at all."

Conner hesitates, then shrugs. "Well . . . press is press. But she gave it the green light. Kaydee vouched for the magazine. Said the write-up could help us expand past the usual circuit."

"Did you know Brad before this weekend?"

"We had one lunch and exchanged a few emails about food vendors. That's it." He shifts his weight. "Kaydee had more history with him than I did."

"Really?" I ask, more sharply than I intend.

"They used to work together. She never brought it up?"

No. No, she didn't.

"I thought he'd be helpful," Conner goes on, voice flattening. "But he stirred the pot. Rubbed a lot of people wrong—including Kaydee."

My stomach coils. First, she said he was the problem. Now Conner's implying she had more history than she admitted. Who's lying?

Before I can ask anything else, Conner shifts gears.

"The reason I'm here," he says, lowering his voice, "is because I heard *you* were the one who found him."

"It wasn't my idea of a good time," I admit.

Conner nods. "I heard he was also your ex. That sucks. I don't know about you, but I wouldn't mind if some of my exes dropped—"

"Don't," I cut in, sharper than intended. "Whatever Brad was, he didn't deserve that."

Conner flinches, then laughs hollowly. "Right. No offense."

Seth slides the basket of wings onto the counter, tone sharp. "That's a messed-up comment, man. Brad treated my sister like garbage, but he was still someone she cared about. Show some respect."

"Respect?" Conner grunts, grabbing his wings.

Seth's jaw clenches. "What's that supposed to mean?"

Conner smirks. "Dude, I was at Sugar and Spice Bakery when you decked Brad. I was on the phone having a meeting to discuss the festival. Don't act like you didn't hate the guy."

I blink. I hadn't seen him there. But I'd been too focused on the fight, on Seth's raised voice, Brad's smug expression. The rest of the bakery could've been on fire, and I might not have noticed.

So that's how Kaydee knew about Seth. Conner must've told her what he saw. I mentally file the detail away. *Could she have told the police to deflect from whatever her relationship was with Brad?*

"I didn't hate him," Seth says, his jaw clenched harder. "But he wronged my sister. What kind of brother would I be if I didn't protect her?"

Conner shrugs, unbothered. "Whatever you say." He takes a bite of his wings. "Hey, these are pretty good. Spicy, but in a good way."

I force a smile. "After you learned what happened to Brad, did you consider calling off the festival?"

Conner's head snaps up. "Are you crazy?" His voice rises in disbelief. "Do you have any idea how much effort goes into planning something like this? How much money's tied up in vendors, permits, advertising? This thing runs on a razor-thin margin as it is. And besides, his death was . . ." he pauses for way too long, "an accident."

"What do you think happened to him?" I ask.

"The guy tripped over a rock, right? Sounds like that could've been an accident."

"You can't be serious." I stare at Conner in disbelief. "If it were an accident, then Detective Wilcox wouldn't have said she was looking into the 'unusual circumstances' surrounding Brad's death."

Conner winces and quickly backtracks. , "It's tragic, but deaths at festivals happen. Take Electric Daisy Carnival—people have died, and they don't cancel."

Seth scoffs. "That's a rave with glow sticks and fifty thousand people. Drugs are common there. This is a family-oriented food festival. It's not the same."

Conner shakes his head, licking sauce from his fingers. "Kaydee and I discussed the ethical implications," he says defensively, "but the financial fallout from canceling was too risky. Unless my lawyers tell me otherwise, the festival goes on."

His response unsettles me. A man died, yet Conner seems more worried about ticket sales.

Because let's be honest. Brad was killed. A healthy thirty-year-old guy doesn't just drop dead. And if it really was an accident, if he tripped and hit his head on a rock, then why was he lying face up? Why was the rock off to the side?

That's not how you fall. You don't face-plant backward. And if this were really an accident, Detective Wilcox wouldn't still be sniffing around, asking Seth about his argument with Brad at Helena's bakery. Why would she be wasting time on an open-and-shut case?

Conner exhales, his voice raw. "Pushing forward like nothing happened looks wrong. I'm not that big of a jerk—I get that. But canceling?" He shakes his head. "Not an option. This weekend is everything. The sponsors have been beyond generous, and we need this festival. If we lose it, we could lose the farm."

I glance at Seth. Something in Conner's words nag at me. "But . . . I thought you said the sponsors have been generous?"

A flicker of something crosses his face before he tamps it down. "They have. But their help only goes so far. It doesn't pay for our feed, utilities, or vet bills." He runs a hand over his already mussed hair. "This farm has been in my family for generations. We barely survived the pandemic. Two years of events wiped out. We lost a ton of revenue. I used up nearly all our savings to keep the place running."

His eyes darken, a shadow passing over his expression. "The farm is more than a business. It's part of the community. People assume, because we have land, we're well off, but they don't see the financial strain my family suffers."

Then, almost as an afterthought, he mutters, "It's not even the first time we've had a tragedy here."

My insides tighten like a fist. "What do you mean?"

Conner tenses, like he didn't mean to say that out loud. "Nothing. Bad luck, I guess."

I exchange a glance with Seth. *Bad luck?*

I wait.

He doesn't elaborate.

"Conner," I press.

He shakes his head with a hollow chuckle. "Couple years back, a contractor fell while dismantling a gazebo after a wedding. Total freak accident, but it blew up on social media. People said the farm was cursed. It nearly tanked us."

A queasy ripple rolls through me. Once is misfortune. Twice starts to feel like a pattern.

His phone dings, but he doesn't check it. "Gotta go do boss stuff," he says, lifting his basket of wings.

"Wait!" I call as he turns. "Are there any chickens in the barn?"

Conner studies my phone as I show him a picture of Teriyaki. He frowns. "Nope. Someone probably dumped her. Happens more than you'd think."

Something flickers in his gaze again. *What is it?* Hesitation? But he turns away before I can read it. "Good luck with that." His voice lowers. "Stay safe."

Swiping on my screen, I pull up our growing list of suspects in our Kluckin' Clues list and add more detail beneath Conner Green's name.

> **Connor Green:** ***Event manager. Family owns the farm. Conner didn't like Brad's questions during the walk-through. Called him condescending. Kaydee had to physically separate them. Seems way more concerned about ticket sales than the fact someone was murdered on his property. Financial pressure + sketchy vibe = motive?***

When I glance up from my phone, the festival is still running like nothing's wrong.

But something *is* wrong.

And the deeper I dig, the more I realize—

This list?

It's only going to get longer.

Chapter Thirteen

The air hums with chatter and laughter, the low thump of bass carrying across the festival grounds. Rylie returned a little while ago, her chicken costume replaced with jeans and a T-shirt emblazoned with Kluck Yeah!

"Who's that?" Rylie asks, boxing up two orders of Golden Oldie Sliders.

I glance out the serving window at a woman standing a few feet away. She's wearing oversized sunglasses, a floppy sunhat, and a baggy sweater that all but swallows her frame. Her phone is held to her mouth as she murmurs into it. I can't see her eyes, but something tells me she's scanning our truck with unsettling intensity.

Then it hits me.

The hat. The glasses. The sweater.

She's wearing the exact outfit as the person I saw on the path right before I found Brad's body.

"Seth, Rylie," I hiss. "It's the outfit," I point at the woman still facing our truck.

Seth leans past me and squints. "What outfit? Half the people attending the festival are dressed like her."

Rylie slaps my brother's shoulder. "She means it's the same outfit she saw yesterday."

At least someone listens to me.

My *Murder and Mayhem* instincts kick in, and I grab my phone. "Rule number 72," I mutter to Rylie, snapping a quick photo.

"'When in doubt, take a picture,'" she echoes. "You never know when you'll need evidence later."

Seth groans and goes to the fryer station, dropping a basket of wings into sizzling oil. "You two sound like you're about to launch a podcast called *Amateur Hour: Live from the Fryer*."

"First of all," I say, "don't tempt me. Second, what are the odds I'd see the same outfit I saw someone wearing right before I found Brad's body? Too perfect. Too intentional."

"You mean the lady in the solar eclipse starter pack?"

"Floppy hat, dark glasses and sweater that screams 'I definitely don't want to be recognized,'" I say. "You don't think that's a little suspicious?"

Seth shrugs. "It's the Bay Area. That's called SPF."

He's got a point. Plenty of people show up to food festivals in wide-brimmed hats and mystery-aura sunglasses.

"I'm with Beth," Rylie says. "The timing is too perfect."

"You two are ridiculous. It's just an outfit."

"It's not *just an outfit*," I tell him. "That woman knows something. My gut is rumbling telling me I'm right."

"Your gut is rumbling from the double chocolate milkshake you sucked down on the drive here," Seth says. "I told you to drink a protein shake."

"Ice cream is protein," I quip.

"Not the kind your body needs," he says. "If you're convinced that woman knows something, then call the police."

"Yeah, yeah." I watch the woman still facing us.

Brown hair peeks from under her hat. She stiffens, seemingly aware I'm watching, then walks quickly to the truck with her phone raised.

"Is it true you found the body?" she demands.

I lean casually on the counter. "Did you know there's only one letter that doesn't appear in any U.S. state name?"

"What?" Her mouth falls open.

"Not Z," I say cheerfully. "Think Arizona. It's Q."

"What does that have to do with anything?" she snaps, pulling off her sunglasses.

"You asked something random. I thought we were trading trivia."

"I need honest answers," she says.

Seth steps forward, wiping his hands on a towel. "Where's your badge?" he asks, his lawyer mode fully engaged.

"What?" she falters.

"You didn't introduce yourself or show ID. Why should we answer your questions?" he says.

With an exaggerated sigh, she flashes a press pass. "Caren Ludwig. Caren with a C."

She's *that* Caren! Brad's predecessor at *The City and Beyond*.

"Freelance journalist," she says, dangling the lanyard like a golden ticket. Alarm bells go off. Not because Peyton warned me about her, but because nosy reporters rarely mean good news.

"Covering what, exactly?" I ask.

"The Rise of the Foodie," she says. "An exposé on Brad Dawson—his career, his influence, and who he really was."

Seth raises a brow. "And you're writing this for . . . ?"

"I'll decide that once it's done," she says breezily.

"Caren Ludwig," I say, letting the name hang.

"Do I know you?" she asks.

"No, but I've heard of you," I say. "You were the food critic Brad replaced."

"I don't see how that's relevant," she says flatly. Sliding her sunglasses back on like armor.

But it's very relevant. Brad Dawson replaced her. If Peyton is right and Caren had a difficult reputation, there's a good chance she didn't leave quietly.

"Makes sense you'd be interested in Brad," I muse. "You two have history."

Her grip tightens around her phone. "What do you know about our history?"

"Just that he replaced you at the mag—"

"I had a career until Brad and that rag torched it!" she snaps. "His death won't overshadow what he did to me."

Rylie whistles. "*Nojenta*."

Caren waves a dismissive hand.

"Why write about another food critic?" I ask.

"It's called rebranding. This exposé is my ticket back into the industry." She scowls. "And if you won't cooperate, I'll make you my prime suspect as I uncover what happened."

I exchange a look with Rylie. This woman isn't persistent—she's desperate. And I don't trust her. Desperate people do desperate things when they feel threatened.

Caren turns and marches off, her phone clenched like a weapon.

"*Ela é louca*," Rylie circles a finger around her head.

"Brad is the gift that keeps on giving," Seth says dryly.

"What's with the chicken?" Rylie asks, glancing at the back steps.

Teriyaki waddles up, clucking indignantly at the commotion.

"That's Teriyaki," I say, watching her hop into the truck.

"She's about to be the next special on the menu," Seth adds.

"Stop being mean," Rylie says, scooping up the chicken. She coos and sings to her in Portuguese while Seth mutters that he's surrounded by crazy people.

"I'll take her." I gesture to Rylie for Teriyaki. "I bonded with her yesterday, but if she is a pet, someone's probably worried sick. I should at least ask around."

I head out of the truck and into the crowd, holding the chicken like a slightly confused purse dog. The festival's in full swing now. Families are everywhere, kids zigzagging through bubbles, balloon animals, and climbing over hay bales like it's an obstacle course.

I set Teriyaki down, thinking she wants to stretch her legs. Big mistake.

A shrieking toddler rounds a corner and barrels toward us like a runaway roller skate. Teriyaki squawks in alarm and flaps wildly before launching herself up and straight onto my shoulder.

"Okay, okay!" I clutch her legs to steady her. "You've made your point. You're a shoulder chicken now."

She settles in, fluffing her feathers like she meant to do that all along.

As we continue our slow march through the fairgrounds, I spot a festival volunteer in a lime-green vest adjusting signage by the entrance to the carnival zone. I make a beeline for her.

"Hi! Sorry to bother you," I say, gesturing to the bird now riding shotgun on my clavicle. "I found this chicken near my food truck. Is there a lost and found for poultry?"

The volunteer looks confused. "Uh . . . no petting zoo this year, if that's what you're asking. People do dump animals sometimes, though. You could try the flower pavilion. That's where folks tend to leave kittens. Last month, someone left four in a wheelbarrow." She shakes her head like it's a weekly occurrence, and maybe it is. She points toward a building ringed by planters. "Try in there. If anyone knows anything about stray animals, it's the pavilion crew."

I thank her and head that way, weaving past a kid carrying a snow cone bigger than his face.

With no leads on her origins and no chicken lost and found station in sight, I wander toward the flower pavilion. The air shifts from fried food and sunscreen to fresh-cut blooms. The scent of roses, lilies, and pollen assaults me before I enter. A sign announces the pavilion's showcase theme: Floral Fantasies. Bouquets spill out of wheelbarrows and teacups, competing for ribbons in the "Whimsical Arrangement" category. There's even a three-tier "cake" made entirely of carnations.

"Excuse me," I say to another volunteer in a green vest, this one with a clipboard and fanny pack. "Has anyone mentioned a missing chicken?"

She looks up at Teriyaki, still perched like a pirate's parrot.

"Cute bird," the volunteer says. "But nope. She's not one of ours."

Before I can respond, Teriyaki takes off again sailing straight onto the back of a lounging alpaca chewing on hay.

I sigh. "Of course, there's an alpaca in here."

The handler nearby reading a paperback doesn't even flinch. "This one's named Chewpaca," he says, turning a page without looking up. "He doesn't mind company. But stay away from Gizmo. She's a troublemaker." He jerks his chin toward a burnt-red alpaca standing with a plastic bucket lodged on its head like a medieval helmet. "Unless you want your buttons chewed off."

Sure enough, Chewpaca keeps munching hay like this happens every day. Teriyaki, perched proudly on his back, lifts her head and gives a content little cluck.

"Well," I say, "I guess Chewpaca's not a speciesist."

With a sharp shake, Gizmo knocks the bucket loose. It clatters to the ground, her ears twitching as her gaze locks on me.

"Uh-oh."

She breaks into a determined trot right for me. I try backing away, but who knew alpacas could move that fast. My retreat stalls when I bump into a flower display, petals brushing my arms. Before I can sidestep, Gizmo's already at my front, biting at the hem of my shirt.

"Hey!" I shuffle sideways. "Not the outfit. This is my favorite chicken shirt."

The handler looks up briefly, then returns to his book. "She likes people. Especially the ones that try to stop her."

"Figures." I gently steer Gizmo away before she can start nibbling on my jeans next. I point to Teriyaki. "Have you seen this chicken before? She kind of . . . showed up."

He glances at her—still perfectly balanced on Chewpaca's back like she belongs there. "Nope," he says and flips the page.

I shift my weight. "Okay . . . what about people? Did you see anyone around here Thursday afternoon? Tan hat, oversized sweater?"

He turns another page, unimpressed. "Half the people here match your description. Gonna need more than 'beige and cozy.'"

"Ugh." I groan. "Thanks anyway."

"Happy to help," he says, already back to his book. "Next time bring a photo."

If I had snapped a photo of who I saw standing in the field by Brad's body I wouldn't be asking around. I'd be talking to the police with proof of Seth's innocence and mine.

Suddenly, Chewpaca lets out a low, bizarre whuff-whinny that sounds like someone stepped on a goose underwater. The alpaca sneezes, hay flying everywhere. Teriyaki flaps her wings in surprise, then resettles, unfazed.

I stare. "Great. Now I've got a multilingual emotional support chicken."

With no one claiming Teriyaki and no chicken-loving flower volunteers in sight, I find an empty bench beneath a hanging basket of ferns. Teriyaki returns from her alpaca adventure and nestles beside me on the wood slats.

"I guess you're with me for now."

"Bawk!"

"You like that idea?"

Teriyaki clucks proudly, as if arriving at her own conclusion.

"You really do understand what I'm saying," I say to her, raising an eyebrow. "Are you a very small, feathered psychic?"

She tilts her head at me before hopping down to peck curiously at a fallen petal.

"Right. Didn't think so." I sigh, pulling out my phone. "Let's see what the Internet has to say about Caren Ludwig."

Caren Ludwig, it turns out, isn't tied to any major publication. She's freelancing, grasping at whatever opportunities she can find.

"Huh," I murmur to Teriyaki, scrolling through my phone.

She tilts her head, her beady eyes full of curiosity.

"Something doesn't add up."

Teriyaki clucks softly, as if encouraging me to keep digging.

I scan Caren's LinkedIn profile, expecting to see a long list of food publications or media gigs. Instead, I find a glaring six-month gap in employment. Her last official job was food critic for *The City and Beyond*.

Scrolling, I find an old press statement in a journalism thread. *The City and Beyond* announced Caren Ludwig's departure due to "creative differences."

"Creative differences?" I scoff. "That's a polite way of saying she didn't play well with others."

Teriyaki fluffs her feathers.

"Look at this," I click on a link to a public food panel discussion from last year. A blurry video shows Caren onstage, mid-argument with another critic. Her voice cuts through the low-quality audio:

"You can't seriously compare some pretentious, deconstructed foam dish to real food with history and tradition."

The other panelist tries to interject, but Caren barrels over him.

"People like you are ruining food culture. You chase trends, not taste. I refuse to dumb down my reviews to fit a magazine obsessed with influencer-approved nonsense."

I raise my brows. She's not wrong, but wow—she doesn't hold back.

Another article catches my eye, an industry gossip piece speculating on her firing. The headline is brutal: "From Food Critic to Persona Non Grata—What Happened to Caren Ludwig?"

The article suggests she was forced out, and *The City and Beyond* had been looking to replace her. Enter Brad Dawson, a critic with a flashier style and larger online presence.

Beth: 1. Caren: 0.

I exhale. "She got blacklisted."

Teriyaki lets out a tiny squawk, as if scandalized.

I look down at her, who's running her beak over a twig. Likely deciding whether to eat it or not.

"You're terrifyingly perceptive for a bird."

She tilts her head at me like a tiny feathered therapist, then goes back to pecking at the dirt, having abandoned the twig.

"No wonder she's bitter. Six months is a long time to be out of work, especially in her field." I click back to her LinkedIn. Under her name, she's listed as a Freelance Writer and Industry Consultant. Which sounds a lot like code for "I'll take any job that pays."

I check her recent activity. Nothing solid, a handful of articles on independent food blogs, a few guest spots on niche podcasts. No stable gig, no major bylines.

She's desperate.

And now she's here, digging into Brad Dawson's life.

I look at Teriyaki. "She said herself she's chasing a comeback."

And I have a feeling she doesn't care who gets in her way.

Chapter Fourteen

After the alpaca incident and a fruitless round of questioning, I give up on finding Teriyaki's rightful home—if she even had one to begin with. Cradling her, I head back toward the truck, weaving through crowds and sidestepping toddlers with bubble guns.

Back at Kluckin' Good, the fryer's sizzling, the line's picking up again, and Seth eyes me like he's waiting for me to crumble. I must look as exhausted as I feel.

"This festival already feels like it's been dragging on for a week," I complain, setting Teriyaki in her box. "And it's only the second day."

Seth gives me a look that says he's worried about me. Probably because I found Brad's very dead body yesterday and seem to have adopted an emotional support chicken. Once things calm down in the truck, he shoos both Rylie and me out like we're foxes in a hen house.

We follow a winding trail toward the arts and crafts area and past the stage, the scent of sawdust and fresh paint hanging in the air. The fresh air helps, but I stop dead in my tracks when I see a another oversized hat. My chest squeezes.

"Look." I point, heart pounding. "That hat!" My pulse kicks up. "That's the same style hat I saw someone wearing near the barn right before I found Brad's body. The person was wearing a hat like that, and when they heard me, they headed for the flower pavilion."

Rylie shields her eyes from the sun and scans the crowd. "And you're sure it was that exact hat?"

"I didn't see their face of who was wearing it," I admit. "But it looked like that." The person turns, and my breath catches. "It's Caren Ludwig."

Rylie squints. "I prefer the name Tabloid Gremlin."

I nod, but before I can say more, Rylie starts turning in a slow circle. "Okay, not to be the voice of reason here, but . . . Beth, look around."

I follow her gaze. And there they are—at least four other women and two men all wearing that same wide-brimmed, floppy sun hat in various shades of beige. Some with ribbon bands, one with a giant sunflower on the side. It's apparently the hat of the festival.

Rylie crosses her arms. "Seth might actually be right. That hat's not exactly one of a kind."

My shoulders sag. "So much for my hat theory."

"It's still a lead," she says, tapping open the notes app on her phone. "We're adding her to the Kluckin' Clues list. She gives off major suspicious energy."

She's not wrong. Caren looks like she's hounding people. She's going full journalist, interrogating a poor jewelry vendor like she's trying to shake loose a confession.

"She's not wasting any time," Rylie says, watching Caren gesticulate like she's calling plays at a football game. "Probably sniffing around for a headline."

"Let her sniff," I murmur, already pulling out my phone. "I've got questions of my own." Caren jabs a finger toward a middle-aged man holding a tray of mini cheesecakes. He recoils slightly, his expression somewhere between confused and irritated. She leans in, and her whole body looks wound tight. like she's ready to pounce on the next soundbite.

I exhale sharply. "I looked her up."

"Oh?" Rylie glances at me, intrigued. "And?"

"Peyton was spot on with everything she said about her. Caren used to be a food critic for *The City and Beyond*—until they fired her for 'creative differences.'" I make air quotes. "Which is a nice way of saying she was impossible to work with."

Rylie's eyebrows shoot up. "No kidding? That's a pretty big gig to lose."

"Yeah, and it gets worse. Since then, she's been blacklisted from every major food publication. She hasn't had a real job in six months." I lower my voice. "She's desperate."

Rylie whistles. "No wonder she latched on to Brad's murder like a lifeline. If she can spin it into a career comeback . . ."

"She'll do whatever it takes," I finish grimly.

Ahead of us, Caren suddenly whips around, her eyes locking onto us like a heat-seeking missile.

"Turn around," Rylie hisses. "We don't want to start anything with her here."

We backtrack toward the stage, slipping into the woods before she can storm over.

As we walk, Rylie pauses. "Hang on, let me finish this last note."

I scroll on my social media feed, waiting for Rylie.

"There, all done. Let me just . . ." She looks up at me. "Why is Seth removed from the shared list?"

"Dunno." I clear my throat, keeping my eyes on my screen.

"Beth," Rylie pushes my phone away. "Why is your brother removed from the shared Kluckin' Clues list?"

"Probably a . . . glitch." My voices comes out all squeaky like a mouse on helium.

She frowns as she scrolls down, then her eyes widen. "Wait—no, he's at the bottom. As a suspect. *O que é isto*?"

"It's nothing," I choke out.

"This isn't the kind of thing you lie about. Tell me the truth."

"Fine! I added him. What choice do I have?"

"How about the choice to not add your twin brother to our suspect list?"

"That's harsh," I say. "You think I wanted to add him? If you hadn't shared the Kluckin' Clues list with him in the first place, none of this would even be an issue. Back when Benji and Sloane were killed, it was just you and me keeping track. Seth didn't see it then—why'd you have to drag him into it now?"

Rylie gapes at me like I've grown another head. "Don't you dare pin this on me. I added him because he's part of the team, not so you could sneak his name onto a suspect list. You did that all on your own."

"You don't think the guilt is gnawing at me?" I ask. "Because it is. We both know how Seth felt after what Brad did to me. We both saw him punch Brad days before he died. Detective Wilcox is sniffing around Seth like he's already guilty, and Seth is totally blowing this off. I added him to the list to keep everything in one place so I can make sure my twin doesn't go down for something he didn't do."

Feeling emotionally drained, I take a deep breath.

Rylie crosses her arms, still glaring. "That doesn't make it right. You can dress it up as strategy, but it's still you pointing a finger at your own brother." Her tone hardens. "And you want to talk about clues? Fine. I hate to admit it, but there was that small window Thursday, when Seth disappeared while we were handing out flyers and samples."

My heart lurches. "What?"

"I didn't think much of it," she says. "There was a crowd of people taking selfies with me. When I turned around, Seth was gone."

I'm almost afraid to ask. "For how long?"

"Maybe fifteen minutes," Rylie pauses. "Beth, you can't think—"

"Absolutely not," I say with conviction. "Seth is innocent."

"Then why did you add him to the suspect list?"

"Like I said, I'm trying to keep track of everything so I can prove he's innocent."

"*Meu Deus*," Rylie resumes walking. "You need to tell him. He has a right to know."

"I will. I just—not yet. Don't tell him," I pause. "Please?"

Rylie shakes her head, rambling in Portuguese. "This is a bad idea. Aren't you the one who said no secrets?"

"This is different." I swallow. "This is a secret to keep from hurting him. I'm trying to protect him."

"Hm," she presses her lips into a thin line. "Seth said the same thing to me when he didn't want to tell you we were dating. You should remember how that made you feel before you decide to keep secrets from him."

She stomps ahead, leaving me alone with my guilt.

I know she's right. But if I can handle this quickly, I won't even need to tell Seth at all.

We make it to the stage area, and a band is wrapping up their set. Unicorn Pixies—judging by their glittery banner—thank the crowd for being "totally awesome." That explains all the unicorn costumes I've seen.

The stage sits in a clearing surrounded by towering redwoods. Sunlight dapples the ground through the branches. This perfect, peaceful time helps alleviate my guilt about including Seth on our Kluckin' Clues list. It's also the type of setting my mom would love.

My phone buzzes, yanking me from my thoughts.

One glance at the screen, and I groan. "Really?" I hold it up for Rylie to see. "My mother is like Beetlejuice. Think about her, and she appears."

Rylie grins at my irritated expression. "Bet she's calling to tell you to drink water. Or reapply SPF."

At least we're still kind of normal, I think, even if Rylie and I just snapped at each other.

"She does keep track," I admit, sending her to voicemail.

My phone buzzes again. I sigh, hitting answer this time. "Hello, M—"

"Did you send me to voicemail?" she cuts me off, sharp as a tack.

"I'm working," I say, shooting Rylie a helpless look as we keep walking.

"Oh, I know. I already talked to Seth. He said you and Rylie are 'on break,' so forgive me for thinking you had a moment for your mother."

"I'm allowed to take breaks," I reply, dodging the guilt creeping in.

"What's happening with the police?" she asks, concern dripping from her voice. "Are you in trouble about Brad? I can come down and explain things—"

"Mom, please," I interrupt. "I don't need you explaining my history with Brad to the police."

"I'll explain how those last two murders were misunderstandings," she insists.

I groan. "Everything's fine, Mom. Seth and I have it under control." I scramble for a distraction. "How's Dad? Or your plants?"

"Oh! I'm testing a new fertilizer on my hydrangeas. I think it's going to give me a super bloom this year."

"Mom, Lazarus was dead for three days and still looked better than those hydrangeas. The HOA probably thinks they're a crime scene."

"They're not dead," she argues. "One has four green leaves! If your truck hadn't parked so close—"

"I stressed them out. Got it," I say.

I spot Helena sitting with Detective Kane at a table. His expression changes as he waves to me. That dimple on his left cheek makes an unfairly charming appearance.

"Have you met any eligible bachelors yet?" my mom asks suddenly.

I think of the cute customer from earlier but decide she doesn't need more matchmaking fuel. "Not yet," I say, waving back at Detective Kane.

We approach him and Helena, and I can already feel heat blooming on my face thinking about our hug in the truck.

Detective Kane's gravelly voice cuts through the air. "Hello there." I glance over to see his trademark smirk in full-dimpled force.

"Who's that?" Mom's voice turns shrill. "Is that a guy? It sounded like a guy."

"Goodbye, Mom," I say quickly, cutting off any chance for further interrogation.

As I pull my phone away from my ear, her voice echoes, "Call Larry!"

I tap the end call button and sigh.

Detective Kane raises an eyebrow. "Larry, huh?"

"Don't ask."

"Beth." Helena looks at me, worried. "I heard you found Brad's body. Have the police been hounding you too?"

I instinctively glance at Detective Kane.

"Wasn't me," he raises his hands defensively. "Some food reporter tipped her off."

"Caren," Rylie and I say in unison, exchanging an eye roll.

Helena nods. "She introduced herself earlier, trying to get me to talk. A classic 'I'm here to help you, tell me everything' routine." She lowers her voice. "But when I refused, she got intense."

"That's Caren," I say. "What do mean, hounding me too? Have the police stopped by your truck?"

"Twice." Her fingers fidget with the end of her braid. "I was half expecting Detective Wilcox to slap cuffs on me then and there."

She's trying to play it off, but I don't miss the way her knee bounces under the table, restless energy buzzing beneath her cool exterior. Is she nervous because she's hiding something? Or is she shaken by the idea of being a suspect? I've been feeling the same way all day—an awful cocktail of anxiety and sadness, muddled by the lingering confusion over Brad's death.

I take a seat across from Helena, and Rylie slides in close beside me. "I talked to Detective Wilcox earlier too. It was basic stuff, standard questions." Seeking reassurance, I steal a look at Detective Kane, who nods encouragingly.

"I was talking to Detective Kane about it," Helena says.

"The police are doing their job," he replies in his calm, steady tone. "It's best to be upfront, even if you think it's irrelevant. Leaving things out can make it look worse than it is."

Helena nods, twisting her braid tighter. Her casual look, ripped jeans and a cat-themed Captain America shirt, contrasts with the tension in her shoulders.

"It was probably Brad's review about my café," she mutters. As she leans to the side, I spot a dried crust on her left sneaker.

I squint. It's dark, rust-colored. Not quite brown.

Goosebumps prickle my arms.

Following my gaze, she hastily brushes at the stain, flicking off the last bit with the edge of her fingernail. "Oh. That," she says lightly, not quite meeting my eyes. "There was a . . . a little accident earlier. I should've been more careful."

My stomach knots. *Accident?*

"What happened?" I ask, keeping my tone neutral.

She waves a hand. "A spill near the compost bins. Nothing major."

I nod slowly, but unease creeps in. If it was a spill, why does she suddenly look like she'd rather be anywhere else?

"I bet the police are asking everyone about Brad," Rylie says, breaking the tension. "They'd be crazy not to, considering how many people couldn't stand him."

Helena huffs. "No kidding. A lot of food vendors here knew him and didn't like him."

I look around and spot more food trucks than I can count. If what Helena says is true, then my suspect list just tripled.

"Not only did he claim our food was 'uninspired' and 'bland,'" Helena continues, "but he *lied*, saying there was cat fur in our cupcakes." She shakes her head. "He may as well have written 'skip it' across our front door."

"Detective Kane is right," I say gently. "Even the smallest grudges can be motive."

"If they wanted to know about my beef with Brad, they could google it." She brushes harder at her sneaker, as if trying to scrub away the conversation along with the dried stain. "They didn't need to stop by my truck."

"You know," I suggest, "you could always talk to Seth. He'd know whether it's a good idea to have a lawyer just in case."

Helena nods but doesn't say anything right away. Her fingers tap an uneven rhythm on the table, her thoughts clearly spinning. Then, as if shaking off whatever's bothering her, she reaches for something beside her.

A hat.

An oversized, wide-brimmed hat.

My breath catches.

"Where'd you get that?" I ask, my voice a little too sharp.

Helena lifts it, holding it up with a proud smile. "Cute, right? My assistant, Trina, gave it to me." She strokes the patterned scarf wrapped around the band. "I think the cat print adds a little flair."

"It's adorable," I say, forcing a casual tone as I take a closer look. The fabric is slightly creased, like it's been folded and stuffed somewhere. A few specks of dirt cling to the brim. My smile is tight. Too tight. "Very . . . charming."

I've seen that hat before. It was worn by the person walking away from the barn before I found Brad.

But it didn't have a scarf then.

Not a red one. Not one covered in cartoon cats.

That scarf is memorable, and I know I would've clocked it.

Which means either the scarf was added after, or this isn't the same hat at all.

Or worse. It is the same hat but altered to look different.

"Trina said there's a woman here selling these," Helena adds. "Guess we're all gonna match by the end of the festival."

I nod, forcing a smile. Which explains why I've been seeing so many. How convenient. Now every oversized-hat wearer is a potential suspect.

Helena glances at her phone and sighs. "I should probably go find Seth and get his take." She gives us a small wave, then heads toward the truck area before I can respond.

I watch her go, my mind whirling.

A suspicious stain on her shoe. A flimsy excuse. And now, that hat.

Coincidence? Or something worse?

I glance at Detective Kane, who follows Helena's retreating figure. Once she's out of earshot, his gaze shifts to me.

"How are you doing?"

"Fine," I say automatically. "Considering everything." But even as I say it, I feel the weight of the day pressing down.

"You need a new hobby. Wasn't finding one dead body enough?"

"Maybe I'll try needlepoint or bird-watching."

"Now, those are statistically low-risk activities," he says, leaning in a little. "I'd fully support that."

I try to grin, but there's a question gnawing at me that I can't quite shake. "I mean, it's not like this is my problem. Brad was my ex, not my responsibility." I pause, my eyes tracing the outline of the distant barn while my thoughts drift closer to home. "Though if anyone needs clearing, it's Seth. He's been so calm, it's unnerving."

Detective Kane gives a thoughtful nod. "I'm sure Seth's used to handling pressure. Comes with being a lawyer."

"Right." I smile faintly, but it feels thin.

The truth is, I hate even letting his name linger on my mental list—the one I pretend doesn't exist but absolutely does.

Thinking about it makes me queasy. But until I can prove, really prove, that he had nothing to do with Brad's death, I have to keep him there.

"This entire thing is an enigma," Detective Kane says, crossing his arms.

"What do you mean?" Rylie asks, tilting her head.

He exhales, his gaze flicking between us. "I'm not officially on this case, but I've heard things. Brad was . . . complicated. Some say he was charming, had his good qualities. Others say he could be a total prick if things didn't go his way." His eyes settle on me. He's grinning almost smug. "Kind of like you."

I blink. "Me?" Did he just—?

"You're short—"

"Vertically challenged," I cut in, arms crossing.

"You look cuddly, but you're actually trouble."

I scowl. "I am *not* cuddly."

"See?" His grin deepens. "You bristle at that, but not at being called trouble. That's what makes you an enigma. You seem harmless—*cuddly*, even—but you're stubborn and don't scare easily."

Rylie chuckles. "Oh, she's scared of things. Just not the things she should be."

I glare at her, but Detective Kane keeps talking without missing a beat. "You're always where you shouldn't be, but you've got sharp instincts. I'll give you that." He lifts his head, considering. "You look like someone who should be running a bake sale, not solving murders."

I cross my arms tighter. "So, what you're saying is . . . I'm deceptively dangerous?"

"More like deceptively persistent." His gaze flickers over me, something unreadable beneath the teasing. "And when you two are left alone, you're bound to cause problems."

I make a thoughtful noise, pretending to be unaffected, but my pulse betrays me with an irritating little stutter.

On the one hand, he called me short. On the other, he also called me dangerous—and maybe he kind of liked that.

I'll let it slide. *This time.*

Another thought flits through my mind. "Brad developed a reputation as the up-and-coming foodie to watch."

"Maybe someone like Caren Ludwig wanted to *derrubá-lo*?" Rylie says, finishing my thought.

"You think someone wanted to bring him down to keep his reputation from outshining theirs?" Detective Kane asks.

Rylie gives me a look like *See, even he knows my language.*

"It's possible." Detective Kane strokes his jaw.

His jaw is so appealing, I could bite into it like a juicy apple. *Whoa!* Cool it, Beth. Maybe Seth is right. I need to find someone.

"Are you okay?" Detective Kane's voice cuts through my thoughts. "You're . . . kind of drooling."

I quickly wipe my mouth with the back of my hand, mortified. "Fine, totally fine!" I squeak, and both Rylie and Detective Kane stare at me like they know I'm lying.

"As I was saying," he continues, oblivious of my treacherous thoughts, "there are several reporters hanging around covering the festival."

He's right. The festival is crawling with media—some reputable, some looking for clickbait, and one very aggressive freelancer who is a total Karen.

With a C.

His expression darkens slightly. "And you need to be careful, Beth."

"So I've been told."

Detective Kane shakes his head. "You're being reckless."

I swallow hard. "I—"

He raises an eyebrow. "Who found the body?"

Rylie points at me without hesitation. "She did."

Detective Kane gives a small smile, but his tone is firm. "Beth, you need to take this seriously. You're the one who found the body, and you're also the one who keeps poking around. The wrong person might take that the wrong way."

I shift uncomfortably. "It's not like I'm—"

"Leave it to Trish," he says, his voice harder now. "Look, I get it. You want to help. But murders don't get solved in a day, and this isn't some TV show where the amateur sleuth always wins."

I scoff. "That's debatable."

"Beth." Detective Kane levels me with a look. "I'm serious."

I tilt my head. "You're worried about me."

"I'm worried about my paperwork if you get yourself killed," he says dryly, but his tone is softer.

"Well, I *appreciate* the suggestion," I say, making it clear I don't. "But last I checked, this isn't your case."

His jaw tenses, but he doesn't argue.

"Exactly." I say, standing my ground.

Before he can respond, he spots a woman and a little boy walking toward us. His entire expression morphs into a smile as he waves. "That's my sister and nephew Mikey," he says as I stare at the little boy, who looks sticky from the cotton candy he's holding.

Before he steps away, he hesitates. Then, in a low voice, he adds, "Watch your back, okay?"

I smile. "What, no statistical breakdown on the odds of my survival?"

"Odds go down when you don't listen."

I watch him leave to join his sister and nephew, an odd mix of warmth and frustration twisting in my chest.

Before I can dwell on his words, Kaydee, the festival manager, plops down in his empty seat. Her usually neat bun is disheveled, a few loose strands sticking to her forehead. She sighs, running a hand over her hair.

"This day." She shakes her head, glancing off into the distance as if hoping to find an escape.

"*Você está horrível*," Rylie says to Kaydee. "Are you all right?"

Kaydee nods slowly. “I’ve never felt so exhausted in my life.”

“The festival taking a toll?” I ask. “You know . . . after Brad’s death and all.”

She glances down, giving a small, weary nod. “They say the show must go on.”

“Must be rough, though, keeping everything on track while the police are investigating,” I say, giving her a sympathetic look. “I think Conner said you were friends with Brad, right? That can’t make it any easier.”

“Yeah, I knew him pretty well.” Kaydee’s gaze shifts to the ground. “We were friendly for a time. What’s happening isn’t ideal, but we’ve still got coverage. Reporters, critics, podcasters . . .” Her voice trails off, staring off into the distance. She seems . . . unsettled.

I glance at Rylie, then pivot casually. “Hey, were you able to get that stain out of your shirt?”

Kaydee shakes her head. “What stain?”

“The one from Thursday,” I say, keeping my tone breezy. “In the bathroom. You were wearing a maroon top with . . . something splattered on it. It looked like it might be tough to get out.”

Kaydee’s brows knit together. “Maroon top?” She thinks for a moment before nodding, like she’s trying to remember. “Oh. Right. Yeah, it was ketchup, I think. I was eating fries backstage while a band was warming up.”

“Huh. It looked kind of . . . thick. Like it had soaked in,” I say. “Didn’t smear like ketchup usually does. It was splotchy and jagged.”

She touches her shirt collar instinctively, she’s wearing a festival graphic tee today. “Well, maybe it was old ketchup,” she says finally, her words measured.

“Could’ve been barbecue sauce,” I suggest lightly, watching her face. “Or something else?”

Her mouth tightens for a second before she forces a shrug. “You’re seriously asking about a condiment stain?”

"I notice stuff," I say. "Occupational hazard."

Kaydee's smile falters, and she fidgets with the chain around her neck. "It was nothing, okay? Just a spill. I already got rid of the shirt."

Rylie raises an eyebrow but doesn't press.

"Really?" I don't hide the shock in my voice. "That shirt looked expensive."

"It was old," she says. "It wasn't worth my time trying to save."

We let the silence stretch for a moment too long. Kaydee shifts her weight, clearly ready to bolt.

"Anyway," she says brightly, "how are you guys enjoying the festival?"

I clock the dodge immediately, my suspicion deepening. But I don't push. Not yet. "It was a lot better before I found my ex's dead body," I say.

"I can't imagine what that was like," Kaydee says. She sounds genuinely sorry for me.

"How long were you and Brad friends?" Rylie asks Kaydee.

"What?" Kaydee looks surprised while toying with the crescent moon pendant on her necklace.

"You and Brad," I say. "You said you were friends. Must've been after he and I broke up."

"I said we worked together," she snaps. "We weren't friends."

Rylie and I exchange a glance. That's not what she said earlier.

"How long did you and Brad work together?" Rylie asks casually while I scroll to our Kluckin' Clues list and jot this down.

Kaydee shifts, fidgeting with the pendant, her thumb rubbing over it like she's trying to polish it. "Not long. I was already working at *The City and Beyond* when it was sold. Brad came on as the new food critic pretty quickly after the new management started cleaning house to match the new look they were going for."

"How long was that?" I ask.

"I don't know, maybe a month?" she guesses.

"What did you do there?" Rylie asks.

"Marketing," Kaydee says quickly. "But it wasn't a good fit. When a marketing position at the Green Family Farm opened, I took it."

I nod, but something about the way she answers feels . . . rehearsed. Like she's flipping past a chapter she doesn't want us to read. And the way she keeps working that necklace—like it's a worry bead—makes me wonder what she's not saying. "So, you and Brad. Did your jobs ever cross over?" I ask.

Kaydee's fingers tighten around her chain. "Why all the questions?" she asks, light on the surface, but there's a flicker behind her eyes. "You're really digging deep, huh? Should I be worried you're writing a tell-all?"

"Not unless you've got something juicy to tell," I say lightly, but I'm watching the way her fingers keep circling that necklace.

Across the way, I spot Adam walking by. I lift my hand to wave, but he stops midstep when he sees us, shakes his head, and keeps moving.

Weird.

Kaydee fishes her phone out of her pocket with a weary sigh. "This festival," she shakes her head. "Looks like I have more fires to put out."

"Everything okay?" I ask as she stands.

"Fine, a late vendor who finally arrived." She rubs her lips thoughtfully before forcing a faint smile and walking away.

As she disappears into the crowd, I tap my phone against my knee.

"Kaydee corrected me fast, too fast," I say to Rylie. "She was firm when she said they weren't friends. They only worked together for maybe a month. Which makes me wonder—what exactly happened between her and Brad?"

I jot down her comments in our Kluckin' Clues list. Kaydee's history with Brad might seem insignificant, but nothing is too small to note—especially when someone is trying to act like they have nothing to hide.

Rylie and I linger longer than planned, caught up in a comedian's open mic routine. For a fleeting moment, the festival feels normal—like a celebration again, vibrant and alive, as if the tragedy hasn't cast its shadow over everything.

But as the evening deepens, the crowds thin, and the warmth of the day fades into something cooler. Uneasier.

My phone buzzes with a message from Seth to our group chat.

Seth: Ready to head out.

I send a quick thumbs-up emoji, nudging Rylie. "Time to go."

We start back toward the truck. The festival is winding down, chatter fading into scattered laughter.

Near the edge of the lawn, under a sprawling oak, a woman sits cross-legged on the grass, a battered guitar resting in her lap. Her voice is soft but clear, carrying through the cooling night air.

The song is slow and aching, each note slipping into the dark like secrets no one dares speak aloud. She sings of promises made under summer skies, and simmering secrets no one can hide. The melody works its way under my skin, settling in my bones.

I stop walking. For a moment, it feels like she's singing straight to me—or maybe to something I don't want to name.

The final chord fades into the rustle of leaves.

"You're thinking too hard," Rylie says beside me.

"Maybe not hard enough," I whisper.

Chapter Fifteen

Thank goodness Saturday is already a step up from the past two days. No dead bodies, no overbearing detectives—just a perfectly crisp morning, fresh coffee, and the satisfaction of beating most of the other food trucks to snag the same high-traffic spot we've had for the last two days.

The festival doesn't officially open until eleven, but Seth's already getting a jump start on the day. He's been preparing for the lunch rush by cleaning the flattop, refilling the deep fryer. Wings, sliders, and fries are locked, loaded, and ready to be served.

Now we're taking a quick break and inhaling some breakfast.

Rylie props her phone up on the prep counter, and the familiar theme song of *Murder and Mayhem* kicks in—eerie strings and the unmistakable voice of Inga Nevarez.

"Welcome back, M&M Squad," Inga says in her velvet-smooth voice. "Today's case takes us to the outskirts of Tampa Bay, where a missing person report led to a backyard full of secrets. In this episode, we're going to talk about the importance of rule number 15: it's better to be rude than dead. If someone gives you the creeps, you don't owe them politeness. You owe yourself survival."

Rylie gives a little fist pump with the burrito she's eating. "Preach, Inga."

I nod, sipping my coffee. "Maybe we should print that on napkins. Or T-shirts. Or possibly life vests."

Seth looks up from the driver's seat with a frown. "Why are we listening to this again? It's not even eleven AM and I've already heard the phrase 'shallow grave' twice."

"It sets the mood," I say, reaching for a hash brown bite. I had slept through my backup alarm and only had time for a shower, so drive-through breakfast it was.

And yes, I absolutely did pull our eighteen-foot food truck through the drive-through.

You should've seen the looks on the teenage employees' faces. They were priceless. They looked like I'd asked them to deep fry a UFO. One kid dropped his headset. Another tried to take our order from the back door before realizing we had a front window.

"Besides, we don't have customers yet," I say now. "No one to traumatize but you."

"You said 'yet,'" Seth points to the walking path with his burrito. "Which means technically, they could walk up any second. Just in time to hear talk of dismemberment."

"It's called ambiance," I say. "Some people play jazz. We prefer true crime."

Seth mutters something about needing hazard pay and goes back to eating.

There are no customers, not yet anyway. And so far, the worst thing to happen is Layla from Roller Burger throwing me side-eyes with an unnecessarily wide berth every time she walks by.

"That's the fifth time she's circled us in the last hour," Rylie mutters, finishing up her burrito. "If she passes by again, we're charging her rent."

"She's probably still salty about Coffeeology," I say.

Rylie hums in agreement. "Twitchy little turf war queen. She seems like the type who's only happy when someone else is miserable."

"Maybe she's trying to overhear our specials." I arch a brow in Layla's direction. "Or maybe she's upset we've snagged the same spot each day of the festival."

"If that's the case she should get here sooner," Rylie says.

"Chicken wing?" I call out, catching Layla lingering about ten feet away, glaring at me like I personally invented cholesterol.

She huffs and makes a hasty retreat.

"What's her deal?" Rylie asks, watching Layla dart off like she's late for a villain convention. "This can't be because we got a better spot than her."

"Not sure," I say. "I mean, sure, she found me kneeling over Brad's body—which, okay, not ideal—but she hasn't spoken to me since. Only glares and dramatic exits."

"She might be trying to kill you with vibes," Rylie says.

I shrug. "Wouldn't be the weirdest thing that's happened this week. Still . . . I don't think it's that. There's something else with her. Like she's offended by my existence."

"Maybe it's your hair," Rylie quips. "You've got a bit of a 'finger in a light bulb socket' look going on." She gestures to my frizzy coif.

"I know, I didn't have time to dry it, but I can't look *that* bad." I reach for my blue baseball cap and tug it on. "Plus, I haven't even found another dead body, so I'm going to count this morning as a win."

"Yet," Seth mutters under his breath.

"Rude! Finish eating, then get back to your prep work, smart aleck."

Seth gives me a mock salute. "Aye, aye, commander."

We're minutes from opening when my phone beeps with a message.

> **Mom: I gave Larry's mom your number. Give the nice guy a chance.**
> **Me: Nice guy is code for boring.**
> **Mom: Boring is good. Boring means Larry won't dump you for his cousin.**

My thumbs fly across the screen.

Me: She was his step-cousin!
Mom: And that makes it better?
Me: Yes! A little bit!
Mom: Besides, with the number of dead bodies you keep finding, you could use a little boring in your life.

Before I can reply, another message lights up my screen.

Maybe Larry Kuntz: Is this Beth Lloyd? This is Larry Kuntz. You never gave me your number, so my mom called your mom. Your mom says we can go out again.

Another text follows immediately.

Maybe Larry Kuntz: If this is Beth, my mom can drive us to the movies on Wednesday, but it won't be weird. She has a van, and we can sit in the backseat together.

"Oh no," I whisper, staring in horror as a picture of a white minivan pops up on my screen.

Maybe Larry Kuntz: See, we can have the entire back row to ourselves. It's like a free limo! And my mom promised not to show you my naked baby pictures again.

Groaning, I drop my phone onto the prep counter and smack my forehead.

Rylie and Seth crowd around, laughing as Larry's texts pop up like unsolicited infomercials.

"Oh meu Deus, that's a terrible comb-over," she says, holding up the last photo Larry sent—a selfie of him lying down in the back row of his mom's van, looking solemn and possibly a little green.

"This is who you let Mom set you up with?" Seth snickers. "If you wanted to be kidnapped, there are easier ways than hopping into a van with this guy."

Beep! Another text comes through.

Maybe Larry Kuntz: FYI, my mom has a no eating rule in her van.

Beep!

"If that's Larry again, I swear I'm blocking him," I grumble, reaching for my phone.

"Nope, it's Detective Kane this time!" Seth dances out of my reach. He clears his throat and reads the message aloud in a deep, fake voice.

Detective Kane: Checking to make sure you're staying out of trouble and, hopefully, haven't found any more bodies.

"Seth," I growl, lunging for my phone, but he grins and holds it over his head.

"Oh, here's another one," he taunts, scrolling.

Detective Kane: BTW, tell your brother my nephew Mikey says he's sorry for trying to milk him yesterday. He thought it was an exhibit teaching kids about dairy farming basics.

Seth lowers the phone. "Rude kid, and his hands were sticky from taffy."

I aim a punch at his gut.

"Oomph!" Seth grunts, doubling over as I snatch my phone back.

Me: Haven't found any bodies yet, but the day is young. I'll pass on Mikey's apology, but if he stops by, I'll give him a free lemonade and fries if he manages to tip Seth over.

Satisfied, I tuck my phone into my back pocket as Rylie zips up her chicken costume, adjusting the headpiece.

"Time for my break. I'm gonna walk the grounds, hand out samples, maybe pick up some chatter while I'm at it."

"Chatter about what?" Seth leans on the counter.

She shrugs a wing. "Whatever people are whispering about. Chickens are very approachable, you know."

"Only if they're as cute as you." Seth flirts, leaning closer to her.

Gag!

"It's the beady eyes," she says, puffing out her feathery chest. "They scream 'I won't judge you.'"

"You can judge me all you want," he says. His voice husky.

Before I can stop him, Seth grabs the edge of Rylie's chicken headpiece and pulls it down enough to kiss her—right through the beak.

"Ugh!" I exclaim, throwing a hand up to shield my eyes. "Do you two mind? That's, like, biologically disturbing."

Seth laughs as Rylie lifts her head and gives him another slow kiss.

I throw my hands up. "Oh, perfect. Sure, let's turn this into the Kluckin' Love Shack while I'm running around trying to keep us afloat!"

Rylie recoils, blushing, while Seth chuckles.

"Sorry, Beth. Some of us find chickens irresistible," Seth says, winking at Rylie as she adjusts her head and leaves.

"Honestly, I didn't need to see that," I mutter, mentally scrubbing my eyes with bleach. Seth stares after her, his lips quirking in a half smile.

I study him. "You need to spend less time kissing your chicken girlfriend and worry more about yourself."

"About what?"

"Um, hello? You're a suspect in whatever this turns out to be," I remind him, waving my hands for emphasis. "You punched Brad. That's a strike right there."

"And you had a public fight with him before he died, *then* found his body," Seth holds up his fingers. "That's two strikes for you, if we're keeping count."

"You're right, neither of us are looking good," I agree. "But this isn't about me. It's about you!"

Seth shakes his head, moving to the serving window. "I already talked to my boss at Buford and Myers. They've got a lawyer on standby. I'm covered. Detective Wilcox isn't who I'm worried about."

"Well, good for you," I mutter. "Then who are you worried about?"

He spins around, pointing at me. "*You*. I'm worried about you poking your giant, nosy nose where it doesn't belong."

I gasp. "My nose is perfectly proportional for my face."

"Sure it is, Commander Schnoz," he quips, shaking his head. "Let the police handle this, Beth."

As if summoned by the mere mention of law enforcement, Detective Wilcox appears. She strides past our truck with her signature purposeful gait, making a beeline for the Sugar and Spice food truck, where she taps Helena on the shoulder in the middle of her specials-sign setup.

I freeze, my grip tightening around a rag I was using to wipe down the counter. "What do you think that's about?" I whisper, watching them.

"If I had to guess," Seth says, peering over my shoulder, "the detective's questioning her more about her history with Brad."

Helena's gestures become more dramatic, sharp, and tense. Suddenly, she whirls and marches toward *us*.

Detective Wilcox, completely unbothered, heads in the opposite direction.

Helena barrels straight for us, the sides of her green cardigan flapping behind her like a cape caught in a windstorm. Her eyes are wide, her mouth set in a tight, trembling line. "Seth, I need to talk to you," she says, her voice brittle with panic. "The police want me to go to the station."

Seth steps out of the truck immediately, concern flashing across his face. I follow with a cup of lemonade, sensing she needs something—*anything*—to ground her.

"Okay, slow down," Seth says, his tone even. "What happened?"

Helena presses the heel of her hand to her forehead. "Detective Wilcox told me," she stops, taking a deep breath. "Brad's death . . . it's officially been ruled a homicide."

I blink. "What?"

"She said a friendly judge put pressure on the medical examiner. They rushed a few things and . . . I don't know!"

"Don't know what?" Seth asks.

"The results change things," Helena answers. "She didn't say exactly what they found, just that it changes everything."

"What kind of results?" I ask, wondering if it has anything to do with our tumbler being found near him. "Did she say if they ran tests?"

"I-I don't know," Helena stammers, brushing hair out of her face with a trembling hand.

"Here." I hand her the lemonade. "Drink and get your thoughts together."

Her knuckles whiten around the cup.

I glance at Seth, who mutters something under his breath. My heart kicks against my ribs. Homicide.

Helena begins pacing, one hand curled tightly around the lemonade. "She said my coming down to the station is to 'assist the investigation,' but the way she looked at me . . ." She shakes her head. "Like I'd done something. Like I was some kind of criminal."

"She asked you to come in, she didn't say that you're a suspect," Seth says gently. "Right?"

Helena hesitates. "She said she had more questions about the timeline. Said I was 'close' to Brad, even though I wasn't. She thinks I might remember something useful. But—" Her gaze flits past us. "I've already told her everything. Twice."

Seth tries to guide her toward the picnic bench near our truck. "Sit down for a sec."

She resists. "I can't. I just—I needed to tell you before I left. Because if something happens . . ."

"Nothing's going to happen," I say quickly. But my voice is thin. I don't even believe myself.

Helena finally takes a shaky sip of the lemonade. "I refused to go with her." She looks to Seth. "That's okay, right?"

"You didn't do anything wrong by refusing to go in. You have the right to remain silent, whether they ask you on the street, at your business, or even if they—"

"Arrest me?" Helena's voice jumps an octave.

Seth sighs. "I'm not saying they're going to arrest you, Helena. I'm saying you have the right to consult with a lawyer first."

Helena exhales shakily. "I don't know. Maybe I should've gone in. Refusing makes me look guilty, doesn't it?"

She's scared. But *why*, if she has nothing to hide?

Seth's voice is calm but firm. "You didn't do anything wrong. But if you're worried, I can introduce you to a lawyer from my firm."

She hesitates, then nods, her grip tightening on the lemonade. "I need to clear my name. Rumor around the festival is that I'm not the only one under scrutiny," she says, casting a pointed glance between us, landing on me. "People are saying you've had it out for Brad for years."

I stiffen. "I wouldn't say I *had it out for him*," I begin defensively, but Helena cuts me off.

"I don't blame you," she says briskly. "After all, how dare he try to rekindle things with you after his cousin dumped him?"

"*Step*-cousin," I correct her automatically. Again, not for Brad's sake—for mine. It makes me feel marginally less pathetic to remind people.

Helena doesn't miss a beat. "Anyway, Seth, did Beth tell you I told Brad he wasn't welcome at Sugar and Spice anymore? And you know what he said?" She drops her voice into a mocking imitation of Brad's smarmy tone. "'Are you sure about that? Because I still haven't reviewed your fine establishment.'"

"So, he threatened you," Seth says, frowning.

"Essentially, yes," Helena admits, her jaw tightening. "Chris had to escort him and that girl he was with out of the café. His review appeared online on the first day of the festival. Such a jerk move of him to pull. Leaving a bad review and listing me as a vendor here at the festival."

My insides twist. Brad didn't just make enemies—he wielded his influence like a weapon.

I try to keep my tone light. "What exactly happened after that? Did he come back? Did you see him at all Thursday?"

Helena's eyes narrow slightly, and her lips press into a thin line. "I already told you—he left."

Something about her tone makes my skin prickle.

Before I can press her further, Seth gently steers her away. "Let's take a walk. I'll introduce you to someone who can help."

Before Seth and Helena leave, I stop them. "Hey, real quick. How did you like the tumbler?"

"Tumbler?" she asks.

Seth gives me a look like I'm crazy.

"Yeah, the yellow one I gave you."

"I . . ." Helena shakes her head. "I'm not sure what you're talking about."

"Remember when you came over to my truck at the start of the festival because you were upset over Brad's review of your café?" I ask, hoping to jog her memory.

"How could I forget?"

"Well, you asked for a drink and told me you were out of cups," I remind her. "Trina was going back to the bakery to pick them up. I poured your lemonade into one of our prototype tumblers and told you to keep it. I was curious what you thought of it."

"Oh." Helena nods. "Yeah, now I remember. It's cute, the laughing chicken. Maybe think about adding some other colors?"

"Good idea, thanks." I'm stalling. "Want me to refill it for you? Where is it?"

Helena opens her mouth, then pauses—too long. "Trina borrowed it?" she says, like she's testing the answer. "No, wait. I think I set it down on a picnic table at the festival and lost it." I stare at her. *Lost it?*

She frowns, like she's only now processing its absence. "I don't know. I was so flustered after Brad's review of my café, then talking to the detective, I must have forgotten where I set it. I really don't know where it is. But it was cute."

Dread settles in my chest. *That's understandable, right?*

Except . . . *why does it feel like a lie?*

Or worse—what if it's the truth, but I *want* it to be a lie? If Helena is lying, and has something to do with Brad's death, then I can remove Seth from my Kluckin' Clues list without a second thought. And he'll never need to know.

As long as Rylie doesn't tell him.

I swallow hard. "Right. Well, I'm sure it'll turn up."

Helena nods, but her eyes flick away too quickly, like she's already trying to forget the question.

"Let's go talk." Seth puts his arm out to guide her away.

As she heads off with Seth, chatting quietly about the police wanting to talk to her, a cold ripple crawls up my skin.

Something's off.

But I don't know if it's her or me.

I try to shake it off as I walk back into the truck, but the feeling sticks. Like a smudge I can't wipe away.

I was right. This wasn't some freak accident that killed Brad. This was murder.

I don't want to suspect Helena. But I can't forget how upset she was the morning of Brad's death. Or how cagey she got when I pressed her about him.

Then there's the rust-colored mud that was on her shoe. *Could it have been blood?*

And the hat. *The hat that looked exactly like the one on the figure near the barn.*

I reluctantly pull out my phone and add it all to my Kluckin' Clues list. I don't want to be suspicious of Helena any more than I do of Seth, but I have to be impartial with something of this magnitude looming over us.

I've barely tucked my phone away when Kaydee appears, clutching her Flavors of the Bay festival tumbler like it's a life support.

"Hey, Beth. Got any hot water?" she asks, holding her tumbler out for me to take.

"Sure," I say, pouring her some. "You okay? You look pale. Careful," I say, handing it back. "It's hot."

She sets the tumbler down quickly, wincing. "Ow. Yeah, I'm fine. Just tired."

"Where's the insulated cup I sold you? It'd be way better than the single walled one the festival is selling."

Kaydee freezes for half a second before forcing a casual shrug. "I, uh . . . gave it to a friend."

Gave it to a friend?

"So, you don't have your tumbler anymore?"

"Is that a problem?"

"No." I shake my head. "No problem at all."

Only two Kluckin' Good tumblers are unaccounted for—one belonging to Helena, the other Kaydee—and one of those was discovered at the murder scene.

She hesitates, then glances at the crowd as if looking for an escape. "And, um, you don't have any tea bags, do you? My stomach's been a little off."

I lean against the counter, watching her. "Fresh out. Maybe Coffeeolgy sells tea?"

Kaydee shifts on her feet. "Right. Thanks anyway."

She grabs the tumbler with a paper towel, then hurries off like she's afraid I'll ask more questions.

I frown, tracking her retreating figure.

She gave away her insulated cup?

My gut tells me she's lying.

And I've learned to trust my gut.

But before I can dissect it further, a stream of customers demands my attention. By the time the line slows, I've lost the thread—but my mind still buzzes with questions.

Secrets are simmering under the surface here.

And it's only a matter of time before they boil over.

"Where's Seth?" Rylie asks, pulling off her chicken head with a dramatic sigh of relief. Her hair is a wavy mess, sticking up in wild angles from her ponytail, but she looks pleased with herself.

"He left with Helena a while ago. Detective Wilcox asked her to go to the station," I say.

Rylie's eyes widen. "Did she go?"

"She asked Seth for advice first. He offered to walk her through what might happen and put her in touch with someone from his law firm who can help." I pause, watching her face. "They're officially calling it a homicide now."

"Wait. What?" Rylie is staring me. "Did she say anything else?"

I shake my head. "She was pretty worked up and seemed unclear about the details. Something about the ME doing a rush and results coming back."

"That changes everything."

"Yeah," I say quietly. "It does. It confirms my gut was right all along. Now the real question is, was Brad's death planned or an accidental homicide?"

"Have you talked to Seth about the Kluckin' Clues list?"

"No," I drag the word out. "Why would I until I need to."

"I think you need to," she says. "Especially if the police are ruling Brad's death a homicide. He has a right to know you've added him as a suspect."

"I will, just," I hold my hands up. "Please, don't tell him. Let me handle this. Okay?"

"Fine, but I don't like this." Rylie exhales, then walks over and sets her chicken head in the driver's seat. "Well. My undercover snooping didn't involve any body counts, but it did turn up dirt."

"What kind of dirt?" I straighten.

Rylie leans in. "I chatted with a few food vendors who knew your shady ex-boyfriend. Turns out, Brad really was shady. He was charging business owners for reviews. Not openly, he'd phrase it as a friendly favor or 'supporting local.' If you wanted five stars, you had to pay."

"Money?"

"Cash only. Or high-end gift cards so it looked less like bribes."

"Like the envelope I saw Wrap City guy giving Brad the other day. I can't believe this."

"It was weird," she says.

"What was?"

"The people I talked with, either liked Brad or they didn't."

"They probably only liked him because they were paying for good reviews," I surmise. "What happened when business owners didn't pay up?" I ask.

"No one would say," she says. "Maybe Wrap City guy might have answers."

"Oh, I'm counting on it," I say, looking out the serving window at the crowds. "My next break, I'm looking for him." A flicker of movement catches my eye.

Kaydee.

She's pale, her arms wrapped around herself as she hurries toward a porta potty. She glances over her shoulder, like someone's following.

Our eyes meet.

She quickly looks away and disappears inside.

Rylie notices my distraction. "What's up?"

"Kaydee," I say softly. "She's been acting off. I don't know her well, but she's always been so upbeat about the festival. Now? It's like she's scared of something."

"Or someone?" Rylie raises an eyebrow.

I nod slowly. "Maybe she knows more than she's letting on."

Chapter Sixteen

The smell of fried food clings to everything. My clothes, my hair, probably my dreams at this point. So I take the first official break of the morning to stretch my legs and look for Teriyaki.

"I'm stepping out for a few minutes," I say, grabbing my coffee.

Rylie throws up both hands, a dish towel slung over one shoulder. "Go. I got this."

"You say that, but if anyone orders sliders and we're out, do not try to make more."

"I know what I'm doing!"

"Rylie, you once set a toaster oven on fire trying to warm up pita bread."

"That was one time. And pita is tricky."

"Throw fries at them and stall until I get back. Do not touch the flattop."

"Fine. But if someone asks for 'extra crispy' anything, I make no promises."

I give her a look and step down onto the grass.

The festival is a swirl of sounds and smells. I scan the area, eyes sweeping around food trucks. "Teriyaki," I whisper. "Don't make me put your face on a missing chicken flyer."

Suddenly, there she is. Waddling out from behind a lemonade stand like she's been on a secret mission. Tail feathers swaying, strutting like she owns the entire food festival.

"Seriously?" I scoop her up, balancing my coffee and a squirming chicken. "Where have you been?"

"Bawk, bawk!"

"That's no excuse." I cradle her against my chest. "You could've at least stopped by to let me know you were safe."

"Buk, buk, buk!"

"Well, I guess you are used to being outside."

She flaps one wing indignantly, and that's when I notice the sticky mess on her foot.

"Is that—" I squint. "Teriyaki. Did you step in caramel corn ?"

She tilts her head then lets out a guilty ba-gawk.

I sigh, wiping her foot on my apron. "You're lucky you're cute. Sticky and cute."

"You know she's not supposed to be wandering around unsupervised, right?"

I turn to find a guy in a rumpled plaid shirt watching me, one eyebrow raised like he's caught me smuggling poultry across county lines.

Wrap City guy.

The same guy who handed Brad an envelope on the festival's first day, then later claimed he didn't know him.

I was hoping to chat with him. Now's my chance.

"Who, her?" I ask, lifting Teriyaki. "She's become part of my team. No leash law for emotional support chickens."

He laughs. "You run the chicken wing truck, right?"

"That's us," I say. "Kluckin' Good."

"Marc," he offers, pointing to the bold letters on his shirt under the flannel. "I own Wrap City. You should stop by and try a roasted red pepper hummus wrap."

"Thanks for the recommendation," I smile. "You were here on Thursday, right? First day of the festival?"

He hesitates, only slightly, but I catch it. "Yeah. Why?"

"I saw you talking to Brad Dawson." I keep my voice casual.

"Not sure I know what you mean."

"He was the food critic covering the festival. Tall guy." I raise my coffee well above my head. "Brown hair, worked at *The City and Beyond*. I saw you two talking near a potted lemon tree."

His eyes dart sideways, "Oh. Right. That guy. We talked, nothing major."

I arch an eyebrow. "Pretty sure I saw you hand him something."

Marc exhales sharply. "You're not a cop, right? You have to tell me if you are."

"Nope," I assure him. "Just curious."

"I didn't kill him!" He shouts, then lowers his voice. "It was cash. I paid him."

"For what?"

He glances around first. "A regular spot in *The City and Beyond*. You can look it up, I'm not lying. I was a monthly featured food truck. It cost me a lot, but it paid off. Two trucks now. Both posted up in San Francisco full-time. That kind of publicity changed everything."

"So, bribery."

"Look, I know how it sounds," he glances over his shoulder. "But everyone does it."

"I don't," I say.

"Well, good for you," he sounds annoyed. "But Brad had a whole system. You think that guy ever paid for lunch? He got envelopes like mine from probably half the trucks here. And not just cash. I've heard stories."

Teriyaki and I tilt our heads in unison. "Like what?"

"Gift cards to high-end retail places, concert tickets, luxury wine."

"Buk, buk," Teriyaki chimes in.

"Good question, girl," I say. Marc looks at me like I'm losing my mind. "Was that all?" I press.

Marc shakes his head, not wanting to answer.

"Look," I sigh, "I'm not a cop. But my brother is a lawyer, and I'm friends with a detective. Either tell me the truth or I'll send Detective Kane a text telling him to visit your truck for a chat."

"Okay." Marc hesitates, face tightening. "It was monthly."

"What was?"

"The payments. It was like a subscription fee. Grease his palms, he boosts your business. If you didn't? One bad review could kill you overnight. Ask around." Teriyaki makes a gurgle sound, and I couldn't agree more. This is sickening.

"The other day with the envelope wasn't some shady one-off. It was routine."

He nods.

He studies me more carefully now. "Were you one of the trucks in his pocket? Is that why you're digging?"

"No, but I do have a stake in this."

He fidgets, wiping his palms on his thighs. "I've got two kids and a mortgage. I'm not proud of it, but if buying good write-ups keeps my family afloat? I did what I had to."

"What happened if someone couldn't pay or refused to pay?"

"You got a deadline," Marc says bitterly. "You had until the next publishing window to get your act together. Otherwise, Brad made sure the public knew exactly what he thought of your food."

"So, he threatened?" I ask.

"Not with yelling or swearing. Brad was slick—he called it honesty. But those reviews? They could sink a business."

"Did he?" I ask. "Sink a business?"

"One truck—Rattle and Pearl, a boba place—refused to pay. They lost over seventy percent of their customers after one of Brad's reviews. They ended up closing."

"Brad bullied them and won," I say.

"They weren't the only ones. There've been others."

"So, yeah, it was a threat," I say slowly. "Or worse—a promise. That if you didn't pay, he'd tank you overnight."

"Judge me all you like, but I wasn't about to take the risk when Brad came knocking."

"What about Layla Gafford?" I ask. "She owns Roller Burger. Did she ever cross paths with Brad?"

"Maybe," Marc says. "Brad crossed paths with a lot of food truck owners. From what I can tell, Layla isn't the type to mess with. She doesn't like anyone."

I can tell.

"What happens now with Brad's shady arrangements?"

"That's what I'm asking myself. Brad's dead. Who takes over? Who decides who gets featured? I can't go back to the shadows after tasting the good life."

He heads back to his truck, then pauses. "For what it's worth? I have an alibi. I already told the cops. I just paid for a headline, that's all."

"I believe you."

And I do.

He's sweaty, nervous, fumbling. But not dangerous. Just another cog in the wheel of the machine Brad built for himself. A machine powered by cash, threats, and leverage.

As I watch Marc disappear behind the stainless-steel flap of his truck, a bitter thought settles in my chest: Brad didn't just manipulate people. He monetized their dreams.

And now that he's gone, the people left behind are still trying to figure out how to survive the vacuum he created.

Teriyaki flaps and squirms until I let her hop down to peck at something shiny on the pavement.

I take my time heading back, letting Marc's words settle like a too-hot sip of coffee I wasn't ready for. "Everyone does it," he said. Like bribing food critics was another line item on a budget sheet. Propane tank, fryer oil, hush money.

What's worse? More and more, I'm hearing whispers that Brad was truly awful. I mean, I knew he was awful from our breakup, but this is next level. He was taking bribes. And the ones who didn't play along? They got slammed in his reviews. Publicly dragged. Business lost.

This feels like another chisel tap in the sculpture of Brad's downfall. Did I ever really know him? Or was I another pawn in his game—a mark to be used for his own gain? I'd thought I was coming out here to stretch my legs. Instead, I got another cracked piece of the puzzle.

Teriyaki clucks beside me, waddling along like she's got somewhere important to be.

"All right, all right," I joke, holding the door for her. "Back to the grease-scented sanctuary."

To my surprise, nothing's on fire.

Rylie's got her feet propped on a milk crate, scrolling through her phone with one hand and sipping lemonade with the other. The flattop is spotless. The fryer untouched. Teriyaki hops into her usual nest of rags under the prep counter like she never left.

"You're alive," I say.

"Barely." Rylie gives me a blank stare. "Two customers. One lemonade, one basket of fries. Not even Plucked and Truffle fries!" She shakes her head, resuming her scrolling. "I've had dreams with more foot traffic than what I had."

"Sorry your solo truck duty was so uneventful." I set my coffee down and lean on the counter. "I ran into someone interesting while I was out."

Rylie doesn't look up. "The ghost of Brad Dawson?"

"Nope. Marc, he owns Wrap City."

Her head jerks up. "Wait, the envelope guy? You found him already?"

I nod.

"Okay, go on," she says, sitting up straighter.

"He spilled the tea faster than a cracked teapot. The envelope was a bribe. He paid Brad for monthly placement in *The City and Beyond* magazine."

Rylie's mouth falls open. "Like, regular-feature bribes?"

"Yup. Acted like it was an investment. Apparently, being in the local foodie spotlight let him open a second truck. Doubled his income."

Rylie whistles. "The rumors are true. Brad was running a full-blown pay-to-play racket."

"And not just with cash," I add. "What you heard was true. Marc said people gave Brad cash, concert tickets, luxury wine, high-end retail gift cards. They had a deadline to pay up or he tore them apart."

"So now what?" she asks.

"Well, Marc might be scummy, but he doesn't strike me as a killer. The cops already talked to him, he says he has an alibi. When I was questioning him he immediately blurted out, 'I didn't kill him.'"

"So either he's guilty and panicking, or he's a terrible liar with zero chill."

"I'm leaning toward the second one," I say. "He's shady, not homicidal."

Rylie sets her lemonade down. "I'll update the Kluckin' Clues list."

Before Rylie can work on the list, the sound of purposeful footsteps makes us both look up.

"Avocado fries and an Arnold Palmer," a voice barks. "Now."

Conner Green slaps a card down on my truck's serving ledge like he's delivering a final notice, not a lunch order.

"Buckawk!" Rylie squawks, making him jump. "Where are your manners? Didn't your momma teach you how to say please?"

He blinks, clearly not used to being challenged. "Uh . . ." His gaze bounces between us. "Please," he grumbles, like it costs him extra.

Rylie huffs, snatches his card, and jabs at the keypad with a little more force than necessary. "*Cara de idiota.*"

I don't need a translation to catch the insult.

"Give us two minutes," I say, tossing avocado slices into the fryer. The oil hisses, filling the truck with the smell of sizzling guac. I pour his Arnold Palmer while they crisp, then slide the basket toward him. "Here. If that's all, we have work to do."

If he can't be polite and show us manners, then he's not getting any from me.

He takes a long sip of his Arnold Palmer and exhales like we're the problem. "Relax. I'm running on fumes. Didn't sleep."

He looks it. The usual too-tight graphic tee and man bun are still intact, but the shirt is the most rumpled I've seen yet. His eyes are bleary, and there's a tremor in the way he lifts the drink to his mouth. Less "guy in charge" and more "guy putting out fires he may have started himself."

"You didn't sleep?" I ask. "Long night?"

"You could say that." He rubs the back of his neck, then catches himself, like he realizes he's said too much. "Anyway. Kaydee's on PR cleanup duty, so at least that's handled."

"PR cleanup?"

He gives me a look like I'm slow. "You think it's a coincidence no one's talking about Brad? I pulled a few strings. Talked to the right people. The story's not going public until Monday."

The words hit me like ice water in the face. "You did what?"

He waves an avocado fry like it's a magic wand. "Lawyers. Media contacts. I asked them to sit on it. Bad for business if people think the festival's a crime scene. Vendors panic, customers stay home, sponsors back out. But this way, we ride out the weekend, keep the profit margin high, then let the headlines fly."

"That's . . . wow," Rylie's speechless.

"You can't make a death disappear," I say.

"It's practical," Conner replies, sharp now. "No one wants to eat pulled pork nachos next to a crime scene banner. I protected the festival."

I study him. He believes that. *Really* believes it. He's not hiding guilt. He's hiding damage control.

"Right," I say. "And I guess Kaydee's supposed to make sure no one notices?"

"She's good at that." His voice softens but not in a kind way. More like someone smoothing over a scab. "Kaydee's always been the one who makes things run smoothly. That's why I trust her. I just need to watch how hard I work her."

"How long have you two known each other?" I ask.

He swipes a napkin across his mouth. "Freshman year at Santa Clara University. We interned here together during junior year."

"You interned?" Rylie asks. "I assumed you'd be handed a job."

"My grandfather was adamant I earn my place," he rolls his eyes. "Kaydee left, did the big-city thing, then asked me for a job when things got messy."

"Messy how?" Rylie asks.

"She said the corporate PR world was toxic. Bad bosses. Bad coworkers. Long hours. It wrecked her relationship." He shrugs, but it's too casual. Too dismissive. "She wanted a fresh start. I gave her one."

"She worked at *The City and Beyond*, right?" I already know the answer, I want to see what he says.

"She did." He narrows his eyes. "Why?"

"I think it's interesting," I say slowly, "that she used to work with Brad, but since the festival started, she steered clear of him."

Conner's jaw ticks. "They barely worked together."

"Still," I say, "it's worth noting who she's avoiding."

Rylie tilts her head. "And if she worked with Brad, she might've crossed paths with others in his circle."

"Like Caren Ludwig," I add.

Conner's eyes flicker—quick, but not quick enough.

"She blames Brad for losing her job," Rylie says. "If she and Kaydee worked together, maybe there's history there."

Conner stiffens. "Stop."

Rylie and I exchange a look.

"You're protecting her," I say quietly

He folds his arms, tapping one finger against the edge of his fry basket. "None of this matters to me. I don't ask questions when someone wants to escape a trainwreck. I needed help. She showed up."

"Maybe you should ask questions," Rylie says, her voice gentle but firm.

"You said you trust her," I press. "But you also said you're careful not to overwork her. Why?"

His gaze sharpens, like a mask slipping. "She's . . . dealing with personal stuff." His tone is too flat, too careful. "I don't want to push her too hard."

"Why?" I ask.

"Drop this." He exhales through his nose. "I've worked too hard to rebuild this place. I don't need trouble before I'm ready."

"Before you're ready for what?" I ask.

No answer. He grabs his food. "I've got things to do. You've got customers." He nods toward the group forming behind him.

We watch him go, his shoulders tight, steps stiff.

Rylie leans close. "He's hiding something."

I nod, still staring after him as I wave the group of teens forward. "Yeah. And I don't think it's just Kaydee."

Rylie and I fall into our natural rhythm, ringing up orders and boxing up food for hungry customers. The sizzle of oil, the clatter of trays, the hum of conversation—it's all familiar, almost enough to drown out the tension curling in my gut.

Then my phone buzzes with a flurry of texts all at once.

Seth: Finished with Helena at the station. If Detective Wilcox tries to talk with you, don't!
Seth: Seriously. Don't engage.
Seth: I'm not kidding, Beth. Say nothing.
Seth: Why aren't you answering me?

"Ms. Lloyd."

"Agh!" I fumble with my phone, barely catching it before it drops into the fryer. I whirl around to find Detective Wilcox standing at the truck window, arms crossed.

Great. She and my mother must share some sixth sense because the second I think about them, *poof*—they appear.

"Hey! Back of the line, lady!" a customer shouts. "I was here first!"

Detective Wilcox flicks open her badge with a practiced motion, silencing him instantly. "Do you have a minute to talk?"

"Umm . . ." I glance over at Rylie, who's already shaking her head.

"If now isn't good," Detective Wilcox says, "we can talk at the station."

My stomach knots. I have no intention of stepping foot in an interrogation room again. "No, no," I blurt. "Give me a minute, and I'll meet you outside."

Rylie grabs three baskets of Golden Gate Heat wings from the warmer. "Are you crazy? Seth won't want you talking alone with her."

"I know," I say, already typing a response but pause when I see the timestamp of his messages. All of them are from thirty minutes ago.

Stupid signal.

Me: Detective Wilcox is here.

Three dots pop up instantly.

Seth: DON'T TALK TO HER!
Seth: Why didn't you reply sooner?
Me: No signal.
Me: She's threatening to take me to the station.
Seth: She's bluffing.
Me: I'll keep it brief.
Seth: BETHANY!!

I shove my phone into my pocket. "He's fine with it," I squeak, then cough.

Rylie narrows her eyes. "Yeah, sure he is."

I grab a water bottle and step out of the truck. Detective Wilcox is leaning casually against a tree, her stance deceptively relaxed. She's wearing jeans and a fitted black V-neck, blending in like any other festivalgoer—except for the badge clipped to her belt and the gun at her hip.

She doesn't smile as I approach. That's the thing about her. No wasted pleasantries. No warmth.

Just sharp eyes and a mission.

"Thanks for taking the time to speak with me," she says.

I twist the cap off my water bottle and take a sip. "I'd much rather do it here than at the precinct." *Play it cool, Beth. She's got nothin' on you.* "So, what can I help you with?"

Detective Wilcox pushes off the tree, stepping a little closer than I'd like. She's trying to unnerve me.

"Tell me again how you found the body," she says. "This time, tell me backwards."

My hackles raise, like a dog who sees the mailman.

Last night, after we'd finished at the festival, Rylie cued up an episode of *Murder and Mayhem* titled "Liar, Liar, Alibi on Fire." We were both starved and I didn't want to cook after a long day in the truck. So Rylie drove us to a late-night burger joint while Inga Nevarez's ominous voice filled her Jeep.

"Here it comes," Rylie had said, elbowing me as she cracked open a soda. "This is the part where they talk about reverse questioning."

Inga's voice had floated through the speakers, calm and eerie. "Some detectives ask suspects to recount events in reverse. It's not to mess with you. It's to catch a lie. Most people telling the truth can replay things out of order. Liars? Not so much."

"I'd flunk that even if I was innocent," I said.

Rylie grinned, her eyes on the road. "Good thing you're not planning any murders, huh?"

"*Murder and Mayhem* rule number 12: If they ask for your story backwards, they think you're lying," Inga said.

A beat of music. Then Inga added, "I first learned this one on a blind date in San Jose. The guy keeled over during dessert—face first into his crème brûlée. The cops grilled me forwards, backwards, and upside down. Granted, this was my third blind date to drop dead in three weeks, so things looked sketchy for me. But guess who passed with flying colors?"

She let that hang for a moment. "Truth has layers. Lies crumble when you rewind them."

Now, standing here under Detective Wilcox's watchful eye, that memory plays on a loop. Is Detective Wilcox testing me? Or does she think I'll accidentally spill something about Seth?

I take another sip of water, stalling.

"Fine." She sighs, reaching behind her back. She pulls out a pair of handcuffs, letting them dangle and clink together. "I'll take your brother to the station and talk to him again about his assault on Mr. Dawson."

My heart slams against my ribs. "Stop," I say, a little more sharply than I mean to.

Detective Wilcox raises a brow, still rolling the cuffs in her hand. "If you want this to stop, then tell me what happened."

I swallow down the panic clawing up my throat. "I was on the phone with 911, checking for a pulse, while Layla Gafford screamed from behind me."

As if summoned, Layla walks by, shooting me a glare.

What's her problem? She couldn't have heard me.

"Before that happened, I went to use the bathroom on the side of the barn where I ran into Kaydee. Before I left for the bathroom, I saw Brad talking to Marc, the owner of the Wrap City food truck."

"How do you know his name is Marc?" she asks.

"Because I met him," I explain.

"What were they doing?" she asks.

"It was quick. Marc handed Brad an envelope. Brad tucked it into his pocket and walked off."

I bet she's asking me to see if my story matches Marc's.

She rolls her fingers in a circle. "Keep going."

"Before I saw Brad and Marc, Adam Parks, er, Ivan Parker as you might know him, and Helena Wynn were at my truck."

Detective Wilcox steps back, thoughtful. "Interesting." She switches gears. "What about Helena Wynn? How long have you known her?"

I tread carefully. "Years. She and her husband were friends with my Aunt Dolly and helped me when I took over the food truck."

That's an understatement. Back then, Seth was knee deep in law school, and Rylie still couldn't boil water without setting off alarms. Helena and Chris were lifesavers, trading recipes and business advice they once shared with my Aunt Dolly.

"Your aunt is Dorothy Hendrix? Is that correct?"

I nod.

Detective Wilcox doesn't react. "Let's go back to your brother. You and your brother seem close, but also ambitious," she continues. "A food truck you received after your aunt's death. A reality show appearance. And yet, there's an unfortunate pattern, isn't there?"

My jaw tightens.

She ticks names off on her fingers. "Dorothy Hendrix. Benji Mayhew. Sloane Owsinski. And now Brad Dawson." She meets my eyes. "That's a lot of bodies connected to you and your brother."

I grip my water bottle. "We had nothing to do with any of those deaths," I say, keeping my voice steady. "My aunt died of natural causes, and the rest—" I shake my head. "We didn't cause any of them."

Detective Wilcox studies me, her expression unreadable.

I exhale sharply. "Look, I get you want answers, but trying to drag my family and business through the mud isn't the way to go."

The moment the words leave my mouth, I regret them.

Detective Wilcox steps closer. My water bottle crinkles under my grip.

Calm down, Beth.

She watches me, then sighs. "You really don't know, do you?"

Something about her tone makes my pulse hitch. "Know what?"

She tsks. "I'm surprised Seth never told you. Your brother punching your ex-boyfriend the other day wasn't the first time it happened."

My insides jolt like I've touched a live wire. "What?"

She shrugs. "I did some digging. Turns out there was a bar fight, back when you and Brad were dating. Nothing major. No charges pressed. But your brother got in Mr. Dawson's face. Got physical." She watches me closely. "Makes you wonder, doesn't it?"

My thoughts spin. Seth never told me. *Why?*

Before I can think twice, I hear myself say, "Is that why you're looking at him? Because of an old bar fight?"

She doesn't answer. Instead, she looks past me, out toward the crowd milling through the festival grounds.

"Is that why Brad's death has been officially ruled a homicide?" I ask.

Her head swivels around, a small smile on her lips. "Someone is certainly asking lots of nosy questions."

"Is it true?" I demand.

She rubs her thumb over the silver cuffs she's still holding. "Yes," she finally says.

My breath catches. "That was fast."

"A judge friend of mine pushed this case to the top of the ME's pile. Scalp hemorrhaging is more common in assault cases than accidents," she shares. "It's preliminary of course. But coupled with the evidence we have, the coroner was confident enough to officially rule Mr. Dawson's death a homicide this morning."

I stare at her, unsure what to say.

It strikes me how different Detective Wilcox is from Detective Kane. She's sharing this information so plainly, while Detective Kane keeps a perfectly sculpted poker face of silence.

Then she speaks again, drawing me back. "Your brother already had bad blood with the deceased. There's motive tangled up in this for both of you. It's not a good look."

Of course she's not sharing this to be kind. She's circling Seth. Watching me. Watching both of us.

Detective Wilcox slips her cuffs back onto her belt. "We'll talk again soon." I stare at her as she strides off into the crowd.

My heart pounds as I try to understand what happened.

I don't know what scares me more—that Detective Wilcox thinks Seth is involved . . .

Or that I don't know what he's been hiding.

Chapter Seventeen

I step into the food truck, the weight of Detective Wilcox's words still pressing on my shoulders.

"Well," I announce, reaching for the overhead shelf where we keep the hand sanitizer, "Detective Wilcox confirmed it herself. Brad's death has officially been ruled a homicide."

Seth is waiting for me, arms crossed, face tight with barely restrained anger. "Are you out of your mind?" he hisses. "I told you not to talk to her!"

I slather my hands with sanitizer. "Well, maybe if you'd been honest with me, I wouldn't have had to!"

Rylie, who's been boxing up an order, freezes mid-motion. Her gaze flicks between us, sensing the explosion before it happens. "*Oh meu Deus*," she firmly says. "Not in the truck."

Seth ignores her, stepping closer. "What did you say to her?"

"No, Seth," I snap. "The question is, what didn't *you* say to *me*?"

His jaw tightens.

I shove my finger into his chest. "Detective Wilcox told me about the bar fight between you and Brad."

"It's not what you think—"

"Ignore me all you want," I say, voice rising, "but is that why you and Brad didn't get along? How long were you planning on keeping that from me?"

Seth recoils like I slapped him, but then his eyes narrow and he fires back, "How about you tell me why you removed me from accessing the Kluckin' Clues list?"

My pulse skips, then races. "Oh, you didn't think I'd catch that?" He scoffs. "I tried to check it yesterday and couldn't. My access was gone. Just like that." He snaps his fingers.

"You don't even care about our stupid list." My voice rises before I can stop it.

"That's not the point!" He slams his hand against the counter, making Teriyaki squawk. "It was ours. The three of us had access to it. You locked me out like I was the enemy."

"This is getting out of hand."

"Why did you remove me from the list?" he asks. "What's on there that you didn't want me to see?"

"I told you to tell him," Rylie says. "I told you he had a right to know and that keeping secrets wasn't a good idea."

He turns his attention to Rylie. "You knew?"

"I told her to tell you," she says.

"That doesn't matter." He looks like he's been slapped again. "When she didn't you should have."

"Leave her out of this." My throat is dry and scratchy. "This was my choice. I didn't want you to see I'd added your suspicious behavior in the first place."

The to-go box in Rylie's hand crinkles loudly as the gawking customer, a teenager with earbuds hanging loose around his neck, finally clears his throat. Rylie practically throws the box into his arms.

"Here. Go!" she yells, and the teen scurries off.

Meanwhile, Teriyaki squawks from her perch near the prep sink. She hops down, wings slightly flared, and wedges herself between me and Seth like a one-bird security team. Rylie scoops her up before she can start pecking ankles.

"She doesn't like yelling," Rylie explains. "And neither do I."

I hold up my hands. "I didn't add you because I thought you were guilty," I tell Seth. "I panicked, okay? I thought if you saw your name there, you'd shut down. Or worse, you'd think I actually believed it. I just wanted to protect you."

"So that's it? You had me listed like some criminal? Fine. Did you add yourself?" Seth asks.

"What? No! I found the body, Seth, why would I—"

"Killers report bodies all the time!" His face is red now, voice shaking. "Don't act like you're above suspicion. Brad humiliated you in front of a restaurant full of people. He strung you along until he dumped you for his step-cousin. You had motive too."

"You think I killed Brad?"

"No," he says flatly, "but you said you were tracking everyone who had motive and opportunity. You didn't put yourself on the list. That's not protecting me, Beth. That's protecting your version of the truth."

I open my mouth, then close it, a gust of air leaving my lungs.

Rylie shifts uncomfortably, still holding Teriyaki, who lets out a small whimper of a cluck. "He's right. You tell us, no lies, no secrets. But you lied. You controlled the list, controlled the story. That's manipulation, Beth."

I stare at her, feeling gut punched. "I wasn't manipulate—"

"You were," Seth cuts in. "You isolated me."

"This secret was supposed to keep you safe," I say.

"No," he says. "It just made me the outsider."

The words hit hard. I drop my gaze to the floor, heat rising behind my eyes. "You're right."

The truck goes quiet.

"I screwed up," I say. "I thought I could solve this before it got worse. Before anyone else got hurt."

Rylie gently sets Teriyaki down, her voice softening. "But trying to solve it alone meant you were willing to keep quiet even when it could make someone else—someone you love—look guilty."

"And if the roles were reversed?" he asks. "If I'd kept something from you because I thought I was protecting you?"

"You did," I remind him. "And I was furious and hurt."

"Why weren't you straight with me from the start?" he asks, his tone filled with pain and anger.

"Something has been off with you ever since we saw Brad at Sugar and Spice."

"You should've asked," he fires back. "Instead of accusing me of murdering your loser ex!"

"I never suspected you of killing Brad." My voice cracks, and I feel raw. "But you've been lying to me—for years, apparently.

Rylie cuts in sharply. "Bethany."

"Okay," I sigh. "I'm asking now. What happened?"

He runs a hand through his hair, pacing the cramped truck. "I didn't tell you because I knew exactly how this would go."

"Meaning?"

"Meaning you'd jump straight to suspicion. Which, congratulations, you did."

"Wow," I say. "We're trying to calm down here and you're really pulling the 'it's your fault I lied' card?"

"You did jump straight to suspicion," he says.

"I'm sorry," I say again.

"Sorry," he mutters, scrubbing a hand over his face. "It's just—this whole thing sucks."

"No argument there," I say. "I really am sorry. Isolating you isn't what I wanted. I messed up, but I'm trying to make it right. So please . . . tell me the truth about what Detective Wilcox was saying. No more dodging from you, and I won't add you to my suspect lists anymore."

Seth hesitates. His shoulders slump. Then finally, he nods.

"It was at a bar," he says quietly. "Couple of years ago. Brad and I obviously weren't friends, but we knew the same people. He didn't know I was there. I overheard him mouthing off about you. You had been dating close to a year at that point. He was telling his buddies how he could get whatever he wanted." His fists clench. "I told him to shut his mouth. He laughed."

I go still.

"Things escalated," he says. "I lunged. Someone pulled me back before it turned into a full fight, but words were said. After that, we stayed away from each other. I didn't tell you then because I knew you wouldn't listen." His voice is tense, controlled, like he's holding back something heavier.

My pulse kicks up. "That's not fair. I would have listened."

"Would you?" He lets out a sharp breath, shaking his head. "Beth, you were in love with the guy. Anything I said would've pushed you closer to him. You were already shutting me out every time I brought him up, saying it's because I didn't like him."

I open my mouth, but no words come. Because deep down, I know he's right.

Exhausted and frustrated, Seth tugs at his hair. "I didn't want to fight with you back then. I figured you'd see him for what he was, eventually." He exhales. "I didn't expect it to be like this."

I can't speak. My throat tightens as memories surface—Brad's digs, his smug jabs, his weird defensiveness around Seth. I'd thought it was petty jealousy over how close we were. Not that he hated my twin.

Seth watches me softer now. "I never told you because I didn't want to lose you over him. While you were devastated by the breakup, I was overjoyed. It liberated you from him."

"I should've listened," I whisper.

He gives a bitter laugh. "Yeah, well. I didn't expect to be dragged onto a suspect list because of *not* telling you."

I look up at him, really look this time. "I was trying to protect you, Seth. I don't want the cops thinking they've got their guy because you had a beef with the victim."

Silence settles between us, heavy.

Rylie exhales and gently sets Teriyaki back in her box of rags under the counter. The chicken stretches her wings dramatically, then fluffs up and settles, satisfied that the yelling has stopped.

A lump forms in my throat.

Before I can say anything else, a slow clap interrupts us.

Caren leans against the serving ledge, smirking. "Well, well. This gets better and better."

Seth stiffens. "What do you want, Caren?"

"Making sure I'm not missing anything juicy." Her gaze flicks between us, sharp and assessing. "Quite the family drama. You know, Beth, people are starting to talk. Wouldn't want the wrong narrative getting out there."

My stomach knots. "Meaning?"

"Brad made his career off drama," she says lightly. "Maybe I should too."

The implication slithers around me like a noose.

Caren gives me a wink before sauntering off, leaving a heavy silence in her wake.

Seth curses under his breath.

I hug myself, trying to shake off the unease crawling up my spine. It feels like I'm looking in the wrong places. But what if I already found it, just haven't seen it?

I turn to Seth and, before I can second-guess myself, pull him into a hug. He tenses, surprised, before hugging me back.

"We're okay, right?" I murmur.

His voice is quiet. "Yeah."

And I believe him. Seth has never been the problem—he's always had my back. I can't let Detective Wilcox get in my head. Trusting the wrong person got me burned once before. And I can't afford to let it happen again.

As I pull away, the pit in my stomach tightens.

I want to believe I've been fair, unbiased. But Seth is right. I've been playing judge and jury without ever looking in the mirror.

Because the last time I ignored my instincts, I trusted Brad Dawson.

And I'm not making that mistake again.

Chapter Eighteen

Seth steps down from the truck with a sharp clang of the back stairs.

"I need a breather," he says, already pulling out his phone. "Five minutes."

I nod, pretending not to notice that he won't meet my eyes.

But of course I notice. My twin—my best friend, the person who knows me better than I know myself—walked away. Because of me. Because I hurt him.

When Seth forgives, he forgives. But I know this will take some time for both of us.

Rylie doesn't say anything, but I catch the subtle sigh she lets out while sliding a fresh basket of wings under the heat lamp.

I'm standing at the serving window staring after Seth when a deep voice cuts through the lull.

"Back again," the man says. "I couldn't stop thinking about your fries."

It takes a second to place him. The beard helps, though. It's trimmed, a little too perfect, like he wants it to look effortless but definitely took effort. He was here earlier, which already feels like a lifetime ago.

"Oh," I say, my voice a little too high. "Hi."

Cool, Beth. So smooth.

He reaches for one of our display tumblers at the edge of the serving ledge. "Could I get this filled with iced tea? And I'd like another order of Plucked and Truffle. Please."

"Absolutely," I say, reaching for the cup and nearly knocking over the tray of straws. "Sorry—I mean yes. For sure."

He laughs, not unkindly. "You okay in there?" He hands me the tumbler, his fingers lingering as they touch mine.

"A little fried." I wince. "That was not a pun. Or it was. Unintentional. Ignore me."

"Too late," his grin curves slow and lazy. "You've officially charmed me with potato-based wordplay."

My laugh is too high-pitched, too fast. I'm just standing here staring like an idiot. Did his brown eyes always have a hint of gold in them?

Ahem! Rylie clears her throat, loudly.

"What?" I ask.

Her head nods to the fryer. "His fries?"

"Oh! Right." I give him a bright, probably too wide smile. "Let me grab those for you."

I spin, trip over my own feet, and bump into Rylie. "I'll get them," she says, steering me toward the drink station. "Before you burn the truck down."

Trying to recover some dignity, I scoop ice into his Kluckin' Good tumbler. "All we've got is unsweet tea. That okay?"

"Perfect," he says, leaning forward on the counter, chin resting on his hand like he's watching a show. "As long as you're the one serving it." The words hit like a match dropped in a fireworks store. My face ignites, my brain scrambles, and for a horrifying second, I forget how cups work.

"Oh," I say brilliantly. "Um . . . well . . ."

"Meu Deus," Rylie groans.

"The cup is limited edition," I finish.

"That so?" Turning, I see his smile deepen, and I swear the temperature inside the truck jumps ten degrees.

"That's $19.50," I blurt, setting the drink on the ledge as Rylie slides the basket of fries through. "Free refills today, ninety-nine cents all weekend. And the tumbler's double-walled. Keeps your drink cold even if the sun tries to melt your face."

"Worth every penny." He pays, tips, and grabs a fry like he didn't just drop my brain in the deep fryer. "See you around."

Rylie nudges me with her elbow. "That was . . . something."

I'm watching his retreating back. "I'm not ready to unpack whatever *that* was."

And of course, that's the exact moment my phone buzzes in my apron pocket. I don't even check the screen before answering.

"Pedro, *please* tell me you're calling with good news about Audrey."

There's a pause. A long one. "Who's Pedro?"

I nearly drop the phone. The voice on the other end isn't Pedro. It's deeper and laced with amusement.

Detective Kane.

My stomach does an Olympic-level flip. I snap my gaze at Rylie, who's now refilling sauce cups at the prep station. I mouth, *Switch with me!* And gesture toward the window.

She frowns but moves into my spot with a cheerful "What can I get you?" as a customer walks up.

I duck toward the back of the truck. "Uh." I clear my throat, gripping the phone tighter. Still reeling from seeing the handsome customer moments ago.

Who knew I had a thing for beards?

"You there, Beth?" Detective Kane's voice cuts through the line.

"Pedro is Rylie's cousin. My car—Audrey—is at his family's shop."

"You named your car?"

"I name all my cars," I say, like it's completely normal.

"Uh-huh." He's grinning, I can hear it. "And what exactly is wrong with Audrey?"

"Her check engine light is on again."

"That could be anything."

"Thank you, Detective, for that insightful automotive analysis."

"Happy to help," he says dryly.

I squeeze my eyes shut. *This is going great.*

Before I can dig myself deeper, he adds, "Check your messages. I sent you something by mistake."

I pull the phone away and swipe to my messages. A blurry close-up of a corn dog fills the screen. "Uh . . ."

"That was meant for Jerry," he explains, referring to his partner, Detective Hamstead. "He's been ranking festival corn dogs for years. His wife wouldn't let him come this weekend—he's gotta watch his salt intake. Anyway, I was tasked with updating him on the competition."

Jerry is a fun guy. We get along great. He even brought his wife, Marcy, to my truck once for a dinner date.

"You called to tell me you sent this picture by mistake?" I squint at the blurry photo. "This is . . . deeply unappealing."

"Not my best work. But I figured you wouldn't judge me for bad lighting."

I laugh, loosening up. "Since I'm in this elite corn dog club now, do I get a vote?"

"Only if you promise to vote my way," he says, voice dropping low.

My pulse skips. "And if I don't?"

"Then I'll just have to win you over," he says smoothly.

My brain short-circuits. *Was that flirting?*

"Whatever it takes," he finishes.

Okay, *that* was flirting.

I bite the inside of my cheek to keep from smiling. I hate that he can make me melt with one line. My face is probably giving me away.

His tone shifts. "Tell me you're staying out of trouble, Beth."

"No trouble here!" My voice jumps half an octave.

"That was the most unconvincing lie I've ever heard."

"I'm working. Totally above-board, noncriminal enterprise."

"And not asking questions about a certain suspicious death?"

"You mean homicide. Detective Wilcox confirmed it. The ME said scalp hemorrhaging—"

"I'm aware," he says, "Just didn't know you were."

"It's nice how she shares information with me," I add. Giving him a subtle dig while leaving out I'm confident the reason she does is because she's got Seth locked in her sights. "Now, please define 'asking questions.'"

Detective Kane sighs, and I'm sure I detect an amused exasperation. "Beth."

I sag against the counter. "Okay, maybe I've . . . been around some conversations."

"Right. And I *accidentally* sent you a picture of a corn dog."

"Are you actually worried about me?" My stomach flutters. "You could've just called instead of fake texting me a picture. Or are you just trying to make my life difficult?"

"Can't it be both?"

I groan again, and Detective Kane chuckles. "Just keep your nose clean, Lloyd."

I open my mouth to retort, but he hangs up.

Rylie is already at the back of the truck, waiting for something juicy. "Sooo," she drawls. "That was *definitely* not Pedro."

I shove my phone into my pocket. "Nope."

"You were smiling," she says. "And blushing, while talking to Detective Kane."

"No, I wasn't. It's just hot in here."

"Two men at the same time." Rylie teases. "You like them."

"I do *not*."

"Uh-huh." She folds her arms.

"I don't know what you're talking about."

"Sure you don't."

"Goodness, it is hot in here," I wipe my brow like that'll cool the flush in my cheeks.

"Funny, I feel fine. But you? You're hot and flustered. Practically steaming."

"It's just the grill."

"It's just the dimples," she sings. "Or maybe the beard. Or both . . ."

"Rylie—"

"Yeah, you're hot all right," she says, waggling her brows. "Hot for Detective Kane and his swoon-worthy jawline. Or are you hot for the bearded customer with fries?"

"Keep it up," I warn, "and you're wearing the cow suit next shift."

She gasps. "You wouldn't!"

"Try me."

I let out a deep breath, still flustered. Detective Kane didn't have to call. He didn't have to check in. He's just being nosy, that's all.

Right? I think as I fan my face.

But then there's that bearded customer who said he couldn't stop thinking about my fries.

Was it just the fries?

I can't stop thinking about the way he smiled and flirted.

Now I don't know which guy I'm blushing over.

I can't help replaying my phone call with Detective Kane on a loop. It felt weird but also *not.* Did he know I was flirting? Did he know *he* was flirting? *Was that flirting?*

A sudden squawk snaps me out of my spiraling thoughts. I whirl around in time to see a blur of white feathers burst through the back of the truck.

"Teriyaki!" I exclaim as my rogue chicken flaps her way onto a storage crate, fluffing herself up like she owns the place.

"When did you leave the truck?" I reach out, gently scooping her up.

She lets out a smug little cluck and nestles into my arms, like she never left.

"Exploring, huh? Well, next time let me know. If something happened to you I'd be worried."

I crouch beside her crate, stroking the soft feathers along her neck. "You're becoming my emotional support chicken, huh? Don't tell the health inspector."

She clucks once and settles in, perfectly content.

Scratching her neck, I coo, "Who's a cute wittle chicky?"

"Wittle chicky?" a voice mimics.

I yelp and jump to my feet, spinning around to find Detective Wilcox standing outside the truck. Her eyes bore into me, sharp and unreadable.

Annoyance floods my veins. *How long has she been standing there?*

"My chicken," I say quickly, wiping my hands on my apron. "What are you doing here? Again."

She doesn't blink. "Why shouldn't I be here? The festival's open to the public, and everyone I need to talk to is conveniently in one place."

I fiddle with the hem of my apron. "And you think the person who killed Brad is still here?"

Her gaze sharpens. "I do. For all I know, I could be looking right at them."

That sends goosebumps down my arms. She wants to rattle me—mission accomplished. But I'm done being playing nice.

"I thought we already established this was a homicide," I say. "So if you've got more questions for me about Brad Dawson, maybe we should do it down at the station. With my attorney present."

Her brow lifts. "Feeling defensive?"

"No," I say flatly. "I'm trying to work. And frankly? This is getting old. You keep circling back to the same questions like you're hoping I'll slip up."

Her jaw tightens. "People don't always say everything the first time around."

"Then maybe you should be clearer about what you're asking." *God, Seth is gonna flip his lid when he hears I said this.*

She doesn't respond, just keeps staring.

I clear my throat. "Detective Kane and I talked about that, actually—"

"All Andy's done is defend you," she snaps, cutting me off. Her voice is sudden and cold, like a slammed door. "I told him I have things under control. This is my case. I don't need some big-city detective swooping in and stepping on my toes."

I blink. "Big city? You mean Clementine?"

She ignores me, taking a slow step forward, up to the back step of the truck. "What exactly did you tell Andy?"

"Nothing that I didn't already tell you."

Her expression darkens. "Sounds like you've got it all figured out."

"Not really," I say. "I still don't know who did it."

She watches me for a beat, then her tone shifts. "Tell me, are you and your brother conspiring?"

I pinch my nose, shaking my head. "Conspiring? To do *what*, exactly?"

"Oh, you know."

"No, I don't know."

Her lips twitch. "What about Helena Wynn? You two seem cozy. Cozy enough to cover for each other?"

"Detective Wilcox," I say, planting my hands on my hips, "if you want to keep this conversation going, I'll need to call my attorney."

Her lips twitch, but she doesn't smile. "Let me guess, your brother? Helena already told me he's your lawyer. How convenient to have an attorney in the family."

"It is for me; I pay him in pizza." Pulling out my phone, I hold up a finger. "If you wouldn't mind waiting, I need to make a quick call."

Detective Wilcox backs off. "No need. We're done here."

"Great," I say as she strides off, kicking the dirt like a kid denied candy.

I fire off a text:

Me: Detective Wilcox is sniffing around again. She's gunning for both of us. Told her if she wants to keep talking, I'd have to call my attorney.

Seth immediately replies.

Seth: Thank you for finally listening to me. For once. Do I need to come now? I'm talking with a client.
Me: Nah, she bailed when she learned I had an attorney. But we need this wrapped up ASAP. She's fixated on us.

Three dots appear. Vanish. Reappear.

Seth: Don't worry about me.

Three more dots.

Seth: Don't do anything stupid.

I roll my eyes and type back.

Me: Who, me? Never!
Seth: Bethany, I swear you're going to be the reason I get arrested!
Me: WOW. I'm trying to protect you!
Seth: I'm already handling this the legal way. Don't drag Rylie into this either.

I shake my head, talking to Teriyaki, "Can you believe him? It's like he doesn't trust me or something."

She clucks softly, already asleep, utterly unfazed.

"Puh-lease." I roll my eyes and go back to texting.

Me: The only thing I'm planning is a post reminding our followers where to find us this weekend.

I arrange one of our Kluckin' Good tumblers next to a basket of Golden Gate Heat Wings, Guac the Line Fries, and a basket of Beats and Bites. Snapping a photo, I upload it to all our social media pages.

Remember! We're at the @FlavorsofTheBayfoodfestival this weekend. Stop by and say hello. Don't forget to try one of our exclusive festival specials! #FlavorsofTheBay #KluckinGood #FoodTruckLife #FoodiesofTheBay

"Wow." Almost immediately, my post racks up likes. Checking the festival hashtag, I'm shocked by how many people have been tagging our truck.

The festival hashtag is full of photos, many of which are the usual food selfies. I also see a lot of happiness. Everyone's posts make the festival look like a blast. While I'm thrilled everyone is having a great time, I have to admit I'm a bit envious. I had fun weekend plans too. Ones that didn't include finding Brad's dead body and making sure Seth stayed out of jail.

My phone pings with a text message.

Pedro: Great news, the parts came in for your car. I should have Audrey up and running by the end of the weekend.
Me: Thanks so much!

At least there's one piece of good news this weekend.

Chapter Nineteen

A big part of me is over this festival—but not enough to leave. My feet ache, my back feels like it's been molded into the shape of our truck's griddle, and I'm pretty sure my hair smells permanently like Kluck-It sauce. But I can't let exhaustion get the best of me. Aunt Dolly would've seen this as another bump in the road. Maybe even an opportunity. She wouldn't pack it in—she'd double down, maybe slap on a feather boa and turn this whole mess into a spectacle worth watching.

So, that's exactly what I'm gonna do.

I paste on my brightest food-truck-owner smile as a couple approaches the serving window, staring at the chalkboard menu like it holds the secrets of the universe.

"Are the Golden Gate Heat Wings spicy?" the woman asks, resting a hand on her very pregnant belly.

"There's a kick for sure," I say, launching into my well-rehearsed pitch. "The wings are coated in a sweet and spicy chili fusion, sprinkled with crispy sesame seeds and green onion slices. They start off sweet but end with heat."

The woman rubs her belly, clearly undecided. "I don't know . . . Baby Boise doesn't love it when I eat spicy food. But they sound amazing!" She pouts at her husband like she's auditioning for a role in a rom-com.

"Babe," he says, with the weary patience of a man who's lost many arguments. "You get *terrible* heartburn if you eat so much as pepperoncini."

"We've got something milder," I offer, sliding a sample of our Crazed Chick Wings through the window. "These wings are coated in a honey brown sugar barbecue sauce—sweet, no heat."

She snatches the sample like I've handed her the winning lottery ticket, takes a bite, and moans. Not a polite, restaurant-appropriate "Mmm," but a full-on "this changed my life" sound.

"I *need* these," she says, turning to her husband. "Baby Boise needs these."

The husband glances at me like he's hoping I'll talk her out of it, but I shrug. I'm not about to get between a pregnant woman and her cravings.

"I'll take an order—" he starts.

"Two!" she interrupts, waving her half-eaten wing for emphasis.

He sighs but doesn't argue. "Two orders of whatever those wings were."

"Two Crazed Chick, coming right up!" I retrieve the baskets from the warming station and slide them through the window. "That'll be $18."

He hands me thirty. "Put the rest toward your Kind Bites board. Let someone else have a meal on us."

"Thank you," I say, genuinely touched. That board is one of my favorite things about running this truck.

As they walk off, I watch him reach for a wing. Without missing a beat, she slaps his hand like a cat swatting a toddler.

"Baby Boise doesn't share," she snaps.

I bite my lip to keep from laughing, turning quickly toward the prep counter. But the image is seared into my brain, guaranteeing random chuckles for the rest of the afternoon.

And then I see it.

A pair of binoculars. Poking out from behind a tree.

Caren.

Again.

I resist the urge to groan. Seriously, does this woman have nothing better to do? It's like she took a master class in being the world's most obvious lurker. Even Bigfoot has better camouflage.

Her name is as annoying as the woman herself. Who spells Karen with a C, anyway?

I duck slightly, watching as she steps out from the shade—not toward me but toward Layla. Of course. Birds of a feather flock together. In this case, vultures.

Layla's and Caren's heads bend together, whispering like they're conspiring to take over the world. Every few seconds, they glance toward my truck, and my stomach tightens. What are they talking about? My truck? Me?

I should march over there and ask outright, but that's exactly what Caren would want—a reaction. And I'm not giving her the satisfaction.

Instead, I snap on a fresh pair of gloves and force a smile as my new regular customer, the dino tutu mom from the first day bounces up to the truck.

"Hey, got any Kluck-a-Doodle Classics?"

"You know it," I say, shaking off my irritation. "Extra basket for ketchup?"

"Yep! My boys are ketchup fiends." She laughs. "Oh! And three refills of lemonade, please." She sets her tumblers on the counter for me.

While I prepare her order, I keep glancing at Caren and Layla.

What are they whispering about? Why do they keep looking at me?

I grab the card she's handing me for her order. "I'm Beth, by the way."

"Charlie," she smiles.

I tap her card on our point-of-sale system, then hand it back.

"See you later," she chirps, grabbing her food and drinks before heading off.

The moment she's gone, Rylie appears, her chicken costume flapping as she bounds inside the truck. She scratches Teriyaki's neck lovingly and asks, "How's *meu pintinho* doing?"

"We have a stalker," I point toward the nefarious pair.

Rylie groans, pulling off her chicken head. "What's it gonna take for her to leave us the cluck alone?"

"If she causes trouble, call Seth," I say, untying my apron and hanging it by the door. "I'm going on break."

"You gonna confront them?" Rylie asks, staring at Layla and Caren.

"Not unless they give me a reason." I glance toward the food stalls. "But if anyone needs me, I'll be following the smell of bacon."

"No promises I won't peck them if they come near."

I wave her off as I step onto the path. Bacon might not solve my problems, but it's definitely not going to hurt either.

The smell of sizzling bacon lures me like a siren's call. I weave through the bustling festival crowd until I reach Bacon My Heart, Vicky Yang's truck.

Vicky's son, Nick, mans the window. His grease-stained cap is pulled low over his forehead. His apron reads: *Don't Go Bacon My Heart, I Couldn't If I Fried!* Which earns a small smile from me despite everything.

"Hey, Nick," I greet him while scanning the menu. "Can I get an order of Ham It Up, but I'd like it with melted Swiss instead of cheddar, a Bacon Me Crazy, hold the mayo but add the spicy garlic aioli, and the Gooey Gambit with an extra side of candied bacon?"

"Sure thing." He punches in the order as I hand over my debit card. But as he leans closer, his voice drops to a whisper. "Hey, so . . . is it true?"

I raise an eyebrow. "Is what true?"

Nick shifts uncomfortably, glancing around like we're in a mob movie and someone might be listening. "That you . . . killed someone?"

I choke on my own saliva. "Are you kidding me?"

"All the vendors are talking about it," he says sheepishly. "Some say you knew the guy."

Pinching the bridge of my nose, I inhale deeply, forcing down the urge to slam my forehead against the counter. "Yes, I knew Brad," I say evenly. "But I did not kill him. And if you could help put an end to that ridiculous rumor, I'd appreciate it."

Nick at least has the decency to look embarrassed.

Before he can reply, his mother, Vicky, appears at the window. "Most of us know better," she says, giving Nick a pointed look. "Go make Beth's order. I'll handle the window."

Nick scurries off like a scolded puppy, and Vicky leans out, her warm smile instantly easing some of the tension coiled in my chest. She's known me since I was a kid, and she's one of the few people here I trust completely.

"Hey, sweetheart," she greets me.

"Hey, Vicky," I reply, forcing a small smile.

"Ignore the gossip. Most of us know it's coming from Layla."

That gets my attention. My brows knit together. "Layla? Why would she spread something like that?"

Vicky snorts. "Because she's scared. Look around—your truck has a line wrapped around the corner. Hers? Not so much."

I glance around until I find Layla's bright orange Roller Burger truck. Sure enough, her crowd is noticeably thinner. But why would that make her desperate enough to drag my name through the mud?

"I don't get it," I admit. "We've never even met before this weekend. I don't want trouble. I just want to serve good food."

"Well, Layla doesn't see it that way," Vicky says. "Every food trucker in the Bay Area knows your Aunt Dolly's reputation. Dolly built Kluckin' Good from the ground up, and people loved her.

And now you and Seth? You've only made it better. But Layla doesn't see collaboration—only competition."

"That's ridiculous," I almost laugh. "Why can't we support each other?"

Vicky gives me a knowing look. "Because people like Layla don't *play* fair. You've heard her nickname, right?"

I shake my head.

"Lying Layla," Vicky says, her tone darkening. "She's known for spreading rumors and stirring up drama. She and I were at a food truck night at Jack London Square years ago, and she nearly ran me out of business."

"What did she do?"

Vicky lowers her voice, eyes flicking around before she speaks. "She spread lies about my truck, said I used artificial ingredients and caused an E. coli outbreak. My business took a huge hit. I could've sued. But as a single mom with three kids, I didn't have the resources to fight her."

I grip the serving counter, anger bubbling under my skin. "That's disgusting."

"She's *worse* than disgusting, Beth," Vicky says, voice sharp. "She's ruthless. She'll do *whatever* it takes to stay on top—lie, cheat . . ." Her expression hardens. "Or worse."

"Worse?" I'm almost afraid to ask.

Vicky hesitates, then nods grimly. "There was a guy—Daniel Price. Used to run a burger truck. He and Layla had a nasty rivalry, and then one day . . . he *left*. Vanished from the food truck scene overnight. No explanation."

I frown. "You think she did something to him?"

"I think he got scared enough to pack up and never look back." Vicky's eyes flick toward Layla's truck. "And I think you should be careful."

A prickle of unease crawls up my arms. Is Layla that cutthroat? That manipulative? And if she was willing to destroy businesses and livelihoods over competition, would she go as far as murder?

Before I can voice the thought, Vicky's expression softens. "I know this festival hasn't been what you expected—"

"It feels like a failure," I admit for the first time. "I've been looking forward to this festival for weeks, and *nothing* has gone as planned. Seth's mad at me, for good reason, the cops are sniffing around both of us, my ex-boyfriend is dead, and my car broke down. And now I'm supposed to watch my back because of Layla? Aunt Dolly would be so disappointed in me right now."

"That so?"

I nod. "Why not? I'm disappointed in me."

Vicky makes a tsk sound. "Is Seth still mad?" she asks.

"I don't know," I say. "Probably not. Hurt is more accurate."

"Do you forgive him right away when he's hurt you?"

I think back to how hurt I was when I learned he'd been dating Rylie behind my back for weeks without telling me.

"Fair point," I say. "I still feel like I've made a mess of things."

"Listen to me," Vicky says, her voice firm. "You haven't failed, Beth. You're in the thick of it, that's not the same thing. You only fail if you pack up, go home, and let people like Layla win because they think they're better than you."

I look down, tracing the edge of the counter. "I want to live up to Aunt Dolly's legacy."

"I knew your aunt long before you were born, so listen carefully." Vicky leans forward, her expression serious. "You think Dolly had it easy? She built Kluckin' Good from scratch, but she had her fair share of struggles and disappointment. People stole from her, lied about her, tried to tear her down. I saw it all. You know what she did?"

I shake my head.

"She got up the next morning and fired up the fryer like nothing happened. She didn't let it sink her."

I'm stunned. "She never talked about that."

"She didn't need to. By the time you and Seth came in, she had thick skin and a loyal customer base. But she wasn't invincible—she kept going."

Her words land like a weight and a balm all at once. I've been holding Aunt Dolly up like she was untouchable, thinking I'd never measure up. But maybe I've been measuring the wrong thing. Vicky smiles. "And trust me, if she were here, she'd be in the truck with you slinging wings and telling people like Lying Layla to kick rocks. She'd be proud of what you've done with her business, Beth. You've got her grit—you just forgot for a second."

A lump forms in my throat. "Thanks, Vicky. Really.""

"We all need a little tough love once in a while," she gives me a wink. "Now wipe that sad look off your face and go show everyone why Kluckin' Good still owns the street corner when it comes to wings."

Nick reappears with my order, setting the bag on the counter. "Here you go!"

"Thanks, Nick," I say, taking the bag. Turning back to Vicky, I add, "And thank you. For everything."

Vicky waves her hands at me. "Go enjoy those sandwiches before they get cold. One taste of Bacon Me Crazy and Seth will forget about everything else."

"You're probably right," I laugh.

As I head back toward my truck my mind is racing. Layla's nickname isn't for show—she's a master manipulator, and if she's behind the rumors about me, there's no telling what else she's capable of.

But there's one thing I know for sure.

If Layla thinks she can ruffle my feathers, she's got another thing coming—because I pluck back!

And if she killed Brad?

I'm going to find out.

Chapter Twenty

"We can't keep her—"

"She's staying!"

Seth and Rylie are toe to toe, locked in what looks like round three of a shouting match, as I climb the back steps of the truck.

"No, she isn't," Seth declares, pointing at Teriyaki, who's currently perched on a crate of napkins. "The only chickens we're keeping on this truck are the ones on the menu."

"Bawk, bawk!" Teriyaki trills, flapping her wings for emphasis.

"*Cala a boca*!" Rylie snaps at Seth.

Seth gasps, his expression morphing into deep betrayal. "How *dare* you!"

"You don't even know what I said," Rylie replies, arms crossed.

"I *know* it was rude," he shoots back.

"What is going on?" I set our sandwiches on the prep counter and brace for impact.

"We're discussing what to do with her," Seth says, pointing accusingly at Teriyaki, who now huddles between my legs like a feathery hostage seeking refuge.

"And he's *o homem estúpido* who won't listen," Rylie huffs.

"First, I agree—Seth *is* stupid," I say, earning an outraged squawk of protest from him. "Second, Teriyaki's well-being is up to *me*. Not you. Until I know what's best for her, she *stays*. Clear?"

Seth glares but takes the Bacon Me Crazy sandwich I shove at him.

"What's this?" he asks, inspecting it suspiciously. "Why didn't we eat the food we already have on the truck?"

Rylie and I gasp, scandalized.

"Seth Evan Lloyd," I scold, channeling our mother's signature no-nonsense glare. "What is wrong with you?"

"How would you feel watching someone eat one of your relatives?" Rylie demands, jabbing a finger at him and nodding toward Teriyaki.

"Is this about that show again?" Seth groans. "Did you two go down another conspiracy podcast rabbit hole?"

"It's called *Murder and Mayhem*," Rylie and I correct at the same time, complete with matching eye rolls.

"And no, this isn't about the podcast," I add. "But I'm sure Inga Nevarez would agree with us."

Seth stares at me like I've sprouted feathers myself. "Beth. We run a chicken truck. People expect us to serve chicken. Rylie literally dresses as a giant chicken to bring them here."

"Exactly," Rylie says smugly, crouching to scratch Teriyaki under her chin. "This is why she loves me so much, *meu pintinho*."

Teriyaki fluffs her feathers, lets out a contented cluck, and waddles back to her makeshift nest.

"Thanks for this." He lifts the sandwich in my direction. "But you'd better not adopt a cow," Seth demands, chewing. "Because you're *not* taking burgers away from me."

Before I can fire back, Kaydee appears at the serving window. "Knock, knock! Checking in to see how the festival is going."

"Hey, Kaydee." Adam walks up before I can reply, his hands tucked awkwardly in his pockets. I wasn't expecting to see him again. Let alone hovering awkwardly near Kaydee like he's rehearsing something in his head.

"Hey," she replies, brushing a strand of hair behind her ear. She glances at him, then away, then back again.

"So," Adam starts, rocking on his heels. "How . . . are you feeling?"

That's a weird question.

"I'm drained," Kaydee sighs.

Adam reaches out, lightly touching her shoulder—then pulls back like she's scalding hot. "But you're okay?"

"Yeah." She nods.

"We, uh . . . still need to talk," Adam says, rubbing the back of his neck.

"Later," Kaydee replies, her tone clipped. She walks off before he can say more.

"That was weird," I say to Adam.

"If Beth's saying it was weird, then it was *definitely* weird," Seth says as I jab him in the ribs.

Adam lets out a frustrated sigh and runs a hand through his hair.

"Maybe she's busy?" I offer, not sure what else to say.

"Probably," Adam mumbles. "But I still need to talk to her."

"About what?" I ask.

"Stuff," he says vaguely.

"Gotcha." I nod, feeling more awkward by the second.

"Can we get you anything?" Seth asks, mercifully changing the subject.

"No, thanks," Adam replies. "I was hoping to talk to Kaydee."

"How's she been since Brad's death?" I ask, lowering my voice.

Adam's expression darkens. "Why are you asking?"

"Because," I blink at the shift in his tone. "She worked with him. That's gotta affect her."

"Yeah." Adam hesitates, then sighs. "Kaydee and I are—or *were*—friends? I don't know."

"How do you *not* know if you're friends with someone?"

"It's complicated."

"Then *uncomplicate* it," Rylie says flatly.

Adam rocks on his heels, staring after Kaydee as she disappears into the crowd. "I don't know what to do," he mutters.

I raise an eyebrow. "Okay?"

Adam shifts his weight, glancing in the direction Kaydee walked. "Seth, can I ask you something? Guy to guy,"

"Sure," he says, giving Adam his full attention.

"If someone you care about is going through something huge—and they shut you out completely—what do you do?"

Seth frowns. "Depends. Did you do something to make them shut you out?"

Adam nods, jaw tightening. "Yeah. Big time."

I glance at Rylie, who raises an eyebrow.

"Three months ago," Adam says slowly, "Kaydee and I were on a break."

Seth immediately asks, "A break? Or a 'break'?"

"This isn't an episode of *Friends*," I tell him.

"What's the difference?" Rylie asks.

"One's mutual," Seth says, "the other is an excuse to act single while still keeping the other person on the hook."

"It was mutual," Adam says quickly. "We both needed space. But while we were apart, Brad hooked up with her."

"Oh," I say softly.

"Wait," Rylie says. "I thought you said you and Brad weren't friends anymore?"

"We weren't. Not really. Not for a while." He runs a hand down his face. "I didn't lie, exactly—I just didn't tell you," he looks at me, "the full story. We started drifting months ago. Brad . . . changed. His ego got louder than everything else. I didn't like the way he talked to people, or how he treated them like pawns in a game."

He pauses, jaw tight. "But the end of our friendship came after Kaydee told me what happened between them."

Seth gives a low whistle.

"I was furious," Adam continues. "I confronted Brad. Words were exchanged. It got physical. Said things to Kaydee I shouldn't have. She quit her job, took one here at the farm."

"And you two patched things up after?" Seth asks.

"Took a while. We talked. A lot. Decided to try again. Then a month ago . . . she told me she's pregnant."

"Wow," Rylie says.

"We were happy," Adam continues. "Then Brad came back—for the festival preview. He learned about Kaydee and joked that he was the dad."

Rylie lets out a sharp breath. "What a jerk."

"I don't know if he meant it. But I snapped. Said some awful things to Kaydee. And now she won't talk to me."

A beat passes.

Seth rubs the back of his neck. "Man . . . if it were me? I'd give her space. But I'd also be real clear I was sticking around. That I wasn't going anywhere, no matter what."

Adam nods slowly, like he's trying to swallow glass. "Thanks."

I watch him. He's not being dramatic. He looks . . . wrecked.

"You think I blew it?"

Seth shrugs. "Maybe. But I've seen people come back from worse."

Adam exhales. "That's something, I guess."

Before I can pry further, Adam suddenly shifts. "You know what? Forget it." He exhales sharply. "That's not even why I came over here."

I frown. "Then why *did* you? I thought you said it was to talk with Kaydee."

"Yeah, that but also," he pauses, his shoulders tense, "to warn you."

"About what?" Seth asks, wiping his mouth.

Adam glances around, then lowers his voice. "Layla."

My stomach tightens. "What about her?"

"She's bad news, Beth. She warned me and Van Ambrose, my drummer, to stay away from your truck unless we wanted salmonella."

"She *what*?" Seth coughs, choking on his drink. "She's going to get hit with a defamation lawsuit if she doesn't quit it."

"I already knew she was trouble," I say. However, judging by our weekend customer traffic, the rumors haven't affected us. "I overheard some other food truck vendors talking about her on Friday. Vicky also told me all about her. She's called Lying Layla for a reason."

Adam lets out a dry laugh.

"She's not just a liar, she strikes me as calculated." I turn to Seth and Rylie. "Vicky Yang, Aunt Dolly's old friend who runs the Bacon My Heart food truck, told me Layla does more than lie. She's destroyed other businesses."

Seth lowers his sandwich. "Define destroyed."

"She nearly ruined Vicky's business," I say, my voice hardening. "And she ran another food truck—Daniel Price's—completely out of the area."

Adam gives a grim nod. "And it gets worse. Layla had a history with Brad."

I stiffen. "What kind of history?"

"Roller Burger was one of the first trucks Brad reviewed when he moved back," Adam says, arms folding. "He torched her. Said her burgers were overhyped garbage. She went ballistic. Threatened to sue, accused him of a smear campaign. It went nowhere, but she never forgot."

I'm curious whether her nasty habit of spreading rumors about other trucks started before or after that.

"Figures Brad would write a review like that," Seth says. "Guy couldn't help but broadcast his opinions like they were gospel."

"I don't know why it still surprises me," I say. "Brad was awful. I never thought I'd be thankful he dumped me." This way, I never had to see how much worse he got.

Adam sighs. "Watch your back, okay? Layla is more than gossipy, I think she's got a target on you."

"Vicky says Layla is probably jealous of how well our truck is doing here compared to hers," I explain.

"Well, if she feels you're a threat she might take action. She felt Brad was a threat at one time too . . ."

"Are you saying you think Layla is involved in what happened to Brad?" I ask Adam.

He shakes his head. "I don't know what I'm saying anymore," he says, then walks away.

I try to process everything Adam dumped on us.

Would Layla go that far? Would she kill over revenge and reputation?

But then there was Adam. He had a real reason to be upset with Brad himself.

Did Adam lose control and attack Brad over him sleeping with Kaydee?

"I'm gonna take Teriyaki for a walk," I announce, securing the makeshift harness I MacGyvered last night out of an old tote bag and some rope, hoping Teriyaki would return. "The entire world is turning into a soap opera, and I need a breather."

"I'll join you," Seth offers, cramming the last bite of his sandwich into his mouth.

"Not a chance," I say firmly, pointing a finger at him. "You're staying here because, even though Rylie's been practicing with the deep fryer, I don't trust her not to set the truck ablaze. And I definitely don't trust you."

"Me? What have I done?"

"Nothing yet, but you'll probably want to 'accidentally' drop Teriyaki off at the barn," I accuse, tightening the rope harness around my squawking chicken.

"Seth!" Rylie gasps. "How *could* you?"

"I haven't done anything!"

"But you want to," I say. "Conner doesn't even have chickens here. It's no place to leave her."

Teriyaki flaps her wings indignantly, as if agreeing with my assessment of Seth's possible treachery. "Bawk, bawk!"

"See? She knows," I say.

"Knows what?" Seth throws his hands in the air. "I haven't even done anything to her yet."

"Yet?" Rylie says and starts lecturing him in Portuguese.

Leaving Seth and Rylie bickering inside the truck about our newest mascot, I set off across the festival grounds with Teriyaki waddling beside me, her tiny feet tapping against the gravel.

A distant cheer erupts from the pie-eating contest near the main stage, followed by the emcee hyping up the next round of competitors. Nearby, a bluegrass band strums a twangy, foot-tapping tune that clashes with the bass-heavy beat spilling from the open mic tent.

A handler in overalls walks past with a fluffy dark brown alpaca in full Renaissance gear—tiny velvet cape, feathered cap, and all. The alpaca hums softly and gives Teriyaki a curious side-eye, but she barely notices. She's too busy preening like she owns the runway.

A little girl skids to a stop, clutching a half-melted rainbow snow cone. "Can she have some?" she asks, already tipping the cone.

"Uh—" I start to protest, but it's too late. Teriyaki sticks out her beak and takes a tiny peck.

"Buk, buk!" she declares with icy confidence.

"I've never heard you make that sound," I say to Teriyaki. "Must've been good."

The girl giggles and dashes off, trailing melted syrup.

I planned to swing by Helena's bakery truck to show off my new feathered companion—she'd *love* Teriyaki—but instead, I drift toward the barn.

It's quieter here, the festival chaos fading into the background. Peaceful but eerie. The yellow police tape is gone, replaced by a large sign that reads:

Do Not Enter. Authorized Green Family Farm Employees Only.

I glance at Teriyaki. "So much for that."

She tilts her head and clucks before pecking at the dirt.

Bending down, I scratch her neck. "If Brad came to interview the owners of the food trucks, why was he by the barn where there are *no* trucks? Bathroom run? Or something else?"

Teriyaki freezes mid-peck, her beady black eyes freezing on me.

"Cluck."

She stretches her neck, scanning the area, then lets out an ear-splitting screech that nearly startles me into falling over.

"What's wrong?" I ask, looking around.

Then I hear it—a twig snapping.

Teriyaki flaps her wings wildly, pulling against her harness as if to charge at whatever spooked her. A second later, I see who's behind the tree.

Caren.

My patience frays. "Are you *following* me?"

Caren steps out from behind the tree, lowering her sunglasses with an exaggerated sigh. "Oh, for the love of—*you're* following *me*!"

We glare at each other.

"I am simply walking my chicken," I deadpan.

"I was looking for the bathroom," Caren snaps back. "Which, by the way, is *closed* thanks to your little crime scene." She gestures dramatically toward the bathroom by the barn. "You probably murdered the plumbing too."

"I didn't murder anyone," I tell her. "This isn't *my* crime scene. And I have no idea what you're talking about. Why are the bathrooms closed?"

I glance toward the restroom doors. Sure enough, they're blocked off with a folding sign. A man trudges out holding a mop and a bucket.

"Whatever happened in there," I say, nodding toward him, "has a lot more to do with lunch choices than murder."

Teriyaki squawks, loud and judgmental.

Caren wrinkles her nose and puts her sunglasses back on. "This whole festival is cursed."

Teriyaki lets out another *bawk bawk* as if scolding her.

Caren plants a hand on her hip, the corner of her mouth curling. "I *swear*, every time I turn a corner, there you are."

"Funny, I was thinking the same thing about *you*."

We stare at each other for a long beat.

"Look, I don't have time for whatever paranoia-fueled theory you're cooking up," Caren says, crossing her arms. "Some of us are actually trying to find out what really happened to Brad."

I narrow my eyes. "And why exactly do you care so much?"

"Oh, I don't know, maybe because it's my job?" She gestures toward herself. "Journalist? Reporter? Ever heard of it?"

"Food critic," I correct. "And an ex-critic at that."

Her expression darkens. "Not for long."

I cross my arms. "So, this is all just a career move for you?"

"Everything is a career move," she says, brushing imaginary lint off her shirt. "That's how jobs work, sweetheart."

She turns, but I step forward. "So, you're telling me you came *all the way out here* for a bathroom break?"

Now that I say it, it doesn't sound as ridiculous as I meant it to. Porta potties are a crime against humanity. Caren pauses, her jaw tightening slightly before she leers. "And you're telling me you came *all the way out here* to let your chicken stretch her legs?"

Touché.

She tilts her sunglasses down just enough to glare over the rim before sliding them back up. "See you around, Lloyd." But as she turns, she grumbles, "Can't believe he posted that stupid alpaca photo."

I freeze. "What?"

She glances over her shoulder, clearly realizing she said too much. "Nothing."

"Nope," I say, stepping forward. "Not nothing. And since we're already being weird and cryptic, let's clear something else up. What exactly were you and Layla whispering about earlier? I saw you both looking at my truck like I'd parked it on top of your grandmothers."

"Relax. It wasn't personal."

"Funny," I say. "Gossip usually is."

She hesitates, then says coolly, "Layla's got opinions. She's been in the game longer than you, and people listen to her. When she says a truck's more sizzle than substance, it gets around."

My throat tightens. "So she has been talking about me."

"I didn't say that." Her voice sharpens. "I said people listen to her."

A beat passes between us.

"She doesn't like the competition," I say, more to myself than to her.

Caren shrugs. "She's been working the circuit a long time. And you showed up with your aunt's truck and a cheeky name. Now you have a real-life pet," she juts her chin at Teriyaki. "She doesn't like you."

Caren starts walking away, but not before tossing one last remark over her shoulder. "You want people to stop talking? Give them something better to chew on."

With that, she saunters off, leaving me with a chicken, a blocked-off barn, and a thousand new questions.

Teriyaki lets out a dramatic *bawk bawk* in response.

I pull out my phone and start scrolling through Brad's Instagram. If Caren saw something on there, I need to find it. Brad's most recent posts are nothing special—generic food shots, overused hashtags, staged grinning selfies. But then—

"Hmm. What's this?" I ask, crouching down and showing Teriyaki the photo. She pecks at the screen, her beak hitting Brad's face with a satisfying *thunk*.

"Hey!" I pull my phone away. "I don't like him either, but don't break my screen."

I pause on a photo taken the day before the festival. The caption reads: *Made a new friend!* He has a goofy grin and his arm draped over an alpaca in the foreground, but it's the background that makes my stomach drop.

Adam and Kaydee are there. They're not posing. They're *arguing.*

Kaydee's arms are crossed, her glare sharp enough to cut. Adam is pointing at Brad, his face twisted with something close to anger.

This must be what Adam was telling me about. He saw Brad not long ago. I check the date when this was uploaded.

A week before the festival.

This must've been the festival preview Adam mentioned.

I zoom in again and look at Kaydee's angry face while Adam is pointing at Brad. This must've been when Brad dropped that offhanded comment about him being the dad and everything blew up.

Adam's been spiraling ever since. Kaydee too. And looking at the photo now—her posture, Adam's expression, Brad's smirk, I can see it.

This is where it started to unravel.

I zoom in. Peeling red paint. Ivy creeping up the fence.

The barn.

All three of them were there, days before the murder. And whatever happened didn't stay in that barn—it fractured something.

Caren's seen this photo, and she's running with it. But this isn't her scoop. It's a dead end.

I know the story behind that moment, and it doesn't involve Seth, or Helena, or me.

So I'll let her chase it.

Because if Adam's already hiding things, and Layla's whispering poison, and Caren's stirring up chaos—

Then someone else out there knows what really happened.

And they might do whatever it takes to keep it buried.

I scratch Teriyaki behind the wings, tuck my phone away, and head back to the truck.

Let them talk.

I'll keep digging.

Chapter Twenty-One

On my way back to the truck, I stop by the carnival section. Bright pennant flags flap overhead, strung between wooden poles like a rainbow-colored canopy. Kids shriek with laughter as they whiz by on a zip line, while a tired carnival barker with a megaphone tries to drum up excitement for the ring toss.

"Win a giant duck for your lucky duck!" His voice is hoarse, like he's been shouting all day.

"You can explore the ground while I check out the area," I tell Teriyaki, giving her leash a gentle tug.

When I was researching chickens last night, I read that they don't have street smarts. Not sure if that's true, but the last thing I want is for Teriyaki to chase a butterfly into a bounce house.

She tilts her head, considering me.

"I just want to see what all the fuss is about," I explain.

"Bawk." She spreads her wings, spinning in a circle.

"I'm not looking for Detective Kane," I say.

"Cluck, cluck." Teriyaki pecks at my shoe.

"Hey, stop that!" I jump back. "All right, fine! So what if I am? I'm curious to see him in a domestic setting." The thought of him in relaxed jeans and a snug black T-shirt playing with his nephew sounds . . . distractingly appealing.

Scanning the area, I don't see him or the sister he waved to yesterday. But I do spot the pregnant couple from earlier. The wife is sitting at a table, devouring a powdered-sugar-covered funnel cake while her husband massages her feet. She rests a hand on her swollen belly and looks blissfully content.

The sight reminds me of Kaydee.

She's been looking queasy all weekend, constantly clutching her stomach, slipping off to the bathroom during quiet moments. But now I'm wondering if it's more than morning sickness.

I mentally rewind the past few days.

Both Kaydee and Adam have lied to me. Neither of them were honest about how recently they saw Brad. Kaydee gave the impression that she hardly knew him when the reality is, she worked with him for three months and hooked up with him.

I still see her zoned out face in the dark bathroom right before I found Brad. Like she'd seen a ghost. Then there's that smeared stain on her shirt, which I've yet to get an explanation for.

Pulling out my phone, I go back to that photo Brad posted. Adam and Kaydee arguing in the background. The more I stare at it, the more I get this prickly feeling. Did Brad push too hard that day with his comments? Did he threaten something? Reveal something?

Or maybe Kaydee was already primed to explode and Brad lit the fuse.

And then there's Conner, telling me that Kaydee is good at making problems disappear. What kind of problems?

I mean, yeah, she's pregnant. But what if there's more to it than that? People do weird stuff when they're guilty. I should know.

I still remember how poorly I tried to cover up eating my dad's very last blueberry muffin. The man had been looking forward to it all day. I panicked and tried to blame my parents' dog Winnie, a pudgy Boston terrier with the criminal mastermind skills of a throw pillow. I even scattered crumbs near her bed like I was staging a crime scene. It was a flimsy coverup.

My point is, guilt makes people act strangely. Over-the-top strange.

Is that what's happening with Kaydee?

Either way, I've got a bad feeling about what that photo really shows. About what it means.

Before I can spiral further, Teriyaki's leash tugs me back to reality. "All right, girl. Time to get back to work."

She waddles along happily, but I freeze when a woman in a wide-brimmed hat barrels toward me, her attention glued to the tablet in her hands.

"Teriyaki!" I scoop her up before the woman collides with me.

"Gosh darn it!" she exclaims, her tablet clattering to the ground.

I recognize her a second too late. "Peyton, right? You're Brad's assistant."

She gives me a puzzled look, then smiles. "Chicken truck, right?"

"Kluckin' Good," I remind her. "I'm Beth."

"That's right. I still need to meet your twin brother and hopefully get a picture of him in his cow costume for the article I'm writing for the magazine."

"Let me know when, I'll make sure he and Rylie are in full livestock mode. Is that gonna be okay?" I point at her device.

Peyton kneels to retrieve the tablet. She brushes a bit of gravel from the edge of the case. "No harm done. At least it didn't land in a puddle this time."

"This time?" I ask.

She grins. "I'm not known for my coordination." She stands and tucks the tablet under one arm.

"Sorry about that," I say, adjusting Teriyaki in my arms.

"No worries. I shouldn't have been looking at a screen while walking in a busy place. And who is this cutie?" She waves at my chicken like she's only now noticed her.

"Meet Teriyaki!" I scratch under her chin, and she nuzzles into my wrist. "She's been my new buddy this weekend."

"She's not going to become a new addition to the men—"

"No!" I cut her off, cradling Teriyaki protectively against my chest. "She's my friend. We don't eat our friends."

"I think Brad would have liked her," Peyton laughs.

I force a fake smile. The thought of him being around Teriyaki does not fly with me.

"He wasn't exactly an animal person," I say.

"That's right." She nods. "After he ran into you at that bakery, he told me the two of you dated, so I guess you know all about his general dislike of animals. But I think he would've liked her anyway. May I?" She reaches out to brush Teriyaki's feathers.

"How's covering the festival going?" I ask.

"Better than I expected," she says. "I've been busy with the event coverage. Editing photos, chasing people for quotes, sampling the various cuisines offered."

"I saw the post you tagged us in. Thank you for that."

It was a compilation post of some of the food being offered at the festival. Our truck along with five others were mentioned by name.

She waves it off. "You and your team have some of the best food I've tasted so far. It was an easy choice."

I smile. "It means a lot. Every little bit helps."

"If you see any good photo ops—especially with your brother and the cow costume—just holler. I want to make the article as fun as possible."

An old-fashioned honking sounds, and I look around to see where it's coming from.

"That's me." Peyton shifts her bag and tablet, taking out her phone. "It's my calendar telling me to do something." She taps on the screen a few times, then sighs.

"Looks like you're busy," I say, catching a glimpse of her schedule.

"Too busy," she says, not quite joking. "And I'm still finishing edits on Brad's last piece. I promised him I'd help make it sing."

That gives me pause. "You're still working on something of Brad's?"

She nods. "He didn't like turning things in until they were perfect. Even his drafts read like polished prose. This was already slated for release next week."

"The magazine will still publish his articles even though he died?"

"At least the next three that were already in the pipeline," she says. "Mr. Collins wants them wrapped by end of next week. Said we owe it to Brad to finish what he started."

"Must be tough."

"It is," she admits. "But it helps, having something else to focus on."

"How is your boss taking the news of Brad's death?" I ask.

"Not good," she says.

"I hate to sound morbid, but," I pause, trying to be delicate as possible, "does this mean you'll be taking over Brad's role now?"

"I'll most likely need to start job hunting," Peyton says, adjusting the hat perched low on her brow. It's a stylish piece, summery but sharp.

"What do you mean?"

"*The City and Beyond* used to be more balanced. But ever since the new owners took over, it's become a boys' club." She twists the band of her festival pass. "Brad was their golden goose. Flashy, loud, always chasing whatever was trending. The kind of guy who'd lick barbecue sauce off a stranger's thumb if it got views."

I wrinkle my nose. "Seriously?"

She nods. "That clip got like two million views last month. Mr. Collins couldn't stop raving about it." Her voice is flat, tinged with something between envy and exasperation. "Brad played the game. I won't."

"Wow," I shake my head, unable to understand why someone would want to do that.

"Clicks talk. And Brad . . . Brad delivered them." Her tone's not exactly admiring, but it's not bitter, just resigned.

"What do you think you'll do next?"

"Not sure," she admits, adjusting the strap on her bag. "I have a contact I can reach back out to, and I still have my blog I can focus on. I'm glad I listened to Kaydee when she told me to keep it going."

"You know Kaydee Foley?" I ask, keeping my tone light.

"Sure." Peyton says, swatting a fly.

"That makes sense. If you guys worked at the same magazine—"

"We actually met through my blog," she cuts in. "Kaydee messaged me years ago about partnering as a micro-influencer."

"No way," I smile. "What a small world."

"Right? We hit it off. Later, I ended up working at the magazine before it sold to the new owners."

"Were you guys close?"

Peyton hesitates. "Work-close, I guess. Friendly, but didn't braid each other's hair on weekends or anything."

I think of how close I am to Rylie. We work together, but we're also best friends. I know how those lines blur.

"Did you keep in touch after Kaydee left the magazine?"

"Kinda," she admits. "Life causes people to drift, but when I texted her I'd be here for the festival, she responded right away. We made loose plans to grab drinks after the first day."

"That's nice," I say.

"It would've been."

"What do you mean?"

"Bawk!" Teriyaki flaps her wings wildly, trying to get down.

The moment I set her down she chases after a food crumb tumbling in the breeze.

"We were supposed to meet up that night," Peyton says, watching her. "I even picked the place. But Kaydee blew me off."

I pause. The first day of the festival was when Brad died. If she knew about his death already, that could've thrown a wrench into everything.

Then again, if she didn't . . .

"Any reason why?" I ask.

"She said she was swamped. But she seemed off even before that. When Brad and I saw her during the walkthrough at the farm last week, she was weird. Jumpy. Distracted. She wasn't acting like herself, maybe scattered is the right word." She looks at Teriyaki, her brows drawing down like she's wrestling with the memory "I don't know, maybe she's stressed." She forces a smile. "It would've been nice, but it's fine."

I stay quiet, letting the silence stretch. Because I know something Peyton doesn't. The truth behind why Kaydee has been acting weird since seeing Brad last week.

But it's not my place to tell Peyton.

Still, a quiet question lodges in the back of my mind.

Why did Kaydee back out of those drinks?

"I gotta go," Peyton says. "But let me know if your brother is open to a photo op as a cow."

Peyton walks away, and I'm about to leave when I spot Kaydee leaning against a tree, staring off into the distance.

I tug on Teriyaki's leash and head over. Kaydee stands with her arms crossed, shoulders curled inward like she's trying to disappear. Her gaze is fixed on a dad holding his infant son, her expression tight.

She doesn't notice me until I'm beside her. "Kaydee."

She looks over, eyes wide and glassy. "Beth. Hi."

Up close, she looks even worse. Shallow skin, chapped lips, and a bone-deep weariness that blurs her usual polish. Exhaustion? Stress? Or something else

Teriyaki clucks, jutting her head curiously toward Kaydee.

"That dad," Kaydee says, forcing a smile. "It's like the world disappears for him." She wipes her eyes, watching the dad dance with his baby.

"You've looked a little . . . off all weekend," I say gently. "You okay? Not eating? Not sleeping? Or does everything smell terrible?"

She flinches, then sighs. "God. Is it that obvious?"

"Morning sickness?"

Kaydee's shoulders sag. "I don't know why they call it morning sickness," she complains. "I feel awful all day."

Teriyaki struts in lazy figure eights around Kaydee's feet. "Sometimes when I'm upset, talking helps."

Kaydee doesn't respond right away. When she does, her voice is barely a whisper. "Everything feels so . . . messy. These last eight weeks have been a roller coaster. How am I supposed to make this work?"

"With Adam?" I keep my tone gentle. "He's worried about you."

Kaydee scoffs. "Did he send you?"

"No. He just mentioned it."

She studies me, as if deciding whether to believe me. Slowly, her shoulders relax. "Adam's the father," she admits. "We've always been on again, off again. When it's good, it's amazing. But when it's bad . . ." She shakes her head. "I even quit my last job for him."

"At the magazine?"

She nods. "Adam didn't like me working with Brad. Thought we were getting too close."

"Were you? During the three months you worked together."

She gives a pitiful laugh at being caught in her lie. "At first, no. But then . . . maybe. I don't know. Brad was like that with everyone. Pushy, magnetic."

"How long have you and Adam been dating?"

"A year, maybe a little longer."

I pause, trying to make sense of it. "So, you knew Brad before you worked with him?"

Kaydee nods slowly. "Yeah. I'd met him through Adam. They were friends, but Adam started pulling back when he got sober. Brad stuck around anyway."

I nod. "When Brad joined the magazine, you ended up working together?"

"Kind of. Our departments overlapped sometimes. I was there three months with Brad before everything went sideways."

"Was Adam pulling away before or after you hooked up with Brad?" I ask.

Her eyes flick to mine. "Adam told you?"

"Seth, actually. All of us were in the same friend circle when I dated Brad," I explain. "But you know that."

She nods. "Adam told me the whole story between you and Brad. Dumped for his step-cousin, that's awful." She wipes her nose. "Adam started pulling away from me a couple of weeks before I slept with Brad. It was his sobriety. He needed space to focus on himself and we agreed to take a break. I was working late nights, so was Brad. Late nights turned into late dinners . . ."

"And late dinners turned into a late-night—"

"Mistake," she finishes. "Brad was a mistake."

I feel that. Teriyaki lets out a disgruntled squawk, fluffing her feathers like she's judging Kaydee.

"So Adam's distance wasn't because of Brad, at least not at first."

Kaydee shakes her head. "No, it started because of his sobriety. Band life doesn't exactly promote clean living, but things with Brad haven't helped."

"What happened after your mistake with Brad?"

"Nothing at first," she admits. "I told Brad it was one and done. He didn't care. It was Adam who blew up."

"You told him?"

"I had to," she twists her necklace. "Adam called a week later about our break, and I told him about Brad. I didn't expect him to take it so hard."

"Really?" I can't hide my shock. "You slept with his best friend—or former best friend, whatever—and didn't think that would wreck him?"

"I know you're right," she snaps. "Don't you think I know that?"

"I don't know what to think," I admit. "But I'm curious, how did you patch things up with Adam?"

"I left the magazine," she says. "It was the only chance I had to make things work with Adam. I took a job with Conner here at the farm. About a month later I found out I was pregnant. For a while, things were okay. Then Brad showed up."

I nod slowly. "I saw a photo. Brad's Instagram. You and Adam were in the background. It looked like you were having a fight."

Kaydee winces. "I didn't even know he'd taken a photo."

"Why was he here before the festival?"

"I didn't know he was going to be," she says. "When the magazine called Conner for a press pass, I vouched for them, but I didn't expect Brad would be so ballsy to show up. He knew I worked here."

"He did?"

"I told Mr. Collins I was taking a position at Green Family Farm. I didn't even give two weeks' notice, I just left. Word spread fast."

She tugs at her sleeve, voice tightening.

"Conner told me the magazine wanted to do a walk-through before the festival. Get the lay of the land. I wish I'd called in sick that day."

"But how does that explain the photo of you and Adam arguing in the background?"

"Adam came to take me to lunch, but I felt awful. Couldn't eat. Hearing him describe food made me throw up. I was dry-heaving by the barn when Brad showed up."

I brace myself.

"He made a scene when he found out I was pregnant. Said maybe the baby was his. It wasn't funny. Adam lost it. He got physical with Brad and said some awful things to me. We've been fighting ever since."

"I can't say I blame him."

Kaydee's head snaps up, her body tensing. "What?"

"You lied to me, what's to say you haven't been lying to Adam?" I cross my arms, watching her closely. "At the beginning of the festival, I asked if you knew Brad, you said no. But you did. You worked with him for three months. You were more than friends."

Kaydee's face darkens. "That was months ago."

"Doesn't change the fact that you lied," I say evenly. "Why?"

She shifts her weight, her eyes flicking away. "I didn't think it mattered," she says, but there's something off in her tone.

I tilt my head. "Didn't matter? Or you didn't want anyone to know?"

She exhales sharply. "Fine. I was embarrassed, okay? Ashamed. Brad wasn't a great person, he was a mistake I hooked up with. And when he died, I panicked. People twist things. Jump to conclusions." Her gaze lifts, wary. "People like you."

I tense. "That's not fair."

"Isn't it?" she asks. "Be honest, Beth. When you found out, what was your first thought?"

I open my mouth, then close it.

She huffs a humorless laugh. "Exactly."

I don't argue. Because the truth is, when I realized Kaydee had a deeper connection to Brad, suspicion hit before logic could catch up. Kaydee shakes her head. "I didn't kill Brad. And I'm tired of people looking at me like I might have."

I hesitate, then press. "Then tell me about the shirt."

Her brow furrows. "What shirt?"

"The first day of the festival, I saw you in the bathroom. You looked out of it. You were wearing a maroon shirt with a jagged stain around your waist."

She exhales, looking away. "I had morning sickness. I threw up right before the gates opened. Tried to rinse it out, but it was a mess."

"That was vomit?" I ask. "On the bottom of your shirt? Please."

"It was," she insists. "Ketchup and vomit. Not blood, if that's what you're thinking."

"And you threw it out after the police spoke with you?"

"In the dumpster behind the staff tent. I didn't want to walk around smelling like that all day."

I study her face. She doesn't flinch. Doesn't look away. For once, she seems . . . honest.

She might be telling the truth.

Or she might be saying exactly what she needs to.

I take a breath. "What did Brad want from you? If he followed you around the barn, he must've wanted something."

"He was looking for Adam, said he wanted to talk about things." Her voice hardens. "But Brad learned I was pregnant and made his comment."

"Kaydee, are you sure Adam didn't—"

"No." Her voice is sharp, final. "He might hate Brad, but he's not a killer."

I want to believe her.

But anger, betrayal, and resentment can drive anyone over the edge. A small cough interrupts us. Conner is standing a few feet away, his expression neutral, and his timing perfect.

"Sorry to interrupt," he says. "I need to borrow Kaydee."

Teriyaki brushes against my leg. I crouch, running a hand over her warm, feathery back, grounding myself. My phone buzzes with a new text.

Rylie: SOS!

Chapter Twenty-Two

I race back to the truck, clutching Teriyaki under one arm, wondering what's going on. Rylie's SOS text didn't provide any details about what's happening, just the three letters. By the time I spot Kluckin' Good, I'm bracing for the worst. Flashing lights, police sirens, and Seth being hauled away in handcuffs.

Instead, I'm greeted by a massive line of customers snaking around the walkway and blocking other food trucks. Relief washes over me. This I can handle.

I duck inside the truck, unhooking Teriyaki from her harness. She lets out a contented cluck as I place her in her makeshift nest of rags by the storage bins.

"Good girl," I murmur, giving her a quick pat before washing my hands and tying my apron around my waist.

"Well, well, look who decided to show up," Seth says, flipping a slider with dramatic flair. "Welcome to the party. What took so long?"

"It's called being fashionably late," I quip, getting wings ready for the fryer. "You should try it sometime. Might make you more popular. God knows you need all the help you can get."

"Right. Popularity is something you know *all* about." He arches his back. "I've been standing at this grill so long my feet are about to file for worker's comp."

"Poor baby," I tease. "Remind me to start a GoFundMe for your suffering."

"Make sure it includes hazard pay," he fires back, gesturing toward the growing line outside. "I've had to dodge three hangry customers and a guy who kept calling me 'chief.'"

"Tragic," I deadpan, sliding beside him at the fryer, I drop a basket of wings into the hot oil. The sizzle is loud, but it's nothing compared to the chatter outside. We move in a well-rehearsed rhythm, frying, flipping, and plating as fast as we can manage.

"Switch me spots," I tell Rylie as I pass her. She's doing a great job handing out orders, but I need her elsewhere. "You can garnish faster than me. Start on those fries, will you?"

"On it," she says, moving to the warming station.

I take over at the window, smiling and chatting with customers as I pass out their orders. Things are moving smoothly until a guy in a baseball cap leans in.

"Can I get two orders of Beats and Bites sliders?" he asks.

"That was the last basket we handed out," Seth calls over his shoulder, digging through the chest freezer. "It'll be another ten minutes."

Rylie's head pops up, her eyes wide with excitement. "I can cook more!"

Seth and I whip around in unison. She's already reaching for a stack of patties.

"Rylie, no—"

"I've got this! I've been practicing with the fryer!" she declares, her voice brimming with determination as if she's about to save the day.

"That's not the same thing—"

"I got this!" She cuts Seth off, her confidence unwavering as she grabs a bottle of oil and squeezes it across the flattop.

The world slows down as the golden liquid pools on the grill. Seth's eyes widen in horror.

"Not that bottle!" he yells, lunging toward her, his arm outstretched for the truffle oil.

But it's too late.

Rylie's already slapped a patty onto the flattop, and the sizzle is all wrong.

A loud hiss erupts, followed by a plume of thick, black smoke rising like a signal of culinary disaster. The acrid smell hits first, sharp and unmistakable.

Then the smoke detector screams.

Seth dives for the knobs, twisting them off in one swift motion. "Kill the heat!"

"Oh no, oh no, oh no!" Rylie chants, frantically waving a spatula like she's trying to part the smoke with sheer willpower. "What did I do wrong?"

"You used the wrong oil!" Seth barks, grabbing a towel to fan at the smoke.

I'm already coughing, stumbling toward the service window. "Open the windows and doors wider!" I shove the service window up as far as it'll go. Sticking my head out, I gasp for fresh air. "Sorry, folks! Quick break!"

Groans ripple from the line of waiting customers, but the chaos inside the truck drowns them out.

Teriyaki decides it's her time to shine. She squawks loudly, her wings flapping as if the end is near.

Before I can react, she launches out of her nest like a feathery cannonball.

"Teriyaki, no!" I duck as she zooms past my head and lands smack on the prep counter.

A container of panko breadcrumbs tips, spilling across the counter like sand.

"*Frango bebé*!" Rylie shouts, diving for Teriyaki, but the chicken flaps out of reach, leaving a breadcrumb tornado in her wake.

Seth is still fanning the smoke detector with a towel, muttering curses under his breath. I grab Teriyaki midflight, scooping her up before she causes more damage.

"Sorry, girl, you're going back to your nest." I place her carefully into her little corner, where she settles with an indignant huff.

"And this is why a chicken doesn't belong in a food truck," Seth snaps, still swatting at the air.

"Teriyaki isn't the problem. She's part of the branding," I argue, glaring at him as I brush breadcrumbs off my shirt. "And ambiance."

"Ambiance? Sure. Until she flies into the fryer one day."

Rylie, meanwhile, stands frozen in front of the grill, staring at the charred patty and the oil-slick disaster she created.

"I was trying to help," she says, her voice small. "What did I do wrong? I oiled the flattop like you guys always do."

"You used truffle oil," Seth explains, his tone softening. "It has a low smoke point. It's only for topping fries, not for the grill. You should've used vegetable oil."

"How was I supposed to know that?" Rylie asks.

"Maybe," Seth says gently, "leave the cooking to us for now."

"I didn't mean for this to happen," she sniffles.

"I know," I say, taking a deep breath. "We'll keep practicing, Rylie. But next time, maybe we'll try it in a bigger, less . . . flammable space, okay?"

She nods, her shoulders sagging. "I guess I'll stick with handing out samples and coupons."

"Great idea," Seth soothes as the smoke detector finally goes silent.

The line outside groans again, realizing there won't be any food for a while, but I glance at Teriyaki. She's now resting in her nest, and I shake my head, equal parts exasperated and amused.

While we wait for the last of the smoke to clear from our truck, the three of us—plus Teriyaki, who is perched smugly on my lap—sit on a bench nearby. The smoky haze lingers in the air, making my throat feel raw, but the real weight pressing down on me isn't from the air quality. It's from everything else swirling in my mind.

"Beth!" Danny calls, striding over from his truck.

"Hey, Danny," I chuckle. It still cracks me up that his name isn't Al. Also, he's not remotely fat. Danny owns Fat Al's Burgers, a truck known for serving half-pound gut-busters and the best Philly cheesesteaks you'll find in the Bay Area. "What's up?"

"I came to offer a trade," he begins, then pauses, sniffing the air. "Three baskets of wings for three Philly cheesesteaks. But, uh . . . I'm having second thoughts."

"Nah," I wave him off. "Our truck will be aired out in another ten minutes. Tops."

He gives me a skeptical look, and I don't blame him. We might be clear of the worst of it, but the scent of singed oil is still clinging to my clothes.

Danny shrugs. "All right, if you say so. Aside from your impromptu smoke show, looks like you've been doing pretty good."

"We've been slammed," Seth says.

"But so have you. Every time I pass your truck, there's a line of people," I add.

Danny laughs. "People can't resist a gooey Philly cheesesteak."

I grin, trying to hold on to the easy energy of the conversation, but then he says it.

"I'll admit, when I heard about the death I was worried it'd scare people off. Doesn't seem to be the case."

"Where did you hear about it?" I ask carefully.

"It's all anyone in the vendor row's been talking about." Danny says like it should be obvious. "No one seems to know what happened. Anyway, I'll be back in twenty minutes with your order." He gives a casual wave as he leaves, oblivious to the fact that he lit a match in my already overactive brain.

I guess it's good that Danny doesn't know I found Brad's body. But if all the vendors are talking about it, how is there still nothing in the news?

Unease slithers down my back. Conner.

"I pulled some strings. The media's holding off."

He said it so casually, like it was nothing. But now I can't stop questioning how much sway Conner has. How long can he keep a lid on something like this?

Rylie frowns. "Danny's right, though. You'd think people would be buzzing about Brad by now."

I turn to her. "They should be. But I haven't seen anything either. I've checked, not a single mention of Brad's death."

Rylie is already scrolling on her phone. "Let's see if the Internet's caught on since Thursday." Her face tightens as she reads. "Hmm."

Seth leans in. "What is it?"

"There's a minor blip about an 'accident' at the Flavors of the Bay food festival, but no details about what happened." Rylie scowls at her screen. "But get this—the article mentions that six years ago, a death occurred at the Green Family Farm."

She clears her throat. "Apparently, six years ago, a worker died while dismantling a gazebo. He was wearing fall protection but didn't connect the D-clip to the lanyard. The family sued, but the lawsuit was dropped. Kevin Green, the farm's former manager, was quoted as saying, 'Legally, the farm had no liability in the unfortunate death, but our prayers and condolences are with his family.'"

She scrolls further. "The article says OSHA, the Occupational Safety and Health Administration, closed the case after ruling it a worker error. No charges were filed."

"It really does seem like it was just a tragic accident," I say.

Rylie's thumb hovers over her screen. "Some of the comments are saying otherwise."

I frown. "Comments?"

She turns her phone so we can see. “Several people are calling it ‘convenient’ the farm wasn’t held responsible. One user says their cousin used to work events here and called it a ‘disaster waiting to happen,’ whatever that means. Another’s wondering if someone in the Green family pulled strings.”

Seth sighs. “Internet sleuths at it again.” He scans the screen. “People are questioning whether the farm can survive, especially after the pandemic hit them hard.”

A cold sinking feeling spreads through me. “Conner told us the farm was struggling, but I didn’t realize the media knew too.”

Rylie chews her lip. “If the first death was an accident, what does that have to do with Brad?”

“The media won’t care,” Seth says. “Two deaths at the same place. They’ll connect the dots, whether they’re worth connecting or not.”

“It doesn’t help Conner is acting like a jerk about things,” I say. “He cares more about his family’s farm than someone dying. How will the public view his attitude?”

Seth’s jaw tightens. “It’s a PR nightmare waiting to happen. It doesn’t matter what Conner does. If he keeps the festival going, he’s heartless. If he shuts it down, he’s hiding something. It’s a lose-lose situation.”

“This article’s already questioning his priorities,” Rylie says, scrolling further. “Someone has caught wind of Brad’s death. If the media keeps digging, this could spiral out of control fast.”

“This is more than Conner’s reputation at stake.” Seth sighs. “Bad press and public perception can ruin everything. When something tragic happens at a major event, the media scrutinizes everyone involved. Vendors, performers, even sponsors. This could kill the festival permanently.”

I nod. “A second death at the Green Family Farm will raise safety concerns, accident or not.”

Seth's expression darkens. "If the farm or festival is found negligent in any way regarding Brad's death, lawsuits could follow. Insurance costs could skyrocket—or they could lose their insurance altogether. No insurance means no festival, period."

I swallow hard. "So when Conner said there was too much on the line for him, he *wasn't* exaggerating." The reality settles over me like thick fog. "If police don't catch the killer, this could be the end of the farm and the festival."

"One scandal can ruin a business," Seth says grimly. "If Brad's death causes the festival to collapse, it's not just Conner's problem—it's an economic hit to everyone. Local businesses, food vendors, surrounding towns. This festival brings in a lot of income for a lot of people."

"That's a lot of weight on Conner," I admit. "But his attitude isn't helping."

Seth shakes his head. "Even if the police catch the killer, it all depends on how the media spins this. And right now? It doesn't look good."

Chapter Twenty-Three

I'm wiping down the counter when a throat clears outside my serving window.

"What can I get you?" I smile, expecting another chicken wing order.

But when I make eye contact, I freeze.

It's him.

Again.

The same attractive bearded customer who's been to my truck twice already.

My hand pauses mid-wipe, gripping the cloth tightly. "Oh! Hi again," I manage, my voice tinged with genuine surprise.

"Hellloooo," Rylie says, inserting herself into the moment. "Nice to see you again. Did you miss us?"

I nudge her back with my hip. "Ignore her," I tell him, my cheeks flushing.

He grins, clearly enjoying my flustered reaction. "Told you that you'd earned a customer for life," his tone warm and teasing.

"Is that so?" Rylie says, pushing her way past me again. "Or are you here for something more?"

"Don't you have something better to do?" I snap, pushing her away.

"Oh, this is more interesting," she says, her eyes sparking as she watches the man.

"Go!" I force her away.

"*Tudo bem, tudo bem*," she laughs.

I turn back to him. That shy smile, part laughter, part something else, pulls me in.

"Sorry about that," I say, laughing nervously. "Didn't think 'for life' would start so soon."

"What can I say? Those were some tasty truffle fries." He winks, locking those golden brown eyes on mine with magnetic intensity. "Can I use this today?" He fishes the coupon from his back pocket.

I notice his beard's thicker than before, adding a rugged edge I hadn't appreciated. His thick, wavy hair looks like it's begging for a touch. Before I can answer, Seth appears, arms crossed. "That coupon is for outside the festival at one of our regular locations."

"Shame," the guy says, tucking the coupon away.

I catch my gaze lingering on how his jeans hug those muscular thighs, and my cheeks flare.

"But I'd be lying if I said I only stopped by to score some free wings," he adds with another wink.

Why is everyone in the world able to wink but me?

"Uh-huh. And just what are you hoping to score?" Seth's tone is dripping with suspicion.

"*Pare com isso*!" Rylie scolds Seth. "Don't listen to him. He's overheating, and the truck's cooling system is terrible." She shoots me a look that says "Get it together," then drags Seth toward the back of the truck.

I swallow hard, forcing myself to focus. "What can I get you?" My voice is steadier than it feels.

"Whatever you recommend." He flashes me another slightly shy smile. "And if I'm being honest, I'm hoping your number comes with it."

"Oh, heck no, buddy!" Seth bellows from the back of the truck.

Rylie's rapid-fire Portuguese scolding drowns him out. "*Burro estúpido!*"

I snort at her calling Seth a stupid donkey—one of the few Portuguese phrases I proudly know—earning an indignant huff from my brother, who apparently knows it too.

Meanwhile, the man waits patiently, still grinning like he knows exactly how much he's ruffling my feathers.

Focus, Beth!

My pulse quickens, and I'm unsure if it's worrying about Seth's next outburst or the flirtatious stranger in front of me.

"Recommendation?" I study his rugged face. "Our weekend special is the Golden Gate Heat Wings. Sweet at first, with a fiery finish."

"Golden Gate Heat Wings," he repeats, his smile widening. "Perfect. I'll take that."

"That'll be $12," I say, ringing up his order, trying to play it cool. Well, as cool as *I* can.

It's hard when his brown eyes are watching me. He's not as handsome as Detective Kane, but that's not really a fair comparison. Detective Kane is in a league of his own. A league that ignores me unless I'm involved in a murder or he wants a free meal.

Maybe I just need a date? That's all this is. I've been surrounded by Rylie and Seth, who are grossly in love, and now this handsome stranger is smiling at me like he wants more than my wings.

That explains everything.

Sure, the guy smiling at me is good-looking, and maybe that's what I need. A date with a good-looking stranger. My last date was with Larry *and his mother*, after all.

He hands me a twenty-dollar bill, our fingers touching briefly. The warmth of his skin lingers on mine.

"Keep the change," his eyes never leave mine.

I nod, turning to prep his order. Tossing the wings into the spiced honey sauce, I shake the bowl with more confidence than I feel. By the time I hand him the basket, I've convinced myself I'm fine.

Mostly.

"Here you go!" Scrunching up my face, I concentrate hard and attempt to wink again.

I'm pretty sure I end up resembling a creepy doll with malfunctioning eyes.

"Umm." He takes his order. "Are you all right?"

My face relaxes, and I open both eyes, blushing furiously. "I'm fine," I say, fiddling with the rag I left on the counter. "I was trying to wink back."

Seth's laugh booms through the truck, and I want to kill him.

The man's confusion melts into a soft laugh. "Maybe stick to both eyes open for now."

"Noted," I mutter, ignoring their laughter.

He lifts the basket, inspecting it for a moment before glancing back at me.

"You seem disappointed," I say, curious.

"A little," he admits. "I was hoping to get your number."

Heat flames my face. Is this what a hot flash feels like?

"I'm working," I say apologetically. "But I can give you my name. It's Beth."

His grin softens into something warmer, more genuine. "It's nice to meet you, Beth. I'm Gavin, but my friends call me Gav."

"Gav," I repeat, testing it out. It feels weird in my mouth, too familiar too soon. "Gav . . . er, Gavin."

He laughs. A deep, warm sound that starts in his chest and spills over, lighting up his whole face. It hits me like a heat wave—unexpected and a little dizzying.

"Not a fan?"

"I don't know," I laugh with him. "You know what?" I grab our supply notepad. "Why not? Here."

I scribble down my number, heart pounding. Just as I'm writing the last digit—

"Lloyd." Detective Kane's voice cuts through the air like a scalpel.

My hand jerks, making my last digit a questionable squiggle. I glance up and see both men standing in front of me.

Gavin, charming and confident, his smile still lingering from our shared laugh.

Detective Kane, all cold authority, his jaw set like he's walked into an ambush.

The sight of them side by side makes my pulse skip like a scratched record.

"Detective," I say. My chest is pounding, and I feel like I've just been caught stealing a red thong again. "What can I do for you?"

"Just checking in," he says, eyes flicking to Gavin, then back to me. "Didn't realize you were . . . busy."

Gavin doesn't flinch. "Just picking up an order."

The tension crackles so hard I'm surprised the fryer doesn't short-circuit.

I tear the sheet from the notepad and shove it at Gavin. "Here."

Detective Kane's gaze sharpens as Gavin takes the paper.

"Is this a new customer loyalty program I should know about?" he asks dryly.

"You're hilarious, Detective," I grit through clenched teeth.

"Thank you," Gavin replies, flashing Detective Kane a cool smile as he tucks my number in his pocket. "I'll call you," he turns and walks away, whistling.

Detective Kane doesn't move. Doesn't blink.

I can feel his stare burning holes through me.

"Something I can get you?" I ask, not looking at him.

"I just stopped by for some—"

"Golden Oldie sliders on the house!" Rylie appears, shoving a basket at him. "Busy day. No need to linger."

He raises one eyebrow at her. "Did I order?"

"Consider it a chef's recommendation," she says. "To go, obviously."

Detective Kane glances at the food, then at me. "Should I be concerned about the customer ahead of me?"

"Nope," I force a smile. "He was just hungry."

His eyes narrow slightly. "Hungry can mean a lot of things."

I blink, caught off guard, my heart racing. "Uh—well, you know, wings are good at filling bellies."

He leans a little closer to the window, voice dropping. "Is that all he wanted? Just his belly filled?"

"Uh, I don't follow."

He chuckles. "I'm sure you do."

"Rylie!" I look at my best friend, my eyes screaming *help me!*

"It's a busy day, Detective," she nudges the basket closer. "We need to get back to work."

Without a word, he places a twenty-dollar bill on the ledge.

I blink, stunned. He actually paid.

"Thanks," he says, voice low but genuine.

As he walks away, I finally exhale.

Rylie hands me a napkin. "You look like you ran a marathon."

"I feel like I tripped over the starting line."

"There's no end in sight to people wanting wings and sliders," Rylie says, grabbing the last basket of each from the warmer. "Where did all these people come from?"

"I don't know," I say, eyeing the new line of customers.

She hands the order to a man. "If you enjoy the food, follow us online and check out our other locations."

The man nods, walking off with our last baskets of food.

"Sorry, everyone, we're sold out of wings and sliders," I announce. Groans and complaints erupt.

"We still have fries and mac-and-cheese poppers," I add quickly. "Or try Fat Al's for one of his cheesesteaks."

More grumbling, but they drift off. "Come back tomorrow!" I call, though no one's listening. Teriyaki clucks sharply from her crate in the corner. "I hear you, Teriyaki," I say. "We're ready to call it a day."

I hear a frustrated grunt, Turning around, I see Seth with a stormy expression. He picks up a griddle scraper and angrily attacks the flattop.

"Something the matter, Seth?" I ask.

"That was completely inappropriate earlier," he snaps.

"What was?"

Spinning around, he points the scraper at me. "Flirting with a customer. It's unprofessional."

I raise an eyebrow. "Gavin came back because he liked the food. That's customer loyalty."

"He wasn't coming back for the food. He was hitting on you, and you were encouraging him. This is a workplace, not a dating app!"

"Oh please." I fold my arms. "You should be glad I met someone on my own. Someone not hand-picked by Mom, like Larry Kuntz." I shudder thinking about the selfies he keeps sending me of him and his mother.

Seth snorts. "Okay, fine. Based on what you've shared, Larry has definite serial killer vibes. But a customer? We're supposed to be professional."

"Right," I say. "Because nothing says professionalism like you and Rylie making out next to the coleslaw."

Rylie, halfway to the sink with a bowl, freezes. "These, uh . . . need sanitizing."

"That's different," Seth flushes. "We're in a relationship."

"Exactly. Maybe Gavin and I could be too. Stop acting like my love life is a public safety threat."

"I thought you had the 'hots' for Detective Kane?" Seth challenges. "Or are you taking numbers like it's speed dating?"

"Oh, give me a break," I shoot back. "You don't even *like* Detective Kane!"

"I like him better than some rando trying to score your number!" Seth angrily waves his scraper around. "And what about Larry and his mom?"

I gasp. "Leave Larry out of this! You're being ridiculous! I didn't hand Gavin a room key and my Social Security number."

Seth opens his mouth, but I cut him off. "You're the one who told me I needed a date. So don't act all holier-than-thou when I take your advice!"

Seth stands there, speechless, frustration flickering across his face. Teriyaki lets out a loud squawk, making Rylie glance over. "Even Teriyaki thinks this argument is ridiculous," she says.

"Maybe she does," I mutter, unclipping my apron. "We're sold out, so I'm going for a walk." I turn to Rylie, ignoring Seth. "You can handle cleaning and closing."

I scoop Teriyaki from her crate, clip on her makeshift harness, and step outside. The breeze cools my temper, but my mind replays Seth's lecture.

"Who does he think he is, preaching from his soapbox like that?" I fume, setting Teriyaki down. She clucks in response, as if listening intently.

"Exactly. He and Rylie are gross all the time, but I smile at a customer and suddenly I'm unprofessional?" My anger ebbs, and I scratch her neck. "Thanks for listening, girl." I stand up, giving her leash a gentle tug. "Let's walk."

Watching Teriyaki waddle beside me lifts my mood. Pulling out my phone I send a group text to my parents.

Me: Just saying I love you.

I attach a picture of Teriyaki.

Me: Meet my new friend!

Dad replies first with two heart emojis, a rooster head, and a drumstick.

Mom, as expected, fires back.

Mom: I'm never going to get grandchildren if you keep spending all your free time with poultry.
Me: It's not my fault all the single men I find are dead.
Mom: Stop being morbid.
Dad: Stay safe, Bethy Boo!

Smiling, I pocket my phone as I run into someone.

"Watch it!"

Layla Gafford, reigning queen of ice-cold glares, looks me over like I'm something stuck to her shoe. "You're still here."

Layla is the last person I wanted to run into. From what I've been learning, she's the kind of woman who won't hesitate to spread malicious rumors, especially if she thinks you've slighted her. For whatever reason, she's had it out for me since day one of this festival.

Teriyaki pecks her shoe. I don't stop her. "We are. It's a food truck festival."

"It must be nice—walking around like nothing's wrong." Her eyes sharpen. "First you find a dead body, now you're stirring up trouble. Throwing suspicion on me to keep it off yourself?"

My pulse spikes. "Excuse me?"

"You're sniffing around like some amateur detective."

I match her stance. "Funny, I recall you screaming accusations when I found Brad. Forgive me if I don't appreciate the hypocrisy."

"Anyone found standing over a dead body shouldn't be here. And I've noticed you keep throwing my name around."

"What exactly do you think I've been saying?"

She studies me, then I notice a red smear on her shirt.

"What's that?" I point at the stain.

Layla tugs at her shirt to look. "None of your business. Now stay out of my way. You don't belong here." She storms off.

Teriyaki ruffles her feathers. "I don't like her tone either," I tell her.

"Buk!"

"Yeah, it probably was ketchup," I agree. Probably. Hopefully.

But that wasn't just attitude. That was a warning. Which means Layla isn't just defensive.

She's scared.

And I need to find out why.

Chapter Twenty-Four

Getting back to the truck, I release Teriyaki from her harness. She huffs, but I give her a pat and step inside. Rylie and Seth have cleaned everything and are knee-deep in tomorrow's prep work.

"I'm feeding Teriyaki," I say, grabbing the box of cornmeal I brought from home this morning.

"Beth, wait." Seth catches me at the door. "I'm sorry. I was out of line."

"About what?"

"If you want to hook up with a customer, who am I to stop you?"

"Wow. Stellar apology," I say. "I'm not 'hooking up' with anyone. If I were, it's none of your business."

"You're right," Seth says. "I was wrong. I'm sorry."

"Apology accepted—but only if you stop treating me like I need a babysitter."

"It's my job to protect you."

"Please, I've been protecting you all weekend. Which is my job because I'm your *older* sister."

"By two minutes!" Seth throws up his hands. "You act like you're two years older, when, in fact, legally you're only seven years old."

"How dare you!"

"*Parar*!" Rylie shouts over us. "Can't you two just agree it's both your jobs to protect the other?"

"Fine" Seth crosses his arms.

"Fine. But stay out of my love life," I tell him.

"What love life?" he teases.

"I hate you!"

"No, you don't," he calls as I stomp out of the truck to feed Teriyaki.

She's exactly where I left her, pecking at the ground. She spots me and waddles over. chirping happily for her dinner.

"You okay?" Rylie asks, joining me outside.

"Your boyfriend's annoying," I grumble.

"*Sim*," Rylie laughs. "But so are you."

"Rude."

She leans against the truck, watching Teriyaki. "While you were gone, I talked with one of the merch vendors. She saw Brad the morning he died, arguing with Helena."

I freeze. "Helena?"

Rylie nods. "The person the merch lady described sounded a lot like Helena."

"What'd she say?"

"Brad snapped some photos of her table, then walked off. The vendor didn't think much of it until some woman—Caren, I'm guessing—showed her a picture of Brad, asking if she'd seen him. That's when she remembered him. She also heard Helena say, 'Don't you realize what this could do to me and my bakery?' Then she followed him."

My spine tingles. I've known Helena for years. She's always been warm, friendly, a free cookie for anyone needing a pick-me-up. But would she confront Brad over a bad review? Follow him to the barn?

"Helena's business is everything," I say slowly. "If she thought Brad's review would ruin it . . ."

"You think she was angry enough to do something?"

"I don't know. But she never told me about that argument."

Rylie's already typing on her phone. "I'm adding it to our Kluckin' Clues list. Let's go over who we've got."

She scrolls, reading aloud. "Kaydee Foley. Festival manager. Control-freak energy. Access to the grounds early and had that weird stain moment in the bathroom. Also bought a tumbler the morning of the festival."

"Which is now gone." I remind her. "She also had a history with Brad."

Rylie nods. "Mystery Person from the path: Big hat, chunky sweater, fast pace, clearly trying not to be seen. Classic murder-y behavior."

"Too many matches for that description here. But I have a strong suspicion they weren't on a nature stroll."

She keeps going. "Layla Gafford. Roller Burger owner and general menace. Arrived right after the body was discovered. Could've been lurking the whole time."

"She also had a bad review from Brad about her truck," I add. "She's not the type to let things go. Could be motive."

"Conner Green," Rylie continues. "Festival director, family owns the farm, and he invited Brad. Might've had the most to lose if Brad trashed the event."

"Let's not forget Conner pulled strings with the media to hold off the story of Brad's death."

"Also not the first death to happen on the farm," Rylie adds.

"He's been too cold and callous for my taste." I say, thinking about his attitude.

"Helena Wynn," Rylie reads. "Local baker with a bad review hanging over her head. We know she argued with Brad the morning of his death."

"I also gave her a tumbler that is also missing," I say. "She thinks she lost it with all the commotion that happened on the first day of the festival."

"I guess that's plausible," Rylie says, even though neither of us buy it. "Next on the list is Adam Parker, aka Ivan Parks."

"Brad's former best friend," I say. "Brad broke the bro code and slept with Kaydee, then implied he might be the dad of her baby."

"Red flag city," Rylie says.

"Caren Ludwig," I read the name on Rylie's phone. "She's the former food critic Brad replaced. Looking to leverage his murder for her own gain. I don't trust her."

Rylie hesitates at the last name. "Seth Lloyd. Argued with Brad, punched him before the festival, police know about his bar fight. Protective of you. Possible motive. Possible opportunity."

Guilt gnaws at me. "I had to be honest about the possibility. But he's not a suspect. Remove him."

"It's what Inga Nevarez would've told you to do." Rylie deletes his name.

"Let's hit the talent show," I say. "Maybe we'll pick up something useful."

"I'll get Seth."

"I'll meet you there. Teriyaki is still eating."

Rylie leaves while I watch Teriyaki peck at the last crumbs. "Are you still open?" a voice asks.

Peyton stands smiling, hugging her tablet to her chest.

"Sorry, sold out."

"Bummer." She shifts the tablet in her hand.

A worn sticker on the back catches my attention—a talking mustache wearing a monocle with the words Foodies Unite.

Doesn't look like Peyton's style. But Brad's? Definitely.

"Did Brad give you that sticker?" I ask, nodding at the tablet. "When we were dating, he always said monocles were the underdog of the glasses world."

She laughs. "It's his. I cracked the screen on mine. So I'm borrowing it while I cover the rest of the assignment this weekend."

"Oh, right," I say. "Speaking of work, remember when you told me about a woman named Caren. Was it Caren Ludwig? How well did you know her?"

Her brows knit together. "Why?"

"She's been hassling me. I just want to know if I need to be more careful around her—if she's the type to twist things to fit a story."

Peyton thinks for a moment. "We worked together occasionally before Brad replaced her. She hated him for it—made a scene when she got fired."

"That fits," I mutter. "What was she like, aside from hating Brad?"

Peyton taps the tablet. "Competitive, nosy, always convinced she deserved more."

"Do you think she would . . ." I pantomime hitting my head.

"Kill Brad?" Peyton laughs. "Caren is nasty and difficult, but I don't think she'd kill someone."

"I hope you're right," I tell her. But I'm not so sure. Caren had motive to hate Brad. And she doesn't care about the truth, only the story.

That makes her unpredictable.

Peyton shifts her weight. "I hope this all gets resolved soon so we can move on and stop worrying."

Me too.

"If you're looking for food, maybe try Fat Al's or Bacon My Heart?" I suggest.

"Thanks!"

Peyton leaves, but the questions keep stacking. What if Caren's planting seeds to control the story? And is she the only one using Brad's death?

The weight of not knowing presses in, heavier than ever.

Chapter Twenty-Five

"Beth!" Rylie waves both arms like she's guiding a plane. "You missed the bluegrass band."

"Oh, bummer."

"Don't worry, there's something even better waiting for you." Her grin immediately puts me on high alert.

"What are you talking about?"

"How does five hundred dollars sound?"

"In cash?" I ask, suspicious.

"Vaudeville act in the talent show," she says.

I blink. "And that involves me how?"

"Rylie volunteered you," Seth says, smirking.

"What? No."

"It's for a cute little old man's illusionist act," Rylie says, smoothing things over like butter on burnt toast. "It's the answer to your car troubles. That clunker of yours costs money, you know."

"Stop calling Audrey a clunker." I glare at her. "She's a complicated lady. Which is her prerogative."

"A lady who sure spends a lot of time with guys under her hood." Seth quips.

"Your car is a money pit you can't afford," Rylie says.

"I can afford my car just fine."

Mostly.

I'd be able to afford Audrey better if her repair bills didn't cost an arm and a leg.

Before I can argue further, Rylie is waving her arms. "Over here!" An old man wearing a top hat and sporting a large white mustache approaches. "Beth, this is Mr. Hodgens. Mr. Hodgens, meet Beth—your new assistant."

"Thank you, my dear." Mr. Hodgens—who looks like he moonlights as a friendly skeleton—extends a bony hand. "Sheryl got sick, but you'll do fine." He gives me a once-over that's somehow both brisk and approving. "Just fine."

"Why don't you help him?" I hiss at Rylie.

"I'm too tall for his costume," she says with zero remorse.

"I suggested it," Seth smiles. "Consider it revenge for the cow costume."

"I'll split the thousand dollars with you," Mr. Hodgens offers. "Provided we win, and you can fit inside my trunk."

"Your what?" My eyes narrow.

"An old oak trunk I use in my act," he explains cheerfully.

"I don't know—"

"It's gonna be great!" Rylie interrupts, dragging me backstage like a kidnapper with good intentions. "Let's get you ready." She shoves me behind a curtain and pulls a blue sequined top down over my head. "Take your jeans off. The skirt won't fit over them."

"Why am I listening to you?" I grumble, unbuttoning my pants.

As Rylie yanks a neon-yellow wig over my scalp—taking a clump of hair with it—I hear angry voices beyond the curtain.

"I don't care what you say. He deserved what he got."

The hairs on the back of my neck lift. I freeze, one arm halfway into a glittery sleeve.

The voice continues, lower now but no less bitter. "All I needed was him out of the way. Now I can get my life back."

I poke my head through the curtain to see who's talking, but I can't see around a leaning tower of prop trunks. .

"Did you hear that?" I whisper.

"Hear what?" Rylie yanks me back.

"Someone said *he* deserved what *he* got. Maybe about Brad. And something about getting their life back."

"Could've been about anything," she says, adjusting my wig some more. "What you heard doesn't prove it was about Brad. You're just nervous about the act."

"Maybe . . ." I'm not convinced.

"C'mon, let's go," Rylie pulls the curtain back for us.

I spot Caren, with her permanently scowling mouth, storming away from the dressing area.

My gut tightens. Maybe I'm not overthinking it at all.

Rylie hands me a mirror. I take one look and scream.

"You look fabulous!" she declares.

"I look like . . . I have no words." My voice is horrified, flat, and utterly defeated. Between the skimpy sequined top, the floofy neon-yellow wig, and the sparkly skirt that wouldn't pass a dress code at a Vegas showgirl convention, I look like I lost a fight with a glitter bomb.

"Why, my dear," Mr. Hodgens says, wandering over and adjusting his top hat, "you look perfect! I wanted an assistant who would stand out among the other performers."

"Yeah," I mutter. "I stand out like a sore thumb."

"We're going to be the best vaudeville act this town has ever seen," Rylie cheers. "We're gonna win!"

"What's this 'we' business? You're not wearing this scandalous 1920s nightmare."

"You don't have a choice," Rylie says. "Pedro called me. Audrey will be ready tomorrow, but the total's gonna be two grand."

"Two grand?" I choke. "That's how much my car is worth!"

"This gig gets you five hundred for free."

"Only if I win," I remind her.

"Then you better be amazing."

The only reason I follow Mr. Hodgens onto the stage is the price tag. I can't afford a new car, and I can't afford not to fix Audrey. Sure, my team won *The Food Truck Showdown*, but the $100,000 prize got split four ways. Then came taxes, Seth's share, Rylie's bonus, and a much-needed girls' trip to recover from the chaos. The truck was closed for almost a week. No work means no income when you're self-employed. Between that and missed shifts during filming, my savings took a nosedive.

Seth's right. My car is stressing me out. But I'd rather eat nails before admitting he's right.

Mr. Hodgens tugs my elbow toward the side of the stage. His cologne is musky and sharp like my grandma's attic.

"Now, my dear," he says in a low, urgent voice, "follow my cues. First, parade around with the giant playing cards. When I say 'Abracadabra,' you wave your hands like this"—he does a little jazz-hands thing—"and I'll pretend to pull a rabbit from my hat."

I nod stiffly, the wig scratching against my scalp.

"Then you climb into the oak trunk. It has a false panel. I'll give the signal of 'Prepare to be amazed,' then hit the trunk. You'll unlatch it from inside, slip through the trapdoor under the stage, and pop up stage left with a bouquet of silk flowers. Easy as pie."

Easy for him to say. He's not the one about to squeeze into an antique box and vanish through a trapdoor in heels. The crowd claps as we step into the spotlight. Stage lights roast me like I'm inside a toaster oven. I shoot Rylie a murderous look over my shoulder and she grins back.

I smile, wave the ridiculous oversized cards, and flutter my fingers on cue. Mr. Hodgens hams it up, pulling a stuffed rabbit from his top hat to wild applause.

Then he gestures toward the trunk.

The ball of nerves in my stomach bounces. The old oak trunk looks even smaller up close. It's scuffed with age and smells faintly of mothballs and lemon oil. I swallow hard.

I don't mind small spaces, but that thing is tiny. Audrey's trunk looks bigger than this old hunk of wood.

"Come on, dear," Mr. Hodgens whispers, holding out his bony hand.

I force my stiff legs to move. My palms are clammy against his dry, papery skin. I climb into the trunk, curling myself into a tight ball as the lid creaks shut overhead, blocking out the blinding lights.

Inside, the smell is stifling—dust, old wood, and something sour, like spilled wine from a performance ten years ago. My knees jab into my ribs. I grope for the false panel, but the cramped space presses against me from every angle, and I fumble.

Where is the latch?

"Prepare to be amazed!" Mr. Hodgens shouts, giving the trunk a hard rap.

I push at the secret panel. Nothing. My heart starts to pound against my ribs like a trapped bird.

Outside, I hear a drumroll. I push harder.

Nothing.

"Any minute now!" Mr. Hodgens says, his voice is overly bright as he hits the lid. The whole trunk shakes. I kick frantically at the walls, my breathing sharp and panicked as the trunk moves about

Almost there—almost there—

Finally, the false panel gives with a groan of warped wood. I scramble through it and drop down onto the platform beneath the stage. It's even dustier under here, with cobwebs clinging to my sweaty arms.

I crawl along the narrow space, following a strip of fluorescent tape toward the side skirting. I find the slit in the curtain and shove through it just as the cymbals crash and the spotlight swings to stage left. I stumble into the blinding light like a creature emerging from a basement crawl space. My wig's askew. The skirt is twisted sideways, and the silk flowers droop pathetically in my hand. I'm sweaty, red-faced, and breathing like I just outran a bear.

For one terrible second, the audience goes dead silent.

Mr. Hodgens stares at me, eyes bugging.

Did I miss my cue? Did I ruin everything?

Then—without missing another beat—he throws his arms wide and bellows, "And behold! The miraculous return of my marvelous assistant. She's frazzled and fabulous!"

The crowd erupts with laughter and applause.

Stunned, I blink.

Okay. That worked?

I stagger forward, nearly trip over a floor cable, and fumble for the mic stand. "Ta-da?"

The mic screeches slightly, and the crowd howls. Cheers and whistles echo off the rafters. Someone yells, "Encore!"

I give the world's messiest curtsy, jerking awkwardly, and half run offstage, cringing as hoots and whistles fill the air. On the last step, I nearly crash into a wall of blue denim.

Detective Kane.

"Oh God," I whisper.

"Quite the act you put on there," he says. "Magic and mayhem? You're a woman of many talents, Beth Lloyd."

Blushing furiously, I stammer, "I—I didn't plan this. Rylie volunteered me. I was ambushed."

Detective Kane chuckles. "It was entertaining. Question: Do you own that outfit, or did you have to rent it?"

"Shut up!" Heat floods my cheeks. "And what are you doing back here, anyway? You're not festival security."

His grin fades just a fraction. "Waiting for Trish," he replies. "This badge lets me go anywhere I like." He pats the gold emblem resting against his hip.

"I need to change," I duck away before he can see how red my face is. By the time I return, he's gone, and Seth and Rylie are waiting backstage.

"You did great!" Rylie cheers.

"I want to go home and wash off the smell of mothballs," I push past the next group heading for the stage.

"You can't," she says, hurrying after me. "The judges will announce the winner after the last act."

"Then you stay," I snap. "This was your idea."

"Don't be a poor sport," Seth says, trailing behind us as we pass a snow cone stand.

That's when I see Caren's phone pointed at Kaydee. "You can't pretend you didn't know him. You worked with Brad. You worked with me. So why lie?"

"I never said I didn't know him," Kaydee replies, arms crossed. "I just have nothing to say to you."

"That's not what your silence tells my followers. You're hiding something."

"Leave Kaydee alone." Conner cuts in.

Caren whirls on him. "Why haven't you told the press what really happened?"

Conner's face flushes with anger. "Enough."

"I'm asking harmless questions," Caren shoots back.

"*Isso é mau*," Rylie mumbles. "This is bad."

We hang back as Caren's voice carries. "Why hasn't the festival made a statement? Why keep this under wraps?" Heads turn and conversations falter.

"Caren," Kaydee says, trying to stop her. "Let's take this somewhere else."

But she doesn't listen. "A man dies during a major event, and there's no coverage. I called KMTN news station. They didn't even know someone was dead."

Gasps ripple through the crowd. "Dead?" someone asks.

"You're harassing people," Conner snaps, signaling a security guard. "It's time for you to leave."

"I'm telling the truth," Caren shouts. "This isn't the first death on this farm."

The air goes still.

"This isn't gonna end well," Seth says, leaning closer to Rylie, his hand going to her shoulder.

"There was a construction worker," Caren tells the crowd. "Six years ago, a man fell to his death while working on a gazebo. The report I read said it was an accident, but you never told the vendors. Did you, Conner? Or the sponsors. Or the community."

Conner's face goes pale. "That has nothing to do with—"

"It has everything to do with it," Caren snaps. "Because I think you covered that up too."

A murmur builds as security moves in. "You've stirred up enough drama," Kaydee says.

"I have as much right to be here as anyone—"

"Not anymore," Kaydee tells her. "You've done nothing but cause problems."

Caren scoffs, but I can see the panic flicker behind her eyes as the security guard marches forward. She lets herself be escorted out but not before throwing a final glare over her shoulder.

The tension slowly diffuses, and I watch as Conner whispers something to Kaydee and they follow the security guard.

"That's our cue," Rylie says.

Seth hands me his keys. "Take my car. We'll bring the truck back to Mom and Dad's."

"Thanks," I say, too drained to argue. "I'll grab my purse, then leave." The exhaustion of this weekend settles in my shoulders as I reach the truck. Once I've got my bag slung over my arm, I cut across the gravel toward the parking lot.

It's quieter here, the festival noise fading. A breeze stirs the branches—

And I go still.

Near the edge of the lot, half in shadow, a figure slumps by a car. "Hello?" My voice shakes as I step closer, shining my phone's flashlight. The beam catches on a snapped gold chain and crescent moon pendant.

Kaydee's necklace.

My heart hammers as the beam finds her on the ground, one hand smeared with blood, the other over her stomach. Frantic, I open my group chat and text with shaking fingers.

Me: HURRY! Parking lot. NOW.

I barely hit send before I switch to dial 911. The screen flickers—dead battery.

No, no, no.

Panic claws at my throat as I slap my phone.

"Kaydee!" I drop beside her, shaking her shoulder. "Wake up!"

Nothing.

"Help!" My voice cracks as I scream into the night. "Somebody help!"

Two figures rush toward me.

"We're off-duty EMTs," a woman says, kneeling beside Kaydee. She shines a light into her eyes. "She's alive, but we need to act fast."

"She's pregnant," I blurt. "Will she be okay?"

The EMT doesn't answer. Her focus is already on Kaydee. "Grab the crash bag," she tells her partner. Then she looks at me. "We're twenty minutes from the nearest hospital. I can't say if your friend will be okay."

Her partner returns, a phone tucked between his ear and shoulder. He drops to the ground and opens the bag.

As they work, my mind races.

Who did this to her?

Chapter Twenty-Six

"We meet again," Detective Wilcox says, her tone sharp as steel.

I stay quiet, leaning against Seth's car. My pulse still hammering. The EMTs called 911 and moved fast—hemostatic pads to Kaydee's head, oxygen, vitals—then the ambulance whisked her away. Seth and Rylie arrived just before Kaydee left and I told them everything. Now the red lights are gone, and the weight of it all presses down on me. Detectives Kane and Wilcox arrived moments later.

"Beth, what happened?" Detective Kane's voice is rough, filled with concern, as he moves toward me

Seth blocks him. "My client has nothing to say."

Rylie sits beside me on the ground, rubbing small circles on my back.

I wish I could hold Teriyaki right now.

Detective Wilcox doesn't miss a beat. "If anyone would be here protecting her, it'd be you. Buford and Myers, right? Impressive firm."

Seth's expression doesn't change. "Glad to know you did your homework."

She shrugs. "I like to be thorough."

He hands her a card. "Then you know questions go through me."

She tucks it away. "Ms. Lloyd, did you disturb the scene?"

I want to answer. *I want to defend myself.* But I know how this looks.

I was alone in a dark parking lot. Kaydee's broken necklace lays on the ground that could have been ripped off during a struggle.

I found her bloody and unconscious.

And I have no witness to prove I wasn't involved.

Detective Wilcox is watching me, waiting. She knows this is bad.

Seth answers for me. "Define 'disturb.'"

"Did she touch anything?"

"She touched Ms. Foley trying to help her," Seth says.

"Do you expect me to believe that your client stumbled onto another body?"

"Kaydee isn't—" I protest.

Seth raises a hand, stopping me. "Ms. Foley is not dead." His tone is razor-sharp. "If you're going to imply criminal involvement, at least be accurate."

"You're wrong, Trish," Detective Kane interjects. "I know Beth. She's not a killer."

"The evidence speaks otherwise," she says.

"Or maybe you're looking at the wrong evidence," Detective Kane pushes back. "First impressions aren't always what they seem."

"What about second impressions?" she asks. "Or third? How many times is Ms. Lloyd going to keep stumbling over bodies?"

Rylie's grip on my arm tightens, like she's trying to shield me from the weight of that statement.

Seth stays calm. "Let's be precise—Ms. Foley was stable when they loaded her in the ambulance. The EMTs said my client's quick action likely saved her life."

Detective Wilcox crosses her arms. "It's suspicious, Mr. Lloyd, admit it."

"What is?"

"Three times, your sister was alone when she discovered a body. How do you explain that?"

Seth doesn't falter. "From my client's perspective, this is all unfortunate timing. While I respect your investigation, Detective, you're referring to cases my client was cleared from and actually helped solve."

Detective Wilcox studies me, her gaze sharp enough to cut. My pulse pounds, but I keep my face neutral.

Finally, she sighs. "I'll need a statement."

"You'll get one," Seth replies. "On our terms."

That's the end of it—for now. Seth takes his keys from me and hands them to Rylie. "Drive her home."

"I've got you," Rylie whispers, sliding an arm around my shoulders as I stand. She steers me toward the car. Her voice is the one steady thing in a night that's splintering apart. As we pull away, I glance back.

Detective Kane is watching, concern etched on his face.

Detective Wilcox, however, looks like a hawk sizing up its prey.

I turn away, staring out the window, but her suspicion rides with me all the way home.

"If you'd listened to me, your neck wouldn't be hurting right now," I say, sipping coffee from my *World's Most Annoying Sibling* travel mug—a gift from Seth.

He massages his neck, wincing from sleeping crunched on my loveseat. Last night, Seth drove the food truck back to our parents' house, where Rylie picked him up before driving us to my apartment. I told them I didn't need a sleepover—a hot shower and a true-crime documentary would do. But Rylie insisted, and Seth backed her up, clearly underestimating the size of my loveseat.

"Not a chance I was leaving you and Rylie alone in your first-floor apartment with that pathetic excuse for a deadbolt," he says, cracking his neck. "I called Dad last night and told him everything."

"You *what*?" Great, now it's just a matter of time before our mom calls.

"He's getting your landlord to install a new lock. You're welcome."

"For what? Snoring so loud I thought you were revving a chainsaw?"

"It was an eye-opener, for sure," Rylie mutters, jamming potatoes through the fry cutter. "You should probably get tested for sleep apnea."

"I'm *fine,"* Seth says, clearly not appreciating the concern. "It was Beth's too-small excuse for a couch that had me snoring."

"Sure, blame my couch," I say, slurping obnoxiously from my mug.

Sunday morning food truck prep feels off. I keep losing track of what I'm doing.

My mind won't stop drifting to Kaydee.

Adam called late last night to thank me for saving her. She was still unconscious, but the doctors expected her to wake up soon. I wonder if she's awake now. Does she remember anything?

"You and the EMTs saved her," Adam told me. "The baby's heartbeat is strong, and the doctors aren't expecting complications."

That was a relief—one less thing to weigh on my mind.

"I can't believe Conner's keeping the festival going," I say, draining my coffee.

"Why wouldn't he?" Seth asks. "This is business. He told us himself—his family *needs* this weekend to succeed."

"I hate to say it, but Caren was right. There's been hardly any news coverage about Brad's death," Rylie adds. "They won't make much of Kaydee's attack. It happened after most people were gone."

"Anyone who saw the ambulance probably assumed someone got sick," Seth says. "No one's jumping to attempted murder."

Two violent incidents in one weekend swept under the rug? It makes my insides knot. Before I can dwell on it, Layla Gafford glares at me, then scurries away like I've suddenly grown horns.

"What's her problem?" I ask.

"She's an opportunist," Seth says. "She sees a chance to turn the tide against you, and she'll take it."

I shake my head, but Seth isn't wrong. Layla's not afraid—she's a shark smelling blood.

My thoughts circle back to Kaydee. Caren's the troublemaker, kicked out of the festival. So why was Kaydee attacked? Did Caren lash out at her? She's made threats to me more than once so far this weekend.

Did she threaten Kaydee too and follow through on it?

But Conner was with Kaydee in the parking lot last night. Right?

Could he be responsible for what happened?

If Conner wanted to stop drama, why attack Kaydee—the peacemaker—not Caren? Unless Kaydee got in his way and took the brunt of his anger while Caren fled. But would he really attack a pregnant woman? He defended Kaydee last night. Unless that was just an act and he didn't care what happened to her.

I shake it off. "Time to get moving," I say, forcing my mind back to work. "Rylie, Seth—get dressed and hand out samples. It's our last day, and we need to make it count!"

Seth eyes the cow costume like it's radioactive. "I should stay behind. There's a sociopath on the loose, and dressing like a dairy cow doesn't scream intimidating."

I shove the costume at him. "I need that moo drumming up business."

Pedro texted me early this morning to say my car's ready. Even with the family-and-friends discount and a payment plan, I'm still staring down a $1,700 bill. I need every sale.

"Hey, Rylie," I call as she zips up her costume. "Do you know if Mr. Hodgens and I won last night?"

"No idea," she says. "Seth and I ran out after your text. I haven't seen Mr. Hodgens since."

Great. Another mystery added to the list.

Teriyaki clucks loudly outside, flapping her wings.

I step out and scoop her up. "Good morning!" She nestles into me like we've been besties for years.

Conner strolls by, stopping when he sees her. "Is that the same bird you showed me?"

"Yes," I say, already bracing for his reaction as he walks over.

He pulls out his phone. "Want me to call animal control?"

"No!" I snatch it. "I'm keeping her."

Conner glares at the phone, his look clearly saying, *Give it back—now!*

"Here." I toss it to him. "I just don't want anything to happen to her," I say, hugging Teriyaki.

Conner shrugs. "People dump animals at farms all the time. If you're keeping her, take her to a vet."

I nod. "What's the plan for the festival today?"

"What do you mean?"

Seth stands next to me, cow costume in full effect. "A death and an attack don't look great. Closing early?"

"No," Conner snaps. "That won't help anything." No hesitation. No uncertainty. Like he already decided long before we asked. "Kaydee woke up this morning," Conner continues. "Aside from a concussion and some bruises, she'll be fine."

"Did she say who attacked her?" Seth asks.

Conner hesitates. "Adam told me to stop pushing her." He exhales sharply. "The police were calling me all night. It was a nightmare. But Kaydee and the baby are okay—that's what matters." He points at me. "Adam said you found her. Thanks."

"Where were you?" I ask him.

"Excuse me?" He folds his arms and stares down at me.

"Where were you when Kaydee was attacked?" I repeat. "When I found her, no one was around. I thought you two walked out together."

"I went as far as the gates," he says. "Once I confirmed Caren left, I turned around. Kaydee must've gone ahead without me."

"What about the security guard?" Seth asks. "Did he stay in the parking lot?"

"How would I know?" Conner asks defensively.

"Maybe the guard saw something," I say. "Is he here today? He should talk to the police."

Conner grinds his molars. "It was dark. The guy probably didn't see anything useful."

He moves to leave.

I press. "Do you remember who it was? I could ask him—"

"No," he says flatly. "Drop it."

That stops me. "Why? Don't you want to know what happened to her?"

"I said drop it." His voice lowers to a cold warning. "We've got a festival to finish."

He walks off before I can say another word.

Seth doesn't move. "I don't like him. There's something off about him."

"I know," I murmur. "But besides him being a jerk, I can't explain what it is."

Before we can speculate, Detective Wilcox strides toward us, her expression fierce.

"If you're here to grill me about last night or Brad Dawson, talk to my lawyer."

Seth adjusts his ridiculous cow head and steps forward, making sure the detective sees him. "And I'm already here, so let's save you a phone call."

Detective Wilcox gives Seth a long, unimpressed once-over. "Of course you are." Then she turns to me. "I'm looking for Conner Green. Have you seen him?"

"Yeah. You just missed him."

"Figures," she says annoyed. "I've been trying to reach him all weekend. Finally got him on the phone last night, and all he said was that I had to go through his lawyer."

"Wait," I'm confused. "You haven't spoken to him?"

"No," she narrows her eyes. "Why?"

I almost answer, but Seth subtly shifts beside me—a reminder to keep my mouth shut.

Before Detective Wilcox can push further, Detective Kane steps up behind her, smiling. "All this talking's making me hungry. I think it's finally time for you to try Beth's wings or sliders."

Detective Wilcox sighs. "Might as well. I've been hearing about them all weekend."

Before I can respond, Rylie bursts out of the truck, tray of samples in hand, fully dressed as a chicken.

"Hot sliders fresh off the grill!" she calls cheerfully, then pauses when she sees the scene in front of her.

Detective Wilcox stares at the human-sized chicken holding a tray of food.

Detective Kane grins like Christmas came early.

Seth, still in his cow costume. "If that's all you have, Detective, we'll be in touch."

Detective Wilcox doesn't react—just shakes her head and grabs a slider off Rylie's tray. Detective Kane snags one too.

She takes a bite, chewing thoughtfully. Then she points at me. "This is good."

A beat.

"Suspiciously good."

Detective Kane chokes on a laugh.

Seth glares. "You did *not* just imply my sister is covering up a crime with food."

She takes another bite. "Just saying. If she were guilty, it'd be a smart tactic."

Detective Kane laughs. "Best cover-up I've ever tasted."

I groan. "You are insufferable."

Detective Wilcox wipes her hands on a napkin, suddenly back to business. "If you see Conner again, call me."

She turns and strides off, but I catch the way her jaw tightens—she's frustrated.

Detective Kane lingers long enough to take another slider. "Well, this was *udderly* entertaining," he says, winking at Seth.

Seth moos at him.

"You *didn't* just say that," I groan.

"Oh, I did." Detective Kane strolls off after Wilcox, chewing happily.

"Moo-ve on, *amor.*" Rylie holds out his cow bell.

Seth throws it on the ground and storms off.

Picking it up, I step inside the truck and grab my coffee.

It's gonna be a long final day.

Chapter Twenty-Seven

Teriyaki sleeps as the food truck hums quietly, the silence broken only by the fridge. I finish cleaning the prep counter when Van the drummer appears at the serving window with a stout man carrying a guitar slung over his back.

"Adam told us what you did last night, thanks." Van says, his voice filled with gratitude. "This is Reggie." He motions toward the man with the guitar.

I wipe my hands on my apron, smiling. "Ah, the elusive guitarist I've heard about."

"Reggie Douglas." He tips his chin. "I've actually been by your truck several times this weekend. You've got the best hot wings I've ever tried."

"We're heading to the hospital to see Kaydee," Van adds. "She's requested a basket of Plucked and Truffle fries and some wings. Any flavor."

"If it's for Kaydee, it's on the house." I grab a basket and drop them into the fryer, the oil hissing and popping as the fries cook. I reach for a bowl and toss freshly fried wings in our tangy Kluck-It sauce. "What's the future of your band look like with Adam starting a family?"

Reggie and Van exchange uncertain glances. "Not sure," Van admits.

"Life on the road is no way to raise a family," Reggie adds, adjusting his guitar strap. "Speaking from experience. But we'll see how things play out."

"That's the good thing about music." Van smiles. "There are different ways to get your fill. But if Adam does decide he wants to quit the band, we'll send him off in style."

"Monte Carlo night!" Reggie nods enthusiastically. They high-five, the clap echoing through the truck.

"We'll hire your truck to cater," Van says. "Can you do a hundred wings?"

"Pfft," Reggie scoffs. "We'll need three hundred, easy."

I chuckle. "Three hundred wings is nothing. I can fry that in my sleep." I grab two boxes for the fries.

"Good to know because we're inviting everyone we know," Van says. "That includes you—for saving Kaydee's life."

Reggie scratches his chin. "You and your chicken crew are on the guest list," he pauses, turning to Van. "But Kaydee made it clear. No more Peyton after their last fight."

"Wait," I stop what I'm doing and look over. "Kaydee and Peyton fought?"

"Fight is an exaggeration," Van says. "It was the same argument. Kaydee is just hormonal with this pregnancy, I doubt she meant it."

"So you knew she and Adam were expecting?"

"Totally," Van says. "Adam told us right away. He was nervous but excited."

"And you know Peyton?"

"Yeah," Reggie says, cracking his neck. "She was around."

"I thought she and Kaydee barely knew each other."

"Why would you think that?" Reggie asks.

"Peyton made it seem casual," I say. "She told me Kaydee reached out to her on her blog inviting her for some cross-promotion stuff. That's how Peyton started working for *The City and Beyond.* Sounded like they were acquaintances."

"No way," Van insists. "They were tight. At least they used to be. Kaydee and Adam were on and off for the past year, and when Kaydee came to our shows, sometimes she brought Peyton."

Reggie nods. "When Kaydee quit that fancy magazine, she asked Peyton to quit too."

"She did?"

"But Peyton stayed," Van, shakes his head.

"Why?"

Reggie glances at Van. "She said she 'owed herself to someone.' Whatever that meant."

I grip the counter. *Owed herself to someone?*

"What do you mean?" I ask.

Van shrugs. "We never asked. Kaydee tried to get Peyton to leave the magazine, but she wouldn't, then Kaydee would vent to Adam about it."

"Do you know what she'd say?"

"We tried not to get involved," Van admits.

"I remember Kaydee saying someone had a hold on Peyton," Reggie adds, fiddling with his guitar. "But she wouldn't explain."

Van nods in agreement. "Kaydee was disappointed. Thought she could save her."

Save her?

My fingers curl around the edge of the counter. Save her from what? Or from who?

"When was the last time any of you saw Peyton before this weekend?" I ask.

"Let me think," Van widens his stance. "Couple of weeks ago?"

"Nah, man," Reggie frowns, "last week, after band practice. The four of us ran into Peyton at dinner. Remember?"

Last week?

"That's right," Van strokes his chin. "She came over and apologized to Kaydee for something that happened earlier in the day."

"Did she say what it was?" I ask.

"Something happened at the farm. Don't know what. But things were tense."

"It got better once Kaydee and Peyton made up," Reggie adds.

"Until she got buzzed," Van reminds his bandmate.

"Kaydee?"

"No!" Van looks at me. "Her and Adam don't drink anymore. Kaydee urged Peyton to quit the magazine." Van sniffs. "Peyton was buzzed, but she said something that stuck with me. She said, 'I think the guy I work for would have to drop dead before that happens.'"

My heart stutters.

"She was joking," Reggie adds. "She laughed after."

That line lands like a gut punch.

I stare at them, my thoughts reeling. Last week. That's when Kaydee was pushing hardest for Peyton to leave. And Peyton made that offhand comment: Brad would have to die for her to leave.

I know Peyton ghostwrote for Brad. She stayed at the magazine even after Kaydee left. And she told me Brad saved her job after Mr. Collins tried to fire her.

What did she give Brad in exchange for that?

She wasn't just loyal to Brad. She was trapped.

Or maybe entangled is the better word.

I barely hear the fryer beep.

All the useless details from the weekend fall away, leaving one glaring truth.

I know who killed Brad.

But why was Kaydee attacked?

My hands tremble as I box their food, but I force myself to focus on the task.

"Here," I say, handing them each two boxes. "There are some extra wings and fries for Adam too." Van and Reggie give me a wave with the to-go boxes and disappear.

The moment they leave, I fumble with my phone, and dial Detective Wilcox's number. It goes straight to voicemail.

"It's Beth Lloyd," I say hurriedly. "I have information about Brad's murder you need to hear."

Hanging up, I immediately try Detective Kane.

Straight to voicemail.

Frustration bubbles. Maybe Detective Wilcox finally found Conner. Maybe Detective Kane is assisting with questioning.

I send a quick text instead.

Me: I have information you need ASAP.

I redial Detective Wilcox and leave another message.

"This is Beth Lloyd again. I need to speak to you immediately. I think I know who killed—"

"Bawk!"

The sudden squawk from Teriyaki jolts me, and the truck shifts slightly.

Behind me, the back door clicks shut.

Chapter Twenty-Eight

Peyton stands in the cramped space.

She looks smaller than usual, shoulders hunched, fingers twisting in the hem of her baggy brown sweater. She won't meet my eyes.

I tighten my grip on my phone. "Peyton," I say carefully. "What are you doing in here?"

She swallows hard. "I need to talk to you."

There's no malice in her voice, just exhaustion. Her words are fragile, like she's afraid the ground will give out beneath her at any moment.

I inch toward the counter, keeping my movements slow. "You can't be in here. Health codes—"

Her eyes flick to Teriyaki. "You're a little past health codes, don't you think?"

Teriyaki clucks uneasily. "What do you want?" I ask.

Peyton's gaze meets mine for the first time, her eyes red-rimmed, wet with tears and something darker—desperation.

"I don't know what to do," her voice cracks.

"Do you want to talk about it?" I ask, keeping my voice gentle.

She takes a shaky breath. "I got a job offer," she says, almost like she can't believe the words herself.

"That's great," I say, though something about her tone makes me hesitate.

"I was supposed to start Monday."

Tension coils in my belly. "What happened?"

"Someone from the new magazine called Brad on Thursday."

I freeze, every nerve on alert.

Peyton lets out a bitter laugh. "He steamrolled me. Telling them I was difficult. I wasn't a team player. I was unreliable."

Her voice breaks.

I recall Brad's mystery calls Thursday, when he stopped by Kluckin' Good. I thought it was about the festival. But it was about Peyton. "I got a call after the festival opened," she says, blinking back tears. "They rescinded the offer."

"I'm sorry."

"It was *so hard* to take a leap and get a new job. But I couldn't keep working with Brad anymore, so I did it. And I loved this new place. It was going to be a fresh start."

"You confronted him," I say.

Peyton nods tightly. "I begged him to fix it. To tell them he lied."

I already know what happened. *Brad wasn't going to fix anything.*

"He laughed. Said I wasn't going anywhere. That I belonged to him."

"Oh, Peyton . . ."

"I told him I didn't belong to anyone. And that he couldn't keep passing off my work as his or making me do his dirty work."

"Good for you."

She sniffles. "I told him if he didn't fix it, I'd tell Mr. Collins everything."

"Why not sooner?"

Her laugh is barely a whisper. "Because I didn't just do my work."

I frown. "What do you mean?"

She wrings her sweater hem so hard the threads strain.

"At first, it was small," she says. "He reminded me how he saved my job when layoffs hit. Said all he needed was a little help from me in return."

I stay silent, letting her speak.

"He had me rewrite other critics' work before it got published," Peyton says, her voice trembling. "Just tweak the language enough to sound like it came from him. Sometimes he forwarded me their drafts—stuff he shouldn't have had, but he sweet-talked the right person. Sometimes he'd take me along to meetings with writers or bloggers from other magazines, under the guise of setting up collaborations. While he distracted them, he'd have me snoop on their laptops when they were away from the office."

"How did you manage that?"

She laughs. "I have a knack for going unnoticed. You'd be surprised how many people don't have passwords on their laptops. Or don't close what they're working on to take a meeting in another room."

Revulsion coils in my gut.

"I'd copy whatever I could onto a flash drive. Notes, outlines, full drafts. Then I'd rewrite them, and Brad would publish first. When their columns came out later, it looked like they copied him. Then he'd cancel their collabs."

Her laugh is bitter now.

"Sometimes he did the stealing himself, other times he pushed me to do the dirty work—said I owed him for saving my job. Said this was how you got ahead." Her voice drops. "It got worse."

A sick feeling crawls up my throat wondering how it gets worse.

"He wanted inside info. Draft press releases, PR schedules, emails about launches or embargoes. Stuff I accessed through editorial. Things not meant to be shared." She presses her fingers into her temples.

"He wanted to look like a one-man show for Mr. Collins. Brad obsessed over proving he didn't need a team—just his instincts.

The better his pieces, the more perks. When that wasn't enough . . ." She swallows hard. "He started eyeing big assignments—celebrity interviews, sports coverage—stuff beyond food." Self-loathing twists her face. "I knew it was wrong. Breaking NDAs. Violating confidentiality. But I told myself it was just helping a friend." Her voice breaks. "But he wasn't my friend. He used it against me."

"What did he do?"

"He threatened to tell Mr. Collins I hacked the system, stole files. That I stole from other magazines, using my flash drives. Said there'd be cameras showing me entering offices while he was in meetings." She hiccups, holding back a sob. "He made me the criminal."

I exhale sharply. "Peyton, you were a victim. You should've come forward."

She shakes her head. "Who would've believed me? The girl fetching coffee and scheduling meetings? No one even noticed me when Brad was around. That's why he could do anything."

Silence hangs heavy between us until her hands start to shake, wringing her sweater's fabric. "I told him I was done, and he need to get my job offer back. He told me I wasn't going anywhere." Her voice trembles. "He grabbed my arm, hard, and said I was going to ruin everything if I opened my mouth."

I catch my breath as she pushes up her baggy sleeve, revealing a fresh, finger-shaped bruise.

"I tried to pull free," she lowers her sleeve. "I shoved him. He yanked me back, and I panicked."

The air is heavy with the weight of her confession.

"I kicked him," she hiccups. "Harder than I meant. I didn't know there was a rock he'd hit his head on."

"Peyton." My fingers flex. I want to tell her it'll be okay, but I can't.

She presses her hands to her face. "I swear, I didn't know it was there," she repeats.

All the pieces click together.

"It was you," I say softly. "Thursday afternoon. The person I saw near the barn. The mystery person in the oversized hat and baggy sweater."

Peyton's breath hitches. "I heard your phone, but I was scared. So I ran. But I swear, I thought he was going to get up."

"If it was an accident," I say carefully, "then you should have done something."

"It was! An accident." Her voice is hollow. "He fell. Didn't move. I panicked—I ran." Her shoulders shake with guilt. "I thought he was going to get up. I *swore* he was going to get up." She wipes her tears roughly. "But then the police called. And I knew. I knew he wasn't ever getting up."

Her words suffocate the space between us. Peyton's unraveling. "And Kaydee?" I ask.

Her face crumples. "I didn't mean to hurt her, I just needed her to listen."

I stay quiet.

"I tried talking to her earlier, but Caren showed up and—"

"Wait," I stop her. "Was this backstage, before the vaudeville act?"

She gives a nod.

"While I was getting ready for my act with Mr. Hodgens, I overheard someone. 'He deserved what he got,' the person said. And, 'All I needed was him out of the way.' I thought it was Caren. But it was you."

"I didn't know anyone heard that." She sniffles, eyes glistening. "I thought if I told Kaydee what happened, she'd understand. But she wouldn't listen, said I was talking nonsense. Then Caren showed up and ended our conversation."

"But that wasn't the end of your conversation with Kaydee, was it?"

She hugs herself tighter. "I was scared. I just needed someone to believe me, to know what Brad was like. I told her everything Brad made me do." She wipes her face, leaving streaks on her cheeks. "But she looked at me like I was a monster. What choice did I have? He tricked me once, then used it against me. I was stuck."

I let the silence stretch, watching the guilt chewing her up. Then I ask, "Why didn't you tell me you and Kaydee were friends?"

"Things between us were complicated," she says. "After she left the magazine, we didn't see eye to eye. She wanted me to quit too, but I couldn't tell her how deep into it I was."

"I don't know what to say."

"Me neither," she wipes under her eyes. "When I told Kaydee everything, she said I made the wrong choice. She wouldn't listen, and I could tell she was planning to go to the police. I was desperate, tired of being scared, tired of Brad ruining my life even after he was gone."

Her hands twitch into fists, then release.

"I grabbed her arm. I just wanted her to stop, to listen."

"What did you do?"

She swallows hard, eyes unfocused. "I didn't mean to shake her so hard. She pulled away, and . . . I don't remember shoving her."

The truth hangs between us.

"Was what happened to Kaydee an accident too?"

"I was shaking her, trying to make her listen. Her ankle twisted on the gravel, and she fell. Her necklace caught my sweater and pulled. I just wanted her to listen. She hit her head, but it wasn't my fault." Her gaze is distant.

Silence crashes over us.

Does she really believe that? It sounds like she's blaming Kaydee for not listening.

Peyton presses a hand over her mouth, holding back a sob. "I ran," she chokes out. "But this time I ran to find help."

I step forward, wanting to offer comfort. But there's nothing I can say to undo her choices. Peyton swallows hard, her eyes glassy with tears.

"I made a mess of things, didn't I?" she asks.

I look at her. Really look at her.

Peyton isn't some cold, calculating monster.

She's scared.

Cornered.

Backed into a place so tight and dark she couldn't see a way out.

"I'm not going to lie. You made a mess. You were scared, but that doesn't excuse the choices you made. You hurt people. Brad, Kaydee."

Her chin trembles.

"But I think you've been hurting too. When animals are trapped, they fight. You've been fighting so long, you didn't know how to stop." I hesitate. "But why come to me?"

She looks at me, and the vulnerability there knocks the breath from my lungs.

"Because you see people," she whispers. "Even if you don't want to. You asked questions no one else did. And maybe—I don't know—maybe I hoped you'd see something good in me." Her voice breaks. "I didn't know where else to go."

"The police would have been a good start."

She swallows. "I know. But I never meant for you and Seth to get wrapped up in this."

One last question lingers, refusing to let go. "Can I ask something? It's been bothering me."

Peyton nods, hiccupping softly.

"How did you get a Kluckin' Good tumbler?"

She looks confused. "What?"

"The police found one of our tumblers in the bushes near Brad's body. It wasn't mine, Seth's, or Rylie's. You said you didn't mean for us to get involved. Did you leave it behind?"

Her brow furrows, then realization dawns slowly. "Yellow, right?"

"Where did you get it?" I ask.

"I saw it on a picnic table. Thought someone forgot it."

I frown. "So, you took it?"

"I was going to take it to lost and found. What's the big deal?"

I shake my head, the pieces slamming into place with nauseating clarity. "You took Helena's tumbler. She told me she set it down and then couldn't find it again. That tumbler came from my truck. It was found at the murder scene. The cops zeroed in on it. You gave them a reason to suspect us."

She opens her mouth, then closes it. Guilt spreading across her face.

"I didn't mean that," she whispers. "I didn't even think—"

"I believe you. But we still paid for your mistake."

"I'm sorry." She swallows, voice softening. "I was holding it when my new employer called. They said they were going another direction. I knew Brad was behind it, so I followed him, and asked him to talk privately. We went to the barn."

"Why there?" I ask, picturing Brad with the alpaca. "You knew it'd be empty."

Peyton nods. "I was with him last week when he did a walk-through with Conner. I knew there wouldn't be anyone to hear us argue."

"Did you plan to fight with Brad?"

"No! I planned to beg him to fix it. But he just laughed." Her eyes darken. "Everything happened fast after that. I must have dropped the tumbler. Didn't even notice."

It makes sense now.

There was no cover-up, no planting evidence. Just fear and a mistake that tied me and Seth to this from the start. The sharp crunch of gravel outside makes us both freeze.

"Beth, you in there?" Detective Wilcox calls.

Peyton looks at me, her entire body trembling, and in that moment, she isn't just the girl who ran.

She's the girl who's been running her entire life.

"What do I do?" she whispers.

"You tell them the truth," I say softly.

Peyton closes her eyes, a tear slipping down her cheek.

For a second, I think she's going to bolt.

I can almost feel the moment she considers it—sees the door, sees the chance to run one last time.

But she doesn't.

She lets out a slow breath, and with quiet resolve, steps toward the door.

Her fingers hover over the handle, hesitation flickering across her face.

"I'll come with you," I offer.

Grabbing my phone from the prep counter, I step outside with her.

Detective Wilcox and Detective Kane exchange confused glances.

Peyton lifts her chin. "I want to tell you what happened to Brad Dawson."

Detective Wilcox searches her face. Then, softly, she says, "Let's go have a talk."

Before she leaves, Peyton hugs me. "Thank you," she whispers.

I watch her go.

Not with relief.

Not with anger.

Just sadness.

"She was just as much a victim as Brad," I say as Detective Kane walks over. "It was an accident."

"That's the problem with accidents," he says. "They still leave wreckage behind." He steps closer, just close enough for his warm scent to envelop me. "You okay?"

Nodding, I breathe in the comforting cedar fragrance.

His expression softens. "Everything will be taken into account when Trish gets her full statement."

"I hope so."

"Trish is a good cop," he reminds me. "She'll see that justice is done for Brad, and for Peyton."

"Peyton made a mess. Lied. Stole someone's work. And I get why Brad used her. It was easy. He trapped her with guilt and kept pushing. But . . . she still made the choice."

He's quiet for a beat. "The monsters who show you who they are? That's easy to deal with. It's the ones who mean well, get in too deep, and can't stop that keep me up at night."

I look at him. "Do we just feel bad and move on?"

He meets my eyes. "You don't move on. But you carry it. And you try to be the kind of person who *does* stop. Even if it's late."

"That feels . . . wildly unsatisfying."

He huffs. "Welcome to my job."

"She could've run," I say. "I think she almost did."

"But she didn't," he says. "That counts for something." He walks off toward the sheriff's deputies.

It's not absolution. But it's something. A soft cluck sounds at my feet.

I look down.

Teriyaki stands there, nudging my leg with her little beak.

I scoop her up, pressing my face to her warm feathers. I can't bear the thought of leaving her behind.

"Beth!" Rylie approaches in her chicken costume. "Is it true? Did Peyton just confess?"

"Yeah." I nod.

"Wow." That's all she says before handing me the keys to Audrey. "She's all yours. Pedro dropped her off twenty minutes ago."

With one last squeeze, I look at my new emotional support chicken. "Let's go home, girl."

Epilogue

The drive home should feel like a victory lap. With Teriyaki perched in her box beside me, I tap the steering wheel, the weight of the last few days finally settling. Audrey, my trusty—or rather, temperamental—Volkswagen Rabbit has been repaired, and for once, I dare to believe I'll get home without incident.

That hope lasts all of three blocks.

With that all too familiar lurch, Audrey shudders, coughs, and rolls to a dead stop. My stomach sinks as the dreaded check engine light flashes back to life, a grim omen.

"You've got to be kidding me," I groan, slumping back into my seat.

Teriyaki lets out a soft, almost judgmental cluck from the passenger side.

"You're right. I should've known better." I sigh, pulling out my phone to call Pedro to get my car towed back to the shop.

As soon as I hang up, Teriyaki makes a strange, low warbling sound. Then louder. Then louder still.

I glance over. "Oh no. Don't you start. We can't both have a meltdown."

She puffs up like a feathery balloon, flapping wildly and letting out a screech so dramatic it would've impressed a soap opera star.

"Teriyaki?" I ask warily. "What are you—oh no. No, no, no—don't tell me you're about to—"

BAM BAM BAM.

I nearly jump out of my skin as someone knocks hard on my window. I turn to find Mr. Hodgens staring in like a startled owl, his crooked top hat slipping farther sideways.

"There you are, my dear!" he trills. "I've been searching for you everywhere, and here you are, parked on the side of the road."

I open the door, more out of instinct than intent, and—

WHUMP.

Teriyaki launches herself from the passenger seat like a feathered cannonball, stumbles on the curb, spins in a circle like a wind-up toy, and squats dramatically.

"Wait, what are you—"

"Buk, buk, buk, ba-GAWK!"

She lays an egg. Right there. On the sidewalk. In front of me, Mr. Hodgens, and of course a passing jogger who slows down just in time to witness the poultry miracle.

"Are you serious? You couldn't have waited five more minutes? Or, I don't know, literally picked any other location that's not directly in public view?"

Teriyaki fluffs her feathers, gives me a smug cluck, and struts away like she's just dropped a Grammy-winning album. Mr. Hodgens gasps in delight. "A fresh Silkie egg! Remarkable!"

I blink at him. "You know about chickens?"

"My late wife raised Silkies," he says fondly. "Fluffy little drama queens, every last one of them. We had one named Beatrice who refused to lay unless *The Sound of Music* was playing." He kneels, inspecting the egg like it's the Hope Diamond. "I don't think it's fertilized," he declares. "Your girl's been living the single life, I assume?"

"I mean, I hope so. We haven't had *that* talk."

He picks up the egg with a reverence usually reserved for newborns. "May I take this home? For sentimental reasons, of course. Not for breakfast. Probably."

I raise an eyebrow. "Sure, just maybe don't poach it."

He chuckles, cradling the egg. "No promises."

Teriyaki, apparently satisfied with her dramatic sidewalk performance, hops back into the car and settles into her box with a contented coo.

"I'm glad I found you. You disappeared after our *thrilling* performance last night."

"Oh. Right. The talent show." In the chaos of the last few hours, I'd completely forgotten about our forced duet.

Mr. Hodgens beams as he flourishes an envelope. "First place, Beth! The judges adored our act—especially your dramatics of pretending to be stuck."

I stare at him. "Dramatics?"

He clears his throat, suddenly very interested in adjusting his hat. "Ah, well, I may have neglected to mention that was an accident."

"You locked me in," I say flatly.

"A minor detail," he concedes, waving a hand. "The judges thought it was brilliant. They called it 'a masterful interpretation of confinement and longing.'"

I groan, rubbing my temple. "That's because I was *actually* trapped. That was real confinement and longing."

"Yes, well, I didn't correct them." His mustache twitches with amusement.

I shake my head, reluctantly taking the envelope. "Well, at least the prize money is real."

His gaze flicks to my car. "And just in time, I see."

I crack open the envelope, glancing at the prize money inside. Not enough to pay off my latest repair bill, but it'll help.

I sigh, chuckling. "Guess I am a professional performer now. But I'm retiring on top. One and done. Gotta leave 'em wanting more."

Mr. Hodgens clutches his chest dramatically. "A tragedy. You have real flair. If you ever decide to unretire, look me up." He adjusts his top hat and backs away.

Before I can respond, my phone vibrates. Adam's name flashes across the screen.

"Hey, Adam. Everything okay?"

"She's awake," he says. "I thought you'd like to know she woke up this morning. The baby is okay too."

Relief courses through me. Even though Connor, Van, and Reggie told me earlier that Kaydee was awake, hearing it from Adam makes it real.

"That's great! Is she—"

"She remembers everything, Beth," Adam interrupts. "And . . . she's struggling with it."

I inhale sharply. "I can't imagine."

"She's angry. Confused. Scared." His voice dips. "She knows Peyton didn't mean to hurt her, but that doesn't erase what happened. She could have lost the baby. I could've lost both of them."

I press my palm against Audrey's hood, grounding myself.

"I'm sorry, I wish there was something more I could say. I hate that any of you went through this."

Adam exhales heavily. "Me too. Kaydee doesn't hate Peyton, but she can't just let it go either. Neither can I, if I'm being honest."

"Of course."

"Kaydee wants to understand," Adam says. "But that's going to take time. Right now, she just . . . she needs space."

That makes sense. Trauma isn't something you shake off with a simple "I forgive you."

"She does want Peyton to get help," Adam continues. "She doesn't want her locked away forever—just to get the help she needs so this doesn't happen again."

Me too.

"I just got off the phone with Detective Wilcox. She's on her way to take Kaydee's statement."

For the first time in days, I allow myself to truly breathe. Kaydee's safe. She and the baby are okay. And now, with her statement, hopefully justice will be done, and Peyton can get the help she needs.

"I talked to the band," Adam continues. "We're bringing in another singer, someone local, so when the baby comes, I won't have to travel too far. Kaydee and I . . . we're going to try this. Try being a family."

A smile spreads across my face. "That's amazing, Adam. I'm really happy for you."

"Yeah." He exhales. "It feels right. I just can't believe I almost screwed this all up with my own insecurities about her and Brad."

"But you didn't," I remind him.

"True." There's a beat of silence on the line. "Thanks again for everything."

After we hang up, I lean against Audrey for a moment, absorbing it all. Peyton was a victim trying to protect herself. Yes, she should have gotten help for Brad when he fell, but sometimes fear makes people react poorly. And from what I learned this weekend, Peyton wasn't the only one.

A tow truck finally arrives to drag Audrey—my cursed car—back to the shop. The driver loads Audrey onto the flatbed, and I gather Teriyaki's box from the passenger seat.

As I turn, another car pulls up, blue and red lights flashing from the dash. Detective Kane steps out, shaking his head. He gestures toward my broken-down car with a look that's somewhere between a smile and a sigh. "Audrey giving you trouble again?"

He remembered her name.

"She's consistent. I'll give her that," I say, battling a grin.

I can't believe he remembered my car's name.

"Come on, I'll give you a ride home," he offers. "Your pet too."

"Thanks."

We climb into his car, and as he pulls onto the road behind the tow truck. "You did good, Beth," he says, glancing at me.

Taking a deep breath, I gaze at Teriyaki, safely nestled in her box in my lap. "Then why don't I feel good about what happened?"

"Because, like you said, Peyton was a victim. She made some bad choices, and she'll have to answer to the DA," he says, taking a left and following the tow truck back to Rylie's uncle's shop.

"It's still sad," I say, looking out the window at the quiet town beyond.

"Death often is," Detective Kane says, his voice detached. "While you did good, I'd feel more comfortable from now on if you stayed out of these things."

"I'll try," I say.

But something tells me this won't be the last time trouble finds its way into my life.

"Further allegations of harassment have been made against the deceased, Brad Dawson. Allegedly, Timothy Collins, owner of *The City and Beyond* online magazine, knew about Brad Dawson's actions and ignored them. Claims allege Timothy Collins silenced complaints with payments."

With a click of my remote button, the TV switches off. I've reached my limit with stories about Brad's awful treatment of small business owners. I can't help feeling like I dodged a bullet when Brad dumped me all those years ago. Yet I'm heartbroken by the person he became and the innocent victims who suffered because of his desire for online fame.

"Bawk, bawk."

I give Teriyaki a gentle pat and glance toward the window, half expecting to see my landlord's scowling face peering in. "You better keep it down," I whisper. "No pets allowed, remember?"

Teriyaki tilts her head and blinks at me, wholly unbothered.

Technically, she's not a pet, she's more like family. But I'm pretty sure the building's strict no animals policy doesn't make that distinction.

The aftermath of Peyton's arrest saw intense news coverage from all angles. Local stations, true-crime podcasters, even a regional news crew from Emeryville wanted a piece of the story. This included sharing interviews where other small business owners recounted Brad's harassment, showing Peyton wasn't alone. Because of these revelations, and her testimony, her lawyer got her a plea deal, but she's still facing prison time. I hope she receives the help she needs to deal with the trauma of everything.

And then there's the Green Family Farm. With two deaths now tied to their name, the media descended like vultures. News anchors rehashed not just Brad's death, but the tragic accident from six years ago. But Conner, ever the businessman, spun the coverage in their favor, announcing their next festival as a "celebration of resilience." Only Conner could turn a crime scene into a PR opportunity.

My phone buzzes, breaking the quiet. It's a notification from Caren Ludwig. I set up Google alerts on her name because I didn't trust she wouldn't try to drag me or my food truck through the mud with her stories.

Tapping my screen, I read the notification.

New episode: "*Crime & Commentary*—The Next Miss Marple?"

I groan and click play, already bracing myself.

"Welcome to *Crime & Commentary*, the podcast that pulls back the curtain on small-town secrets! Today we have a special guest with us, Caren Ludwig. Caren worked tirelessly behind the scenes to uncover the truth and scandal around Brad Dawson, Rise of the Foodie. Caren, tell our listeners a little about yourself."

"Thank you. I'm Caren Ludwig, resident detective—unofficially, of course. With everything that's gone down in sleepy little Grover County lately, it's clear we need someone asking the hard questions. Think of me as the next Miss Marple, but with a better social life and a stronger Wi-Fi signal."

I roll my eyes. Caren, the next Miss Marple? Sure. Because if there's one thing this world needs, it's a former food critic meddling in crime.

"No thanks." I close my podcast app. "I don't know about you, girl, but I've had enough of Caren Ludwig."

"Bawk, bawk!" Teriyaki chirps from her cozy blanket nest on the couch beside me, her feathers puffed and her eyes half lidded like she's already dreaming of mealworms and sunbathing.

I let my head fall back against the cushions, the tension in my shoulders finally starting to unravel. The apartment is still, the kind of quiet that feels earned.

The thing is . . . Caren did ask questions. Not the right ones, and definitely not for the right reasons. But she wasn't wrong about something rotten hiding beneath the surface.

And yeah, maybe I did a little digging too. Not with a press badge or a podcast mic, but with a stubborn streak, a chicken costume, and a tendency to be in the wrong place at exactly the right time.

Maybe there's a little Miss Marple in all of us. Though frankly, I'd settle for just getting through a week without stumbling over a body.

Teriyaki lets out a soft, wheezy snore from her spot.

I glance at her, a grin tugging at my lips. "Same, girl. Same."

Recipes

Plucked and Truffle Fries

Serves: 4

Ingredients

For the Fries:

4 medium Idaho Russet potatoes
2 tsp kosher salt
3–4 cups high–smoke point oil (avocado, canola, grapeseed, or EVOO)
2 tbsp black truffle oil (or any truffle-infused oil)
¼ cup Parmesan cheese, finely grated
1 tsp sea salt

For the Parmesan Lime Aioli:

1 cup mayonnaise
1 tbsp fresh lime juice
¼ cup Parmesan cheese, finely grated
¼ tsp fresh thyme, chopped
½ tbsp fresh garlic, minced
½ tsp sea salt

Preparation

Make the Aioli:

In a mixing bowl, whisk together the mayonnaise, lime juice, Parmesan, thyme, garlic, and salt until smooth. Cover and refrigerate until ready to serve.

Prepare the Fries:

Step 1: Wash and Soak
Peel and cut potatoes into ¼-inch to ⅜-inch strips. Place them in a large bowl of cold water, swishing to remove excess starch. In a second bowl, dissolve 2 tsp kosher salt in warm water, then add cold water until the bowl is half full. Transfer potatoes to this salted water bath and let soak for at least 30 minutes (or up to overnight in the fridge).

Step 2: Par-Fry the Potatoes
Heat oil in a large skillet or deep fryer to 300°F. Drain and pat the potatoes dry with a clean towel. Working in batches, fry potatoes for 3 minutes until softened but not browned. Remove and spread on a baking sheet. Chill for at least 30 minutes before the final fry.

Step 3: Fry Until Crispy
Increase the oil temperature to 375°F. Fry the potatoes again in batches until golden brown and crisp, about 3–4 minutes per batch. Drain on paper towels.

Step 4: Toss and Serve
While still hot, place fries in a large bowl. Drizzle with truffle oil, then sprinkle with Parmesan and sea salt. Toss gently to coat. Serve immediately with chilled Parmesan Lime Aioli.
Tip: For the crispiest fries, make sure they're completely dry before frying and don't overcrowd the pan!

Golden Gate Heat Wings

Serves: 4–6

Ingredients

For the Wings:

3 lbs chicken wings
3 tbsp unsalted butter, melted
2 tbsp sesame oil
2½ tsp garlic powder
1 tsp kosher salt
¾ tsp freshly ground black pepper
¼ tsp cayenne pepper

For the Sauce:

4 tbsp unsalted butter
½ tsp crushed red pepper flakes
⅓ cup honey
⅓ cup sriracha sauce
1 tbsp soy sauce
1 tbsp fresh lime juice
1 tbsp rice wine vinegar
1 tsp cornstarch

For Garnish:

2 tsp sesame seeds
¼ cup sliced green onions
Extra honey and lime wedges (optional)

Preparation

Oven Method:

Step 1

Preheat the oven to 400°F. Line a large, rimmed baking sheet with parchment paper or a wire rack for extra crispiness.

Step 2

Pat the wings very dry with paper towels—this helps them crisp up.

Step 3

In a small bowl, whisk together the melted butter, sesame oil, garlic powder, salt, black pepper, and cayenne. Pour over the wings and toss to coat.

Step 4

Arrange the wings in a single layer on the baking sheet.

Step 5

Bake for 50–55 minutes, flipping halfway through, until the wings are golden brown and crispy.

While the wings bake, prepare the sauce.

Step 6

In a small saucepan over medium heat, melt the butter.

Stir in the crushed red pepper, honey, sriracha, soy sauce, lime juice, and vinegar.

Bring to a light simmer, stirring constantly.

Add the cornstarch, stirring until slightly thickened (about 30 seconds). Remove from heat.

Once the wings are done, immediately toss them in the warm sauce. Let them sit for a couple of minutes to soak up the flavor.

Sprinkle with sesame seeds and sliced green onions. Serve hot with lime wedges and extra honey if desired.

Air Fryer Method:
Preheat air fryer to 380°F.
Follow steps 2–3 above to coat the wings.
Arrange wings in a single layer in the air fryer basket. Cook for 24–28 minutes, shaking the basket every 8–10 minutes, until wings are crispy and golden.

While wings cook, prepare the sauce (see step 6 above).

Toss hot wings in the warm sauce, then garnish with sesame seeds and green onions.

Tip: Want them extra crispy? Let the seasoned wings sit uncovered in the fridge for 30 minutes before cooking.

Acknowledgments

This book—and really, this series—is my love letter to the Bay Area, my home. It's a celebration of the melting pot that makes this corner of California so vibrant and delicious. Hot Wings and Homicide is loosely inspired by FoodieLand, a real food festival that takes place every summer in the Bay Area. It's a food lover's dream, and I hoped to capture a little of that magic in these pages. I just recommend attending your next food festival without the side of murder.

None of this would have been possible without the unwavering support of those who believed in me and helped bring Beth and Seth's story to life. Thank you, all of you.

To my amazing agent, Lindsay Guzzardo. Your belief in me and my wild chicken-fueled ideas continues to be my greatest motivation. You've been one of my biggest cheerleaders, reminding me it's okay if everything doesn't work the first—or fifth—time. We'll get there. (Also, this incredible title? Hot Wings and Homicide is all thanks to you!) Thank you for your wisdom, patience, and for our many chats that kept me going.

To my wonderful editor, Faith Black Ross, thank you for shaping this story into what it is today. Your sharp insights and thoughtful edits brought depth and flavor I couldn't have achieved alone.

I'm beyond proud to be part of the Crooked Lane family. Here's to many more books that make readers (and you) crave chicken wings and fries.

To the outstanding team at Crooked Lane Books. Thank you for your patience, kindness, and expertise in bringing this story to life: Dulce Botello, Mikaela Bender, Beata Garrett, Rebecca Nelson, Stephanie Manova, Elena Silverberg, Shannon O'Neill, Matthew Martz, and Thaisheemarie Fantauzzi Pérez. You all made Beth and Seth's latest adventure shine, both in front of and behind the scenes.

Danielle Paige, years ago I sent you a message on Twitter just to tell you how much I loved your Dorothy Must Die series. I never could've imagined that one day we'd become friends. You've been nothing but kind, generous, and encouraging—long before I even knew what I was doing (and let's be honest, I'm still figuring it out). You're the perfect example of authors supporting authors, and I'm endlessly grateful for your friendship, love, and belief in me. Thank you for being my friend.

Heedayah Lockman, thank you for the fantastic cover. I absolutely love it!

To my best friend Elisabeth Din, the real-life inspiration for Helena Wynn. You have your own clowder of cats and helped name the ones in the café—so naturally, yours will all show up in future books. This past year has been filled with love, laughter, and loss, and your strength, faith, and heart have been an inspiration. I love you, my sister. Po-tay-toes!

To the real-life Rylie—Jennifer Natanauan—thank you for being my best hype woman and proudly rocking that chicken suit at my book events. Don't worry, we've got plenty more adventures ahead. And Joel Natanauan, I hope you're ready for your cow costume!

Irma Perez, who's more than a bestie, you're family. Thank you for your endless excitement about this series. You're always there for the highs, the lows, and the pie-fueled gossip sessions. Speaking of which, I think we're overdue for another. Love you!

Acknowledgments

To my critique partner and fellow author Michele Skaggs. What started as a buddy read turned into a friendship I'll treasure for life. Thank you for the brainstorming sessions, the book chats, and for making writing less lonely. Now . . . what's our next buddy read?

Jennifer Van der Kleut—who would've thought a simple online message between two Crooked Lane debut authors would lead to such a supportive bond? Your silly chicken memes, pep talks, and encouragement to "just apply anyway" have buoyed me when I needed it most. Sharing the debut author's breakfast with you at Left Coast Crime made it all the more special. So glad we met!

Heartfelt thanks to everyone who read and commented on early drafts, especially Maureen Euless. Your insights, jokes, and memes were invaluable. Big hugs and endless gratitude!

To Ashley Brown and Melissa Kapture, whose medical and police insights brought a level of authenticity I couldn't have achieved without you. Your enthusiasm, wisdom, and willingness to dive into every gritty detail made this story stronger. I'm not sure who gets more excited when we start tossing around ideas—you or me!

Cathy and Samson Nelson, thank you for sharing your pet chickens with me! Who knew Silkies had such dramatic personalities? Your photos and videos helped ensure Teriyaki stayed true to her feathery self.

To the cozy mystery readers who've embraced this series, thank you. Your warmth, encouragement, and tagging me in every food truck or chicken photo you found always made my day. You've made this journey less scary and infinitely more joyful. Special thanks to Jennifer Linn, Ashley Blank, Lori Leaf, and Anna Champagne, for their words of support, enthusiasm, and chicken puns when imposter syndrome came knocking. You've all kept me going.

To my moms, Lenda Fletcher and Linda Dutra. Thank you for your endless support, from crocheted chicken bookmarks to handmade aprons and tote bags. I appreciate you taking the boys, so they didn't have to endure every author event, and especially Linda for driving countless miles just to see me, requesting my books at libraries, and cheering me on in every crowd.

Thank you to my cousins Cynthia Lima and Tanya Martinez, who drove six hours to surprise me for a book event—complete with cow costumes and signs that read "Read More Chicken." I'm sorry the event was canceled at the last minute, but I loved every minute of our weekend together!

And finally, to my family: Levi, Lucas, and my incredible husband David. Levi and Lucas, thank you for your hugs and for reminding me that dinosaur breaks are mandatory. David, I couldn't have written this—or survived revisions—without your love and support. From early mornings to late nights, you kept me fueled with homemade coffee, snacks, and encouragement. I love you three thousand.